Gareth took a step closer to her and Zetta instinctively stepped backward. Every fiber of her body was aware of the bewildering excitement that charged through the chamber and into the heart of her being. Even as she continued to retreat from his steady advance, she could feel her heart rate speeding up and her stomach tightening, readying, as a hotness filled her.

When she felt the cold, stone wall at her back, she let out a small whimper of frustration, but, at the same time, she had to hold on to it to stop her knees from giving out from under her.

Gareth's eyes narrowed and she noticed that the broad chest that now filled her vision was moving with great speed, as if he had been running hard. The sight of his muscles working under the soft fabric of his tunic made her mouth go dry. Nervous, she ran her tongue over her parched bottom lip.

It was a provocation that Gareth couldn't ignore.

"I've wanted to do this since I lay in the mud and you made me burn with just a touch," he murmured, lowering his head. He noticed with distracted satisfaction that Zetta's eyelids fluttered closed just before his lips claimed hers. For a moment, she was still beneath him; then suddenly she gave a little moan and reached up to wrap her arms around his neck. It was like a fire in his blood to know that she wanted this as much as he did. . . .

Books by Sarah Brophy

MIDNIGHT EYES

DARK HEART

Published by Kensington Publishing Corporation

DARK HEART

Sarah Brophy

Zebra Books
Kensington Publishing Corp.
www.kensingtonbooks.com

ZEBRA BOOKS are published by

Kensington Publishing Corp.
850 Third Avenue
New York, NY 10022

All Kensington titles, imprints, and distributed lines are available at special quantity discounts for bulk purchases for sales
promotion, premiums, fund-raising, educational, or institu-
tional use.

Special book excerpts or customized printings can also be created to fit specific needs. For details, write or phone the office
of the Kensington Special Sales Manager: Attn. Special Sales
Department. Kensington Publishing Corp., 850 Third Avenue,
New York, NY 10022. Phone: 1-800-221-2647.

Zebra and the Z logo Reg. U.S. Pat. & TM Off.

ISBN-13: 978-0-8217-8095-4
ISBN-10: 0-8217-8095-6

First Zebra Mass Market Printing: February 2008

10 9 8 7 6 5 4 3 2 1

Printed in the United States of America

Prologue

"And that's it, is it?" Robert said, his face unyielding.

Gareth lounged casually in the chair, throwing dice from one hand to the other. He sighed. Robert had obviously decided he wasn't going to make it easy. "I'm not sure what else to say, my friend," he said with a lop-sided smile. "I've already explained that my brother, Baron Lanfranc de Hugues no less, has asked me to see to the family estates in the south and I have agreed. I leave next week."

"And that's it!" Robert bellowed, thumping the scarred oak table with both hands as he stood up. "After all this time, you're just going to leave us without a backward glance. We are your family, God damn it. You've been like a brother to me *and* you're Katherine's godfather. Family! And yet you are going to leave all that because some brother, who has certainly never bothered about you before, starts making anxious noises about a parcel of land in Devon he probably hasn't thought of in years. He wants you to go and look after it like some . . . some nursemaid in full armor. You'd be insane to go!"

Gareth couldn't stop a smile from lighting his face. "And I'm going to miss you too, Robert, but let me assure you that with all my experience of the species, you are much more than a brother to me."

Robert's anger deflated in an instant. He even managed to smile a little sheepishly as he sat down. "I just don't understand why you're going," he muttered grudgingly.

Gareth's eyes were carefully trained on the cubes of bone he weighed in his palm as he spoke. "Like you, I feel we are brothers. But, unlike you, I feel the need to move out of my overprotective brother's shadow." He shrugged his shoulders. "Or perhaps I'm just tired of this endlessly cold country you call home. Can you imagine it, sunshine that actually warms you clear to the bone?"

"Now you sound just like Matthew. All he ever does these days is complain about the weather." Robert glared at Gareth belligerently. "But you don't see him leaving, do you?"

Gareth snorted derisively. "That is only because he would have to move farther than ten paces from the fireplace. He hates to go out to the bailey for fear he will die of exposure." He stood, stretching his muscles. Carefully he placed the four dice in a row on the edge of the table before meeting Robert's eyes. "Don't be such a mother hen, Robert. I was never going to stay here forever; we both knew that. I'll be fine, you'll be fine, and your home won't evaporate on you just because I've dared to leave you."

Robert stood and slowly walked round the table. "When will you be back?" he asked gruffly.

"Not sure," Gareth said, then smiled again. "Or perhaps I'll become so addicted to being warm that I'll never travel farther north than London ever again." He openly laughed as Robert's hackles rose. He grabbed the other man in a hard, backslapping embrace. "Don't worry, old man, I'll be back to flirt with your wife in no time."

"Don't even think of it," Robert growled but returned the hug with fervor.

They both stepped away from each other quickly, more than a little uncomfortable with the open display of emotion and neither entirely sure what to do next.

Gareth cleared his throat and gave Robert another lopsided grin. "Well, I best go and get on with packing. I'd hate to leave some lady's favor behind where Imogen might find it and get the wrong idea."

Robert smiled halfheartedly at the feeble joke, his eyes dropping to the table. "Don't forget the dice."

"No. They are fine where they are. I'll be back to get them when I have finished Lanfranc's business." He smiled again and left the room before things got any more sentimental.

Robert slowly sat on the edge of the table, his hand reaching for the dice. He threw them experimentally, then chuckled as he threw them again.

It was typical of Gareth, really.

The dice were loaded.

Chapter 1

Zetta sat on the damp ground, hunched against the cold, as she leant back against the small structure she had made from blankets and fallen branches the evening before. It wasn't much, but at least it had kept them relatively dry through the long night.

She stared balefully out at the misty rain, trying to will it to stop, even if just for a moment. The incessant sound of moisture dripping had kept her awake throughout the night and if it didn't cease soon, she might just run mad.

She dragged her damp cloak around her small form more tightly and tried to ignore the chorus of sleeping noises coming from within the pathetic structure. She couldn't help but envy Joan and Edrit's ability to sleep regardless of the conditions. She hadn't been able to sleep more than two hours together since they had left London.

She couldn't stop the small wistful sigh from escaping as she closed her eyes and conjured her best memories of that great, dirty city. London.

Zetta was missing it more than she could have thought possible. Hell, she even missed their small crowded chamber beside the fishmongers. They hadn't lived there all that long, only since Joan's illness had forced them to move yet again, but Zetta had still hated having to let it go. The room had been small, too cramped for three people to live in comfortably, and the smell of fish had permeated everything, but none of that mattered now. She missed it.

She inhaled deeply, but all she could smell were the scents of the wet forest. Opening her eyes slowly, she glared at the offending trees with wholehearted hatred. Zetta detested this place and all of the other places like it. She'd seen far too much of their sort lately. She hated their isolation, their strangeness, hated the dangers that she didn't know how to fight, and the vulnerability created by her ignorance. But most of all she hated the awful silence that filled the air like the final judgment of God.

She would give all she had, which, granted, wasn't much, to wake again to the sounds of merchants, thieves, lords, and prostitutes going about their business. Anything was better than this endless silence.

Just as the gloomy longing filled her, the sound of a bird starting to screech out its early morning chorus startled her. A superstitious shiver went down her spine at the thought that her unvoiced request had been answered. She barely resisted the urge to cross herself but the feeling quickly passed. Her eyes narrowed when she spotted the feathered offender on the ground, close to their camp. She reached out for a small rock and, ignoring the voice inside her that said she was just mean and petty, took careful aim.

"Zetta, what are you doing?"

With a guilty yelp that frightened the bird out of harm's way, she dropped the rock and turned on her brother. Edrit lay comfortably among their makeshift beds, his eyes unfocused with sleep. "You fool!" she whispered with a hiss of shock. "You just frightened me out of a year's growth."

Edrit smiled lazily up at her and let out a relaxed yawn, stretching his good hand over his head like a well-rested cat. "I was just asking what you were doing," he said cheerfully, entirely unaware of Zetta trying to shush him.

"Quiet, you oaf. Mother needs her sleep," she whispered frantically.

Edrit climbed up from the oddments of cloaks and limped over to where Zetta sat, then hunkered down stiffly beside her. He looked out at the dawn with a contented sigh before turning to her. "I won't wake her, Zetta. These days she sleeps like the dead and nothing I do will wake her till she is ready to be woken."

Zetta winced at his almost prophetic words but knew that he didn't mean it the way they sounded. She looked over to his large, innocent face and smiled fondly at this strange man-child she called brother. He might be older than her, but nothing she did ever disturbed his own innocent understanding of the world. To him there was no evil, no death, no sadness.

She grimaced as she all too well remembered her attempt to explain to him just how frail Joan really was. She had wanted to prepare him for the fact that disease was slowly eating her body away from the inside. Zetta had told him as gently as possible that the expensive apothecary they had consulted in desperation said that there was nothing more to be done. Joan was dying. Edrit's stubborn inability to comprehend, however, remained absolute.

She couldn't help but envy him a little.

He didn't want to know that his world had to change, and for him it was that simple. He didn't want to lose his mother, so in his mind he had convinced himself that he wouldn't. He had blithely set out on this nightmarish journey with all its stops and starts, not understanding that Joan had come home to this godforsaken place to die.

She reached up a hand and ruffled his sandy blond hair affectionately. "You still need to be quiet."

"I'll try, Zetta," he whispered obediently, then asked at normal volume, "What's to eat?"

Zetta looked away from his open face, even as her own stomach knotted with the all too familiar ache of hunger. "I told you last night, Edrit," she said with careful calmness, "that there would be no more bread and cheese left for this morning."

"But I'm very hungry," he said with puzzled concern and looked at Zetta as if on the strength of that alone he expected her to be able to conjure food out of nothing.

It was a look she was becoming all too familiar with, she thought with despair and placed a comforting hand on his arm. "I'm hungry too, big brother."

"So when do we eat?"

"Edrit . . ." she said warningly, then took a deep breath, trying to still her exasperation. Once calm, she started again. "Edrit, I can't get you food when we don't have any left. We have run out because I didn't plan on us traveling all this way only to get kicked out of the rotten village Mother was born in. Perhaps if we had stayed longer as I had planned. . . ."

"That wasn't my fault, Zetta. I told you that," he protested. "That man's laugh was so nice and he was so friendly that I didn't want to say no when he offered me that drink even though I knew you wouldn't like me to . . ."

She placed a gentle finger against his lips and stopped his very familiar protest. "I know it wasn't your fault, Edrit. That mean man got you drunk on purpose, so that makes it his fault we have got into this mess."

He smiled at her beatifically and lifted her finger away. "But you'll get us out of this mess, Zetta. You always do," he said confidently.

She let out a dry chuckle and shook her head. "That's very nice of you to say so, but for the life of me I can't see how I'm going to manage it this time."

"Why don't you go and steal us some food like you usually do?"

She closed her eyes and gritted her teeth. "Edrit, I've warned you before about talking like that when Mother can hear. You know she doesn't like it. It has to be our little secret that I sometimes do . . . things that are wrong."

"She didn't hear me. She's asleep," he said dismissively and looked at her with an alarming trust. "So when will you go and steal us some breakfast?"

"And where exactly do you expect me to go and steal you some breakfast from?" She looked around their meager camp pointedly. "I can hardly steal food from the trees, now can I? And the people from the village promised to burn us all as witches if we dared to show our faces there again."

Sometimes it felt like she had spent her whole life trying to connive them an existence. She could barely remember a time when the ever-pressing need for food and money hadn't fallen to her to provide. Somehow, she was always able to make things stretch that little bit further. Until lately, that was. She could find no pride in their current meager existence.

They had run into one disaster after another since leaving London. It was becoming monotonous. Everywhere they went they were met with fear and hatred. They'd been kicked out of almost every village and town between London and Exeter, culminating with Edrit getting drunk in Dartton and accidentally starting a fight. It had taken all the money they'd had, their promise never to return, and Joan's small decorative dagger to get them out of that mess.

Not that Zetta had dared to tell her mother that her most beloved possession was gone. The older woman had always placed such value on it that she would be devastated to know that it had been handed over to the ignorant villagers of Dartton to buy their freedom.

Zetta frowned. And now they had run out of places to go. After nearly a year of tedious travel they had reached their destination only to be kicked out again. Not once, however, had Joan shown just how much this particular rejection must have hurt her. That didn't stop Zetta from feeling it all the same. When Joan had last been in Dartton, she had been a Saxon nobleman's daughter, the pride of them all. Now she was a vagrant and a threat that needed to be expelled.

It was unfair. People had only to look at Edrit and they crossed themselves to ward off the evil eye. They were all fools. Sometimes Zetta could hate the whole world for the blind ignorance that infested it.

She glanced over to Edrit and tried to see what strangers saw that could create such hate. His entire left side had been damaged from birth, but to Zetta, the scars of half-grown skin and the strange immobility in his face and limbs were as familiar to her as his beautiful soul. She felt only sadness as she watched him try to walk on the stiff, stunted leg that forced him into a painful hunch. Many nights she held his wasted hand close, trying to infuse it with the warmth it couldn't seem to produce on its own.

To her, his physical deformities held no horror, not when she found nothing to fear in his wide, innocent eyes. It was impossible for her to understand how others could not see his loving simplicity. He was a man grown now, older than Zetta, but in his mind he was but a child and that meant he had to face his life without any weapons. When he suffered, he suffered as a child, without understanding or hope.

Other people might recoil in horror at the sight of his stunted limbs, but the only terror she felt was at the pain they caused Edrit.

She reached out her hand now and fiercely clasped his larger one in her own. Unquestioningly, he clumsily moved so that his arm was around her. There was nothing in this man to fear, she thought protectively, and those who did were ignorant fools.

"Damn," she muttered, ignoring Edrit's giggle at hearing the word that always made their mother wince. "I have no idea what to do next."

"Sure you have an idea. You always have ideas," he said confidently and settled himself into a more comfortable position, his stiff leg out in front of him. "Although I think you'd think better if you had something to eat."

"I'd think better if you'd stop jawing and let me," she snapped, sounding sharper than she had intended. They sat in silence for a moment while Zetta tried hopelessly to solve the seemingly unsolvable.

"What about the road?" Edrit said suddenly.

"What about it, brother dear? You surely don't suggest we eat the rocks, do you?"

"Don't be silly," he said with a scowl. "I didn't mean

us to eat the actual road. I just thought there might be someone on it whom we could steal from."

She opened her mouth to tell him to be quiet, then closed it again quickly.

"That's actually not a bad idea," she said slowly, a plan beginning to form in her mind. "I mean it isn't exactly the busiest of the king's highways and I'm not entirely sure how you steal from someone on a horse, but still, it isn't a bad idea."

"I know."

She smiled and gave his hand a gentle squeeze before letting it go. "One good idea doesn't mean you can go and get cocky on me."

Feeling the tight ball of hopelessness lodged in her stomach beginning to ease, she took a deep breath for the first time in days. She stood up quickly, paused a moment, then reached down and grabbed the rock she was going to throw at the bird earlier. With a small smile, she popped it into a pocket.

"Now, Edrit, I might be gone for some time, so I want you to stay here and look after Mother," she said sternly, trying to will him to understand. "If she wakes up, just tell her I've gone to *buy* something for us to eat."

"But it was my good idea," he said indignantly and got slowly to his feet. "I should go with you."

"But if you go with me, who will look after Mother?" she said gently and reached up and squeezed his shoulder. "Don't worry, Edrit; I'll be back before you notice I'm gone."

"I'm hungry," he growled petulantly, and Zetta smiled at him.

"I know you are, but when I come back I will have enough food to fill even *your* enormous stomach."

She grabbed her hat, shook off the worst of the mud,

and crammed it on over her ears. She gave him a quick hug, moving away before he could return it with his usual enthusiasm. Without a backward glance she started briskly toward the road. If she looked back to Edrit's forlorn figure, she would start to worry about leaving the two of them alone and undefended in this strange place.

Worry made her clumsy. And this time, she assured herself sternly, she wouldn't make a mistake.

Gareth sat comfortably in the saddle, impervious to the rain that ran down his face, neck and shoulders in little streams. The gentle rain had been stopping and starting all morning and in no way relieved the monotony he had been suffering since the start of this endless journey. And now, finally, he was nearly at journey's end. That thought alone should have been enough to lift his mood, but instead it seemed to be turning his bad temper foul.

He'd been traveling slowly down the length of England for weeks and with each mile his normally good humor had turned further in on itself and worsened till he scarcely recognized the brooding man he was becoming. Everything seemed to be a source of irritation to him in this new mood, and the only entertainment he could now find was when he dwelled on the things that were making him so exquisitely miserable.

Starting with the horse Robert had given him.

It had to be the stupidest animal to be found in the whole of the kingdom. The big warhorse seemed to think he was perpetually in some kind of grave danger. He shied from everything up to and including his own shadow with such alarming frequency that Gareth had found himself chasing after the wretched beast more than he rode it.

And when he had the horse under some semblance of control, the isolation and loneliness of the open road wore on him intolerably. But when he reached a town, the crowds of people irritated him until he started to have lurid fantasies about pulling heads off just to ease some of the tension that was building inside him.

He knew it was all illogical, but that didn't make it any less real. And the knowledge that if he turned around and went back the way he had come this strange mood would disappear only galled him. He grimaced and looked balefully around at the trees that seemed to press in all around him, the overhanging branches crowding out most of the muted dawn light. By his estimation, for the last hour he had been riding over family estates, and the signs of neglect were all too obvious.

The road itself seemed to be frequently used, but with no one to maintain it, it had become overgrown. Undergrowth pressed in from all sides, providing a perfect cover for all kinds of threats. Any landowner who cared for his land and the people on it would have seen the potential danger removed long before it would have reached this stage, Gareth thought with grim disgust as he ducked his head to avoid a low, overhanging branch.

He couldn't comprehend such cynical disregard for what was obviously good, fertile land, but, at the same time, it came as no surprise. The de Hugues's concerns in England had always taken a poor second to their continual maneuvering for power in Normandy. Throughout his childhood, the importance of their position as Norman nobles had been drummed into him relentlessly until he had almost believed in it himself.

And obviously Lanfranc still did. Even now, when he desperately needed the funds these lands could raise, he didn't dare leave the Norman estates for fear of damaging his hold on power. It was at such times when younger brothers suddenly had a purpose, Gareth thought, then smiled cynically as he swatted at another branch. He half wished he had told Lanfranc to go to hell when he had ordered him, in the name of family loyalty, to sort out the mess that was their English estates. He still wasn't entirely sure why he hadn't.

Instead, he had leapt on the excuse his brother had sent him like a drowning man grabbing a rope thrown from shore.

It had seemed like a heaven-sent solution to the restlessness that had been plaguing him for months. He had hidden it well, he hoped, but he had been aware of a need for more than the pleasant life that Shadowsend could offer him. And, perhaps foolishly, he had hoped that once he picked up the threads of some kind of existence of his own, one entirely separate from Robert and Imogen's loving circle, he might actually thwart the hollowness that was threatening to destroy everything inside of him.

It was a reasonable enough assumption that he could outrun himself, but it hadn't worked out that way. The damn hollowness seemed to be portable, he realized dourly, and he couldn't stop himself from believing that somehow it was all bloody Robert's fault. All that mawkish sentiment hidden behind angry bluster had eaten its way into him with each passing mile till all he wanted to do was to turn around and go home.

He let out a groan that echoed eerily in the silence as he realized with exasperation that he was doing it again. He was thinking of Shadowsend as home. If it was the last thing he ever did, he would get it into his thick head that it was a home, but not his. The sooner he understood that, the sooner it would be that he could shake off the strange feelings that haunted him.

And he had to start now.

Carefully he straightened in the saddle and tried to concentrate on the road, hoping that the world outside his own brooding thoughts would create enough of a distraction to lift the oppressive mood he had drifted into.

He just caught sight of a figure moving through the undergrowth when his horse suddenly reared up onto its back legs and let out a strangled sound of fright.

With a curse Gareth grabbed hold of the reins tightly, just barely managing to retain his seat as the horse landed back onto the ground with the sharp crack of hooves on hard, wet earth and started out blindly at a dead gallop.

Gareth's raw volley of swearing filled the air as he pulled on the reins with all his strength, trying to stop the animal, but the horse proved impervious to the leather that bit cruelly into the sides of his mouth.

He was so intent on stopping the horse that he never saw the low-hung branch that caught him full on the chest. It lifted him bodily out of the saddle, tearing the reins painfully from his ungloved hands. Suddenly, all he could feel was the burning that filled his lungs and robbed him of all air. He was barely aware of the road rising to meet him with alarming speed.

Then everything went blessedly black.

Zetta frowned with concentration as she systematically emptied all of the valuables from the fine wool cloak she had removed from the stranger. The small pile that was forming beside her was hardly worth the effort, she realized with a growing sense of desperation. It would, of course, be entirely in keeping with her current luck that she would rob the only merchant in Christendom who believed in traveling lightly.

Or, more likely, everything of worth was still attached to the back of the damn horse.

She had been stunned at the horse's reaction to the stone she had lobbed hopefully at its flanks. She had only wanted it to take fright and dislodge its rider. Instead, it had taken off like it was being pursued by demons from hell, making her run at full speed just to keep it in sight. It had taken her a full ten minutes before she had come upon the stranger sprawled across the road, knocked out cold. There had been absolutely no sign of the horse itself, only light hoofprints in the fresh mud.

It would probably still be running a month from now, taking everything of worth with it into the next shire, she thought with a sigh.

After quickly stashing into her own pockets the small loaf of bread and the dagger she found, she rolled the cloak up into a ball. She held the fabric tightly in her hands and glanced nervously over to where the stranger lay sprawled in the mud. Even lying down he was an imposing figure. She had made certain that his hands were tied securely in front of him before she had dared to check that the fall hadn't killed him.

A heated flush rose up her neck and covered her cheeks as she remembered the strange feeling of leaning her ear against his broad chest to check if his heart was still beating. It had filled her body as she had absorbed the heat of his hard muscles beneath her cheek and a seductively masculine scent had filled her senses.

She tried to ignore the strange tingling that still filled her as she carefully approached him, but by the time she knelt down in the mud beside him she was oddly out of breath.

Looking at him now in the harsh dawn light that penetrated through the tree canopy, she had to admit that she had never before seen such beauty. Not that there had been much room for beauty in her life, she thought with a derisive snort at her own sentimentality, but at the same time she found herself trying to memorize every detail of the stranger's perfect face and form.

Even sprawled in the mud, she could tell that he was well over normal height. He was also broad and muscular enough to be a very dangerous male animal, she thought with a shiver that had nothing to do with fear. He didn't look like a merchant up close, for all his fine clothes. She looked down at the hands tied over his abdomen and noticed the calluses that covered them. Calluses no merchant could have. Calluses caused from a long acquaintanceship with swords.

No, not a merchant then, but a warrior. The kind of man she should get away from as fast as possible if she had any common sense.

Instead, she was unable to resist the urge to reach out her hand and run it along the capable strength of his. Her fingers trailed over the frayed leather that held him captive and up the corded muscles of his arms. Her breath caught in the back of her throat when her fingers reached his soft, strangely vulnerable throat.

Watching her pale fingers move over his lightly tanned skin was the most intoxicating experience of her life.

Her hand had been moving lightly over his collarbone for several seconds before she noticed the leather thong round his neck and the pouch that was just visible under his tunic. She knew that a pouch meant coins, but she hesitated a moment, then reluctantly reached for it with both hands.

She carefully untied the knot that held it closed and tipped the small pile of coins into her palm. To her it represented a lot, but she was uncomfortably aware that despite his fine clothes, the stranger couldn't be all that wealthy. This small pile meant that he could ill afford to be robbed of what he had.

Zetta swallowed hard and her hand tightened around them. She needed the silver, she told herself sternly. They wouldn't survive long without some cold, hard currency. Ignoring the guilt that tightened her chest, she carefully began to split the pile into two. One she stuffed into her own pocket and the rest she carefully returned to his pouch.

It was only when she had returned the bag to where she had found it that she dared to look up into his face again. She was glad his eyes were closed. She couldn't face the accusations she would find in their depths. She ran her hand over his powerful brow, pushing his damp hair gently back. He still seemed to be unconscious, but his color was slowly returning and his breathing was slow and steady, as if he only slept.

Without even trying to rationalize her actions, she moved her fingers down his face, grating against the gentle stubble that covered the firm line of his jaw.

Biting her own lip nervously, Zetta ran a finger over his sinfully full bottom lip, not understanding the dart of fire that flowered inside her at the simple caress. She lifted her gaze from his mesmerizing mouth and tried once more to memorize the simple perfection of his face. Her eyes roamed over his straight nose, along the

dramatic slash of his cheekbones and through the soft
curling of his damp, dark blond hair.

When she found herself wistfully wondering what
color his eyes were, however, she snatched her hand
away and stood up. This was not the time to indulge her
strange curiosity, she told herself sternly. She grabbed his
cloak, flicked it out of its roll and covered him with it,
not daring to question her desire to try to keep any rain
off the already wet stranger.

Now she should leave.

But she hesitated for a second. She gave one last lingering look at the beautiful man she had just robbed
before turning and running quickly back into the cover
of the forest undergrowth.

Zetta never saw Gareth's sky blue eyes snap open and
follow her retreating figure with a narrow look.

He didn't even bother to look down at his bound hands.
With a burst of pure rage he clenched them against the
feeble knot, letting out a snarl of satisfaction as it gave
easily. He stood quickly and snatched up the cloak, swinging it round his shoulders in one easy movement.

His mind boiled with rage at what had just happened.
He had only been momentarily stunned and winded by
the fall and had come to fairly quickly, but he had known
immediately that he wasn't alone. His dazed senses hadn't
been able to discern how many attackers there were, so he
had kept his eyes closed and waited. He needed to know
what exactly was happening before he started bashing
heads together.

Well now he knew, he thought with clenched teeth as
he began to stealthily follow after his little thief. He
tried to get some control over the rage that had started
to fill him as he lay there listening to her systematically
rob him.

And it had been a she, despite the boyish clothing he had seen as he had watched her count his money through barely opened eyes. He had known that his thief was a woman from the moment she had touched him.

Her small, tentative touches had been butterfly light, but Gareth had felt them all the way to his soul, and when she had dared to caress his lips he had barely resisted the urge to open his eyes and give her what she was silently asking for by touching any man so intimately.

It had only been his anger that had stopped him cold even as his body had started to heat with arousal; anger that some baggage dared to rob him then touch him as if he were her lover.

As he moved silently through the undergrowth after her, his wounded pride demanded revenge. He had just been unhorsed and robbed by a woman and he couldn't allow that indignity to go unpunished. He found himself smiling darkly, hardly realizing that the hollow feelings that had been plaguing him were suddenly gone. Her touch had burned away all his vague feelings of dislocation and irritation, transforming them in an instant into desire for revenge.

The woman, whoever she had been, had suddenly given him a purpose and he supposed he should be grateful to her. Perhaps he would even thank her once he had satisfied the hungers she had raised in him.

All of them.

Chapter 2

Zetta's steps slowed the closer she got to their small camp. She was painfully aware of the small hunk of bread in her pocket. Its very lack of weight taunted her. It wouldn't have been enough of a meal to satisfy the small hunger of a well-fed person, much less have any effect on three starving, cold people.

The coins she had taken from the stranger were good, but right now they weren't as important as food. You couldn't eat metal, no matter how great the pain in your belly was.

Edrit was going to be devastated when he saw just how little food she had managed to get, but it wasn't his reaction that had her dragging her feet as she entered the clearing. No, it was her mother's calm acceptance she dreaded seeing the most.

Joan would eat her small share, uncomplaining, while the harsh lines of deprivation that already marked her face would bite that little bit deeper. Zetta felt Joan's silences like physical blows. The sadness in them was impossible to tolerate for long. In those dignified silences she heard the eternal knell of her own failure. There was nothing she hated more than these increasingly frequent disasters, and the small amount of bread in her pocket was nothing if not that.

Her hand moved to the dagger at her waist and she tried to find some satisfaction in its reassuring weight. It felt very good to no longer be defenseless, and that the weapon was well made and solid was all the better.

The stranger's dagger was far larger than the one the villagers had taken from her. It was clearly a man's weapon, rather than a mere woman's helpmate. The intricate knot carvings over the hilt that made ridges and patterns on the skin of her palms clearly bespoke of substantial amounts of money. Clearly the stranger at some point had coin enough for an elaborate and costly weapon.

And then the hard times must have come for him just as they came for everybody. Perhaps all he had managed to hang on to while his world fell apart was one small relic of a better past, just like Joan. That his hard times were being made all that more difficult by the loss of his horse, his saddlebags, costly dagger and half his coin was a fact that Zetta was trying desperately to ignore. It was, however, proving futile. Guilt rose inside of her and she was unable to escape the memory of just how vulnerable he had looked lying helpless in the middle of the road. It was an image that refused to be wished away.

She swallowed hard. She'd never found thieving easy, but this all-consuming claustrophobic feeling of guilt about what she had done to the stranger was new to her. She envied the thief who could be entirely devoid of conscience and she had known many. They had shriveled souls, totally unhampered by inconvenient morals. They did what they had to and never thought

of it again. Zetta had never been so lucky. The conscience her mother had instilled in her plagued her
endlessly. She found herself squirming at odd times
with the memories of what she'd done.

But this time the feeling was infinitely worse and she
could not understand why. Perhaps it was because he
had been so easily rendered helpless despite his size.
Or perhaps because he had so little to lose. Or maybe
it was because of the strange feelings that had risen in
her as she had knelt beside him.

Whatever the cause, the guilt was like a living presence in her being, stretching her with its fears. She
wanted to dash back to him and give back all that she
had taken. She could go and check that he was well.
What if he hadn't yet awakened? What if the fall had
hurt him more than she had realized? What if . . .

She ruthlessly quashed all such thoughts. Guilt was a
luxury she couldn't afford, not now or indeed ever. Setting her jaw defiantly, she walked briskly into their small
campsite.

Edrit rushed out to meet her, his face alight with anticipation. Zetta gritted her teeth and walked past him
without a word, unable to meet his eyes. Seeing the
dreams in them would only make her feel the failure
more than she already did.

She pushed aside the worn blanket that served as a
door and ducked her head as she entered their tempo-
rary dwelling, painfully conscious that Edrit had followed her eagerly. She quickly crouched down next to
Joan, who sat bundled up in their best blankets against
one damp wall. After a pause she pulled the bread out of
her pocket and placed it on the ground in front of her.

She didn't have to look up to know that Edrit stared
at her expectantly, waiting for her to produce more.

There was no need for her to see his face fall as he
slowly realized just how little she had brought back for
them, not when his unusual silence screamed its own
condemnation at her.

"Well, doesn't that look lovely and fresh," Joan said
gently as she gave Zetta an inquiring glance. "But I'm
surprised you found someone willing to sell it to you."

Zetta cleared her throat. She needed her sluggish
mind to come up with the lies now before Edrit blurted
out exactly how she had come by the food. "Ahhh, a
serf's wife, a short distance from here, didn't mind part-
ing with the remains of yesterday's loaf for coin," she
mumbled fast, shooting Edrit a warning glance. She
need not have bothered. He wasn't listening to the incidental details of where the food came from. The entire
force of his attention was focused on the bread and the
hunger it would at least start appeasing.

"Zetta, I don't think you got enough," he said with
confusion. "I could eat that all by myself and still be
very hungry."

"Edrit," Joan said with gentle sternness, "mind your
manners. I'm sure Zetta has done the best she could. It
looks a very nice way for us to break our fast."

Zetta said nothing as she pulled out the dagger and
began to cut the stale bread.

"Zetta, that is not my dagger," Joan said softly, but
Zetta was uncomfortably aware of the rare thread of
steel running through her normally soft voice. This
time she would not be distracted by inept lies.

She flushed guiltily but kept her focus trained on the
bread. "I . . . ah . . . lost it." Zetta cleared her throat and
tried again. "I don't know . . . in Dartton somewhere, I
think. Or maybe in Exeter," she added, grimacing

when she heard her pathetic attempts explain the inexplicable out loud.

"Oh, my dear, I wish you hadn't." Joan sighed. "My father gave me that dagger all those years ago, yet I managed to keep it safe. I do wish you had been more careful with it."

"Sorry," she mumbled and shoved half of the bread to Joan, hoping it would distract her enough to change the topic. The other half she gave to Edrit. He grabbed it with both of his hands and let out a loud lusty sigh of relief that the food was now safely in his possession.

Joan hesitated for a second, staring at her share of the bread with confusion, then pinned Zetta with an astute glance. "Aren't you having any?"

Zetta tried to smile but knew she failed. She plowed on regardless. "No, I ate on my way back. I couldn't wait."

Joan's face drew tight and Zetta knew that she didn't believe her for a second. Hardly surprising. Joan was too well acquainted with all of the signs of hunger after many long years of painful intimacy with all of the stages of starvation to not recognize them on the face of her own child. Zetta's resolute stare dared her to say anything.

After a moment, Joan dropped her eyes and took a small bite from the hard bread. At the sight of a small crumb falling onto Joan's blankets, Zetta felt her mouth begin to water and her stomach cramp with need. Just the sounds of eating caused a headache to burst into life at the back of her skull, and the pain pounded relentlessly. She got shakily to her feet.

"I'm going outside to . . . to see if it's still raining," she said clumsily. She didn't wait for a reply. She fled the confines of the shelter as if chased by the devil himself.

Outside she drew hasty breaths of the fresh air, trying

to expand her stomach enough to stop the cramps that threatened to cripple her.

She was so focused on controlling the pain that it took her a second before she realized that she wasn't alone. A man stood in the shadows. Even from a distance Zetta could tell he was tall and strong. She could almost touch the menace that radiated from him.

The stranger!

Zetta's first feelings were, contrarily, those of relief. Her stranger was all right. She had done him no lasting damage beyond that to his dignity, and she was glad. Quickly on the heels of that relief, however, came a very real sense of fear. The man was enraged and she would have to be a fool to ignore that. He wasn't here to reassure her, she told herself sternly; he was here because he was angry.

Very angry.

Zetta felt the last of her strength drain into nothing. She had lost. She had played a game that she had always known would one day have a very dangerous outcome, and she had lost. Now there was nothing she could do but to face up to the consequence of her defeat.

Another failure. She was becoming so familiar with the experience that she could already tell this catastrophe would surpass all else she had ever failed to achieve.

She wished she had stabbed the stranger when she'd had the chance.

Gareth watched with satisfaction as the girl's face went white with shock. Obviously she thought she could get away without any kind of punishment, but he was pleased to see the truth was slowly dawning on her.

He walked toward her with deliberate, unhurried strides, but she seemed too stunned at seeing him again to take any opportunity to flee, just as he had known she would be. He stopped only when he stood deliberately too close to her, the stark differences in their physical sizes making his silent threat very real.

For a moment she cowered, shrinking into the oversized cloak she wore; then her face cleared of all emotion. He couldn't help but admire the way she didn't back down, even when faced with her inevitable defeat. She even managed to narrow her eyes as if she dared to threaten him, but Gareth couldn't honestly say that he felt all that intimidated by it. In some odd way he enjoyed her blatant defiance.

He could afford to because this time he was the one in control. And after the way she had fondled him, he was ready to take full advantage of that fact. He was amazed by how small she was. He found he had little liking for the idea that a slip of a girl had bested him, but the fact couldn't be denied. She stood in front of him ramrod straight, and her head still only reached the center of his chest.

Beyond her lack of height, however, everything about her person was something of a mystery, though to judge from the way her clothes swamped her, she was very slender. The gray worn cloth hid her so well, and with her hat crammed down to her ears and her chin thrust out in a hard line, he was hard-pressed to prove to himself that she was in fact female.

Hard-pressed, that was, until he looked into her eyes.

They might be spitting venom at him now, but their wide, green depths could belong only to a woman. They glowed from her pale and pinched face, telling him to do his worst, but the long sweep of her lashes, the soft plumpness of her lips, and the slight upturn of her nose called to the primitive, completely male part of himself.

It was that very basic part of him that also noticed the white lines of tension radiating from her mouth, marring the perfection, and for the merest of a second he indulged the irrational urge to stroke them away. But only for a second. Quickly he snapped his gaze back up to hers, reminding himself with a stern rebuff that this beautiful little baggage had just unhorsed him, robbed him blind, and then left him lying in the mud.

She deserved none of the strange compassion that she was conjuring in him just through the power of her eyes.

He opened his mouth, wanting to break the spell she had cast over him before he did something silly, but was stunned back into silence when she shushed him with an impatient wave of her hand. She nodded her head sharply to the other side of the clearing away from the pathetic camp. She started walking away from him before he had time to gather his scattered wits.

A simplifying anger at her damn impertinence flashed to life, and he narrowed his eyes as his large strides began to eat up the distance between them.

Just as suddenly as she had walked away, she turned on him. Her hands rested on her hips and she glared at him rebelliously.

"Well, what do you want?" she asked with stiff formality. He was startled by the clear, almost cultured sound to her voice. It didn't in any way match her apparel.

Gareth let his brow rise questioningly. "Well, I suppose on the whole I'd want, as a general rule, not to be waylaid by women and divested of my possessions, but as to what I want now, well . . ." He smiled at her, taunting her. She paled even further.

"I'll give it back." Her hand fell to the hilt of the dagger that hung at her waist. "I'll give it back if you will leave here and forget all of this happened," she added with resolute firmness. Then she seemed to remember something and ruined the effect by adding with begrudging impatience, "Except the bread. I can't give you that back."

Gareth crossed his arms over his chest, carefully hiding his bemusement at her abject gall.

"You dare to bargain with me?" he asked softly. He knew the satisfaction he felt as she flushed was petty, but he didn't really care.

She nodded her head stiffly. "Yes. I bargain if I have to. And take when I must." With a jerk she pulled the dagger free and held it out to him. "Do we have a deal?"

Though he wasn't sure she knew it, her voice wavered with both fear and doubt, yet she still dared to meet his gaze without flinching. For reasons that transcended her not inconsiderable fear, she wanted him gone, now.

He smiled at her tauntingly. "I don't see any need for a hasty decision, do you?" He let his arms drop to his sides and moved with deliberate and irritating confidence over toward the meager fire that she had built, calling over his shoulder with mock pleasantness as he crouched down beside it, "Perhaps we should sit down and discuss all of our options first."

Her growl of irritation reached him as he stirred the embers back to sluggish life and a laugh rolled up inside him as she bristled at him. It was the first time since he had left Shadowsend that he had wanted to even so much as grin, but he was careful to let it out only as a small chuckle. While he was enjoying taunting the girl, he didn't think he should push her too far, too fast.

Not that he should be enjoying himself, he told himself sternly as he watched the flames try to burn their way through the wet wood. This was supposed to be about justice, not pleasure.

Perhaps the bump on his head was worse than he had realized.

He was taken by surprise when the girl suddenly came up behind him and began tugging with impatience at his arm. Her slight weight didn't move it so much as an inch, but her panicked desperation seemed to vibrate through her body and into his. He looked up at her with calm inquiry.

"You can't stay here," she hissed at him, frantic now. "I've offered to return the dagger and coins and you'll have to be satisfied with that. I have nothing else to give you."

A voice in his head that he thought may have been his father's from too long ago whispered that a woman always had something more to give. He found himself looking into her worried face and becoming terribly aware of how her body pressed against his arm. A warmth began to move through his veins.

He was no stranger to raw desire, but he could think of few situations that were less suited to it than this. Still, for some unknowable reason, his body and blood had burnt into sudden life and his loins were responding by thickening with a need that was becoming increasingly uncomfortable.

He wanted this girl, Gareth realized in surprise. He had thought that his only reason for following his thief was so that he could extract some justice, but clearly he couldn't have been more wrong. And the evidence of that mistake was now pressing itself urgently against the front of his hose.

The girl seemed impervious to the sudden shift in the atmosphere, too intent on moving the immovable object that Gareth had become. Her gaze kept nervously returning to the pathetic structure she had emerged from.

"Please leave," she whispered with a gruff desperation.

Before he could clear his head enough to answer, the sound of an infuriated roar filled the air. Gareth barely had time to turn and see this new threat when a large unyielding body slammed into his.

Zetta's hand was torn from the stranger's arm and she watched in horror as two large male bodies fell to the ground. They struggled against each other, both desperately trying to gain supremacy. It was blatantly obvious that while Edrit had the advantage of surprise on his side, he was no real threat to the warrior he now grappled with in the mud. That sudden knowledge galvanized her into action.

With her hand tightening painfully on the dagger she still held, she moved with quiet stealth over to where the men were struggling and waited for her chance.

She didn't have to wait long.

With little effort the stranger pinned Edrit on his back. He straddled his waist, one of his big hands holding Edrit's good hand impotent while the other encircled Edrit's throat.

Zetta slipped behind him. With one quick movement she pressed the blade of the dagger up against the tanned skin of the stranger's throat, trying desperately to ignore the way her front pressed up intimately against the ironlike strength of his back.

"Let my brother go," she said softly in his ear, her breath catching as his muscles moved and shifted against her as he lifted his hands from Edrit. "Now get off him."

"Ah, but what are you going to do now, my dear virago? If I stand up, how will you manage to keep that blade at my throat?" he said gently. Then he corrected with cold stiffness, "*My* blade."

Zetta gritted her teeth as she realized that the damn man was right. Unless she was prepared to use the dagger and kill the stranger, they were at a stalemate. She wouldn't win in a physical struggle with this man. She stood no more chance than Edrit, even with a blade pressed against the bronzed skin of his throat. She could feel the restrained strength of this warrior pressed against her.

Indeed, as each second passed like this she was becoming more and more aware of the intimate contact. Zetta scowled in irritated confusion. As if the stranger recognized her moment of weakness, he suddenly knocked the weapon from her hand. In one smooth movement he shook her off like she was no more substantial than an insect. He rolled off Edrit, who lay on his back gasping for breath, and gained his feet and began to stalk with threatening intent toward where Zetta was trying to scramble to her feet.

Instinctively she knew this was no longer time for heroics. She began to back away, watching with something akin to despair as raw fury tightened his face till it resembled a mask.

As the stranger got ever closer, she looked over to Edrit, frantically hoping for his help. He still lay on his back, too stunned to do more than try to breathe.

The stranger was actually smiling as he reached her. She watched almost from a distance as he lifted a hand toward her, knowing in that instance that she had run out of chances.

"Zetta, what is happening?" Joan asked softly as she stepped out of the shelter, pushing her thin, sleep-knotted hair out of her face.

The threatening hand suddenly went still, then dropped from her sight. The physical threat had passed, but Zetta could only stare at the man as a new terror dawned before her.

Her mother couldn't find out! She couldn't ever know that Zetta had resorted to robbery and violence. If she ever found out the depths to which Zetta had sunk in order to provide for them all, the shame of it would kill her.

She looked into the fathomless blue eyes of the stranger and knew there was only one thing she could do. She swallowed whatever pride she had left. "Please," she begged in a ragged whisper, "please don't tell her. Take your revenge on me however you will, but for God's sake, don't tell her."

His face remained oddly passive as he searched hers questioningly for a moment; then a roguish smile appeared. He even had the audacity to wink at her before he turned to face Joan. Zetta held her breath, then blinked in surprise as he gave the older woman a perfect, courtly bow. For such a big, muscular man his movements were graceful and practiced, as if this strange meeting were happening in front of the king himself rather than in the middle of their wretched little campsite.

"Greetings, madam. I'm sorry to intrude upon your privacy, but I was just taking this opportunity to renew an acquaintance with your . . . Zetta."

Zetta felt her lungs freeze. He knew her name. He might as well hold her soul in the palms of his hands. Joan's glance darted between the compelling man, her daughter, and Edrit, now struggling to stand up. Zetta had to turn her face away from the all too knowing look on her mother's. She couldn't let her see the raw panic that held her paralyzed.

"You know my daughter?" Joan asked, doubt coloring her voice.

"Yes, Mother," Zetta said at a rush. "Didn't I tell you about him? I met him in Exeter. He . . . ah . . . he . . . er . . . He helped me to get away from that landlord. You know, the scrawny one who threatened to call the justices if we didn't pay three times as much as we had agreed on." As her gaze darted to his, then away again quickly, she was more than a little disturbed by the very real amusement she could see lurking in the depths of his eyes.

He was laughing at her, she realized with dull dread, but there was nothing she could do about it, not when her mother stared at her with an increasingly worried look. It didn't matter whether he found the whole situation an amusing little farce or not, just as long as he went along with it.

With one side of his mouth lifted in a wry grin, he bowed once more to Joan. Zetta watched with amazement as all doubt fled her mother's face and the normally composed woman flushed prettily. "Sir Gareth de Hugues at your service, madam. It is a pleasure to meet Zetta's beautiful mother at last."

Gareth.

Her stranger was a stranger no more.

He too had a name. A nice, strong name for a man who at that moment seemed nice and strong as well as graciously kind. Damn. She wished she didn't know that. Robbing from a stranger was hard, but robbing from a man named Gareth who was actually treating her mother with gentle respect, well that made her feel like the worst sinner from the bowels of hell.

As "the stranger" she could almost rationalize away the guilt she felt. Robbing him had been neither good nor evil. It had been an act of faceless desperation. Now that her victim had a name as well as a purse to be lifted, her crimes could not be so easily dismissed.

Her gaze moved over him fleetingly as she tried to understand the incomprehensible. He was prepared to go along with this farce without even knowing why she'd asked it of him. It was an act of kindness that she didn't deserve from him, not after all she had done.

But only seconds ago he had been about to throttle her, Zetta reminded herself with ruthless practicality. She had to remember that and not be drawn in by the apparent charm of a beautiful *stranger*.

It shouldn't matter to her that he looked like a fallen angel and it shouldn't matter that he now had a name. The one thing that should matter was that somewhere along the line he had taken control of the situation. It was well past time for her to try to wrest it back again.

She stepped forward and thrust her hand out at him. "Well, thank you very much, de Hugues, for all of your help, but we can't detain you from your journey any longer." Her voice was purposeful and gruff, but she couldn't seem to stop her eyes from scanning his face nervously.

His gaze strayed down to her hand, then slowly ran up till it met hers again. Clearly enjoying her flush of embarrassment, he smiled at her with easy charm. Her wish that she had killed him flashed through her mind with perfect clarity.

"Now, Zetta," he murmured, his voice deep and dark

like a rich red wine as it caressed her name, "is that any way to treat your . . . rescuer?"

"Oh yes, Zetta, we can't be rude to a man who has helped you so much," Joan said with practiced brightness, feeling more confident now that she had found something that she could understand in this strange encounter. "Of course you must stay and break fast with us, Sir Gareth. It is the least we can do for you after all of your kind service."

"He can't break fast with us as we have already eaten that tiny loaf Zetta brought," Edrit said bluntly, limping over to Zetta's side, his good arm wrapped protectively around his winded stomach.

Zetta looked him over with a start, guiltily aware that she hadn't spared her brother a thought till now. She was relieved that there seemed to be no signs of any permanent damage. If she dealt with the stranger now, then everything would be all right, she thought with a desperate need to make it true.

Despite all of her outward bravado she found herself reaching out blindly for Edrit's bad hand, trying to take whatever strength she could find in his solid support.

Joan scowled at Edrit, a red flush sitting unnaturally bright on her pale, papery cheeks. "Don't be foolish, Edrit. We must have something that we can share with this kind man."

Edrit looked down at Zetta's worried face and shook his head with resolute certainty. "I don't think Zetta thinks he is a kind man. You don't, do you, Zetta? You didn't look like you liked him when I came out." He scowled at Gareth. "I don't like it when people touch Zetta, because she doesn't like it when people touch her."

Zetta closed her eyes, her defeat now complete. She could see no way out of the disaster that Edrit was talking her into. If Gareth abandoned his story now, Joan would start asking questions and everything would unravel.

"Oh, Edrit," Joan murmured with confusion, torn between her instinctual good manners and her certain knowledge that Edrit was entirely incapable of a falsehood.

Much to Zetta's surprise it was Gareth who deftly fended off the impending disaster.

He met Edrit's gaze with a level look. "Zetta and I were only touching because she was thanking me for giving her such a nice dagger," he said gravely.

"So you weren't going to hurt her then?" Edrit asked, his skepticism clear.

"No." Gareth smiled slightly. "And with such a strong brother to look after her so well, I doubt anyone would dare."

"They do dare, but I soon get them gone," Edrit said proudly. Then he added with his usual ruthless honesty, "Normally. You are very strong."

Gareth murmured that he'd been lucky and Edrit glowed with pride.

It was in that moment that Zetta realized that she was in more than mere trouble. She was in the center of a disaster of such enormous proportion that she wouldn't have dared imagine it, not even in her worst nightmares.

Nothing had ever made her more afraid than the sight of Gareth being nice to her family, claiming them in some strange way. He had stalked her only to extract some revenge, so she could only assume that this perfect act was some treacherous and subtle part of his vengeance. He was going to use her people against her. That was the only sense she could make of his behavior. Why else would he deliberately mask any reaction to Edrit's too evident disabilities? Why else would he talk to him man-to-man as if there was nothing strange in doing so with a man-child?

His pleasant behavior had to be a trick, but it was one that Zetta knew no way to defend herself from. It didn't help that Joan too was entirely unaware of the impending disaster that surrounded them. Her face was radiant with her best smile as she nodded at Gareth graciously.

"Well, now that we have that sorted out to everyone's satisfaction, perhaps Zetta we should . . . ah . . ." Joan's gaze darted around the campsite for some inspiration as to what should be done next. That there was no hospitality that could be offered beyond a sluggish fire and questionable shelter made Zetta want to cringe.

Zetta straightened her shoulders defiantly. She would be damned before she would cower before any man. She opened her mouth to tell him that he could be on his way when he cut her off.

"Good lady," he said to Joan with such perfect good manners that Zetta wanted to hit him, "now that we are all friends, perhaps you would do me the single honor of breaking your fast at my holdings not far from here."

Joan beamed a smile at him, grateful for such a simple solution to all of their problems. "Why, Sir Gareth, I know we would be honored, though we would hate to impose. . . ."

"You could never impose, good lady, of that I am sure." He smiled at her with gentle compassion and Zetta rolled her eyes. He chose that moment to glance her way, and she could see by the merriment in his eyes that what she was feeling was what he intended her to feel. This was revenge of the most diabolic kind.

"My mother can't walk any great distance just to break fast," Zetta said with deliberate rudeness, but it only made his smile all that much broader.

"Sadly, I seem to have misplaced my steed, or I would offer to let her ride," he said with expert smoothness, "but as the land we are standing on belongs to my family, and the de Hugues castle is only a ten-minute walk from here by my reckoning, I think you'll find it is a solution that will suit us all."

For the first time since Gareth had started to dazzle her, Joan's smile fell. "You are the Norman lord of this holding?"

"No, madam, merely a younger brother sent to sort out a mess." His gaze thoughtfully traveled over the forest that pressed in on them from all sides. "Though, I have to say, having seen its beauty for the first time, I do feel some small envy of my brother at owning it all."

"Yes, it always was beautiful," Joan said, and Zetta could tell the exact second her mother's mind slipped back into unseen memories. They were claiming her with alarming frequency and were the newest symptoms of the relentless disease claiming her. Zetta felt her throat thicken with a sad anger as she realized with each passing day she was losing her mother to her illness.

Even when Joan murmured politely, "Sir Gareth, we would be honored to eat at your table this morn," Zetta knew Joan had retreated to the place in her mind where nothing could reach her.

At the mention of food, however, Edrit's face broke into an enormous grin and he even laughed as he gave his wholehearted agreement to this new plan. Zetta, however, remained sullen and silent. Gareth was the only one who noticed. Sardonically he raised a questioning brow at her, his compelling eyes glittering with challenge. He had very deftly bested her, and now he was silently crowing at his all too easy victory.

He had won. With very little effort he had maneuvered her into a position where her small family was letting him turn them into his most willing hostages, and she would have to hand herself over to her enemy likewise if she wanted to keep them safe. But she would be damned before she would be gracious enough to give him his victory on a silver platter. She continued to glare at him as she crossed her arms over her chest and stood mute.

It didn't matter. In the bustle of Gareth helping them break camp no one else seemed aware that a trap had just snapped shut around her neck.

Some instinct had guided this man directly to the point where she was weakest: Edrit and Joan. She would do anything for them, and Gareth had smoothly seen to it that he held them in the palm of his hand. It really was the ultimate revenge.

She watched Gareth offer Joan his arm and disappear into the damp green forest and morosely began to follow more slowly behind. There was nothing else she could do.

Chapter 3

"Will that be all?" the girl asked with well-trained politeness, trying unsuccessfully to hide her curiosity.

Zetta stared at her with blank confusion. She had no idea what to say. Instead, she stared with ill-disguised envy at the long, clean brown hair that hung tidily down the girl's back in waves. She had noticed it from the moment the servant girl had entered the chamber and silently set about her work. Zetta could only be very grateful that her hat hid her own short mess. She had to fight hard the urge to pull it down even farther to stop her from catching even a glimpse of it.

She had never felt so intimidated in her life.

Not that the girl seemed aware that the situation was in any way odd. She treated Zetta as if she was indeed an honored guest. But Zetta couldn't let that fool her, not even in the face of this faultless politeness. Her status here was little more than a prisoner and she couldn't let herself lose sight of that fact despite the illusion of all these faultless manners. It had no basis in reality.

"Is there anything else I can do for you?" the girl asked, and this time Zetta awkwardly waved her away, pretending a sudden unshakable interest in the commotion outside the tower window, though she was very careful not to look down for fear the sight of the drop would make her sick.

The creaking sound of the heavy wooden door closing echoed ominously through the chamber. Zetta let out a loud, gusty sigh of relief, and some of the stiff unease that had held her upright since this fiasco had started left her body. Without her polite witness Zetta was free at last to turn from the nauseating view from the window. She gave the chamber a baleful once-over. Its neglected elegance made her feel bad in much the same way the well-scrubbed maid had. She had never felt so out of her depth.

The chamber hadn't been built for the likes of her and that made her want to lash out against it. Its very richness filled her with a petty urge to steal something in the vague hope that by doing so she might turn the world back to something she could understand.

This ornate place was too alien for her to comprehend.

She had never seen a tapestry before and could be called no real judge of them; however, she could tell by the way the ones on the chamber walls still shimmered with color, even under heavy layers of dust, that they were of the finest quality gold could buy. That a chamber as relatively small and unimportant such as this one could boast six appalled her.

Then there was the bed itself.

It almost looked as if it had grown where it stood. The four dark, wooden pillars were each larger than Zetta's thigh and richly carved with strange, exotic-looking creatures that she couldn't identify.

She turned her head to the side and ran a fingertip

over a creature with wings, scales and a snout. It wound itself into a knot and appeared to stretch round the bed-post trying to bite its own tail. Just above it a huge exotic flower blossomed into lush fullness but remained confined by thorns. As the design moved up the post the pattern of strange beast and imprisoned flower was repeated again and again, culminating in a ferocious bird with talons and outstretched wings that seemed to embrace the world even as it threatened.

Zetta tried to look away, but she found her gaze returning to them time and again with a childlike fascination. By comparison, the bed curtains were of relatively plain red and gold brocade, but as there was enough material in them to dress half the population of London, Zetta wasn't fool enough to think them paltry.

She couldn't resist the urge to run a reverent, light touch over the rich fabric, but as she did so a thick cloud of dust rose around her, hung suspended in the air for a second, then started its slow, stately fall back to earth. As she coughed and waved it away from her face she watched it settle on every available surface including herself. Zetta felt relieved.

Now dirt was something that she could recognize. Dirt she knew, dirt she understood. She felt more in control of a situation when there were such clear defects along with its ostentatious decoration.

Zetta looked down at her own filthy clothes with a sigh and thought despondently that her newfound appreciation was a phenomenon born of a desperate need to cling onto something familiar. But just because she knew it didn't mean that she liked it. She had been tempted to ask the serving girl to bring up some water for her to at least wash the worst of the grime away, but in the end she had lost her nerve. Besides, with the way dust coated everything in the chamber it would have been a waste of effort anyway.

She smiled as she realized that the high-and-mighty returned lord of the castle wouldn't be pleased with the state everything was in, then grimaced as she realized that once again she was thinking about the damn man. In the long hours since she'd had the misfortune to knock him off of his horse he had become the sole focus of all her mental energies.

She began to pace up and down with agitation, setting the stale rushes rustling as she went. Zetta had no idea what her next move should be, but she knew that Gareth was enjoying watching her squirm. He hadn't stopped smiling since they had arrived!

In a burst of pure frustration she kicked out at the tapestry hanging haphazardly half off the wall and watched as another cloud of dust was launched into the air. It only went to prove that Gareth had absolutely no reason to gloat about her predicament when he had problems enough of his own. Even to Zetta's untutored eye, his castle was in a disastrous condition. But she had to grudgingly admit that from a distance it was one of the most magnificent things she had ever seen in her life.

The first glimpse she'd had of the castle, just as the clouds had briefly parted to bathe the grim structure with the full force of the dawn light, had taken her breath away. The forest opened up to reveal just one small section of the stone edifice. The way it towered effortlessly over the ancient forest seemed nothing short of majestic.

She had never seen the like before. Not even London's finest palaces and royal buildings could compare to the de Hugues castle. How could anything in London compare when the city's buildings pressed in against each other? There was no room for true grandeur.

Here, however, was more than enough space for the gray soaring walls to dwarf the forest surrounding them into insignificance.

As they had slowly approached through the light misty rain, the morning sun had rested in the trees behind the fortress and the shadow cast by it had seemed to swallow up all in its path. As she had moved into the cool of it she had shivered and pulled her cloak around herself tightly to stop her bones from freezing.

It was almost beyond her comprehension that just one family could own something so large. But one family did claim it as theirs alone, and all of the power it represented was invested in each member of the de Hugues family. In that second when she had first been surrounded by the stone evidence of Gareth's power, Zetta had learned more about fear in this role of passive prisoner than she had ever known before.

Perhaps it was just as well that the closer they had gotten the more apparent the invincibility of the fortress had been marred by neglect, but with a perverseness she didn't dare analyze, she had felt disappointed as her first awe-inspiring impression had faded into unforgiving reality.

The gates themselves were battered, and though impressive enough in design, were so rotted they moved with a gentle sway in the light breeze. The walls themselves seemed strong enough, but the forest moss was swallowing up their austere surface. She had even managed a smile when Gareth's demands to be admitted were ignored for the first ten minutes. He, however, hadn't seen anything funny in the situation as minutes sped past without anyone within even bothering to inquire what all of the noise was about.

She supposed she could, with grudging bad grace, admit that he had held his temper remarkably well, considering that it was his family castle that he was having trouble gaining admittance to. After all, it didn't bode well. If they had been an attacking army, to judge by the garrison's lack of response, the portals of the fortress would have been stormed and all would have been lost before the garrison would have become aware that they were under any threat.

Gareth had had to bellow before someone bothered to poke his head over the battlements and testily demanded he shut up. Gareth had smiled up, friendly enough, as he had called out, "If someone doesn't open the gates and allow the de Hugues party into the de Hugues castle, then I'm going to take great delight in kicking what is left of the gate to smithereens. Then I'm going to take even greater pleasure teaching each of you just how angry I am. Painfully. It's your choice."

The response to this startling declaration had been almost instantaneous. Within seconds the gates had been flung open wide and Gareth had guided Joan inside with a solicitous smile.

Edrit had followed close behind, his cloak drawn tight to hide his damaged arm and leg from prying eyes but only after Zetta had sharply told him to do so. He had been too happy with this sudden change of fortune that promised decent meals to remember those things he had been doing all of his life.

Only Zetta seemed to sense the air of impending doom all around them. She had hesitated for a moment, trying desperately to think of some way to escape what would become her prison the second she crossed the threshold. But there had been no escape, not when Joan and Edrit were already inside. With great reluctance, she had passed through the shadows of the gate and into the sunshine of the inner bailey.

There, pandemonium had reigned supreme.

The news that one of the de Hugues family had finally arrived to take control of the fortress after decades of neglect had obviously spread like wildfire. Everyone from the custodian to the stable boy had found their way into the inner bailey, all eager for their first glance of their new master.

Gareth had seemed entirely impervious to the alarmingly large crowd, or perhaps he had just never expected anything less. Zetta hated the feeling of being pressed in from all sides and with an instinct that she hadn't stopped to question, she reached for her dagger only to remember that Gareth had picked it up from the mud where it had fallen in their brief struggle. Cursing its absence, she moved herself closer to Gareth. Suddenly he seemed like the only safe island in an increasingly dangerous sea.

Nothing at all had seemed to ruffle his calmness. He had smiled at all like the most genial of lords, but, at the same time, he'd managed to take immediate control of the situation. It wasn't surprising, Zetta thought darkly. After all, it was that exact same ability that had brought her to his castle in the first place. If she had been able to stop him they would all be back in the forest, safe.

And starving.

She groaned aloud and began to pace around the dusty chamber, restless.

As much as she hated the fact, she couldn't deny that Gareth had saved them from the creeping death by starvation that had been stalking them with relentless intent since they'd left London. She supposed she should be grateful. Whether he'd expose her nefarious activities to Joan was still very much uncertain, but at least for the moment, he didn't intend them to starve.

Within minutes of arriving he had organized everything up to and including a very substantial meal for them all in their separate chambers. Zetta glared balefully over at the straining tray of food that remained untouched where the serving girl had left it, its very presence seeming to mock her.

The food on the sturdy tray was of such quantity and quality that she had actually been struck entirely dumb when she had first seen it. There were cold meats, bread still warm from the ovens, local cheese and butter and even a late-season apple. To Zetta it seemed like a repast fit for a king. It was clear that while the rest of the castle might have been left to fall into neglect, the inhabitants had seen to it that they were all still well fed.

The smell of food made Zetta's stomach cramp with hunger but she made no move toward it—not yet. To do so, to eat what Gareth provided, would be a defeat and right now she needed to claim some victory from this shambles, as petty as that victory would be.

And she had lost too much already.

She had even lost the comfort of having Edrit and Joan with her as they faced this new disaster. Gareth had calmly ordered for them all to be taken to different chambers, ostensibly to allow them time to eat and rest, but Zetta hadn't been fooled for a second.

This was her prison and Gareth had carefully isolated her from her only allies. It also hadn't escaped her notice that while Joan and Edrit had been taken to the solar, she had been put up in one of the tower rooms, where escape was impossible unless she somehow acquired the ability to fly.

She wandered over to the window once more and stared out at the forest, careful to ignore the sheer drop to the ground. Freedom was so close, yet as distant as the moon. Her hands gripped the window ledge with all her strength as her eyes scanned the landscape with empty longing. Whereas yesterday she'd seen a detestable, alien scene, Zetta now saw an exquisite freedom that she'd foolishly let slip through her fingers. That it was a freedom she hadn't been able to survive in only made it all seem that much more unreachable.

In London she had managed to look after them all well with relative ease, but here, surrounded by this beauty, the country, she'd failed. She could never leave without Edrit and Joan, but even if she did connive an escape for the three of them, she had no idea of where to go, or how they would survive. And that was another power Gareth now held over her.

Truly she had been led by the devil himself when she had chosen Gareth to rob, or maybe she just should have aimed the rock to hit him instead of his horse!

Without being aware of her own actions, she wandered over to the tray of food and picked up the apple. With absentminded distraction she began rubbing it up and down against the front of her cloak before she realized what she was doing.

She glared at the yellowed red skin.

To eat it would be a defeat; to not eat would be to get weaker. She didn't want to eat Gareth's food, but the brutally practical side of her said that it was only a fool who turned down a good meal. There was no pride to be found in starving to death, and with that thought in mind she took a large bite from the fruit and began methodically to chew, taking some slight satisfaction in the fact that the apple was wrinkled and stale tasting.

One more thing that wasn't perfect in the prison Gareth had made for her.

Gareth didn't bother knocking.

He had too many long years of training to make such a tactical error. God alone knew that he had made far too many of them already when it came to his intriguing little thief.

The door creaked as soon as he pushed against it, and Gareth sighed as he realized he had just given up the small advantage of being found by surprise. Still, he did manage to catch the glimmer of fear and trepidation in Zetta's eyes as she turned to face her intruder. But only for a moment. As she wound her arms round her middle and stared up at him from her pale, defiant face, she showed no emotion other than impatience.

It was obvious that she too was contemplating her tactics, for once she was sure she had herself under control, she attacked. "What do you plan to do with me?" she asked, her chin rising imperiously, but Gareth wasn't fooled for a second. She might be trying to appear calm and brave, but he had seen fear too many times not to recognize it now.

He closed the door behind him and strolled into the room, trying to hide his own discomfort with the fact that he was the cause of her fear. He hated the thought that this strange, entrancing woman looked on him as if he would destroy her.

Not that she didn't have every reason to be afraid, he told himself sternly as he stopped in front of her. He raised his brow with sardonic amusement. "What exactly do you think I should do with the person who robbed me and left me lying in the mud?"

She scowled at him. "You have made it clear that it doesn't matter what I think," she spat out. "I offered to return your dagger and coins, but that wasn't enough. I don't see what else you can hope to gain by holding me here against my will."

"Hmmm," he murmured noncommittally, still not sure what he wanted of her. His body, however, wasn't confused by that uncertainty in the slightest. It knew exactly what it wanted. Just being in the same space as her had it tightening with a savage need. He had been taken aback by that reaction in the clearing and it still felt startling in its newness.

And yet it also felt right.

Still, he just wasn't sure what to do with this sudden white-hot desire, and he turned from her, trying to hide his body's fierce reaction from her, but as he caught sight of the large bed that dominated the chamber he had to suppress a groan. It took him several deep breaths before he could bring his body back under some semblance of control.

"What do you think of the room?" he asked, grimacing as he realized just how odd the question sounded, but it was the first safe one to enter his head that had nothing to do with the erotic images the bed had conjured. She blinked her eyes in confusion at the strange turn in the conversation.

"It's dirty," she said, clearly expecting Gareth to take it as an insult.

He walked over to the bed and flicked the curtain with his index finger. He watched with a slight smile as the brown cloud he had created danced in a sunbeam.

"It is, isn't it?" He shrugged his shoulders. "But compared to the rest of this place, it's not so bad."

He turned back to her, his gaze intense as he scanned the room minutely. "The fortress is going to need a hell of a lot of work," he said, his voice soft but vibrating with excitement. "The neglect is staggering. It's almost criminal." He laughed. "Indeed, some of it *is* actually criminal. The man who my father left in charge, John Parchi, has been robbing the place blind for years, from what I have seen this morning."

What he didn't add was that he had actually started to develop a level of respect for the sniveling little bastard. It took a perverse kind of courage to stay when it was obvious that the game was over. Instead, John had held his head high as he had taken Gareth with methodical care round the fortress all morning, knowing that it would be all too blatant that he had been abusing his position and the trust that had been placed in him.

Besides, even with all the visible signs of neglect, Gareth had been so dazzled by the fortress itself that he hadn't really noticed all the work that would be needed to undo all the damage the decades of neglect had wrought. It was magnificent. It had been built as a bold statement of authority at a time when the conquerors had wanted the defeated to know their place, but it was also so much more than that. Everywhere it was clear that no care or expense had been spared. Having seen that, it was inconceivable to Gareth that his father had turned his back on it all and returned to Normandy as if he was leaving nothing of importance behind him.

"It has so much potential," he said, his gaze finally focusing back on Zetta.

"But what does any of that have to do with me?" she asked, growing increasingly nervous.

"My dear thief, as I scarcely understand what it has to do with me yet, I cannot tell you where you fit into all of this. I have no answers to your questions." He turned the full force of his charm into his smile and Zetta felt an overwhelming desire to scream.

"Enough," she ground out. "I don't know what you are doing, but I have had enough. Just get on with whatever punishment you have planned and stop treating me like a . . ."

The word for how he was behaving escaped her.

"Like?" he asked with gentle curiosity.

For the first time since he had confronted her in the clearing, she knew her guard had slipped. "I don't know."

Gareth saw the strange welter of emotions pass over her face and felt his chest tighten as he realized again that he was the cause of her fear and confusion. He wasn't sure why it should matter, not after what she had done to him, but it did, very much.

Her slim shoulders slumped in defeat, as if the rod of steel that had been holding her up had been removed. She was defeated and he hated it. All thoughts of revenge evaporated and he found himself wanting to give her a victory, anything to take away the hurt.

It was at that moment that he knew he hadn't brought her here for any sort of revenge at all. He didn't understand it himself, but, at the same time, he knew it was perfectly right.

"Do you have in your possession any suitable clothes?" he asked and tried not to smile as her confusion dissolved into a very feminine irritation.

"What I am wearing is perfectly suitable," she said with stiff dignity.

"For a not very discerning vagrant, perhaps. It is not,

however, worthy of any woman." He walked round her, assessingly. "No, these won't do at all."

Zetta glared at him when he returned to face her. She didn't like the way his eyes twinkled merrily at her, almost as if he was inviting her to share some private joke.

She placed her hands on her hips and tried to ignore the pain that went through her when she realized that he was laughing at her. She had no pretensions to being pretty or feminine or desirable, but she didn't like standing by while some man laughed at her because of her failings.

But she could do nothing about it, she realized with angry frustration. She was powerless with this man, and not just because he held her and her family in a very gracious prison, she realized with a start. All of a sudden Zetta became very aware of just how large and strong he was. At the slightest provocation, he could turn into the warrior who lurked just under his calm, amused exterior. That alone was enough to give him power over her.

She took a deep, steadying breath and regarded him levelly.

"What have my clothes to do with the fact that I robbed you?"

"Not much really. And don't think that I have forgotten that not inconsequential fact," he said, with a calm infuriating shrug. "But right now, I have other things on my mind."

Gareth took a step closer to her and Zetta instinctively stepped backward. Every fiber of her body was aware of the bewildering excitement that charged through the chamber and into the heart of her being. Even as she continued to retreat from his steady advance, she could feel her heart rate speeding up and her stomach tightening, readying, as a hotness filled her.

When she felt the cold, stone wall at her back, she let out a small whimper of frustration, but, at the same time, she had to hold on to it to stop her knees from giving out from under her.

Gareth's eyes narrowed and she noticed that the broad chest that now filled her vision was moving with great speed, as if he had been running hard. The sight of his muscles working under the soft fabric of his tunic made her mouth go dry. Nervous, she ran her tongue over her parched bottom lip.

It was a provocation that Gareth couldn't ignore.

"I've wanted to do this since I lay in the mud and you made me burn with just a touch," he murmured, lowering his head. He noticed with distracted satisfaction that Zetta's eyelids fluttered closed just before his lips claimed hers. For a moment she was still beneath him; then suddenly she gave a little moan and reached up to wrap her arms around his neck. It was like a fire in his blood to know that she wanted this as much as he did.

And God knows, he wanted this!

As his lips moved over hers in possession, Zetta felt as if the world had stopped turning. She had gone from fear to need in an instant, and she had never felt anything as completely right as the feel of his tongue moving hotly over her lips. She didn't bother to question the instinct that led her to open her mouth for him. All she knew was that she wanted more of him, needed to absorb more of this heat, and she would do anything to get it.

He accepted her invitation with alacrity.

As he wrapped himself around her she realized that it was what she wanted, but, at the same time, it wasn't enough. She needed more.

Her arms tightened their hold on him, trying to drag him closer. She could feel his smile against her as he complied. His hands shifted down to her buttocks and pulled that newly throbbing part of her against his groin.

She buried her hands into his hair and let out a moan of frustration as his mouth left hers and began to rain heated kisses along her jaw. It was only then that she became aware that his hands had left her buttocks.

They were moving upward. Gently they caressed her ribs and then suddenly he was cupping her breasts, his heated strength engulfing her.

She felt as if she had been plunged into cold water. The delicious warmth that had been filling her fled as raw, dark memories of another's touch rose up inside her, destroying all of her arousal with loathing. Before she had time to think about what she wanted to do her hands dropped to her sides and her knee flew up toward his groin with cold, calculating accuracy. For such a large man, he moved with surprising speed, swiftly shifting the vulnerable area out of her reach. Her knee slammed instead into his rock-hard thigh and pain shot through the knee, making her whimper.

Stunned, he stepped out of her arms. She could only imagine what he saw as he stared at her with confusion. She leaned with helpless abandon against the wall, her lips moist and bruised from his kisses. But it wasn't defiance she felt in her quaking soul. She couldn't understand what had happened to her. One moment she had been more than willing; the next she had attacked him with the only weapon at her disposal.

She realized sickly that he had every right to be angry with her. How could he believe that she hadn't deliberately led him on and then tried to geld him? He couldn't. As she waited for the inevitable blow to fall, a feeling akin to grief went through her as she noticed that his face was now entirely free from any sign of the brief, sweet passion they had shared.

But no blow fell.

Instead, he just stared at her for a second, and then he threw back his head and began to laugh, the deep, rich sound curling around her, warming her almost as much as his passion had done. When his laughter finally faded, he reached out a calloused hand and ran it gently over her pale cheek.

"Ah, my little thief, I've barely known you a day and already you have me in a near fatal state of confusion. You are never what I expect you to be, are you? When I expect fear, you give me defiance. When I expect strength, you give me vulnerability. When I expect anger, you give me passion." He shook his head and dropped his hand away, but Zetta still felt pinned by his gentle eyes. There, light blue depths held an intoxicating mix of compassion, laughter. And something else she couldn't even begin to name.

Whatever it was, it stole her breath away. She had to swallow hard before she could find her voice. "I don't understand you either," she said, her voice strange to her own ears.

"At least that is something in which we are equals. That gives me some comfort." But even as he said those words, he knew them to be a lie.

He didn't feel equal to anything. At that very moment he felt as if he had been neatly cleaved from himself. The kiss had stolen all peace from him and yet completed him. He had never felt anything like it before.

For the first time in years, he actually felt whole and alive. Gone was the vague hollowness. Every gap inside him seemed to be filled with the woman who stood in front of him and looked at him as if he'd lost his sanity.

Her lack of understanding was to be expected, he supposed. He had a bruised thigh to prove that perhaps his little thief hadn't quite yet reached that same conclusion he had. It seemed she needed a little more time to see, what seemed to him, perfectly obvious.

"I'll send some appropriate clothes up for you," he murmured with an appeasing smile, while his eyes flicked down over her well-hidden figure. He couldn't help but be intrigued by the thought of being able to see the surprisingly luscious little body that, just moments before, he had felt pressed up against his.

Long experience told him it was going to be well worth seeing.

"What about Edrit and my mother?"

He wanted to smile at the way her voice still quavered with passion as she spoke, but he knew that, at this moment, she wouldn't appreciate his odd humor.

"Don't worry about them for the moment. They have eaten and are now getting the rest they need. You will see them soon." He reached out and held her unresisting hand in his. "It would be well if you did the same."

Although he was frightened that he would scare her even further, he couldn't stop himself from turning her hand palm up and placing a lingering, possessive kiss at its center.

"Rest, my little thief."

With one last, long look at her bewildered face he turned and left the room. He closed the door carefully behind him, and as he walked away he felt himself smiling broadly.

All of a sudden it was very good just to be alive.

Chapter 4

"Zetta, come and have a look at what I've found!" Edrit called out to her, his voice vibrant with excitement as it reached her. Despite her ever-present worry, Zetta was smiling as she followed the sound into the dark stables.

It took a moment for her eyes to adjust from the light of the bailey to the gloom. When she still couldn't find the large figure of her brother among the horse stalls, she called out softly so as not to disturb the horses, "Edrit, where are you?"

"Over here!" he yelled back. Zetta rolled her eyes as his loud voice caused the highly strung horses to move restlessly, several of them whinnying a loud protest at the disturbance.

"Shhh," she hushed Edrit when she found him in an empty stall, hunkered down staring intently into the hay. She moved to crouch beside him, but only after she had made sure that the hem of her dress was well clear of the muck on the floor.

The dresses might not have been her idea, but over the three weeks she had been wearing them she had come to learn their ways with surprising ease. She still felt like a player in a part, but she was getting used to them.

She placed a hand gently on Edrit's back. "You mustn't talk so loud. It frightens the horses."

"Sorry, but you did ask. I had to answer you, didn't I?"

She smiled at him and shook her head, knowing that she would never make him understand. "I suppose." She leaned into him just a little, being careful not to knock him off balance. "So just what was all of the noise about anyway? I was looking for you in the bailey. Why are you skulking around in here instead of outside getting fresh air like I told you to?"

Edrit very carefully reached out with his good hand and moved aside a little of the hay. Zetta's smile broadened as she spotted the three little black kittens nestled on top of each other, sleeping warm and content among the hay.

"I found them yesterday, Zetta, when you were busy with Mother and sent me outside." His hand was ever so gentle as it stroked one of the soft, downy heads. "Aren't they nice?"

Zetta nodded with great reluctance, her own hand itching to pick up one of the dear little bundles. She didn't. If she did, she would only begin to become attached to it, and there was no room in her life for useless, needy little things that would be entirely dependent on her and could contribute nothing.

With a sinking heart she watched as Edrit did pick up one and held it to his chest with his good hand. She knew where all of this was leading but didn't know how she was going to stop it. The kitten mewed a little but, with an already well-developed self-preservation instinct, realized that it had found itself a soft, warm place. It staggered around a couple of times in a spindly legged fashion before snuggling down and closing its eyes.

"They don't seem to have a mother. There wasn't one here yesterday either. If they don't have one . . ."

"Oh, they have one all right, Edrit," Zetta said, trying to stop the request she already knew was coming. "They are far too fat and content looking to have been abandoned. Their mother must have just popped out to find herself some nice, plump mice for her lunch, knowing that they are warm and safe enough sleeping here. She will be back before they have even had time to miss her."

"Oh." He looked at the kitten nestled with sweet trust against his tunic, and then lifted his face to Zetta, hope burning bright in his eyes. "Maybe she won't miss this one? She has got two others."

"Edrit . . ."

"Well, three is a lot of babies to look after at one time. She might even be pleased if I took just one. . . ."

"No." Zetta sounded stern and final, but this time she just couldn't seem to stop her hand from reaching out to stroke the kitten, and she melted a little. Edrit beamed at her, knowing her resolve was teetering.

"What the hell are you two doing?"

All softness disappeared from her, and she snatched her hand away from the soft, enticing fur of the kitten. With an instinctive haste she stood up and moved to stand between Edrit and the threatening man who filled the stall's doorway.

It was the head groom and he glared at her with fury as he waved a pitchfork at them. Zetta tried not to let the lethal-looking tines of the pitchfork distract her, but she couldn't stop staring at them as they moved closer, not when he had them leveled at the center of her chest. She began to pray that just this once Edrit would manage to stay quiet.

"It is no business of yours what we are doing," she said stiffly, struggling to make herself sound unaffected.

"It's my business when the likes of you are lurking around in my stables," he growled, and Zetta could see his hand tightening around the pitchfork. A part of her wanted to get herself and Edrit out of there with as much haste as possible, but that wasn't an option as long as he stood blocking the door. So instead she stood her ground and regarded him with cold dislike.

"These are not your stables. They are Sir Gareth's and, as you know, he has given us permission to go wherever we like within the castle walls. And that includes *his* stables."

"Well, Sir Gareth ain't here now, is he? And I am. So if I say I don't want you and your brother in here, you witch, I don't want you here. I suggest the pair of you just clear off." He lifted the pitchfork at Zetta and his smile had a leering quality that made her shiver. "Or else I might decide to hear just how loud you can scream."

He wouldn't really hurt them, she told herself. He was a bully and if she took him on he would back down. If she didn't, he would then only wait for another chance to play his little games. But with Edrit crouching defenselessly behind her, she wasn't prepared to put her theory to the test.

She turned round and placed a gentle hand on her brother's stooped shoulders. "Come on." She tried to keep all anger and fear out of her voice so as not to frighten him further. A wave of relief went through her as Edrit put the kitten down and got to his feet with a clumsy stumble and let her lead him past the angry man without saying a word.

The man kept the pitchfork leveled at them as they passed, and only once they were back in the stable ward did she sag with relief. She should be used to it by now, she told herself with stern realism as she made her spine stiffen once more. They had been treated by almost everyone in Castle de Hugues as if they were an evil invasion. Everyone was afraid that just by having Edrit or herself near they could somehow become tainted. It had been made clear from the very start that they weren't welcome, despite all of Gareth's insistence that they were to be treated as honored guests.

The irony that he was the only person who treated them with any respect was not lost on Zetta. After all, he was the only one who had a real crime to lay at her feet rather than some childish babble about witchcraft. Instead of revenge, however, he had shouldered the burden of the three of them along with everything else as if it was only natural that he should do so.

There was nothing natural about the situation as far as Zetta was concerned. If he had despised her, shunted the three of them off to some obscure corner of his castle and left them there to rot, then she could have understood him. Instead, he played the genial host, going out of his way to lavish them with his hospitality.

The long journey had sapped the last of Joan's strength and she hadn't left the solar chamber since their arrival, but each evening she seemed to glow a little because Gareth always went up and sat beside her bed or coaxed her into a chair. Wherever she was, he regaled her with funny stories and silliness until she was giggling like a young girl and calling him a "dear man."

Edrit he treated like a friend. He never once complained about the way Edrit had taken to following him around like a lost soul. He actually encouraged it by always trying to point out something new that Edrit might find entertaining. And half the time it was in fact him seeking Edrit out for nothing more than a conversation, as if Edrit was his equal and a friend.

It amazed Zetta that not once did he patronize her brother or stare at his poor, twisted limbs as if he was disgusted in any way. He talked to him man-to-man, and because of it Zetta would have willingly given him anything, everything, he asked for.

But strangest of all was the fact that he never asked for anything in return. It seemed that he could give of himself without expecting payment in kind. The concept was so alien to her that she had spent the first week waiting for him to come to her and demand settlement for all of his considerably generous gifts. She still wasn't sure how she would have responded if he had, not when the passionate kiss they had shared had somehow branded her and was still plaguing her with the temptation it represented. Night after night she woke, hot, anxious and remembering that too brief kiss as if it had become the whole reason for her existence.

But her response to a demand of payment was not tested, because not once did Gareth make any move to claim her. In truth, he seemed to be avoiding her. While he bent over backward to spend time with her family, he only ever seemed to find her by accident and she found herself becoming increasingly irritated by his behavior even though she knew it was perverse to be so.

The truth was she never regretted anything like she regretted the way she had stopped his soul-shattering kiss. He must have been so appalled by her behavior that he had banished everything about their kiss from his mind. If she was honest, she couldn't blame him for that.

So instead she watched him from a distance, her admiration and respect growing despite her best efforts to suppress them. She couldn't explain, not even to herself, the tight, light-headed nervous feeling that assailed her whenever she saw him, even if it was from the other side of a crowded chamber. He didn't have to say one word to her, and yet her heart would start to race. And strangest of all, she hated her weakness but found it addictive at the same time.

"Zetta, I want the kittens," Edrit said suddenly, cutting her free from her gloomy thoughts for the moment.

She sighed as they continued to walk away from the stables and slipped her arm through his. She gave him a gentle, reassuring squeeze. "I told you that we couldn't keep them, now didn't I?"

"Yes, but . . ."

"No buts about it. We can't keep them, and that is final."

"But I don't trust that man. He is mean and I know he will hurt them if he notices them." He stopped still and turned to her, pinning her in place with his pleading eyes. "Please, Zetta."

She stared up into his begging blue eyes and found herself floundering for a second, then forced herself to shake her head. "No, Edrit, we can't take them."

"Why?" he demanded with a rare anger.

"Because . . ." She searched her mind for some reason that he might understand. Then it came to her. "Because they're Sir Gareth's. And you wouldn't want to take away one of his kittens, now would you?"

He stared at her for a second, then shook his head. Zetta could have groaned with relief. She hated lying to him, but she couldn't risk him taking on the groom to go and get his kittens. But her relief was short-lived, and her eyes narrowed with renewed worry when the mobile half of his face split into a sudden grin. He grabbed her hand and began to drag her across the ward.

"We will ask him, Zetta. If we offer to look after them and keep them safe he is bound to say yes and then I can have them."

Zetta tried desperately to extract herself from his grip but it was futile. His hands were at least twice the size of hers, and because his right hand had to compensate for the lack of strength in his left, his grip on her was unbreakably strong.

He dragged her on in his wake, and she tried to resign herself to the fact that it now didn't matter what Gareth thought about her. He was going to see her whether he liked it or not.

Gareth smiled with satisfaction as Anthony's sword overreached itself, leaving his side open and unprotected. Taking advantage of the lapse, he brought the full impact of the flat of his sword against the other man's hip, knocking him to the ground.

Gareth dropped his sword point to the ground and smiled at the fallen man. "You are getting better," he said as he reached out his left hand to help the kneeling man find his feet.

Anthony let out a long groan as he stood, holding a hand to his bruised hip. He glared at Gareth balefully, hating the way that he had defeated him without even breaking into a sweat.

"How can you say I'm doing better when I'm still eating mud every time I go a round with you? Sure, I'm doing better than some of the others, but that's not saying much when you still manage to bring me to my knees every time."

"Yes, and I have also noticed that each time you are lasting a little longer and that you never seem make the same mistake twice. This time you lasted a full quarter of an hour"—he clapped his arm around the other man's back and grinned at him—"and to my way of thinking, that is quiet an achievement. Three weeks ago you could barely last ten seconds."

Anthony gave a rueful laugh as he ambled toward the edge of the practice yard. He grabbed his tunic from where it rested on the fence and mopped his face with it. He leaned back against the new timber fence and watched Gareth move his broad sword through the basic positions then swing it with purpose as if against some unseen opponent. Anthony could only envy the other man's ease and skill.

"Well, Sir Gareth," he said after a moment, "we can only hope that we are not attacked or faced with a real enemy till you have taught the rest of us what the hell to do with our swords. Until then, I'd say we are as good as defenseless."

Gareth's laugh was loud and carefree as, with a practiced final flourish, he slipped the sword back into the scabbard that hung low over his hips.

"Well, I'll see what I can organize with the rest of England, but until then let's hope that once the gate is fully restored, the world is put off by the castle's stout wall, as indeed they have been for the past forty years." He squinted up at the sun. "And in the meantime, could you see if you can find Mark. It would seem that he is going to be late for his practice. Again."

Anthony nodded, throwing his tunic casually over his

shoulder as he left. Gareth wandered over to a barrel of water and filled up a pitcher.

He would never admit it to anyone, but he was enjoying this new life very much. Each morning he woke up anticipating what the day might bring and he was working harder than he had done for years. Not since his days of fighting with Robert's company of mercenaries had he put in so much hard work, but he was thriving on it.

And best of all it was paying off. All around him he could see signs of improvement. It might have been only three weeks, but already he could see the shape things would take when all was running smoothly.

When he'd first had the practice yard cleared and had assembled the garrison there, he'd had to admit that he'd doubted his own ability to make a difference. He had never seen such a pathetic group of fighting men in his life. They had all grown impossibly soft and were next to useless when it came to arms and fighting. He had found a certain grim enjoyment in the incredulous look on their faces as he had informed them that, from now on, their easy life was over. That they would all be organized into groups and would be spending at least two hours of every day in the practice yard.

Gareth took a long drink from the pitcher, then tipped a little of the water over his head. Those first sessions would live in his memory in all of their pitiable detail for many years to come. It might have actually been funny had it not had such a lethal potential. Only eight of the men had known what a sword was and had been able to at least wield it with some level of professionalism. Unfortunately, that same eight had the average age of fifty. They should have been retired years ago, and under normal circumstances Gareth would have given them all a cottage and let them get on with their dying in peace, but he couldn't afford that.

Not yet.

He couldn't allow their skills to be lost, not when the only training the younger men seemed to have received consisted of having been given a sword and told not to hurt themselves.

Or anyone else, Gareth thought, with a wry grin.

Most of them had been unable to hit anything smaller than a six-foot wall, and those first training sessions had been deeply depressing, but he had been lucky. Some of the men had started to show their potential sooner than he could have dared hope. Who knew, maybe in six months' time they would actually be able to defend the castle.

He drained the pitcher and leaned back against the fence. He closed his eyes, preparing to enjoy these few, stolen moments of peace and quiet before the next session.

"Gareth," Edrit called out, entering the yard in his usual unstoppable rush.

Despite the fact it broke into his peace, Gareth was smiling as he opened his eyes and turned to greet Edrit. He almost laughed out loud when he saw the long-suffering look on Zetta's face as she was dragged on remorselessly in her brother's wake. Instead, he let himself enjoy the simple pleasure of just being in her presence. The way she had changed in the past weeks was staggering. It was almost impossible to remember the time when she had looked like a beggar boy.

The change that brought him hours of unexpected pleasure was, however, the dresses she now always wore instead of her boy's rags. What had started as a whim was fast becoming something of an obsession. When he had ordered the housekeeper to see some suitable clothes sent up to his guests, he had only been doing what had seemed like the right thing to do.

However, when he had first seen her standing self-consciously pleating the material of a green dress the housekeeper had found, all sense of altruism had died. She had looked so beautiful, yet so hesitant and vulnerable that he had lost yet another little piece of his heart to her. In that moment, he had wanted to give her everything that was within his power to give. Each week he spent a small fortune on rich fabric, but to see her growing more confident and beautiful with each passing day had made it all worthwhile.

Today, her dress was a deep russet and was laced so that when she walked the gentle outline of her body appeared for a brief tantalizing moment, then disappeared again. That glimpse was enough to prove that no one would mistake her for a boy again. The soft flair of her hips from the pinch of her waist and the graceful line of her breasts declared her all female. The effect was devastating.

Her face too had started to fill out. The hollows etched by near starvation were now all but gone. Where there had been angles there were now the start of sweet curves, and when she smiled she even had a small dimple on her left cheek that would only deepen as her body blossomed.

He frowned as he noticed that the violet circles under her eyes were more stubborn. The bruises were still there, giving her a hunted look, but he was sure that with a little more time they too would go. Even with them, she still radiated a health and vitality that was magnetic.

When Edrit and Zetta came to a jumbled stop just

in front of him, he could feel desire stirring in his veins as her unique scent reached him. He had only to see her across the main hall and he would go into a slow burn. While it wasn't comfortable to want so much without getting, he found he could well stand the torment just as long as it meant that she was near.

But he didn't want to frighten her, not again. So he had tried to control his raging desires with an iron will, and when that had failed, he avoided her altogether. That hadn't worked, either. His need for her was as strong and disquieting as it had been from the first time she had touched him, but at least by giving her time she was starting to lose the startled look of a hunted deer. Even now, when he wanted nothing more than to pull her to himself and devastate her with a kiss, she looked almost peevish as she tried to extract herself from Edrit's grip, but certainly not afraid.

He almost groaned out loud his desire when the sun chose that moment to reappear from behind a cloud. Zetta's short curly hair, free from her hat, suddenly blazed to life in a riot of reds and golds. She looked, for all the world, like a temptress who had been sent to earth with the sole purpose of tormenting poor mere mortals like himself.

He had to forcefully drag his eyes away from the vision she presented and focus in on Edrit instead. He too was looking better but, Gareth thought, with a grin, he failed to have the same effect on Gareth's senses as his sister. Still, as Edrit's eyes blazed with his childlike excitement, Gareth smiled at him.

"What can I do for you, my friend?"

"Can I have your kittens?"

Gareth's brow rose in confusion. "Sorry?"

Zetta cleared her throat, clearly embarrassed by the

situation, but as usual standing stoutly by her brother. "Um, you might not realize it, but there are some kittens in the stables and Edrit has become quite taken with them and would like to keep one." She rolled her eyes with expressive exaggeration. "Well, actually, he'd like to keep them all, but I have explained to him that they are yours and he can't have them."

"Ahhh," Gareth murmured, trying to suppress the urge to laugh. He understood exactly what Zetta was trying to do and he could only admire her bravery. He had already learnt just how hard it was to distract Edrit when he had set his mind on something. Sometimes it felt a little like trying to change the tides.

Only when he was sure that he had himself back under control, he nodded his head with deep seriousness. "Yes, well, I'm sure . . . er, *my* kittens are very happy where they are. And I'm also sure that their mother would prefer it if you didn't move them or else she might not be able to find them."

Zetta cast him a grateful look and Gareth realized just how pitiful he had become when he felt his chest expanding at the small sign of approval. Really, he was becoming more and more like a dog begging for scraps of her affection with every passing day.

"No, Gareth," Edrit said firmly, ignoring all of the other undercurrents and staying fixed on his heart's desire, "their mother wouldn't want them to stay there, not when there is a mean man with a pitchfork. He might hurt them. What then? He threatened Zetta too. So he wouldn't be nice to kittens, I think."

All humor fled from Gareth's face and his eyes burned with an intense focus. Zetta felt her stomach knot as he changed into a cold, deliberate man.

"Who threatened Zetta?" he asked Edrit with chilling

insistence, who rushed to answer, sensing a new way to get what he wanted.

"It was the old groom, the one who looks like a rat. He held a pitchfork at her, pointy bits out, and said that we had to leave or else. I don't think that's the kind of man you would want to look after your kittens. He won't be nice to them." He smiled at Gareth beatifically. "I'd be very nice to them."

Gareth shifted his gaze to Zetta, his face vibrant with an intensity that she had never seen in him before. "What happened, Zetta?"

She swallowed hard and lowered her gaze. Unfortunately, this brought her eyes level with his naked, muscular chest, which she had been desperately trying to ignore. Her mind was so distracted by the unexpected sight of his lush beauty that she found herself mumbling, "Nothing much really. Nothing for you to worry about . . ."

"What. Happened." He enunciated each word very carefully, and she shivered as she realized just how much willpower he had to exert to keep his temper under some semblance of control.

"The head groom took exception to us hanging around the stables. . . ."

"Right," Gareth said, his voice vibrant with fury, and Zetta stared in helpless openmouthed shock as he walked off toward the stables with Edrit following close behind.

Gareth hadn't bothered to put his tunic back on and she couldn't stop herself from gaping at the beautiful way his skin seemed to absorb the sunlight, looking, for all the world, like burnished copper. She found her gaze drawn helplessly down the long line of his spine, following it till it disappeared into the top of the sword belt that rode low on his hips. She had never thought of a back as being sensual before, but the way Gareth's muscles worked under his taught skin as he strode toward the stable was the most exciting thing she had ever seen.

It took her several moments to realize that she was ogling him like some tavern wench. A flush appeared high on her cheekbones and she picked up her skirts to run after them. By the time she reached the stables Gareth had the groom pinned to the wall with his forearm. He seemed to exert no effort at all to hold him there with one arm, and she watched with horrified fascination as he reached down with his other for the pommel of the sword with casual ease.

". . . but, Sir Gareth, I did nothing wrong!" the man protested, his words struggling to make it past his constricted throat. "I was just trying to stop those . . . those people from upsetting your horses."

"You should be more worried about trying not to upset me." Gareth's voice was at once soft and lethal. "And I find it most upsetting to discover that scum like you would dare threaten a woman who is my guest and under my express protection."

"But, sir . . . I would never do that. . . . But you don't understand. They are evil. . . ."

Gareth leaned down hard, cutting off the rest of the feeble excuses. He watched the man struggle for air and, with expert knowledge, let him go just before he lost consciousness entirely.

The man slid, all but senseless, down the wall and slumped on the floor as he tried desperately to get air into his starved lungs.

"Get out of my sight. I want you gone from my land by nightfall. Is that understood?"

"But where will I go?" the man whined piteously.

"To the very devil, for all I care," Gareth said with a snarl, turning from the man, who scurried away before Gareth could change his mind and decide to kill him.

Gareth drew a deep, steadying breath, trying to regain some control over his temper as he moved toward Zetta.

By the time he reached her, his eyes were warming, and if she hadn't been able to see the shadow of his cold fury still lurking in their very depth, she might almost have believed that it had never existed. She found it hard to understand that this man had just done violence for her, to protect her. No one but Edrit had ever done that before, and it took a moment for the shock of it to dissipate before she could speak.

"What the hell did you do that for? I can look after myself, you know," she hissed, hating the sound of her own ungratefulness but, at the same time, she didn't dare trust in the kind protection he seemed to be offering.

He smiled into her eyes, and despite her indignation she could feel a part of her melting. "I know you can, Zetta, but from now on, I would like to do it for you."

She watched in bewildered fascination as he sealed his pledge by lifting her hand and placing a soft kiss on the back of it, all the while holding her gaze. His bottomless blue eyes burnt her with their intensity. She swallowed hard. She didn't know what to say, how to behave. This experience was too far beyond her ability to make any sense of it.

Before she had to find some way to answer the impossible and make a fool of herself, however, Edrit ran into the stable from where he'd been waiting outside. He was so impervious to everything but the mission he was on that he wasn't going to let the sight of his friend Gareth holding Zetta's hand distract him. He headed straight

for the stall that held the kittens and let out such a loud,
distressed cry that it penetrated even Zetta's addled
senses.

She tried to get her hand back and when she failed
utterly settled for pulling Gareth along so that she
could find out what Edrit's new problem was.

As she reached his side he looked up at her with a
very disgruntled look.

"The mother is back," he said and plopped himself
down beside the kittens. He sounded so tragically sad
that Zetta knew better than to show her relief.

"It's for the best, Edrit," she said gently, knowing only
too well just how little a consolation that could be. She
wasn't surprised that Edrit found no comfort in it.

"But I wanted a kitten."

Relinquishing his hold on Zetta's hand at last, Gareth
hunkered down beside Edrit, smiling as he watched the
kittens greedily drink from their very contented mother.

"They're a little young yet to be taken from their
mother, Edrit." Gareth's voice was full of soft compassion and Zetta began to panic as she felt the ice around
her heart begin to melt a little more. "But I can promise you that you can come down here and play with
them whenever you like until they are larger. Then you
can pick the one you like and keep it with you in the
solar."

"Can I please?"

"Of course." He threw an arm around Edrit's shoulders and the two of them watched the antics of the kittens in companionable silence. Zetta could feel her
throat tightening as she watched them. She knew she
should be angry at Gareth for making Edrit believe that
they were going to stay here, but it just didn't seem to
matter at such a moment.

The sight the two of them presented held her spell-bound. It struck her in some way she couldn't quite place that the two of them were even a little alike. She held her head to one side. They were both of a similar size and vaguely similar coloring, and she realized with a tightening heart that Gareth might very well have been the kind of man her brother would have grown into had his life been different.

Not that what she felt for Gareth bore any similarity to her love for Edrit. But with each passing day, Gareth was inching his way a little bit further into her heart and there was nothing that she could do to stop it. Now she lacked the will to even try.

He seemed to have forgotten that she was his pris-oner, and it confused her. She didn't understand him at all. Now the groom, on the other hand, she could understand all too well. He was a perfect example of the men she had known all her life. The men from her world were mean, violent bullies who got their way by using their fists. Having the brains that they so patently lacked was why she had managed to survive so well.

In those very rare instances when that wasn't enough to extract herself from a situation, she had been able to rely on Edrit to provide the brute force she needed. While he didn't have a violent bone in his body, in his defense of her he seemed to find what he needed to use the uncertain strength hidden in his twisted limbs. Be-tween the two of them there had been few mountains they hadn't been able to conquer.

Until Gareth.

She had never before known a man who smiled more than he frowned other than Edrit. His big, boom-ing laugh seemed to fill any room with light. The way it curled round her, warming her dark heart, was addictive. How he could find so much to amuse him in life defeated her, and she would have dismissed him as a half-wit were it not for the fact that his eyes gleamed with intelligence.

And with kindness.

And with compassion.

And more often than not, when he thought she wasn't looking, with a passion that she longed to drown in. Even right now, as she pretended to have her full concentration on the kittens, she watched him from under her eyelashes as he watched her.

His hot gaze moved over her body, lingering on the slight swell of her breasts. Though she knew the contours of her body to be well hidden by the fabric of her dress, she could feel her breasts peaking as if he had stripped her bare and it was his hands that touched her, rather than just his heated gaze. Before, when she had actually felt his touch upon her breast, she had been frightened by memories of her past humiliation as the victim of crude, unwanted caresses. But now those dark moments had lost their sting, and when she thought about him touching her again, she felt only a melting desire. She felt entirely mesmerized by the realization that she actually wanted him. She closed her eyes, savoring the new sensations, and when she opened them again he snared her gaze and held her helpless in the depths of his blue eyes.

He knew. He knew that her body was even now preparing for his touch. His eyes smiled at her and told her that he knew, and that he wanted to touch her just as much as she wanted to be touched. But he made no move toward her.

He would wait, she now realized with certainty, until she was ready to come to him. He would not force her, or harm her, and for the first time in her life she almost believed that such a man existed. He would continue to wait until she came to him. Then, and only then, would he give her everything she wanted.

And more.

She had only to find in herself the bravery to take the first step.

Chapter 5

The noise inside the main hall was almost offensively loud, and as Gareth took a sip from the tankard in front of him he struggled to hide his growing boredom with it. All around him the men of the garrison were eating, drinking and generally making merry, just as they did every evening. The serving women moved among them freely, laughing as they swatted away busy hands with expert ease. They would let nothing distract them from the all-important deed of bringing yet more food for the table.

Gareth had on previous evenings felt a mild fascination with the way that there seemed to be a tireless stream of serving girls from the kitchens till nigh on midnight. He had never seen so much food consumed in all his life, yet the men seemed to take it for granted. Every night the same thing happened, and while he had no idea how it was possible to produce food in such vast quantities, he had enjoyed watching the pageant and ritual that rivaled that of the royal court.

Until tonight.

Tonight all he felt was an irritation that grew more restless with each passing minute.

He placed his tankard back down on the solid oak table with careful control and narrowed his eyes as he surveyed the scene before him. Everything was just as it had been since his arrival, yet now all seemed tainted and sinister.

Until now he had smiled indulgently at the drunken antics of the men, but tonight he found a deep, cold rage growing inside of him, and the noise of merry-making sounded more and more like the hiss of an angry mob intent on drawing blood. Everything was different and menacing now. And he was only too well aware why it had all changed.

The memory of the dismissed groom loomed large in his mind. He could still see the look of absolute con-viction that had been on the man's face as he had tried to tell him that Zetta was evil. No matter how much Gareth wanted to forget that look, he couldn't. The threat it represented was far too real.

And he had seen that self-same look on the faces of most of the people in this room at some time. Right now they were smiling, happy and relaxed as they often were, but that changed whenever Zetta or Edrit hap-pened to cross their paths. He had seen their fear, hatred and repulsion before, but until he had con-fronted the groom who had dared to threaten them with a pitchfork, he hadn't truly understood just how dangerous a combination those feelings were. That was a mistake he now regretted.

He had dealt with the groom, but he knew with a cold certainty that he hadn't made Zetta and her little family any safer. He could see threats to them all around and he didn't know how he was going to defeat them all. But he would try.

He didn't for one moment question this need to keep Zetta safe from every conceivable danger. It just was. Still, he knew he couldn't turn everyone out of the castle just because of this newfound need. No, he had to find some other way to protect her, but for the life of him he couldn't think how it was to be achieved.

He stared darkly at the far wall and its ragged war banners, relics from the conquest, which he had yet to replace. The problem was going round and around in his mind, blinding him to everything else about him. Still, he was aware of Zetta the exact moment she entered the hall.

She came in unannounced and made no move to approach him, but still he knew she was there.

For the moment all of his brooding thoughts dissolved in the immediate sense of well-being that filled him just knowing that she was near. He felt himself smile as he noticed that she had changed her dress since her afternoon with the kittens. The gown she now wore was of a light blue silk that flowed over her gentle curves more exactly, and he was grateful to be distracted from his dark thoughts by the far more pleasant speculation of what lay beneath the expensive fabric.

His smile died, however, when he realized what she was about.

She moved with nervous speed among the tables, taking a little bit of food here, a little bit of food there, putting it all carefully onto the tray that she carried with her. More than once, her hands were slapped away by the men, and when any of the women saw her, they shrank away, shivering as she passed.

Zetta didn't let it stop her. She continued to filch

food until she had what she deemed to be enough, then disappeared back into the shadows as quietly as she had appeared.

Gareth's jaw clenched with raw fury.

She shouldn't still be struggling to provide for herself and her family, but it was all too evident that she was. Her every movement had been furtive, as if she were stealing instead of taking what had been freely offered. He had thought that he had made it clear to her and her family that they were his guests and as such were entitled to their share of the castle's bounty. He understood her reasons for not wanting to eat with the rest of them, but he had assumed that they were being served in the solar.

Yet here she was, forced to all but beg for the scraps off his table. The sudden realization created in him a new anger that demanded an immediate outlet, but he had enough sense left to know that banging heads together would do no good. They wouldn't understand and it would only push their ignorant fear further underground, where it would be all that much more treacherous. It wouldn't just disappear because he willed it to do so.

All the same, he was having a hard time suppressing his more violent urges. Just as he was beginning to indulge in some truly lurid and violent fantasies, a serving girl leaned over to refill his tankard. An even better idea began to form in his mind.

"Would you like some more ale, sir?" she asked, keeping her eyes respectfully lowered, but her sideways glance was pure invitation.

He smiled his most charming smile at her. "No, thank you. What I would like is for you to go back into the kitchens and gather together the best food and drink there is. I would then like you to take it up to the solar."

"The s-solar, sir?"

"Yes, the solar. Get whatever help you need, but I want it done now."

"Yes, sir."

"Good." Gareth was still smiling as he pushed back his heavy wooden chair. The men staggered in their haste to get to their feet, but Gareth didn't bother to acknowledge them as he turned and left the hall. The snub was subtle, but he didn't doubt for a second that every man there knew exactly what he had just done.

In a moment, no doubt, they would also know exactly where he had gone. There would be much muttering about enchantments and other such nonsense, but he didn't care.

How could he? As he climbed the steps two at a time, the elusive sense of peace returned. Somehow, Zetta always made him feel like that, and he knew that if he wasn't careful, he would soon find that he couldn't live without it.

But he didn't care.

"Thank you, Hilda," Joan murmured, her voice soft and fragile.

Zetta remained silent as she finished wrapping the shawl around her mother's too thin shoulders, trying to make her as comfortable as possible in the chair by the fire.

She no longer tried to correct Joan when she mistook her for someone else. It was better to be a Hilda from the past than to see the puzzled look in Joan's eyes turn to frustration and fear as she groped to remember just who her daughter was.

Zetta turned from Joan and picked up the tray full of food she had gathered from the hall, relieved that at least tonight she had managed to fill it with enough to see them through till noon tomorrow. She sat herself cross-legged in front of the small fire and with meticulous fairness began splitting the food into equal portions, putting the three lots that were for tonight's supper on the plates she had stolen along with the tray.

She didn't bother to look up when Edrit entered the room with his usual exuberant noise, but she sighed with relief all the same. She worried about him wandering around the fortress by himself after dark, but he had made sure that she couldn't stop him by not telling her what he was up to. He had crept away with surprising stealth while she had been bathing Joan and preparing her for bed.

By the time she had realized he was gone there had been nothing she could do about it. So she had waited and worried, but of course Edrit was impervious to the fact that he may have caused her any anxiety. He smiled at her in a merry fashion and sat down beside her in a whoosh of movement.

"The kittens have grown so much, Zetta. They are so huge now," he said in a rush, reaching out his good hand to try to snatch away some of the cooling meat from the food she was putting aside for tomorrow.

She slapped it away but smiled over to him, enjoying his uncomplicated presence. "They have grown since this afternoon?"

He nodded his head enthusiastically. "Enormous. You should see them, Mother. They are wonderful."

Joan smiled at him vaguely, then lowered her eyes

in confusion. Zetta quickly handed Edrit his plate, hoping it would distract him just long enough so that he wouldn't realize his mother didn't quite recognize him for the moment.

It worked, but not in the way she had planned.

He looked down at the modest helping on his plate, frowning. Zetta held her breath, but for once he didn't complain about the smallness of his portion. It was as if he was now resigned to the fact that he never had enough to fill the enormous empty cavern inside him.

She looked quickly away from his disappointed expression and got up to steady Joan's plate on her knee. She fussed over her mother for a second, trying to make her more comfortable, before settling down by the fire once more. Zetta picked up a piece of bread and began to eat it slowly. With a sigh that reverberated through his whole body, Edrit followed suit.

For a moment, silence filled the room as they ate. With the first pangs of her hunger satisfied, Zetta looked up and realized that Joan wasn't eating and all of her own hunger fled.

"You haven't eaten anything, Mother," she said as calmly as she could, trying to quell the panic rising inside her.

For a second Joan seemed to look past Zetta; then she struggled and focused in on her. For the first time all day, she recognized her. Her eyes were knowing and sad as she shook her head.

"I'm not hungry. Perhaps Edrit would like to have my share."

"No, you must eat it. You have to eat something." Zetta tried to keep her voice soft as she spoke, but inside she was yelling.

It had been days since Joan had eaten properly and

Zetta was afraid that if things continued as they were she was going to disappear. Each day she got a little vaguer, a little frailer. And Zetta could do nothing to stop it. That didn't prevent her from trying, through.

Pushing aside her own plate, she moved and knelt beside Joan's chair. "Please, eat," she whispered, her voice broken and scratched. "Even if only for me."

Joan opened her mouth to speak, but whatever she was about to say was drowned out by the opening of the door, and the distant sound of the main hall filling the room.

Zetta watched in despair as Joan recoiled from the clamor, her eyes returning once more to look at a world of her own construction. Zetta closed her own eyes and dropped her head, defeat weighing heavily on her. Then her head snapped up. With a growl of rage she stood up and turned to the door, preparing to vent her frustration on whatever fool had dared to intrude. Her jaw dropped in surprise as she watched Gareth direct serving girls carrying heaped trays of still-steaming food. "Put it over on the table near the first window," he said, his usual inviting smile in place, as if this were a perfectly normal occurrence.

Once everything was arranged to his satisfaction, Gareth waved the girls away. Zetta barely even noticed the way they all fled the room as if chased by devils. Her whole concentration was focused on the beautiful man in front of her.

Only once he had shut the door behind them did Gareth meet her gaze.

Never before had a man looked at her as he did in that stolen moment. His blue eyes smiled at her, and in their depths she could feel emotions that she couldn't name. He stole her breath away. She stared at him, transfixed, as she tried to draw a deep breath, abstractly aware that there suddenly wasn't enough air in the room.

She lowered her eyes, trying to find some balance, but quickly raised them again. She wasn't able to deny herself the sight of him, not even for a moment of sanity.

"Gareth . . ." Her voice was no more than a whisper but it seemed to have been what he had been waiting for.

A slow smile spread over his face. "I was sitting down in the hall, feeling all lonely despite the people all around, when it suddenly occurred to me that I would much rather be up here with you. I hope you don't mind my small invasion, but I have brought dinner with me."

Edrit got up and answered with haste, as if afraid Zetta would somehow foul it up. "We don't mind as long as you have brought more food than Zetta."

Gareth spread his arms wide. "Help yourself, my friend."

Edrit didn't need to be invited twice. He grabbed his plate and began heaping it with food with unseemly haste, just in case the bounty should suddenly disappear.

Zetta couldn't move, and for a second, Gareth's gaze searched hers. Then as if he understood her every thought and fear, he walked over to Joan. Zetta felt her heart swelling at the sight of the gentle, warm smile on his lips as he knelt in front of the old woman.

"Is there anything I can get you, my lady?" he asked her softly.

"Oh, I'm not . . ."

"How about trying some of the little savory tarts that I brought up for you specially?"

"Well, if you have brought them . . ."

"Excellent," Gareth said, and before she could change her mind, he had a tart on her plate.

Zetta watched in amazement as Joan smiled up at

Gareth and then with effort lifted the tart and began to eat a little of the delicacy. Gareth waited by her side, and when she politely asked him for another, he filled her plate with several more.

Zetta supposed she should feel put out by the fact that Gareth could charm the world into functioning as he felt it should when she had failed, but she was far too relieved to be that petty. She didn't care how it had been achieved. Joan was eating and that was all that mattered as far as she was concerned.

"I like your smile. You should do it more often." Gareth suddenly appeared at her side.

"Thank you so much, for . . ." She looked around at Edrit and Joan eating with contentment and was lost for the words to explain the depths of her gratitude.

Gareth just shrugged his shoulders.

"Don't thank me for something that I'm doing for my own selfish benefit. I was being honest when I said that I'd much prefer to be here. With you. Now let's see what we can do about your . . . hunger." He led her away from the fire, ostensibly to fill her own plate with food, but Zetta didn't believe that for a second.

Furthermore, she didn't mind his less than subtle subterfuge.

She was so lost in the feel of his arm around her shoulders that it took her a second to realize that he was still speaking.

". . . I suppose I have gotten so used to living within a family that I miss it."

She watched enraptured as his strong, capable hands put some food on her plate as she listened to the deep, rich flow of his words, and she realized she was becoming helplessly curious about the man who hid behind the smiling knight. She wanted to know everything about him.

"Were you with your family before you came here?" she asked with an awkwardness that exasperated her. Gareth didn't seem to notice but instead looked surprised by her question.

Then he shook his head. "No. What I meant was the time I've spent in the north country with an old friend and his family."

She nodded and waited for him to say more. Instead, he walked toward the window and stared out into the night. She followed reluctantly behind, being careful that she wasn't close enough to the window to see out.

When he turned back to her, his face was austere and serious. "And where were you before you took to robbing the king's highway?"

She flushed and couldn't hold his gaze, lowering hers to her hands. "London." She cleared her throat and tried again. "I have lived in London all my life, but Mother wanted to return to the place of her birth. So we came here."

She wanted to add something to explain stealing from him, but she couldn't find the words in her addled brain. There was nothing that could excuse what she had done. From the way he smiled gently at her, she suspected he heard all that she had left unsaid. The silence stretched between them and she could almost believe the forgiveness she saw in his eyes.

He reached out a surprisingly unsteady hand and ran his knuckles along the contour of her cheek.

"Zetta, you are so beautiful that I can almost believe that you are a witch sent to torment me with visions of heaven." His hoarse voice sent tingles down her spine.

She couldn't stop herself from lifting her own hand

and holding his to her face more firmly. He turned his hand and curled his fingers around hers, then lifted them both to cover the slow, steady beat of his heart. She looked at their hands entwined against the rich fabric of his deep brown tunic and shook her head.

"No, I'm no witch. Merely a woman."

Gareth smiled and his hot gaze fell to her mouth. "Trust me, there is nothing 'mere' about the way you make me feel every time I see you."

It was then that she made her decision.

She knew that she would have to leave Gareth and soon. This wonderful time couldn't last forever. At best they had only a few more stolen weeks of being together, but for as long as she could, she was going to have this man any way he would take her.

If he wanted a lover, then she would be his lover. If he wanted a friend, then she would be his friend. Whatever he wanted, she would give all that was in her power to give. She had never been so certain of anything in her life, and this certainty brought with it a peace like she had never before known. She didn't care that she was staring at him with open longing. She was so dazzled by the complete clarity that possessed her that she didn't even notice Edrit had come to stand beside her until he reached out and touched her arm.

She looked down with surprise at his twisted hand against the fabric of her dress and realized with a guilty start that she had been so caught up in her own emotional turmoil that she had forgotten everything else. Reluctantly she removed her hand from Gareth's warm grip and he let her go.

"Mother's fallen asleep," Edrit said in a loud whisper. She nodded, moving back over to the fire. Even though the fire she had laid and lit earlier still blazed, she felt cold away from Gareth's gentle touch.

For the first time in longer than Zetta could remember, Joan seemed to be sleeping peacefully and, to judge from the empty plate that still balanced on her knee, she had also managed to have a proper meal.

Zetta moved to wake her so that she could put her to bed, but Gareth stopped her with a hand on her shoulder. "Let me," he said. Removing the plate, he picked up the old woman and with one efficient and effortless movement placed her onto the bed after Zetta hastily pulled back the furs. Joan only woke when he brought the covering up over her narrow shoulders.

She opened her eyes and seeing Gareth smiled at him as if she saw a dream.

"Humphrey," she said so low that only Gareth heard it.

Startled at hearing his father's name he opened his mouth to ask her if she knew him, but closed it again when he realized that she had gone back to sleep. Questions could wait, he decided as his mind hurried to return to the invitation that he had seen blazing in Zetta's eyes. Right now, that seemed far more important. He turned and watched through hooded eyes as she helped Edrit set up his pallet by the fire. Gareth had offered him his own chamber, but Edrit had stubbornly refused to leave his mother, saying that his sore hand preferred it when he slept near the warmth of a fire.

Gareth, however, had given Zetta no such choice. He had never dared question why he insisted she still sleep in her own tower chamber when he certainly didn't think of her as his prisoner. Now he could only commend himself for his wisdom, and as he watched her adjust the furs and place a kiss on Edrit's forehead, he felt his body tightening, readying with his always heated need for her.

While she turned to place a log on the fire, Gareth grabbed some apples and stuffed them in his pockets for them to eat later. He waited with tamped-down impatience by the open door till she had said her final good nights and all but pushed her out into the noisy passageway.

Obviously, the men still lingered in the main hall below and Gareth knew he should see about having them cleared out for the evening, but right now he didn't care all that much for the petty detail. How could he when a whole new world was being offered to him in the depths of Zetta's forest green eyes.

He closed the door behind them and turned to her. She stood with her hands held together so that her knuckles stood out stark white against the pale, pink satin of her skin. He took her hands in both of his and he felt his chest tightening unbearably as they unfurled and held on to him instead.

"Can I escort you up to your room?" he asked, leaving all of his other questions unvoiced.

Her yes answered them all.

A surge of hot fire flamed through him and he had to fight off the urge to throw back his head and let out a battle cry of victory. Instead, he settled for placing his arms under her knees and swinging her up against his chest. Without hesitation she threaded her arms around his neck. He looked down into her eyes and saw all of his own desire mirrored in their depths.

After that he didn't dare look at her again.

He was afraid that the molten fire that was burning its way down his spine might flare into flames. If that happened, he knew that there would be no force in all of England that could stop him from telling her that he loved her.

There would be time enough for that later, he promised himself as he swiftly walked up the stairs to her room. When the lady was won, there would be all the time in the world. Right now, he had to concentrate on claiming the lady who had her head buried against his throat. His hold on her tightened as he imagined all of the ways he was going to woo her.

She felt so right in his arms, her warm body being held up against his battered heart.

He had thought that he had known love before and when it had eluded him that it was lost to him forever. He had buried his desires, had hoped that just by ignoring them they would somehow just disappear. If every now and then he had been made all too well aware that there was a gaping great hole in his soul where his heart had been, he had enough pride left to make sure that no one else would have guessed of its existence.

Now, the hole was gone. He knew it wasn't wise to once more rush headlong into unknown waters, but he also felt a certainty that things were different this time. This time he would be loved as much as he loved. The woman in his arms had already done so much to fill the spaces inside him, that, given time, she would fill them to overflowing.

This time, he swore silently to himself and to Zetta, they would find everything love had to give.

And more.

Chapter 6

Gareth stopped short in front of Zetta's chamber door, but it took her a moment to notice through the distraction of the strange sensation of being held in his arms. When the fact did finally penetrate her daze, she looked up at him puzzled.

"You've stopped."

"I know," he growled, his frustration mounting as he contemplated the problem at hand. "I can't seem to hold on to you and open the door at the same time," he said at last, when no solution presented itself.

"Well, you could put me down."

"No," he said firmly, his arms tightening around her ever so slightly, "but perhaps if you could reach down to the bar. . . ."

"No," she said quickly. "I'd like to help, but there is absolutely no way I am going to look down."

Her panicked tone distracted him from the problem for a moment. "Don't you like heights, dear one?"

"Can't stand them." She stared resolutely at his chest. "If I'm off the ground so much as a breath and I look down I start to feel like I'm not standing at all but falling. Let me assure you, it is a feeling that goes right to the stomach."

Gareth found himself smiling gently at the calm, sensible way she described what she saw as a weakness as well as a deep fear. No swooning, fainthearted cowardice for his Zetta. No, she was made of the stern determination he had always thought was the exclusive domain of the male of the species.

"Would you like me to put you back on the ground?"

His voice rang with so much reluctance that Zetta managed to look up past his chest and meet his gaze, her cheeks flushed with a blend of embarrassment and desire.

"Don't you dare, Sir Knight." As if to emphasize her point, she inched up even farther in his arms and placed a soft, warm kiss on the side of his neck. When he groaned, she flashed him a coy look and then provocatively ran the flat of her tongue down to the hollow of his collarbone.

"I think you should be doing something to get that door open, don't you?" she said with a throaty purr.

He was galvanized into action. Ignoring her startled squeal of protest, he swung her up and over his shoulder with one quick movement. As she hastily closed her eyes against the nauseating view, he manhandled the bar on the door with one hand, and the other he splayed possessively over her buttocks. He let out a primitive roar of triumph when the door opened and he marched into her chamber, feeling like an all-conquering army.

Only once he had her safely inside and the door shut did he restore to her some of her dignity when he started to put her down the right way up. He held her for a second just above the ground, smiling devilishly into her eyes, and then slowly he slid her down the length of him till she stood on her own two feet.

He turned and barred the door, before focusing all of his attention on her once more. He stared at her flushed face with awe for a moment, not entirely sure if he could believe this moment was real.

He was no stranger to passion or lust, but he had never seen in the face of any other woman emotions like those that burned in Zetta's dark green eyes. It was a smolder that demolished all the pretension and artifice that had always before accompanied the animal act of fornication, leaving him stripped of all his own practiced seductions. All that was left was a vulnerable, aching man who wanted only this woman as his own. He should have been alarmed by the intensity of his need, but much to his bemusement he found himself only intoxicated by the freedom of it.

And in that he wasn't alone. Zetta's face had a similar look of amazement. Her lips parted slightly as she suddenly seemed to become short of breath, but her gaze focused on his. She wanted him, he realized, and his own desire surged up to answer hers. His manhood began to harden and lengthen as his lungs pumped like a bellow.

He could only hope that she didn't think he was out of breath from having carried her slight weight up the tower steps. Such a thing should be nothing to a man used to fighting in full armor. It would be, he thought wryly, if the woman in his arms had been anyone but Zetta.

Slowly he covered the distance between them and took her in his arms. He searched her face with wonder for a moment, then lowered his head to claim her lips for a kiss.

She met him halfway.

Her mouth was already open and waiting for him and he ruthlessly plundered all that she offered. His soul found what it had been seeking all of his adult life in the mating of her tongue with his. His hands began to roam restlessly over her body, seeking out the essence of her. He wanted to make it all for him alone. One hand moved to hold the back of her head, his long fingers tunneling through her hair and moving soothingly along the soft skin of her scalp. The other he couldn't seem to stop from moving down along her spine and mimicking that action on her firm, high buttocks.

He pulled her closer to his straining erection, trying to show her just what she did to him with a single kiss. He wasn't sure if he meant it as a warning or a promise, but the feel of her warm belly pressing up against his hard manhood was almost his undoing.

She absorbed his groan of need and matched it with one of her own. She wrapped her arms around him more tightly, her small hands moving urgently along the tense muscles of his back. She followed the line of them upward until she was stretching to reach his shoulders. She spread her fingers as wide as she could, but still she couldn't cover them. With a sigh of satisfaction she moved them down over the side of his biceps, testing his dense muscles with her fingertips.

It was a small thing and he had never thought of his arms as particularly sensitive or erotic before, but he felt her touch through every part of his body. He changed the slant of his mouth, trying to draw her even closer, though he was beginning to doubt whether he could ever be close enough to her. The most primitive part of him clamored for possession, needed to make her his irrevocably.

He hesitated. The last vestige of sanity inside him warned him not to forget how she had reacted the last time he had allowed himself to be lost to his lust. He had to be careful or risk losing her altogether. And he needed her too much to jeopardize it all now. If he couldn't take this to its only natural conclusion, he had to pull back now or else face the very real danger of combusting.

He hated the part of him that could remain sane even in the midst of such divine madness, but all the same he carefully lifted his hand away from her buttocks. The pressure of her sweet body lifted from his, but even as he regretted the loss of the intimate contact with her body, he resisted the urge to haul her back. But he couldn't let her go entirely. He deepened the kiss and ran a possessive hand over the dip in her spine, trying to find satisfaction in just her mouth when he wanted so much more.

Hell, he wanted everything.

He let out a growl of protest when she suddenly pulled her mouth free of his. Instinctively his body tensed as his mind searched desperately for what he may have done wrong this time.

He could find no hints in the smoldering depth of her eyes.

"I want more," she said finally, her voice ragged with passion.

As she said those words, he saw something in her eyes that he hadn't realized he had even been searching for. At the same time, he knew it like it was a part of himself. For a second, the rawness of his passion mellowed and flowed through his veins like honey. Gently, he lifted his hand from the silken strands of her hair and ran it unsteadily along the curve of her face. A smile played over his lips as she leant into his caress.

"Are you sure, Zetta?" he asked gruffly. He didn't know what the hell he would do if she said she wasn't, but, at the same time, he could not abide the thought of her doing anything with him against her will. It seemed that he had to protect her from everything, even if that meant protecting her from himself.

Slowly she turned her face toward the palm of his hand, and Gareth watched almost mesmerized as she gently nipped the mound of skin at the base of his thumb. Any sting he felt she carefully soothed with the flat of her tongue. His already swollen manhood seemed to grow even larger, the pain relentlessly demanding that he plunder and invade what was being offered to him of free will.

He held back.

She stared at him searchingly for a moment, then carefully lifted his hand from her face and stepped away, leaving him bereft and alone as she walked over to the fireplace.

It amazed him abstractly that he was able to let her go when every ounce of his body demanded that he pull her back, demanded that they be as close as two bodies could be together and that he never let her go again.

Still, his pride didn't want her to know just how easily she had brought him to a state where he would willingly fall down on his knees and beg if that was what it took to feel her in his arms once more. He drew a ragged breath into his starved lungs and tried to find a small rational part in the confusion that was his mind. He needed that part of his disintegrating intellect to tell him that it was better they stop now if she was uncertain. It was better to suffer that than for her to continue with something she didn't want because she felt she had no other choice.

His hands clenched impotently at his sides as he valiantly fought off the urge to haul her back and force her to feel the passion that he felt. He was so caught up in his own thwarted desires that at first he didn't realize what she was doing. It was only as she slowly turned back to him that bewildered comprehension dawned.

He watched as she undid the laces at the front of her gown with slow, deliberate moves. Once the front of the dress gaped enticingly open she began to haul up the fabric of her skirts, revealing first a perfect little ankle, then the white purity of a knee. He watched with fascination as the dress moved relentlessly up, slowly revealing each tantalizing inch of her beautiful thighs. He almost groaned out loud when the light fabric of her chemise obscured the rest of her from his view, creating frustrating shadows in the dim light from the banked fire.

For a moment her face disappeared beneath yards of fabric, and when it reappeared, her short, curly hair stood on its ends, forming a halo. He almost forgot to breathe when she casually dropped the dress to one side and began to remove the chemise. She lifted the thin fabric over her head, and his mouth went dry as the delta between her thighs was at last revealed to his hungry gaze and the chemise joined the dress on the floor.

He dragged his eyes greedily up her pale, sensuous body, then frowned when he saw the tight, white cloth that covered her torso from armpit to the middle of her flat stomach. He hadn't felt the binding when he had all too briefly touched her breasts on their first day in the castle because he had been so thoroughly distracted by his need to protect certain, vulnerable parts of his anatomy from harm.

He moved and reached out a hand, running it lightly over the course, abrasive material.

"Why?"

She caught his hand and held it away from her, a flush staining her cheeks as she plainly searched for an explanation. He laced his fingers through hers and waited patiently.

"Because, Gareth, in the world where I come from, women have but one purpose and that is to sell their bodies for coin." She smiled at him sadly and Gareth felt his gut clench helplessly. "I watched my mother sell hers to keep bread on our table. I watched as she grew older and the bread grew less and the times between meals grew ever longer. I watched, and I knew that I had no choice but to follow her, but when I came of age I found I couldn't do it. I didn't want to be a whore and my mother, my poor, foolish mother, lacked the will to force me."

She swallowed awkwardly. "I wanted to stay a child, stay safe, but there are some things that you can't escape. I became a woman and no matter how much I wished it otherwise, it was soon clear for all to see. One night when I was nearly fourteen, Mother sent me down to the local market to buy some food. I was looking at the stalls when this man grabbed me and dragged me into a small side alley. No one stopped him. No one noticed or cared. I was just one more noisy whore with a client."

She laughed and the harsh, high note made Gareth flinch. "I actually offered him my money. I thought that he just wanted to steal the piddling few coins I had. Needless to say, it wasn't my money he wanted."

It was a common enough tale, but Gareth was filled with outrage. He had never hated anyone in his life as he now hated the faceless man who had dared to harm Zetta. The fire of his hatred burned through his brain, blinding him with its intensity. He could all too easily imagine a younger, vulnerable Zetta with no one to protect her.

But the blatant hypocrisy of his anger made him feel sick.

He had seen rape before, seen it used as an accepted weapon of war. He had never done it himself, preferring willing flesh to terrified compliance, but, at the same time, he had never thought anything of it. Now he looked at the single trembling hand Zetta held to her stomach and it was no longer acceptable.

But he couldn't let Zetta see how close he was to losing control of his temper. The last thing he wanted to do was to frighten her again. She didn't need him reminding her of the dangerous, angry man who had hurt her all those years ago. She was frightened enough already by the memories. Her face was pale and her deep, green eyes, which only a moment before had burned with passion, were now full of remembered pain and fear. No, she didn't need to see his own tumultuous emotions.

Instead, he was careful to keep his voice neutral as he asked the question he didn't want the answer to but, at the same time, knew he had to ask.

"Did he hurt you?"

Her gaze focused back on the present and she looked up at him as if surprised to see him there. Then she managed a small travesty of a smile. "Not for long. As you know, I'm not entirely defenseless, and, unlike you, he was a lazy tub of lard. That time my knee didn't miss."

She looked down to their entwined hands. She carefully let go.

"Two weeks later my mother's 'protector' came to our rooms and told her that it was time I earned my keep. I sat huddled in my bed and listened as he offered precious coin and my mother tried to distract him. It worked, but the next night we had to disappear. But I knew it wasn't enough. It would just be a matter of time. I didn't want to face it. That is when Mother suggested this." She gestured vaguely to the bindings as if they were of no great moment. "I think she hoped merely to give me a little more time to accept my fate by hiding me as a girl child for a while. It was my idea to wear Edrit's cut-down clothes and hide as a male child. It was easy enough done." She searched his face. "I knew that I was breaking God's law and that if I had gotten caught in the charade the punishment would have been severe, but without the freedom it gave me I don't know what I would have become."

For the first time in his life, Gareth found himself entirely without anything to say. He stared at her mutely, unable to even begin to express the world of anger, compassion, and understanding that filled him. Perhaps she understood, though. After taking another unsteady breath, she lowered her eyes, and began to remove the bindings with calm efficiency. She seemed entirely unaware that her hands shook as she unwound her fabric's chains.

Gareth saw it.

When the last of the material fell away, she didn't let it go as she had her dress and chemise. Instead, she stood awkwardly in front of him with it bunched tightly in her fists. She moved as if to cover her breasts again, then stopped halfway and let her hands drop uselessly back at her sides.

She lifted her gaze back to his.

"You can touch me," she said so softly that Gareth almost didn't hear it. She shrugged awkwardly. "If you want to."

The magnitude of her gift stripped him of his last defense against her. How she could decide to trust him when she had lost all trust with the world was beyond his ability to fully comprehend. He had no understanding of just how much courage it would require to do such a thing, but he knew that Zetta was perhaps the first truly brave person he had ever met. He felt humbled before her.

When he could find no words inside him to express all he wanted to tell her of his awe, he closed the small gap between them and reverently took her in his arms.

This time when they kissed Gareth felt almost as if he was participating in an act of worship. The feel of her soft, naked body held against his clothed one was something sacred to be treasured. Without breaking the kiss, he swung her up into his arms with gentle care and placed her in the center of the large bed. Only then did he lift his head from hers and with a quick nipping kiss step away, but he didn't let go of her gaze. Smiling a lopsided, self-deprecating grin, he began to divest himself of his own clothes.

It was her turn to watch.

She followed his every move with hooded eyes. The flush on her cheeks grew deeper, and Gareth noticed with some satisfaction that it had moved downward to spread over the top of her breasts. He removed his nether garments and almost smiled as her worldly, sad eyes widened with surprise when his erection was finally freed.

He had undressed in front of women before, indeed had even been undressed by a woman once or twice when he'd had the time to dally, but never before had he felt as naked as he did in front of Zetta's frankly curious gaze. He felt oddly discomfortable by the feelings of vulnerability that seeped into his consciousness and by the way his already engorged erection seemed to swell even further as she looked upon him. He was almost embarrassed by its straining breadth.

Never before had he felt so potent. They had not yet engaged in the clever titillation he had always appreciated from a skilled woman, but Gareth felt as if he were on fire.

It would seem that small things when done with Zetta had more effect on him than sex with the most enterprising ladies of the court. He was almost afraid that the ecstasy of sinking into her heat might kill him. Even so, it was a risk that he was willing to take.

He quickly climbed into bed beside her and pulled her almost roughly back into his arms.

When his lips found hers again everything became clear once more. In that instant, he knew that he held the only thing that mattered in the whole world. He pulled away from her gently and smiled at her passion-fired eyes. "Zetta," he murmured in wonderment just so he could hear the magic of her name. Leaning up on one elbow he ran a calloused finger over one of the marks the coarse binding had left on the soft flesh of her breasts.

She arched with a gasp as he moved provocatively near one of her nipples, trying to force him to take her flesh fully into his hands. Gently he took the weight of her satiny breast into his palm, filling it to overflowing. The small, puckered nipple almost branded his skin with its heat.

"Don't ever bind them again," he said hoarsely as he lowered his head to kiss them. "Such rare beauty should not be treated so cruelly."

She whimpered in pleasure as his tongue moved over each breast, following and soothing each and every mark made by the binding. By the time he finally took one of her aching, straining nipples into his mouth she was pleading inarticulately for him to ease the restless ache that was consuming her. She lifted a hand to the back of his head and held him against her fiercely.

Smiling, he ran his teeth along her taut flesh, while one hand now dared to move softly along the taut skin of her belly. He could feel her muscles tightening and contracting underneath his touch, as the very center of her body prepared itself.

For him. It was all for him.

He slid a finger over her curls and into her warm, wet delta. She was ready for him. She didn't even try to stop him as he slid his fingers along the sensitive membranes of her womanhood and slipped inside the hot sheath of her body. As he did so, he sucked hard on the needy flesh of her breasts. She once again arched up like a plucked bowstring, driving his finger farther into the incredibly tight sheath of her body. She spread her thighs, opening herself to him more fully, begging wordlessly for the pleasure he wanted so badly to give.

He slipped a second finger inside her, stretching her, testing her as he pressed the heel of his hand against the small bud of her pleasure at the top of her sex. Her inarticulate whimper of passion made him want to yell out his own primitive triumph.

He wanted to watch. He needed to see that it was he who was giving her this pleasure. He lifted his head from her breast and looked into her face. She had closed her eyes and held her bottom lip between her teeth, as if trying to stop herself from screaming.

"Show me," he said through gritted teeth, his own breath coming in static bursts. "Show me your body's first pleasure."

She opened her eyes and looked deeply into his as her body grew steadily tauter, straining toward its fulfillment. She let go of her bottom lip and opened her mouth as if to let out a scream, but he heard no sound.

He didn't need to hear it. He watched with savage satisfaction as her whole body sang for him. She hung suspended for a moment, and then her body seemed to dissolve into a boneless mass and collapse back into the mattress.

He didn't stop.

His hand, now slick with her fulfillment, kept moving intimately against her. She was helpless as he ruthlessly brought her body back to a fever pitch of desire.

Now it would be his turn. He was going to be inside her when her body found its release again. Watching her had brought his body to a point where desire was actually a physical pain, and there was only one way his ache would find easement.

When her hands gripped and twisted themselves into the blankets and her hips moved restlessly against his palm once more, he carefully slipped his fingers out of her.

"No. No," she whispered, her voice hoarse and broken with her passion. Carefully he lifted his body to cover hers, fitting intimately against her.

She opened herself to him urgently, her knees holding on tight to his waist, moving against him, instinctually knowing what he wanted. The feel of her hot, wet sheath against his straining erection was almost his undoing. For the first time in his life he found himself in serious danger of spilling his seed before the deed had begun.

He had to be inside her. Now.

Gripping his hands into the blankets on either side of her head, Gareth silently compelled her to look at him. Just as he needed to see her first pleasuring, he now wanted to look her in the eye as he claimed her. His hips had begun to slowly move forward, carefully nudging himself inside her, but even with the blind need of passion, he couldn't bear to give her any pain. Every muscle in his body strained with his restraint, and a sheen of sweat covered him as he excruciatingly slowly began to enter her.

Just as he felt the barrier of her maidenhead, a sound in the corridor stilled him cold. His desire froze at the base of his spine as his passion-clouded mind tried to find itself in the welter of desire and make sense of the sudden wary alertness that had held him suspended somewhere between heaven and hell. There should be no one else in the tower.

That afternoon, when he had realized the depth of hatred Zetta inspired, he had declared that the east tower was not to be entered without his express permission.

Someone had disobeyed him.

When he heard another noise, this time against the door, every instinct in his body yelled that Zetta was under threat. He wanted to howl his frustration, but somehow he contained it. The absolute need to keep Zetta safe was the one thing that overrode his own body's heated demands. Agonizingly he removed his straining body from Zetta's, drawing from her a startled gasp of protest. He signaled her to be silent as he climbed out of the bed and grabbed his dagger from the pile of clothes on the floor.

Zetta sat up, her face flushed and glowing with perspiration, but her eyes cleared of passion when the distinct sound of a footfall in the hall came through the door. She pulled the furs up to hide her breasts and watched with a taut calmness as Gareth moved silently over to the locked door.

"Stay there," he whispered back to her. She simply nodded her head as she gathered the furs more firmly around herself, her knuckles showing up white against the taupe surface.

All was silent as Gareth leaned an ear against the door. Quietly he removed the bar and grabbed hold of the rope and wood handle. Gathering around himself the calm stillness of battle, he counted to three and then yanked the door open, hoping to surprise whoever was on the other side.

The corridor was empty.

He stepped outside and, unconcerned by his nakedness, began to run down the stone stairs. The silence all around told him what he needed to know. Whoever had been loitering outside Zetta's door had escaped into the lower levels of the fortress. A muscle flexed in his cheek as he realized that it would be impossible to work out who had dared to ignore an express order from him.

Gritting his teeth in frustration, he began to pad his way back up the cold steps, worry and anger warring to gain control of his mind. Anger that someone had dared to defy him, and worry about what might have happened had that person gotten into Zetta's chamber while she had been all alone.

As he turned the last corner, he wasn't surprised to

see that Zetta hadn't obeyed him. She stood as far away from her room as the small width of the stairs would allow. She stared with blank horror into the chamber.

It was only when he reached her side that he saw what held her so transfixed.

Hanging from the metal braces of the door by a frayed rope was the body of the black cat they'd watched nurse her kittens only hours before. Its throat had been cut and Gareth noted with almost clinical detachment that its belly had been very neatly slit open, its entrails left to dangle down past its back legs.

He felt bile rising from the pit of his stomach, and he was almost relieved when Zetta suddenly moved to him and wrapped her arms tightly around his middle. Her shaking plea for comfort forced his concentration away from the horrific sight. Her shoulders trembled as she buried her head against his shoulder, and he lifted a hand into her hair. He fervently wished that he could somehow remove from her mind the sight of the poor cat's mutilated body.

God knows, it was etched in his own, but he couldn't look away. He stared at it and was terrified by the threat to Zetta it represented. Someone in his castle meant her harm, and right at that moment Gareth didn't have the first idea how he was going to protect her, not when he didn't know where the threat was coming from.

But somehow he would.

He pulled her more firmly against his body, trying to reassure himself that she was safe. Whoever was responsible would experience exactly what they had inflicted on the poor, innocent cat, he vowed silently.

Only more so.

Chapter 7

Gareth's eyes remained carefully trained on the practice below the window as he deliberately ignored the growing nervousness of the man who remained waiting anxiously on his knees for Gareth's focus to return to him once more.

Gareth smiled with malicious pleasure.

He was in no hurry to end John's torment. He had even enjoyed the way John looked as if he had accidentally swallowed his own heart as he'd entered Gareth's chamber. And it turned out that Gareth wasn't above twisting the knife. That was why he had chosen that this particular audience take place here, in the main bedchamber. Until Gareth had arrived, John had been running his little nefarious empire from this very chamber. Now he was back to sleeping in the communal long hall with the rest of the mere mortals.

Gareth wanted to make the man squirm, wanted him to be afraid of just what might happen to him. Perhaps then he would tell all that Gareth needed to know.

Gareth found a more comfortable place to rest his hip on the windowsill and waited, appearing to concentrate all of his attention on the men in the practice yard below, but only noticing with absentminded disinterest that one or two of the men were now at least holding their sword like they knew what one was.

The silence stretched interminably.

"Well, are you going to tell me who was responsible for last night's abomination?" Gareth asked suddenly, his patience stretched as far as it would go. He needed more.

The sound of the fat man's breathing filled the chamber and he cleared his throat with loud discomfort but, with surprising stubbornness, said nothing. Once he was certain that his face showed no emotion, Gareth turned around and pinned John with a cold look.

Perspiration glistened visibly on John's face despite the relative chill of the day, and Gareth found it amusing to watch the pompous little man falling apart. Or at least he would have had John not remained obstinately silent.

"Well?" he asked, marveling at his own restraint. His right hand was clenched on the hilt of his sword, but with amazing restraint let it remain in its scabbard.

Still, John saw it. His face blanched as he stared at it with a fixated fascination.

"Please don't ask me, Sir Gareth," he pleaded, his chins quivering with his distress.

Gareth smiled coldly.

"But I already have asked you, John, several times. And now I expect you to answer me. That is not unreasonable, I would have thought. Not when you consider that as the custodian of this castle you owe all of your loyalty to me and my family. *Only*. Not to whatever scum you are protecting now." He paused thoughtfully. "As yet I haven't punished you for all of the years that you have been abusing the trust we placed in you. But do not think that it is too late for me to change my mind about my decision to be lenient. Now, I will ask you only once more who was in the east tower last night and I want you to remember exactly what you owe me before you answer."

Several moments passed and Gareth lifted his hand from the hilt and crossed his arms over his chest. He regarded the man grimly. "Well, John, what is it to be? Are you going to answer me, or are you prepared to face the consequences of your continued silence?"

Tears started to fall down John's face and he was almost groveling in his fear. "I am loyal to you, Sir Gareth," he whined, "but I can't tell you who went into the tower last night and did . . . that. I wish I could, honestly I do, but I can't."

"Not good enough."

Gareth's voice sounded calm, but John paled as he heard the thread of steel that ran through it. His shoulders slumped and he dropped his eyes.

"I can't tell you, Sir Gareth," he said, his complete annihilation written in every quivering contour of his body.

Gareth glared at the kneeling figure, fighting the urge to grab him and slam him against the wall till he told him all he knew, but he knew it would do no good. Still, the frustration that was building inside him demanded an outlet. He had spent the whole morning asking the same questions, but no matter whom he asked, or how, he got exactly the same response.

They wouldn't answer him. From the lowest kitchen wench to the man who knelt pathetically in front of him, they had all said the same thing.

And it wasn't that they did not know what had happened last night; quite the contrary, Gareth thought grimly. Everyone seemed to know exactly who was responsible for last night's horror, but each and every one of them had refused to give him the names he needed.

He had tried everything he could think of. He had threatened, cajoled, smiled, roared, fumed and was now trying to be coldly calm. Nothing worked. For all his efforts, the cloak of silence that had shrouded the events of the previous night remained entirely undisturbed.

Either they were all involved or, more likely, they were too afraid of those who were to speak.

Gareth was fast getting to the stage where he was tempted to start creating some mindless fear of his own just to see where that would get him. At least he could at last vent some of the frustration this morning's entirely wasted efforts had built inside him. He shook his head in disgust at the pathetic man in front of him.

"Get out of my sight!" he said through gritted teeth and John didn't have to be told twice. He got clumsily to his feet, and as fast as he could, he went out of the room, patently afraid that Gareth would change his mind and kill him anyway.

Gareth watched him leave through hooded eyes. When the door shut he let out a string of expletives and turned to stare sightlessly out of the window again. Everywhere he turned he ran into another stone wall, and it seemed there was nothing he could do to knock them down, no matter how hard he might try.

His hands clenched impotently against the stones of the windowsill as he faced the unacceptable fact that his hands were tied. He wanted to protect Zetta, but he could not. The power he held as the lord of the castle came to nothing when faced with the raw, unbreakable strength of superstition and fear that ruled all of his people.

He hated it. He hated the fact that somewhere under his roof there lived someone who had dared to threaten Zetta.

Those responsible, whoever they were, sat in Gareth's hall each night, took the protection the castle offered, ate his food and no doubt thrived. All the while they dared to threaten the woman Gareth was coming to love more with every passing day.

He closed his eyes and slammed his fist into the stones. The pain that went up his arm was almost a relief from the pain of the twisted torment that ate into him.

He should be with her right at this moment. It was what he wanted more than anything.

He wanted to tell her that he loved her, explain it all to her so that she would understand just how much she meant to him. But what right did he have to do so when he couldn't even look after her? Even as he held her in his arms someone had dared to threaten her and he wasn't able to do anything about it.

The pain in his arm faded too quickly, leaving him alone with his need to hurt something, a need to bang some heads together. He opened his eyes and focused on the men practicing below his window. A hard smile came over his face.

It was perfect. He could release some of his pent-up frustrations and, at the same, perhaps teach the men something of what it was to be a knight. Perhaps if he could drill them hard enough so that some of them were actually able to defend more than their own backsides, he could at least offer Zetta some protection, even if it was only from the world outside the castle walls.

Now if only he could keep her safe from the dangers within, he would really have achieved something, he thought with a disgusted snort as he strode from the room.

Somehow he suspected that the exercise wouldn't be enough to free him from the demons of anger and thwarted desire that were eating him hollow. He could reduce his body to a sweating mass of flesh and still it wouldn't be enough. It would never be enough, because it wouldn't change the fact that the person who had threatened Zetta was still living and breathing.

But it wouldn't stay that way, he promised solemnly. Someday, soon, he would see personally that justice was done.

Zetta watched silently as Edrit carefully placed the kittens back into their small wooden box by the fire. She was pathetically grateful that the poor little bundles of fluff would most likely survive now that they were safe. They were still far too young to have been taken from their mother, but at least they were able to lap the milk Edrit religiously brought them every two hours.

If they hadn't been able to, they would have had to be destroyed, and then Zetta would have been forced to tell Edrit at least some part of the truth about what had really happened. How could she tell him that they had been taken away from their mother only to be killed? She shivered and wrapped her arms around herself tightly. Curling herself a little farther into the big chair by the fire, she doubted very much that she could ever find the words to explain all that had happened last night.

How could anyone explain the beautiful fire of ecstasy she had felt in Gareth's arms? How could anyone understand the way her body had burned even brighter still when he had covered her and had prepared to make her his?

How could anyone comprehend the cold harsh fact of the slaughtered animal that had brought reality crashing back down around her ears?

She shivered again as the hated image rose once more before her eyes. No matter how she tried to suppress the memory, it wouldn't go away. She had only to close her eyes and it was there, burnt into her mind with an acid brilliance. No, she would never find the words to explain to herself all that had happened last night, much less to Edrit, she thought dully.

"They have gone to sleep now, Zetta," Edrit said in his loud whisper, drawing her from her own bewildered musings. She tried to smile and could only hope that he didn't notice how badly she failed.

"You have done well," she said softly, and Edrit puffed his chest out with pride.

"I told you I could do it. I told you I could look after the kittens really good. I'm glad that the mother cat decided to leave them with me." He beamed a smile at her. "I was so happy when you and Gareth woke me up last night to tell me. I had been dreaming about them, and then there they were. I *knew* I could look after them."

She nodded, glad he had found some happiness with the kittens, and they seemed to be happy with him. It wasn't how she had wanted things, though. She had tried to prevent this from happening. She had not wanted him to become attached, because then he would be devastated when they had to be left behind.

The silly thing was she had also worried about how he would deal with the day-to-day care of them, certainly not wanting to end up doing it herself if he proved unable to. The last thing she wanted was something else to worry about.

Despite those fears, however, her first thought after the initial shock and horror of finding the dead mother cat had started to pass was that she had to make sure that the kittens were safe and had escaped their mother's fate. She had pulled herself from the comfort of Gareth's arms and begged him to go and see what had happened to them.

He had simply ignored her pleading.

With gentle stubbornness, he had taken her hand and drawn her back into her chamber. She'd turned her head away from the bloody mess on the door, but Gareth had seemed to experience no such squeamishness. He had dressed quickly, brusquely telling her to do the same. As she had struggled to get back into the dress, he had stood tapping his toe impatiently, his arms crossed over his chest while she struggled to lace herself up again.

Eventually he had let out a sigh and had gently slapped her hands away and started to do it himself.

In her haste to get dressed, she hadn't bothered to put the binding back on.

She had soon come to regret that haste. The bodice hadn't fit as well, clinging to curves that she normally hid. As he had laced up the front she could all too easily feel the heat from his hands on the still-hot, aching flesh of her breasts. When his knuckles had brushed over a swollen nipple she'd had to bite her bottom lip to stop herself from moaning out loud. Even after everything, he had only to touch her and she was on fire.

When he had finally finished and lifted his gaze to meet hers, he had been smiling.

"You didn't use the binding linen," he had said and she had felt the words like a physical caress.

Mutely, she had shaken her head, unable to speak, and instinctively her gaze had dropped to his mouth, and she had wanted him to kiss her, to ease the ache that was growing inside her.

He hadn't.

Instead he had hustled her out of the tower room with an almost detached urgency. It was only when he had had her safely ensconced in the solar that he had finally left her to go and see to the kittens. She had been staggered by the relief she had felt when he had returned with the three kittens nestled safely against his chest. The sound of hungry mewing had woken Edrit and he had been so excited by the unexpected gift that he hadn't seemed to notice Zetta's kiss-bruised lips or her rumpled and missing clothing, or the way that Gareth's gaze, filled with banked passion, followed her.

She supposed she should be grateful for the fact that Joan had slept through their invasion. She was too experienced not to have known instantly what had taken place and Zetta didn't think she could have borne her all too knowing look.

Indeed, Zetta hadn't been able to meet her eyes all day for fear that last night had somehow indelibly marked her. She had gone about her daily tasks quietly, trying not to draw attention to herself, hoping that her mother wouldn't notice that today she was different. It was impossible for her to believe that her newly discovered wantonness hadn't changed her.

She might still technically be a virgin, but in Gareth's arms the previous night she had in truth lost the last of her tarnished innocence.

Not that she had truly "lost" it. No, she'd willingly handed it over, she amended with a sigh. Just thinking about what she had done brought a rush of heat to her face, but she couldn't fool herself into believing it was shame that caused her to blush.

How could she when the heat of her face was matched with the growing warmth between her thighs? She could feel her body moistening and readying itself for him. That made a lie of any shame she might have felt in the cold light of day. She still wanted him, and last night she had been more than willing to give herself to him fully and without hesitation. He had brought to life needs that she had never known existed, and now that she did know them, she didn't see how she could ever go back to her previous icy state.

That fact alone was enough to frighten her. She had always known herself well. Known her own strengths and weaknesses, known exactly who she was and what she wasn't. She had lived always on her own terms, gone her own way.

Last night she had met a stranger within herself. She had become another person in his arms, and a part of her ached to be that person again. This newly discovered wanton wanted it no other way. She wanted him in whatever way he would have her. He only had to say the words. Instead he lowered his sensual eyes, bowed politely over her hand and returned quietly to his chambers.

Weaknesses and fears she hadn't even known she possessed now rose to consume her, doubts and insecurities swallowing her confidence whole. She had known it was entirely irrational to do so, but she had resented the way he had so swiftly changed from hot-eyed lover to chivalrous knight. Whether he meant to or not he had conjured her own private demons but appeared entirely untouched by any of his own when back in the real world.

He continued on organizing the world as he saw fit as if nothing had changed. In the space of a few hours he had seen to it that a guard was put on their doors, had bedding brought up for her to make a comfortable pallet, instructed Edrit on how to look after the kittens and given strict orders to all concerned that they weren't to leave the solar without him. If it hadn't been for the one, hot look he had given her just before he left the chamber, she could almost have believed that she had imagined all that had passed between them.

She doubted that he had suffered as she had for the rest of the long, endless night. She had found no sleep at all. Her body was now a traitor and tormented her with its new needs, needs that she knew only one person in the whole world would ever be able to appease.

That he slept in the chamber next to the solar had played on her mind. She had been tempted to steal over to the source of her pain and beg him to take it away. Pride alone had kept her lying restlessly among her furs.

She had already abandoned so much of herself, and she would be damned if she would give him that last piece of her will. Besides, if he could live with it then she would rather die before she would admit that she could not.

"Zetta?" Edrit said with surprising softness, mercifully interrupting her tortured thoughts. She looked up at him and he smiled at her apologetically. "I'm sorry about the mother cat."

Zetta paled. She searched Edrit's face for some sign that he had found out what had really happened to the cat last night. He had seemed satisfied enough by Gareth's vague story, but Zetta knew better than to assume that he wouldn't see that something more sinister had happened.

"Edrit . . ." she started, but he clumsily raised his hand to silence her.

"I know you didn't want me to have the kittens and I know you must be angry with the mother cat for leaving them with me, and I'm sorry that it makes you look so sad."

Zetta smiled shakily as relief flooded through her. He didn't know. He had just been worried about her moodiness, moodiness that had absolutely nothing to do with him, she realized guiltily. She climbed out of her chair and, for the first time in an age, gathered Edrit close for a hug. He laughed with surprise and all but smothered her as he wrapped his arms around her and squeezed. For once, she let herself burrow into his simple, uncomplicated strength and love.

This was what her life was about. The love that Edrit felt for her was the only thing she had any right to truly call her own, and she wouldn't let herself betray that trust.

She couldn't let herself be seduced by dark temptations. But even as she told herself that sternly, she doubted her ability to entirely deny the new being that Gareth had conjured last night. She wanted him and she didn't know if she could fight it off.

She held Edrit tighter and silently prayed for the strength she was going to need, for in the very near

future she would have to leave Gareth and his temptation behind.

Gareth nodded to the guard as he quietly opened
the solar door. His hair was still damp from his morning's exertions, but he felt as if he had found a way
through the maze his life had become. He knew what
he had to do. Softly he closed the door behind him.

He smiled a little when he saw Edrit sitting on the
floor with his legs spread wide, oblivious to anything but
the three kittens that tumbled over and around him.

The last of his tension faded as he watched Edrit's
straightforward happiness as he played with the kittens.
His need to speak to Zetta was still urgent, but he
couldn't bring himself to disrupt Edrit's joyful game. Instead, he leaned against the wall, content to watch his
friend enjoying himself.

Several minutes passed before Edrit noticed Gareth
waiting patiently. With an uncomplicated grin of greeting he scooped up all of the frisky kittens and stuck
them carefully back into their box. They protested their
sudden abandonment, then curled themselves around
each other and began to purr contentedly.

Once he was certain they were all right, Edrit got up
off the floor and limped over to Gareth, his eyes bright
with happiness.

"Thank you so very much for the kittens, Gareth."

He shrugged his shoulders casually. "You don't have
to thank me, my friend. I'm just glad you can look after
them for me. And they certainly seem to like you."

Edrit nodded his head vigorously. "Oh, they do,
almost as much as I like them."

"That's good," Gareth said with a smile, but already

the tension was starting to seep back into his bones. He took a deep breath. "Do you know where Zetta may have gone? I need to speak with her."

Edrit's smile dissolved and his face was unusually serious as he slowly nodded his head. "She said that she needed some fresh air and that as Mother was sleeping for a bit, she could go for a walk if I promised to behave myself. I did promise, and I have been behaving."

Gareth's gut tightened painfully. He couldn't believe that she could have been so foolish as to leave the safety of the guarded solar after last night, especially when he had expressly told her not to. God knows, the sight of the poor murdered cat was engraved on his own mind and it defeated him how she could so easily dismiss the threat it represented.

He tried to keep his voice free from the increasing concern he felt, seeing no point in upsetting Edrit with it. "Did she tell you where she was going?" he asked softly.

"She said that she would walk down in the old herb garden, as no one else ever went there." He paused thoughtfully, his blue eyes solemnly regarding Gareth, who began to feel strangely discomfited by the shrewdness he could see in the other man's normally childlike eyes. As if he had reached some important conclusion, Edrit nodded his head.

His bad hand gripped Gareth's upper arm with surprising strength and his face twisted into a smile. "You should go to her, talk to her. You make her happy. When she's with you, it is as if she is smiling from the inside."

Gareth didn't know what to say to such a statement. All of his usual flippancy was disarmed by the other man's simple honesty. Edrit stared into Gareth's face for a moment, and then he nodded his head again. He gave Gareth a small shove.

"Go to her, make her happy again," he said simply, then turned and went to kneel over his box of kittens.

He felt as if Edrit had just given him some kind of blessing. Filled with a renewed sense of purpose, Gareth quickly turned and left the room.

He would go and find Zetta, make sure that she was safe, and then, he promised Edrit silently, then he would find some way to keep her that way while making her happy.

Make her smile from the inside. Just as Edrit wanted.

Restlessly, Zetta walked among the weed-covered garden beds. The skirts of her dress rustled noisily among the long, unkempt grass and the very sound of it seemed to mock her.

She had changed so much that she scarcely knew who she was anymore, and the damn dress was just the beginning. When she felt it catch on a bramble she gripped her hands into the skirts and ruthlessly pulled it free, taking some satisfaction from the sound of ripping material. The blasted thing was just another sign of changes that made her someone she scarcely recognized.

The unfettered movement of her gently rounded breasts was another.

That morning, for the first time in years, she didn't go through the ritual of denying her sex, and as she walked now she could feel her breasts moving slightly against the soft material of her chemise.

The thing she found most galling was the fact that she liked the changes. For the first time in her life she felt comfortable in her own skin, felt some understanding of what it was to be a woman.

She had to leave, she realized grimly—and soon. She turned and began to pace back toward the walled entrance of the garden, trying to ignore the despair that rose in her at the thought of leaving Gareth.

She couldn't afford to let herself indulge in sentimentality. Reality was where she had to focus all of her thoughts.

And the reality was that escaping would be no great deed, she realized with a mirthless laugh. They were hardly treated like prisoners and, no doubt, everyone other than Gareth would be most eager to see the back of the witch and her entourage.

The idea of running away from him was attractive, but it wasn't possible, not for the time being. She couldn't leave, not now while Joan was so ill. There was no way that she was up to another journey. And as Zetta wasn't about to leave her behind, she was going to have to stay here and face up to all of her worst fears.

Zetta turned and continued her agitated pacing, swatting out at the long grass in a fit of bad temper. It didn't help. Her frustration was still climbing steadily toward boiling point.

"And whose head are you pretending is on the top of the grass stalks?" Gareth asked casually as he strolled into the walled garden. He smiled at her, clearly expecting an enthusiastically warm welcome, she thought darkly, hating him and loving him at the same time.

"Yours," she said with cold relish, taking another swipe to emphasize her point. He raised a brow inquiringly as he reached her side. Quickly she turned away from him and continued her pacing. Gareth easily fell into step beside her.

She tried to ignore him, but her traitorous body seemed incapable of doing that. She could no more stop her heartbeat from leaping with expectation than she could stop a cloud from moving across the sky. Just being so near him and his warmth seemed to bring her body to life. She crossed her arms tightly over her chest and tried the impossible task of dismissing both him and her body's own clamoring for him.

She wasn't surprised that she failed, and it angered her even more that Gareth seemed impervious to her silent struggle. Instead, he walked beside her, entirely at ease with the tense, unnatural situation.

Zetta could have hit him, and only the knowledge that it would hurt her more than him stilled the impulse. She continued to seethe silently for a few minutes till she could stand it no longer. Suddenly, she stopped in her tracks and turned on him. "Just what the hell are you doing?"

Gareth smiled at her lopsidedly. "Walking with you, I believe."

She rolled her eyes. "Yes, I can see that, but why are you walking with me? Surely there are many other, far more important things that the great lord and master could be doing with his time."

"Not really." He shrugged his shoulders, a small devil lurking in his eyes as he added solemnly, "Do you know you are very, very beautiful when you are angry?"

"Well, that's very, very lucky, because in a second I'm going to become almost enraged, so you can well imagine just how much that is going to improve my looks." She covered her face with her hands as she struggled to get herself back under control. She dropped them and tried again. "Look, Gareth, I'm not in the mood for this right now, and I would really appreciate it if you would leave me alone to deal with my bad temper without any witnesses."

With a sincere appearance of regret, Gareth shook his head. "Sorry, Zetta, but I can't do that. I thought I made it clear to you last night that I don't want you to wander about alone at any point. It is not safe. So if you want to walk, then I will just have to walk with you."

Zetta just rolled her eyes. "For God's sake, I'm not some fragile lady of the court who can't look after herself. I'm a street urchin, Gareth. One way or another I've been looking after myself for most of my life, and I'm sure I'm perfectly capable of walking among some weeds without your gallant protection, if you don't mind."

"Well, unfortunately, I do." He casually slipped her resisting hand through his arm and began to walk once more. "Besides, this will give me a chance to talk to you."

"I have nothing to say to you."

Gareth's rich laughter rang out and Zetta had to suppress her shuddering response to the glorious sound.

"My God, woman, you are the most stubborn person I have ever met." He patted her hand consolingly. "But not to matter. You can keep your stubborn silence if you like. It will give me probably my only chance of telling you all that I have to tell without you interrupting."

Zetta bit her tongue and glared at him mutinously.

"Good, now firstly, no more going out by yourself. I want you to only leave the solar if you are accompanied by either myself, Edrit or one of the handful of loyal guards I will have looking after you all.

"Secondly, from now on you will dine at my side. I want everyone in this hellhole to know that you are under my very personal protection. I don't want anyone to forget that fact, and I think seeing you dine in the place of honor at my side should make my point quite nicely.

"Which brings me to my third and final point. From now on you sleep in my chamber."

Zetta stopped short, tugging her hand free of his.

"No!"

Gareth took another couple of steps as if he hadn't heard her, then stopped. Zetta couldn't help but stare at his broad, muscular shoulders. Truly they were a thing of beauty, and even as she tried to fight the way he made her feel, she knew she would always fail with this man.

He turned toward her slowly. She was surprised at the seriousness of his light blue eyes. She almost didn't recognize this unsmiling man.

"I didn't hear any 'nos' last night."

Zetta's face flushed as she remembered her own wanton behavior, but she lifted her chin defiantly.

"Last night was last night."

"It meant nothing to you?"

She looked away from him for a moment. It would be all too easy for her to say that it hadn't, easy for her to deny her own actions, but for some reason she couldn't lie to him about something so important.

She swallowed visibly. "Yes, it meant something to me, but I can't let one night blind me to all other truths."

"What other truths are there, Zetta, that matter a damn when compared to what we could have together? I don't understand what you mean."

She searched desperately for the words to explain all that she felt. She slowly lifted her gaze back to his, hating all that she had to say to him, but knowing that she had to say it, all the same.

"The body of a cat affixed to my door, that is my reality and I would be a fool to ignore it for dreams." She shook her head wretchedly. "Already they call me a witch. They make signs to ward off my evil eye whenever I cross their path. They treat Edrit as if he were the devil himself sent to tempt them. These are my truths, Gareth."

He gritted his teeth in frustration. "Do you think I am unaware of this? Heaven knows I would stop it if I could, but I don't know any way to destroy these foolish superstitions. That is why I want you sleeping in my chamber. We can sleep chastely if you insist, but at least if I'm there beside you, I can protect you from them."

"But who will protect you, Gareth?" she whispered urgently. "If you publicly take me to your bed and make me your leman, then they will say at best that I have bewitched you. At worst, they will say that you have made a pact with the devil. Either way, they will turn against you, and I can't even begin to imagine what they will do to you. I will not let that happen because of me."

The tension that had filled Gareth's massive body seemed to ease and he even managed a slight chuckle. "Zetta, I don't need you to protect me. I'm well big enough to fight my own battles."

"But this battle isn't yours."

He closed the distance between them, his voice low and compelling. "It is if I make it so. I want to help you fight it. Let me make it clear that you are mine and then just let them dare try to harm you."

Zetta stared at him in bewilderment, her brows drawn in confusion. She didn't understand how he could offer so much of himself and seemingly expect nothing in return. She wasn't so vain as to assume that the delights of her body were enough to entice him to risk everything to claim them. If it was willing flesh he wanted, then there wasn't a woman in the castle who wasn't his for the asking.

And they would bring with them no danger, unlike herself.

She tried to understand why he would willingly offer to shoulder all of her burdens only expecting the poor coin of her body in return.

He reached out for her and took hold of her shoulders gently, holding her a little away from him, but the warmth of his large hands seemed to pour straight into her bones. He appeared to be trying to compel her to do what he wanted, to let him make this sacrifice.

It was hard, but slowly she shook her head. "No, Gareth. I won't sleep in your chamber. We won't stay here much longer." She quickly raised a hand to his lips and stilled his protest. "I will leave. I must, but not right now." Her voice broke as she fought back tears. "My mother is dying and I will take your hospitality for now, as it makes her passing easier. But once she is gone . . ."

He tore her hand from his mouth and held it tightly in his.

"Don't leave ever. Stay with me. Stay here, be my companion, my friend, my lover. I want you, Zetta, as I have never wanted anything in my life. I will have you. Nothing you say or do will stop me. Do you understand?"

"It is you who don't understand!" Her voice rose with frustration, but despite her rejection of him she couldn't stop her fingers from lacing through his.

He smiled down at their joined hands and slowly lifted hers to his lips. "It will hurt, but I will give you time. I want you, but I am prepared to wait. A little while." He drew a deep, steadying breath. "All right. For the moment you may sleep in the solar, but know that when you are ready, I will be waiting for you." His eyes hardened slightly. "But you will dine with me no matter where you sleep."

She nodded her head dumbly, and the feel of his hot breath on the back of her hand was like a brand on her soul.

He smiled at her gently. "And you are wrong, my little thief. I do understand. I understand the only thing that matters to me."

He pulled her almost roughly into his arms and was seemingly content just to hold her against his large body. What he said against her ear, however, burned into her brain, blasting into fragments the last of her certainties about her life.

"Zetta," he whispered softly, "I understand now why you have managed to tie me into such knots since the moment I first met you. The reason you can bring me to my knees with just a glance is that you are quite simply the other half of my soul. If it takes me all of this life and the next, I will woo you till you know that you are the woman I was born to love. I will continue to love you till the day I die, and nothing—*nothing*—will ever take you from me."

Chapter 8

"How far away are they?" Gareth asked Anthony brusquely, mounting the stone steps up to the castle's parapets two at a time.

"About two hours, I'd say." Anthony panted, struggling to keep up. "They don't seem to be moving all that fast."

Gareth only grunted in reply. He pushed open the topmost door with a bang and walked out onto the stone fortifications. The wind roared into the stairwell and Anthony was shivering by the time he reached the top of the stairs. He couldn't help but be envious of the way Gareth seemed entirely unaware of the cold as he leaned against the stonework, scanning the horizon intently.

It didn't take him long to find what he was looking for.

The glint of armor through the trees was almost blinding, and soon the banners and pennants also came into view, their patterns and colors intermittently appearing and disappearing among the foliage as they fluttered boldly in the breeze.

Gareth had seen all that he needed to see. He braced both of his hands on the battlements.

"Damn. Damn. Damn," he growled as he slammed his hands against the stones in frustration.

"It's the king, isn't it?" Anthony said as he came up beside him, a faint awe creeping into his voice.

"*Damn,*'" Gareth muttered again. "I was hoping that I would be given a little more time before this happened," he added cryptically.

"More time for what, Sir Gareth?" Anthony asked quietly, and Gareth looked over at him sardonically.

"Time to make this castle monarchproof." He shook his head with disgust and exhaled loudly. "As it all stands there is absolutely nothing I can do to defend this castle from Henry. He can walk in and claim the lot, and I would have to smile very politely and thank him for his benevolence."

He laughed dryly and ran a hand over his tired eyes. "We can only hope that King Henry is so worried about the deteriorating situation between himself and his brother that he is more interested in allies than ill-defended castles."

Anthony looked speculatively at the company slowly advancing through the forest. "Do you really think that the king would try to take the castle?"

"A king always wants one more castle, especially when he is planning to go to war in the immediate future." Gareth smiled cynically. "And our king has been preparing to do battle with his brother Robert for months now. They both seem to think that they should be ruling Normandy, and they are prepared to kill the other to settle the matter once and for all."

Gareth's hand tightened on the stone fortifications. "When their little family disagreement reaches war stage, this castle will become particularly attractive. Not only is it one of the finest that has so far been built on this isle; it is also very well placed, strategically speaking. If Henry loses the war, he will need in his possession as many of England's southern fortresses and castles as he can organize if he is to have a hope of defending the isle from his, shall we say, unhappy brother."

"And if we had had more time to prepare, Sir Gareth, what then? Could we really hold out against the king?" Anthony asked eagerly and Gareth smiled at his naiveté, suddenly feeling ages older rather than the few years that were truly between them.

"Honestly, I don't know. It probably wouldn't have made all that much difference. The men are so raw that I don't know if twelve years would give them enough time to be ready to defend the castle." He turned away from Anthony and his smile slowly faded. "But I would have liked to have had more time all the same."

"So what will we do?" Anthony's voice vibrated with so much confidence that Gareth would have all the answers that he gave him a quick grin that he was far from feeling.

"Well, if we can't repel them, we had best go and see that everything is ready to receive our uninvited royal guest." He raised a questioning brow in Anthony's direction. "Which brings me to our most pressing concern. What, if any, dealings have you had with royalty before now?"

Anthony shifted uncomfortably. "Not much," he muttered, then flushed a bright red as a real smile spread over Gareth's face. He added with a stammer, "Nothing at all, really."

The sound of Gareth's laugh sent a flock of birds resting on the fortifications up into the air. "Well, then, you are in for quite a treat, aren't you?"

"Somehow, I doubt that," Anthony murmured dryly.

Gareth was still chuckling as he headed over to the door and yelled good-naturedly over his shoulder, "I believe you could be right about that!"

But as he wound down the stairs, a serious look returned to his face. He knew with chilling certainty that the coming days were going to be some of the most dangerous he had ever lived through. One false move and everything he had been slowly building over the past three months with Zetta was going to come crashing down around his ears and there was not one damn thing that he could do about it.

That was just the kind of excitement a king brought to his subjects, Gareth thought with black humor. It was an excitement he could well do without.

Zetta moved farther back into the shadow of the stone wall and silently watched the king swing down from his large warhorse, his silver armor glinting in the sun. The outer bailey was full of people trying to catch a glimpse of the unexpected visitor.

No one noticed her in this hiding place, deep within the shadows of the wall.

She had been drawn from the walled garden into the bailey by the sound of so many horses' hooves on stone and her stomach had sunk as she had realized just who had arrived at the castle. She had never seen the king before, but, like every other Londoner, she was all too familiar with his standard. She had recognized it the second she had seen it fluttering in the breeze of the outer bailey and known who their visitor was long before his squire had announced him.

As she watched, Henry benignly surveyed the crowd that had gathered and a cold feeling filled her core.

She knew that she was watching the event that would mark the end of one of the happiest times in her life. The king, however, seemed entirely untouched by any such premonitions, smiling as he motioned for his men to stay where they were.

He alone mounted the stairs that led up to the main doors, and his shrewd gaze seemed to take in every detail around him. Zetta could almost see his mind calculating the exact worth of every single stone. Her heart missed a beat when the doors were thrown open and Gareth, dressed simply in tunic and hose, stepped out into the sun.

The differences between the two men could not be greater.

Henry was a short, stocky man who would no doubt become fat as the years passed. Right now, however, he still radiated the health and strength of a man in the prime of his life. His dark hair was cut so short that it barely moved in the breeze and his hand rested with comfortable familiarity against his sword hilt. Clearly, for all his scholarly reputation, he was very comfortable with his role of warrior monarch.

Zetta shivered, almost fancying that she could feel the power that radiated from him. Gareth could also make her shiver, but his power over her was of a totally different kind. She didn't even try to stop her gaze from taking in every detail of him. He was at once achingly familiar and exotically unknown.

He stood a good head taller than his king and she found herself smiling as she thought that his broad, lean, muscular frame would never run to fat.

With a grace that was always surprising in such a large man, Gareth dropped down to his knees. Despite the subservience of the act, Gareth seemed to give it a dignity that made Zetta swell with pride as she watched. As he bowed his head, his dark blond hair fell forward, hiding his face for a moment, and Zetta realized with a start just how much he had let it grow in the last few months. He no longer wore it short like the knights who crowded all around, and although she didn't quite know what that small change might mean, she found herself liking it.

From her hiding place in the shadows she couldn't hear what passed between the two men, their words being snatched by the wind long before they reached her. She didn't need to hear, however, to know just how comfortable Gareth was dealing with royalty. In no time at all Henry was laughing uproariously at something Gareth said and pulling him casually back to his feet. With a singular sign of favor he threw an arm around Gareth's shoulder.

As the two men moved toward the open door, Zetta turned away. She didn't need to see any more. Quietly she walked back into the walled garden.

She would wait till the bailey had emptied before daring to return to the solar. That way, she could delay the unavoidable confrontation with this new world in which there was no longer any place for her.

As she began to pace through the long grass, the image of Gareth standing tall and proud beside the king filled her mind no matter how hard she tried to push it away. It was the part of reality that she had been so carefully trying to deny for the past months, but the truth could no longer be ignored.

Gareth could never be hers, not really.

The world of kings, castles and wealth was his by right. Her place was in the small, dark world of thieves, prostitutes and parasites of all persuasions. Between those two worlds was a chasm so wide and so deep that she would be lost if she tried to bridge it. She had known that from the beginning, had continually warned herself not to believe in mirages, to stay focused on the truth.

And yet, somehow, Gareth had slowly made her lose sight of that.

He had filled her days with himself so effortlessly that she had almost come to believe that the dreams he whispered to her might become real. She had lost sight of the impossible and had let herself be seduced by a future that was entirely built on air. His wooing had been so subtle that she hadn't seen what he was doing.

She had almost begun to feel like a lady. No, not just a lady, she amended sadly, but *his* lady.

Well, she had to forget all of that.

By treating her like she was the most precious thing in his life he had almost destroyed her. Now that she would have to rediscover herself, she almost wished he had behaved as every other man of his world did. If he had brutally seduced her, used her and then thrown her away, at least then she would have been able to walk tall now. Her hate would have seen to that.

Instead, he had held her hand; spent time with her and her family; walked with her; talked with her; and, but for the heat of his gaze, had not once tried treating her as anything less than a lady. For someone with her past it was almost incomprehensible.

That would be gone now.

The arrival of the king meant that they both had to face facts and she knew she should embrace that notion. She should be glad that the strange, fey world they had let themselves slip into would now be righted. Instead, she felt like crying.

Zetta was about to lose the most precious thing she

had ever experienced. She could find no consolation in the fact that she would always treasure these days spent with a man who treated her like she was worth something. She wrapped her arms tightly around her middle and sat down stiffly on the cold stone bench, trying to prepare herself for the world she would find outside the garden wall.

A single tear slipped down her cheek and she furiously scrubbed it away with the back of her hand. Another slid down to take its place, but this time she did nothing to remove it. Or the next. Just this once she would indulge herself. Just this once she would allow herself to grieve.

Her sadness was her own. She wanted no one to know that she felt as if a knife had been thrust into her heart. If she kept all that pain on the inside, then she would protect the only thing she could truly call her own: her pride. It was hers and she intended to walk away from Gareth and his dreams with at least that one small thing.

Her heart, however, would have to be left behind in his tender hands.

Gareth strode toward the solar, but he knew that no matter how fast he was, he wouldn't beat the gossip. Zetta would already know about their unexpected guest and God alone knew what she was thinking about this new event. He had been working so hard to win her trust, but for all of his efforts he knew only too well just how fragile a thing it still was.

He could only wish now that he had warned her that something like this was going to happen. He had always known that at some point the outside world and all of its complications was going to intrude, and perhaps if Zetta had known that as well then she would at least have been able to prepare herself for it.

But he hadn't warned her. He had been so afraid that it would disturb the delicate trust that had slowly been growing between them that he had deliberately ignored the existence of any threat at all. Now he saw that his cowardice had put in jeopardy everything he had been trying to protect.

He could only hope that Zetta would give him a chance to explain to her that none of it mattered.

His steps slowed, then stopped when he reached the solar door. He pushed it open cautiously, reluctant to see what awaited him inside, but he knew it had to be faced. He sighed with silent relief when he saw Joan was still in her bed and that Zetta was sitting in the chair beside her. The older woman was quietly mumbling and singing to herself and Gareth felt a strange tightness in his chest as Zetta laughed softly and reached out to tuck a strand of gray hair behind her mother's ear.

Only now that he knew for certain that she had at least waited for him to explain things to her did he admit to himself just how worried he had been that she might have disappeared before giving him that chance. When she looked up, her deep, green eyes regarded him solemnly, and his stomach dropped to his knees.

She whispered something to Joan and then rose gracefully from her chair. She smiled at him, but it was such a small, sad little smile that his concern only intensified. He nodded to Joan politely as he grabbed Zetta's hand and all but dragged her over to the window.

He didn't bother to prevaricate.

"You know, don't you?" he said softly, trying to read her thoughts from the closed expression on her face.

She nodded stiffly. "I saw him. I was in the walled garden when he arrived. It must be quite an honor to have the king himself come and visit you."

"No, it is a complete pain in the backside, but nothing to worry about," he said lightly. But he knew she wasn't fooled, not for a second.

He knew her like she was the other half of his soul, yet he had never been entirely sure whether she felt the same. Searching her eyes now, he thought he saw a glimmer of understanding. It was all he needed. He pulled her hand up to his chest and said earnestly, "You do know that this changes absolutely nothing between us, don't you?"

"I know," she said calmly, but she dropped her eyes so that they no longer quite met his. "I was thought to be your whore before the king arrived. The only difference now is that more people will believe it to be fact."

"You are not my whore," Gareth growled, holding her cold hand more tightly in his. "I don't think of you that way and there is no reason why you should call yourself such a thing."

She smiled at him as if he were a simpleton.

"But there is, Gareth. If I am anything to you, it is your leman. And because you've waited for me to come to you, I haven't even been a very successful one of those. There is no other place for me in your life and I've told you that before. Maybe this time, you will listen."

A muscle twitched in his jaw as he regarded her; then suddenly he dropped her hand and turned to look out of the window as he tried to fight the fear that threatened to swamp him. It was just as he had expected. All the time he had taken, all the pain he had suffered denying his ever-present desire for her, all to show her how much he valued her. He had hoped that by acting the knight gallant it would show her that it mattered to him not at all where she came from, or what kind of life she had led until they had met, but it was all gone in a moment. He didn't know how he was going to now prove to her that the only thing that mattered to him was that he loved her with all of his body and soul.

His jaw tightened painfully, but it in no way matched the pain that was slowly growing inside him. The feel of her hand against the taut muscles in his back seemed to burn him like a brand but he didn't move away from it. It was a sign of just how desperate he had become, he thought with savage self-deprecation, that the feel of a woman's small hand on his back could make him want to cry. "If you will give us other accommodation," she said softly, "we are ready to vacate the solar so that your important guests may have it."

He was glad that she couldn't see the look that passed over his face.

When he was sure that he was back under control he slowly turned back to her. "You are not leaving here; I don't care what you say. Nothing has changed as far as I'm concerned. You stay in this room, you have your dinner with me each evening and, most importantly, you are still the woman I love."

Despite the fact that she knew his declaration changed nothing, she couldn't help but smile at the steely way he said something so beautiful.

And when he had said it a couple of days ago, she almost believed him. Now she could only shake her head. "Don't be a fool, Gareth. Everything has changed. The real world has arrived." Even as she rejected everything he offered she couldn't seem to stop herself from raising a hand and holding it to his tense jaw. "You will have to let me go. I was only a visitor in your world. It was a beautiful dream, but now it's all over and you have to let go."

He covered her hand with his and gently held hers away from his face. "And nothing I say now will make you believe otherwise, will it?" His grip tightened almost painfully on her hand. "But you are wrong, Zetta. You are wrong."

He dropped her hand and started to walk away from her but paused for a second at the door. He hesitated a moment, then slowly turned back to her.

"You will come down to the main hall this evening as usual, is that understood?" he said stiffly and Zetta could feel his anger like a physical presence in the room, menacing her from the other side of the room. He didn't bother to wait for her reply and the door slammed noisily behind him. She flinched as if she had been slapped.

"What have you done to upset him now?" Joan asked softly, her voice thin and wavering, but blessedly lucid. Zetta glanced at her and saw that, for the moment, her eyes were clear. She looked at Zetta as if she was actually seeing her.

Despite all of her own worries Zetta felt an easing of the hollow pain inside her. These periods of lucidity were so few and she knew from bitter experience that this one wouldn't last long, so she intended to enjoy it while she could.

"He has many concerns at the moment," she said with careful casualness as she quickly walked back to the bed. She didn't want to waste this moment on something that neither of them could change.

Joan's brow furrowed. "Concerns that involve the men and horses I heard arriving this afternoon?"

Zetta's eyes widened but she quickly hid her surprise

by nodding her head brusquely. She sat in the chair by the bed, desperately hoping her mother would leave it at that.

She wasn't entirely shocked that she wasn't that lucky.

"Who has arrived?" Joan asked. Her clear eyes never once left Zetta's face, and she knew that she wouldn't be able to lie. When Joan was herself she would only be satisfied with the complete truth.

"The king and a regiment or two of his bachelor knights," Zetta said neutrally. "Nothing to do with us."

Much to Zetta's surprise, a slow smile spread over Joan's face. "Oh, my dear girl, it has everything to do with us." Seeing Zetta's look of complete bewilderment drew a dry chuckle from the older woman, and the chuckle turned into her first full-throated laugh in longer than Zetta could remember.

The laugh turned into a racking cough and she fell back against her pillows, her chest heaving violently as she struggled to breathe. But even as she labored, she managed to look like a cat that had caught a fat mouse. Slowly her breathing returned to normal

"I don't understand. What does this have to do with us?" Zetta asked, entirely baffled by her mother's strange reaction.

Joan ignored Zetta's question, and once she had regained control, her pale watery eyes stared at her intently as she asked with a surprisingly strong voice, "And you are going to have dinner with Gareth as usual? And the king will be there?"

Zetta nodded her head, her concern growing with every passing second. She was almost afraid that what she had taken to be a moment of lucidity was in fact a new manifestation of her disease.

"Perfect." Joan smiled and reached for Zetta's hand, and held it tightly. Zetta shivered at the coldness of her mother's skin against her own but found herself holding on just as securely.

"Now, Zetta, you must listen to me and do exactly what I tell you to. Do you understand me?"

"No."

"That doesn't matter, just as long as you do what I tell you to. You will do it, won't you?"

Zetta searched Joan's face and was almost frightened by the stern stranger she saw staring out of her mother's eyes. She nodded her head slowly, and Joan rewarded her by giving her hand another hard squeeze.

"Good. You are to go and bathe and get ready for tonight's dinner. You are to put on the best gown you have, and you are to make yourself look like the beautiful young woman I know you to be. You are then to enter the great hall as if you are a lady born."

"But I am not a lady born. I'm from the gutters and everyone in the castle knows it."

"They think they know it, but I know more than they can even begin to guess," Joan said, her face hard and unyielding. When she saw Zetta's confused and worried face, she lifted a weak hand to Zetta's hair. "Don't worry, my little girl. You are a lady born. I was a gentlewoman before the war that brought these Normans to power and your father—well, that is a story for another day—but let me tell you that your bloodlines are not anything to be ashamed of, ever. They may not be legitimate, but they are among the finest in this country. Remember that and walk into the hall tonight like you are equal to any king."

Joan's hand dropped back against the furs and she leaned against her pillows, exhaustion etching into old lines on her face. "You will do what I ask? You will speak to the king tonight?"

Zetta didn't understand any of it, but she nodded her head anyway. She could not deny her mother anything. Joan closed her eyes with satisfaction.

"Good. Now when you speak to the king, you will mention my name. You will tell him that your mother is Joan of Bovey. Tell him how old you are. Tell him where you were born. Tell him . . ." She started to cough again, but this time she didn't have the strength to fight it off.

It was a long time before the coughing faded into ragged breathing.

Zetta carefully brought the furs up around her mother's thin shoulders and brushed the sweat-soaked gray hair off of her face. That pale, lined face was more familiar to her than her own, but, at the same time, it was alien. It seemed impossible that this old woman was the vibrant mother who had brought so much color and grace into Zetta's childhood.

She had no idea what her mother hoped could be achieved with this masquerade, but, at the same time, there was no doubt in Zetta's mind that she would do exactly what her mother had asked her to do.

Joan had rarely asked anything of her before and had always given so much of herself that Zetta was incapable of denying her anything now, even if doing what she wanted was more than likely going to lead to humiliation. Once it was clear that Joan had slipped back into a troubled sleep and was going to say no more, Zetta got up and tiptoed away.

She quietly crouched down in front of the clothes chest at the end of the bed. The well-oiled hinges made not a sound as she pushed open the lid.

It took her only a second to find the dress she was looking for. Carefully, she lifted it from the chest and shook it free from its folds. Seeing it again, she wondered if she was brave enough to wear it.

The rich, green silk shimmered beautifully in the dying light of the sun, and the gold threads that glowed in the brocaded bodice were mesmerizing.

It was a dress fit for a queen.

She could remember saying something like that when Gareth had given it to her.

When he had presented it to her with a flourish she had been so stunned that she hadn't been able to speak for a full five minutes. Never in her life had she seen anything so beautiful, and when she had told him so he had laughed and told her that it wasn't as beautiful as she was.

Said by any other man, it would have sounded like so much empty flattery, but Gareth had managed to infuse it with such sincerity that Zetta had blushed helplessly and stuttered as she had tried to find the words to thank him. She had then tried to explain that he shouldn't give her such expensive and beautiful things, but he had simply bowed over her hand and said that he would leave her alone till she was able to say something that he actually wanted to hear.

Within half an hour she had sought him out and thanked him for the beautiful dress and had promised that she would keep it always.

But until now, she hadn't thought to actually wear it.

Such a dress was not meant to be worn by a thief from the stews of London. It was a glorious thing that she shouldn't even be touching. Such a dress was made for an elegant lady like the one whom Gareth would one day call his wife, and no matter how glorious the cloth, it could never disguise how far she was from that woman.

Everyone in the great hall tonight would all too easily see through her beautiful disguise and no doubt laugh at her. That was, if they didn't see something far more sinister in her actions.

Already they thought her a witch. If they also started to believe that she was trying to seduce the king over to the devil, then there was no knowing what they would do to her as punishment.

She closed the chest and carefully laid the dress over it.

She didn't have to do what Joan had asked, she told herself desperately. After all, the old woman's mind had been wandering for months. It would be easy to dismiss what she had said as just more of her nonsense. Surely it would be more sensible to just ignore it all, to not go through with this bizarre masquerade her mother wanted.

Joan wouldn't ever know that Zetta had disobeyed her. It was logical, but even as she thought it, she knew she couldn't betray her mother in such a way. She would do it.

She straightened her shoulders.

The hardest part would be that for this one evening alone, she would be a lady like the one Gareth needed by his side. She would have a tantalizing taste of what it would be like if the world were different and Gareth were truly hers. For one night she would cease to be the thief who would bring only complications and pain to his life and would become a lady.

His lady.

And when morning came all pretenses would be over. She had no idea how she was ever going to live with the painful memories of this one evening out of time. It would break her heart beyond all mending and haunt her till the day she died.

At the same time, she would treasure it as the most perfect night of her life.

Chapter 9

"You have a fine castle here, Sir Gareth," Henry said as he cast an appreciative look around the main hall.

The large space had no trouble accommodating the fifty-odd knights the king had brought with him. And the place was looking almost magnificent, Gareth thought as he realized with irritation that the improvements of the past few months were finally beginning to show. He could only now wish that he hadn't been so keen on getting the place looking right.

As Henry lifted his tankard once more, Gareth could almost see his calculating mind taking in every detail, up to and including the number of steaming dishes that were continually coming up from the kitchens.

"Very fine indeed," Henry said with slow satisfaction. "Much better than I had been led to believe."

Gareth murmured noncommittally and quickly offered Henry some more of the roast meat in the vain hope that it would distract him.

It felt as if he were balancing on a tightrope. One false move would send him hurtling headlong into the crevasse that had suddenly opened up under his feet.

He could even end up fighting in the damn war the king had brewing.

This was no mere social visit. Henry was here to acquire another ally for the coming war with his brother, the Duke of Normandy, and Gareth could even find it in himself to admire the cold, ruthless tactics the king was using.

While the French duchy was to be the prize, Henry realized that his only true power came from his English throne. He needed to make that throne as secure as possible, because if he lost the coming war, it would be all he had and he would have a real struggle to keep even that.

If Henry lost, then the world that Gareth knew would be torn in two. If he won, well, then Normandy and England would be unified again as they hadn't been properly since the death of the Conqueror.

It was as if that world was balanced between two vastly different fates, and if he wasn't very, very careful Gareth knew he could find himself on the wrong side of the widening crevasse that was forming.

It was only logical that with his life centered in England, the less powerful king was far more important to him than the almighty duke, but right now, it was the king who was presenting the far greater problem.

Gareth scanned the hall and sighed silently.

The two groups of knights had blended together for the evening, taking full advantage of the opportunity for new conversation and stories, but Gareth could still all too easily identify the men who belonged to the castle.

Henry's knights were all hardened warriors, the veterans of innumerable wars. It showed in the very way they held themselves. By comparison, the men of Gareth's garrison all looked like farmers and serfs.

It would have been glaringly obvious to the most casual of observers that although his men outnumbered Henry's three to one, the royal knights could wipe them out entirely if there was the least sign of resistance. And Gareth wasn't a casual observer. He had the sinking feeling in his gut that not only was the tightrope he had to walk over a crevasse, but also that both his hands were tied behind his back.

"And your brother has asked you to stay here as custodian for how long?" Henry asked politely, interrupting Gareth's gloomy thoughts.

"Lanfranc and I haven't discussed a specific length of time as yet, Your Majesty," he murmured politely.

"Hmm." Henry looked over at him thoughtfully. "And you are happy with this arrangement? I find that most surprising."

"I'm content enough with my lot."

"You are something of an enigma, aren't you, Sir Gareth?" Henry said with a smile that didn't quite reach his eyes. "You spent years as a mercenary with Robert Beaumont, as his second in command, did you not? Not many men of your birth would have tolerated being an inferior to a man of no birth or rank. Yet, I have to admit that the pair of you proved to be a very efficient team. And I suppose I can understand the attractions of such a life, even if it isn't quite what you were born to. But overnight"—Henry snapped his fingers—"you both give it up. Now, Robert's decision makes sense. He had the land he wanted and no doubt has settled down very well to the life of farmer, but that doesn't explain you to me. Why would you join him in his profitless retirement?"

"You don't believe I too was happy playing at farmer?" Gareth asked politely.

"No, hardly likely. But whatever your reason, your retirement seemed to prove one thing: your first loyalty was to your leader. Admirable, but now, suddenly you abandon your leader to act as your brother's lackey. This sudden change makes me very curious."

"Well, it made perfect sense to me till you started to explain it," Gareth said with a smile, but his gut tightened. There was something about the curiosity of kings that made him nervous.

"Come, I think that if you were honest, Sir Gareth, you would admit that you are as confused as I am. Surely you have occasionally wondered why it is that you have achieved so little in your life. I mean, I know better than most that it is not easy being a younger son, but as I have proved, birth is no permanent impediment to greater things. Why haven't you become master of your own destiny? Why are you so content to be the pawn of others?"

"I lack ambition?" Gareth suggested airily.

"I doubt that." Henry narrowed his eyes and assessed him carefully. "No, I can certainly see no lack of ambition in you. So why are you here now?"

Gareth shrugged his shoulders, unable to explain to Henry something that didn't contain the only two things he truly understood: money and power.

"I must say that I am surprised, Your Majesty," Gareth said with a lopsided grin. "I never realized that you spent so much time and effort pondering the fates of your subjects."

"Only the interesting ones, Sir Gareth, the ones I think will be of some use to me and my country."

Gareth chuckled dryly. "I suppose I should be flattered that you see me as useful."

"But you're not?"

"Long experience with this world has taught me that it is very rarely advantageous for the individual to be of use to kings." Gareth lifted a brow. "Especially intelligent ones like yourself."

Henry threw back his head and laughed loudly. "Oh, Sir Gareth, I really must see more of you. My court is in sad need of men like yourself."

"It pains me to refuse you, Your Majesty, but your court will have to do without me for the time being. My commitments to my brother mean that I am to stay here for the foreseeable future."

"And what if I offered you more than your brother? What then?" Henry asked softly.

Carefully Gareth put his tankard down on the table. "What, Your Majesty, could possibly have more value to me than my own honor and the honor of my family?"

"Don't be a fool, Sir Gareth. You know perfectly well that there are many things that are worth more than your honor, things that I alone can offer you. If you want wealth, it can be yours. If you want a higher rank, that can be yours as well. If it is land you want, well then, I think I will soon be able to offer you one of several very nice estates in Normandy." Henry smiled at Gareth benevolently. "Choose whatever you want and it can be yours. Yours, that is, if you agree to follow me."

Gareth quickly looked away, not wanting Henry to see how tempted he was by the offer. Obviously the king had been right when he had said that he wasn't entirely without ambition, Gareth thought wryly, although only a fool wouldn't be tempted by such an offer.

Of course he was tempted.

If he gave Henry his allegiance, then at last he would have the settled security that had always eluded him. If he had an estate of his own, then perhaps his restless dissatisfaction would be gone for good. He could settle down, become his own master.

It was as if Henry had looked into his soul and found a weakness that he had only just found himself. It had only occurred to him of late just how little he had to offer Zetta as a landless knight. If he took the security that Henry was offering him, he could marry Zetta and give her a world free of hardship.

The image it conjured was very tempting, but Gareth was not fool enough to fall for the illusion without seeing the dark scheming behind it.

It wasn't really Gareth whom Henry was after, so much as what he represented as a member of the powerful de Hugues family. Just one member of that family on his side and Henry's importance would increase instantly. Of course, the current baronet would have been perfect, but at this stage Henry needed anyone who could claim close ties to one of Normandy's most respected families. The de Hugueses were powerful enough in their own right that even a younger son was a valuable connection to have.

That this younger son was also in control of the de Hugues English castle was an added bonus. The massive fortress could be a very important asset, and now having seen it for himself, Henry would no doubt be most eager to add it to his arsenal.

It was all ruthlessly logical and Gareth knew that those things that made him a very desirable ally also put him in a very dangerous position. He couldn't take what was offered without throwing himself headlong into a war he wanted no part of. One wrong step and he would have even less to offer Zetta than he did now—that is, if he was alive to offer her anything at all.

He smiled engagingly at Henry. "Well, sire, you have certainly given me much to think on."

"Don't think too long, Sir Gareth. I am not a patient man and you will do much better if you don't forget—" He suddenly stopped speaking and his eyes widened in surprise as he looked at something over Gareth's shoulder. "My God, who is that woman?"

"Don't tell me you have taken a fancy to one of the serving wenches. They are not available, Your Majesty. At least, not until after they have finished serving the meal," Gareth said with a relieved smile, glad that Henry's lecherous nature had finally asserted itself and created a distraction. Knowing Henry's reputation, he could only wonder that it had taken so long.

The king was rumored to have at least a dozen bastard children scattered around the kingdom, and their mothers were of both high birth and low. It was only to be expected that the royal bed would not be empty during his stay.

Gareth followed the king's glance, more than prepared to organize everything as quickly as possible with the wench to give himself more time, and then his heart stopped. Zetta stood hesitantly just inside the great doors.

As she began to slowly walk the length of the long hall, every eye turned to her, but she seemed to be totally impervious to the interest she was arousing. Gareth found himself in complete sympathy with the stunned silence that fell over the hall. He was feeling a little like he had been hit betwixt the eyes with an axe himself.

When he had bought the green cloth and had had it

made up into a gown he had had some vague thought that it would suit her red hair well. Now he realized that he hadn't even begun to understand the beauty of the woman he loved.

She looked magnificent, and it wasn't just the green of the silk that suited her. The dress clung to her lush curves and the unusual square neckline revealed a daring amount of her throat and breasts. Her pale, translucent skin seemed almost to glow in the candlelight, outshining the gold thread that glimmered on the bodice.

But neither shone like the vibrancy of her hair.

In the past months it had grown. Gone was the pixie short hair, and now the vivid waves hung almost to her shoulders, moving sensually with each step she took.

For a moment Gareth forgot how to breathe.

He had always known she was beautiful, but he was awed to see her in all of her glory. His chest expanded with pride as he watched her walk across the room as if she were a queen. He wanted to claim her as his own in front of everyone.

Though he knew she wouldn't thank him for doing so, but he couldn't stop a silly grin from spreading over his face. Anyone looking at him would all too easily interpret the smug, self-satisfied look on his face as he watched her walk toward the dais.

"Who is she?" Henry demanded, forcing Gareth out of his daze with a jolt.

"She's a young woman under my, ah, protection. Her name is Zetta."

"By God, I'd like to have her under my protection for a night or two," Henry growled appreciatively as she reached the dais.

Without giving Gareth even the smallest glance, she dropped into a faultless curtsy.

"Your Majesty," she said softly but somehow made it heard throughout the hall.

"Now, now, my dear, we two need not stand on ceremony. Rise." He smiled at her with wolfish charm as she gracefully rose up. "Come and sit beside me and I'll even share my trencher with you." He moved hastily to make room for her on his bench seat.

With quiet dignity she climbed the dais step and sat herself down beside the now-beaming king. She kept her eyes carefully lowered as Henry set about charming her with the full force of his personality.

Gareth watched with growing unease as she blushed with ladylike decorum and modestly demurred after each of his increasingly extravagant compliments. Something wasn't right, but for the life of him he couldn't even begin to guess what that was.

She seemed calm and relaxed but he could almost feel the tension she was trying to hide like it was his own. It coiled deep into his stomach like a block of ice and grew as, for the next long hour, he was all but forgotten by the pair.

He had to sit silently by while Henry tried to sweet-talk himself into her bed, and his cold fear was soon melted by his growing anger when he realized that Zetta was playing some kind of game. She sat there serenely, almost glowing in the candlelight, and not once did she try to put some distance between herself and the man who was fawning over her. It took Gareth a little while to identify the anger as a form of jealousy.

It was the first time in his life that he'd ever experienced the emotion, and he couldn't say that he was enjoying his introduction to it all that much. It was the dark side of love that he could well have done without.

He reached for his tankard and drained it while he watched with increasing frustration as the woman he loved more than life itself demurred as Henry offered her more wine. Briefly. Then shyly she reached out her hand and took the goblet and sipped from it delicately.

She did it all perfectly.

Her every gesture was the perfect balance of good manners and sophisticated elegance. She acted innocent, but there was just that small something that left a small tantalizing doubt, and Henry was clearly speculating what exactly she was offering. Indeed, if Gareth hadn't been one hundred percent certain that she was in fact an innocent, he too would have been speculating himself.

And if he hadn't met her while she was trying to steal from him, he might also have been beginning to believe that she was in fact a lady of the finest aristocratic blood.

". . . and you do look a little tired, doesn't she, Sir Gareth?" Henry turned his attention away from Zetta for the first time since she had arrived in the hall, and Gareth found himself gritting his teeth when he recognized the red-hot look of lust in the other man's eyes.

"I didn't quite catch what you were talking about, Your Majesty," Gareth said through clenched teeth.

"I said, it was perhaps time that this young lady retired for the night as she is looking decidedly tired." Henry grinned wolfishly. "Indeed, I think I might be a little fatigued myself."

If he hadn't looked so damn smug as he added that last bit Gareth might have just been able to control his temper. And if he had managed to control his temper he might have tried to extract Zetta with a little more finesse.

But Henry did look decidedly smug and Gareth felt the last piece of his sanity snap. Finesse be damned, he decided with relish. Brute force would just have to do.

He stood abruptly and slammed his tankard down on the table.

"You are right, Your Majesty. She looks decidedly tired. I will escort her back to her rooms myself."

Henry began to protest loudly that he would love to help the lady to her bedchambers, but Gareth ruthlessly talked over him. "No, I couldn't ask you to put yourself out. Stay and enjoy the rest of your meal. Zetta is my responsibility."

Before Henry had a chance to argue, Gareth jumped down from the dais and went round to Zetta's side. Zetta didn't look pleased to be rescued, he thought darkly. Indeed, she glared at him like he was a viper straight from hell.

"Gareth . . ." she hissed savagely, but he ignored her. Bowing very politely before her, he held out his hand to her.

She hesitated for a second, casting a despairing look at Henry's angry, red face, but there was nothing else she could do. Reluctantly, she stood and stepped down from the dais, taking Gareth's hand. He barely waited for her to finish her curtsy and stammer her good nights before he started to march her down the length of the main hall.

She waited till they were far enough away from the main hall to not be heard before pulling up short and snatching her hand from Gareth's.

"Just what the hell did you do that for?!" she yelled at him.

He turned on her and she almost took a step back when she saw the anger that glowed in his own eyes. Out of lifelong habit she held her ground, but it wasn't easy as he closed the gap between them.

"Forgive me, but I was laboring under the perhaps misguided belief that you didn't want to be ravished by our beloved monarch. It might seem foolish, but I thought I had better remove you before he ate you up along with the roast boar." He crossed his arms belligerently over his powerful chest and shook his head with disgust. "I'm sorry if it interfered with . . . whatever it was you were trying to do in there tonight."

She closed her eyes, suddenly feeling as tired as she had been pretending to be.

Gareth was right. She had been in over her head. She had thought that if she acted like a lady she would get a chance to fulfill her mother's request, but she hadn't been sitting down for more than five seconds before she had realized that Henry hadn't wanted to talk to her. He had obviously decided that she would be a very pleasant bedfellow, and he had been trying to sweet-talk her with every charm he possessed.

She hadn't expected that to happen and she'd had no idea at all of how to defend herself against his royal advances. She had needed rescuing badly and Gareth's intervention had been timely.

She sighed deeply. "No, Gareth, you didn't make a mistake," she said softly and opened her eyes. "I am actually almost grateful for your ham-fisted interference."

That she agreed with him seemed to take the wind out of his sails, but he continued to scowl at her threateningly, not prepared to let it go so easily.

"Well, you didn't look terribly grateful to me," he growled tightly. "In fact, you looked like you were enjoying yourself. My God, woman! You all but offered yourself to him on a silver platter. With the way you were hanging on his every word all evening, is it any wonder that he thought you were available?"

"I did not offer myself!" Zetta said indignantly. "I never once did anything that could have made him believe that I'd be willing to . . . well . . . you know what I mean."

"Yes, I know what you mean," he said with a sneer. "And you are right. Your offer was terribly polite. You were all demure looks and ladylike smiles, but that didn't mean that you weren't offering yourself to him all the same."

Zetta rolled her eyes in exasperation. "God, what nonsense! Your precious king decided that I was on offer before I even so much as opened my mouth. Indeed, he is the kind of arrogant man who believes that every woman who is breathing wants to fall at his feet." She threw her hands up in the air. "But if you want to believe that he was the innocent victim of my seductions, then that's fine with me. Now, if you don't mind, I'm exceptionally tired and I think I will go to bed now. Alone."

She picked up her skirts and moved to sweep past him, but Gareth had other ideas.

Instead of moving aside to let her pass, he reached for her with surprising quickness and hauled her up against his chest.

A shock of awareness ran through her. In that second the tempered passion that had marked the past months exploded, and now she couldn't believe that the politeness of it had ever existed. A fire that had been burning low in her belly suddenly roared into mile-high flames. Her skin flushed as every nerve ending came to sudden life, her breath catching deep in her chest.

"This is what I really want, Zetta," he ground out, then lowered his lips to hers, claiming her mouth in a savage kiss.

Without conscious thought she opened herself to him completely, and the moment his tongue touched hers all thoughts of anger and irritation were consumed by her need for this man. Tonight's earlier fantasy of being Gareth's lady was destroyed utterly by the reality of being Gareth's woman.

She wound her arms around his waist and possessively splayed her hands over his buttocks, loving the feel of his hard, taut flesh against her palms. She squeezed and he groaned into her mouth his satisfaction with her boldness. The only thing that could have made it better would have been if he had been naked and her hands had been touching his hot flesh instead of cloth.

He slanted his mouth over hers, probing even deeper as if he was trying to permanently claim her as his own. She whimpered her need and he answered that need by pushing her up against the wall and grinding his engorged erection intimately against her soft belly.

He pulled his lips from hers and the sound of their ragged breathing filled the corridor.

"You pierce my soul," Gareth growled, his hands moving to cup either side of her face. He tunneled his long fingers into the curls of her hair and drowned her in the heat of his eyes. "One second you have me feeling like a chaste knight errant with his ladylove, and then you have me almost in a murderous rage of jealousy. Now, you have burned me to the core with just one kiss."

His heated gaze dropped to her moist, parted lips and he lowered his head again. "I don't know what to do with you," he whispered against her mouth before claiming her once more.

This time he wooed her. He teased her with light touches that gave her only glimpses of the dark kisses she needed more than she needed to breathe. It wasn't enough, and with a frustrated moan, she turned aggressor. She reached onto the tips of her toes and plunged her tongue deep into his mouth.

She swallowed his agonized growl of pleasure as he hauled her even closer, lifting her feet off of the floor.

By the time she pulled her head away to catch her breath, she felt as if she were drowning in this man. He was her only reality. The only thing she could feel was his body pressed up against hers, the smell of his blood-hot skin engulfing her senses, and the taste of him lingered on her tongue, making her crave more.

He was driving her mad.

"I want you," she said as clearly as her ragged breathing would allow. "I want to be your woman. I want to feel you inside me. I want you."

Gareth didn't say a word. He simply swung her up into his arms and began to stride toward his room. When he reached the stairs, he took them two at a time as if her weight was no burden at all.

It was only after he had carefully laid her on his mattress and gone back to bar the door that he spoke to her. He stood at the end of the bed, his hot gaze burning her like a brand. "Are you sure?"

For a second she didn't quite understand what he asked, but then a slow smile spread across her face. "I notice that you ask me that question only once you have me safely locked inside your chamber."

"I've wanted this too long to be a fool now," Gareth said shortly, and he frowned at her so ferociously that

Zetta could almost feel his impatience from across the room. "Well?"

She smiled at him broadly. "I am sure."

Scarcely were the words out of her mouth when in one quick movement he closed the distance between them. He covered her completely, and when he claimed her mouth once more he was no longer frowning. She caught a glimpse of his broad smile just before she closed her eyes and gave herself up to the joy of this kiss.

He didn't bother undressing either of them. While his tongue entwined sensuously with hers, his hand dragged the delicate cloth of her dress up and bunched it around her waist. With ruthless determination he laid claim to what he had uncovered, slipping his fingers deep into the center of her passion.

She tore her lips from his and moaned his name as his fingers moved knowingly over her, bringing her need to a boiling point.

"Zetta, you are so hot and wet," he growled. "So ready for me."

"Yes. Yes. Yes," she moaned mindlessly, her whole being concentrated on the movement of his hand against her.

"Do you want me inside you now, Zetta?" he said huskily, his fingers slipping teasingly inside her a little, then withdrawing again. Zetta couldn't find her voice, and when his questing hands found the small tight bud of her passion she thought she was going to die. He drove her past the point of all rational thought.

He leaned over her, the wall of his chest a hair's breadth away from her straining nipples. As if drawn to the warmth of him, she arched up to complete the contact, then moaned in frustration as two layers of fabric kept her from him.

"Well, do you really want me? Do you want me so badly that you could die of that want? Do you want me till you no longer know who or what you are, till you have ceased to be anything but your need? A need that only I can satisfy. Tell me, Zetta. I've waited so long that I need to hear it now." His breath was hot against her skin as he whispered in her ear, and his fingers, wet with her passion, began to move against her faster. "Tell me."

"I . . . want . . ."

It was enough.

He lifted his hands from her and quickly released his straining erection.

Poised above her, he stilled for a second, letting her accustom herself to the sensation of him against her so intimately. Then he began to move.

At once it was the most perfect thing she could imagine, but, at the same time, it wasn't enough. She wanted more; she wanted to fly in his arms. She arched herself up against him, trying to bring him into her fully, but he stubbornly refused to be rushed.

With aching slowness he stretched her, claimed her, taking her closer to the edge but denying her the one thing in the world that mattered to her at that moment. When he reached the fragile barrier of her maidenhead, he stopped altogether.

She moved her hand restlessly down his back, trying to press him into her. Under her fingers she could feel his tunic clinging to his sweat-covered back as he kept himself under tight control. She looked into his anguished eyes, and in an instant she understood what he was trying to do. He thought this restraint was what she needed.

She smiled gently and ran a finger over his damp temples.

"Now, Gareth," she whispered throatily. "Now."

He couldn't deny her simple request or his own burning need. With one swift movement he filled her completely. The sharp flare of pain surprised Zetta even though she had expected it, but compared to the sensation of completeness she felt having him buried in her up to the hilt, it was nothing. He began to thrust and the sensation of completeness was eroded by a burning need for something that seemed just over the horizon.

She wrapped her arms around him and gave herself up to him. As his body moved in and out of hers his mouth worshiped her. The heat of his kiss fell on her lips, her eyelids, her nose and then down the line of her throat. At the hollow of her collarbone, he paused a moment, heating the sensitive skin with the flat of his tongue; then he moved down to the neck of her bodice, encircling it with a necklace of kisses.

When she began to moan her desire aloud, he let out a deep, rich laugh and claimed her lips once more. They were so closely joined that his laugh almost felt like it came from inside her, her joy doubled by his. She was a coiled spring that was being steadily winched tighter. The entire focus of her soul was on the fire that was building deep inside her.

Gareth lifted his head, his face dark with his passion as he stared intently into her eyes. "Give it to me. Give it all to me."

She didn't understand what he meant but couldn't find the words to ask him to explain. It didn't matter. Her body, of its own accord, gave him what he wanted. Mindlessly she called his name as the fire at last consumed her. Wave after wave of completion crashed over her and she lost herself completely to their passion.

Only then did Gareth find his own release.

With one last, hard thrust he buried himself inside her as deeply as he could and spent himself while her sheath contracted around him, milking him greedily of his seed. As the full weight of his body fell on her, Zetta realized with dazed amazement that she had made a terrible mistake. She now knew what it was to be Gareth's woman and knew what it felt like to lose herself completely in his arms.

Knowing all that, how could she ever return to a life without him?

Strangely, as she stroked her hands along his passion-soaked back and felt his manhood slowly start to soften inside her, she couldn't make herself care about such things. Right now she was too consumed by her love for this man to worry about the future. No doubt it would come to claim her sooner than she wanted, but she didn't care.

Chapter 10

Gareth smiled gently as the early morning touched Zetta's hair. She was sleeping with her head resting on his chest, and the waves of her short hair were splayed over his skin like pieces of exotic silk. Gently, so as not to wake her, he ran his hand over its softness. It felt cool, but the effect on him as it moved over his naked torso was more like a fire. When a curl sprang round his finger, chaining him to her, he sighed with contentment.

He was exactly where he wanted to be.

The last hour he had spent just watching over her as she slept. A part of him had wanted to wake her up with kisses, wanted to appease the hot desire that still rode him even after all of last night's exertions.

But he hadn't.

Instead, he had found himself content just to feel the way she rested trustingly on his chest, her limbs entwined with his. Which proved what a pathetic creature he had become, he thought wryly.

Not so pitiable, however, that he wasn't aware of the fact that lying with her in his arms was also driving him a little mad. He had spent the last hour in a state of arousal, but then, he acknowledged, he had been in that state almost constantly since the day she had tried to rob him. He had wanted her from that moment, but more than that, he realized now, he had loved her. And now she was his.

His arms tightened around her as he placed a light kiss on the top of her head, luxuriating in the perfume from her hair that filled his senses.

"You're squeezing me," she said in a gruff voice, and he was smiling as he loosened his hold, a little.

"Sorry."

"So I think you should be."

"Do you always wake up grumpy?" he said with a chuckle.

She yawned and rolled over onto her belly, regarding him with a baleful glare. "Only when I'm woken by some idiot trying to squeeze the breath out of me," she said tersely. She crossed her arms over his chest and rested her chin between them as she eyed his smiling face with disgust. "And are you always this disturbingly happy in the morning?"

"Only when I wake up and find you sleeping by my side. The rest of the time, I swear, I'm like a wolf with a bad head."

His lopsided smile brought a strange, fluttery feeling to her stomach but she tried to ignore it as she ran a hand over his smooth chest. "This doesn't feel like your side."

The laugh that came from deep inside his chest was almost a growl. "No, it's not my side, but it still feels damn good," he murmured huskily as he reached down for an all too brief kiss.

She let herself savor the taste of him on her lips and

the feel of his muscular body under hers for a moment and then let out a long sigh. "I had best be getting back to mother and Edrit. I should never have let myself go to sleep like that. I don't know why I did, really. I haven't slept this well since I left London."

"Well I'm glad that I was of some purpose, even if it was only in the place of a sleeping draught." He sounded so put out that if he weren't such a large, masculine man, she almost would have said that he was pouting like a child.

She was still smiling at that thought as she clambered off his warm, enticing body and out of the bed. "Well, while I wouldn't want you to share that talent with just anyone, I have to say that you did a truly excellent job."

She grabbed a fur off of the bed and wrapped it around herself, securing it with a quick tuck knot as she began to search for her clothes. After they had made love the first time, Gareth had carefully slipped off every piece of their clothing and thrown all the items over his shoulder as he set about kissing every inch of her body.

Which, of course, led to them making love again.

At the time, she hadn't cared one iota what had happened to the green silk dress, but when she found it lying over by the window crumpled she let out a squeak of distress. Snatching it up, she tried desperately to undo the damage that a night on the rushes had done to the delicate fabric.

"Oh God, Gareth, you've ruined it! You have torn all of the lacing and these creases in the skirt will never go away. It was so lovely!"

Gareth rolled onto his side and leaned up on his elbow. "It is only a dress, Zetta."

She glared at him. "It isn't just a dress. It is the most

beautiful thing I have ever seen, and it must have cost an absolute fortune, so don't you dare say that it is just a dress!"

Gareth smiled at her tenderly. "I'm glad that you liked it so much."

She ignored him, continuing to fuss over the dress until he let out a long, tired sigh. Reluctantly, he threw back the furs and swung his long legs over the side of the bed.

She was so intent on the damaged dress that she didn't even look up when he walked over to her side.

She let out a small mew of surprise when he suddenly pulled her back against his naked chest, but she couldn't stop herself from settling herself against him. She didn't even raise a protest when he reached down and plucked the dress from her hand, threw it carelessly onto the floor and wrapped his arms round her waist.

"Don't worry about the damn dress," he whispered huskily into her ear as he gave it a nipping. "I'll buy you another one, another hundred, just as long as I can hold you like this forever."

"You won't be giving me things anymore," she said stiffly.

Gareth stilled. "Why not? You have accepted my gifts before."

"Yes, but things are different now."

"I know things are different. They are better."

She slowly lifted his arms from her waist and stepped away from the protective warmth of his body. She took a deep, steadying breath before she dared to turn and face the anger she knew that she would see in his eyes. "I can't do it, Gareth. I can't accept . . . things . . . for fornication."

"Good God, woman, what the hell are you talking about?"

"You know exactly what I am talking about."

He crossed his arms over his chest and glared down at her belligerently. "You're talking about whore's fare." He shook his head in disgust. "When have I ever treated you in such a way that you would think about us like that? Why in hell's name would you cheapen it by thinking of it as just some whore's trick?"

"You forget, I know all about whores' tricks," Zetta said softly, trying to keep her voice even. "My mother was a whore. I am the product of her whoring. I have been among whores all of my life, Gareth, but until I came here, until last night, I never once sold my body. I stole, begged and lied, but not once did I sell my body."

Wrapping the fur more firmly around herself, she walked over to the dress. Carefully she picked it up and began automatically to fold it as she searched for the words to explain it to him. "I can't live with this, with us, if there is even the remotest hint of whoredom in it. I want you, and although I know I can't have you forever, while I can, I want it to be an open, honest, daylight thing. If I feel that you are buying me in any way, giving me trinkets to keep me in your bed, then you will ruin what little I have. You will ruin me."

Gareth rolled his eyes in exasperation. "You do make the simplest things intolerably complex, don't you?" He snatched the dress away from her again and holding it up between his hands tore it cleanly in two, filling the room with the loud scream of fabric. Throwing the ruined dress away, he pulled her against him again, ignoring her spluttered protest.

At odds with the violence of his actions, his kiss was agonizingly sweet. His lips moved over hers with such gentleness that Zetta felt she was the most precious thing in his world. When he finally lifted his head she stared at him dazedly, her mind a jumble of dislocated thoughts and fears that no longer seemed to belong to her.

"Now that I have your attention, let me make a couple of things clear to you. Firstly, I do not think of you as a whore. Everything about you, from your past to now, tells me that your soul would never allow you to be a passive victim, for ultimately that is what a whore is. You are far too argumentative and aggressive for that." His loving smile softened the harshness of his words. "Secondly, and I think more importantly, what is between us is about love, nothing else. If I give you trinkets or dresses or castles, I do it because I love you more than life itself. Why would I buy your body for a moment when I want your soul for forever? I will not give you up, not now that I have finally found you. And that's where my thirdly comes in."

He stepped away from her a little, trying to give her the space she would soon need, even though his instinct cried for him to crowd her, swamp her and compel her to do what he wanted. He settled for holding her gaze firmly in his as he lifted her small hand to his lips. "I have decided that, seeing as I love you so much and cannot imagine a life without you, the only thing for me to do is to marry you and keep you with me always."

Zetta's mind went completely blank.

Marry? He wanted to marry her?

She repeated the word over and over again in her mind, but she couldn't seem to make any sense of it. Marry. It was a word from a foreign language of which she had no knowledge.

He couldn't mean it.

It just wasn't possible. Men like Gareth, men of

wealth, status and power, just didn't look in the gutters for their wives. They married equally well-bred ladies and sired children with perfect pedigrees. Once their duty to their name was done, they might then turn to the gutters to satisfy their baser needs.

What Gareth was suggesting was utterly impossible.

"If you don't say something soon I'm going to think that you don't want to be my wife," he said gently.

She had to swallow several times before she could find her voice. "It's not a case of what I want or what I don't want," she said, her eyes filling with unshed tears. "What you are suggesting just can't be, Gareth. It is a dream that you cannot make a reality."

"Why not?"

At that moment she almost hated him. How could he be so cruel? To have such a beautiful dream dangled in front of her and to know that it could never be hers— it was a physical pain.

"Don't be absurd, Gareth," she said grimly. "Of course you can't marry me. There are so many things that make it impossible. I am a bastard. I have lived all my life in the stews. I am a thief, a liar. . . ."

"I love you. That is all that matters." He smiled at her cajolingly and gave her hand a small squeeze. "Marry me, Zetta. Become my wife."

"Gareth . . ."

"Marry me."

She looked deep into his eyes and in their depths saw her own greatest weakness. She knew it was unattainable, knew all the reasons why it could never be, but she lacked the will to destroy the love and hope she could see in his eyes.

Slowly she nodded her head.

Gareth let out a whoop of triumph.

He felt a hundred feet tall, and even though he wasn't wholly sure of his victory, not when he could still see doubt and fear in Zetta's eyes, for now it was enough that she had said yes. He pulled her against him in a crushing hug and silently promised to himself that he would overcome every last ounce of her resistance.

She let him hold her for a second, then gently pushed him away.

"Now, I will have to get back to the solar," she said firmly, needing to hold on to something real if she was not to drown in this strange dreamworld. She looked over at the tattered remains of the green dress and grimaced. "But thanks to you, I have nothing to wear to get there."

Gareth's grin was almost boyish. "I like you naked. I like you naked and in my bed even better."

Zetta glared at him. "Well, I can't parade around the fortress naked, no matter how much you like it. I need something to wear."

"Well," Gareth said grudgingly, "I suppose I could loan you one of my tunics."

"Perfect."

He sighed dramatically, dragging his feet reluctantly. "Well, if I must . . ."

"You must," Zetta said firmly, but inside she felt like she was flying. Despite all of her doubts, she suddenly felt a lightness. Everything dark and familiar had been swept away in an instant and she couldn't seem to find it in herself to regret its passing.

She should be worried. She should be making plans to save herself from the disaster that would no doubt claim her the second she began to actually believe in Gareth's fairy tales. Instead, she found herself smiling as Gareth began to reluctantly lift tunics from the chest at the end of his bed, assessing each of them as if they were the finest gowns gold could buy. When he held one up against her and turned his head to its side speculatively, she actually laughed out loud.

He was truly amazing, this man she loved. He was a man of smiles and light and she knew that she had made the right decision. Whatever pain ultimately lay in store for her, the wonder she had now would be worth it.

And she was going to take full advantage of it. How long this lasted was a matter that God alone could decide, but it was in her power to enjoy it while she could, and damn it, she was going to enjoy it to the hilt.

With a sigh of relief Zetta pushed open the solar door. Even though Gareth's massive tunic almost reached the middle of her calves, she still felt terribly exposed running around in it, and she could only be glad that she hadn't met anyone on the way back.

It was odd: having everyone assuming that she was Gareth's woman was one thing, but actually sneaking back from a night in his bed was another altogether.

She closed the door as quietly as she could, not wanting to disturb Edrit and Joan from their sleep. She didn't know how she was going to explain what had just happened to them and she was coward enough to want to put it off as long as possible.

"Zetta, is that you?" Edrit said quietly. Zetta winced as she turned toward the fire, where she expected Edrit to be. Her brow rose in surprise when she saw that his pallet was empty and realized that he must be in the curtained bed with Joan.

"What are you doing in there?" she asked softly as she pulled open the heavy curtains. Edrit sat holding Joan upright, and in the early dawn light his face was a mask of pain. Joan rested against his chest with only his good arm holding her firmly in place.

"Where have you been, Zetta? Mother started coughing and she wouldn't stop and I couldn't get her to stop. I held her up, and that seemed to help her breathe, but I have to keep holding her up. It helps her breathing, but it doesn't stop her coughing for long."

Zetta felt all color drain from her face as she realized that while she had been resting peacefully in Gareth's arms, Edrit had been struggling to keep Joan alive. The knowledge was like a weight pressing down on her, but she couldn't let herself indulge her sense of guilt, not now.

"How long has she been like this?" she asked, quickly moving onto the bed as Joan's thin body was once more wracked with coughing.

Gently she wrapped her arms around her mother's shoulders and lifted her slightly, letting Edrit out from underneath. Clumsily, he crawled to the end of the bed, trying to stretch out his cramped muscles.

"She has been like this forever," he grumbled unhelpfully. "But I didn't leave her, Zetta, not once. Not even when my bad leg started to hurt and then went numb. I didn't leave her. I stayed."

Zetta nodded her head and tried propping Joan up on the pillows, but she couldn't seem to get her to stay. It was like every bone in her body had turned to dough and could no longer support even her meager weight. As soon as Zetta stopped supporting her, she slumped forward and started to struggle for air.

"Edrit, come back here and hold her, for God's sake." Her voice was like chipped ice, but Edrit didn't seem to be offended by the tone so much as the request.

"I have been holding her," he complained petulantly, but he quickly scrambled back up the bed to help. Once more he took Joan's weight and settled back up against the wooden board behind the bed head, a resigned sigh escaping him as his body returned to its cramped position.

Zetta got off the bed and went to the chest. After hauling it open, it took her only a second to find the small but expensive bundle of herbs they had brought with them from London. When she tipped them into the kettle on the fire to brew she noticed they were almost all gone. She had been using them more and more as Joan's condition had deteriorated, but as far as she could see, they had done very little good.

But she had to do something.

It took all of Zetta's determination to coax Joan into swallowing the noxious brew and a further hour before she started breathing freely enough that she could be laid flat, but that was the only victory Zetta achieved.

By that evening she finally admitted to herself that there was nothing she could do. Joan was dying. She refused to ask for any assistance, however. Several times through the long day Edrit had quietly suggested that perhaps if they got Gareth he could help, but each time Zetta had told him to shut up. She refused to give in to that weak part of herself that wanted Gareth desperately, wanted to be held in the security of his arms while she watched her world fall apart.

Still, she felt tears of relief fill her eyes when he arrived just before the evening meal.

She didn't look around, keeping her entire force of focus on the slow rise and fall of Joan's chest, but she knew he was there even before he came to stand beside her.

"I waited in the hall for you to appear, and when you

didn't I thought I had best come and remind you that you promised to always dine with me, but . . ." He paused awkwardly, then let out a sad sigh. "How bad is she, Zetta?"

He waited a moment and when she didn't answer he placed his hand on her shoulder.

The warmth of his touch went all the way to her heart. She swallowed painfully, not knowing what to say. Still she tried.

"I don't know. She has had these attacks before, but never this bad. She has always come through them before but she's already so weak. . . ." Her words slowly faded away. She couldn't bring herself to say it out loud. If she told Gareth that her mother was dying, then it would be true.

She needed it not to be true. He gave her shoulder a gentle squeeze and Zetta knew that he understood. "Would you like me to stay?" he asked softly, and she hesitated.

Her gut response was to say no, that she would be fine without him, just as she had always been. She didn't need him disturbing the tenuous balance she had achieved. Right now, she was blessedly numb, but if Gareth showed her too much sympathy, the numbness might dissolve, and she didn't know how she would stop herself from falling apart if it did.

But still she hesitated.

As hard as it was for her to understand, she wanted him to stay. His presence at her side made her feel a little less alone, a little less afraid, and for the first time in her life she wanted to borrow someone else's strength.

Edrit would be with her, of course, but his support was that of a child. She looked over to where he slept at the end of the bed, and she knew that love her as he did, he could never offer her all of the support that she needed.

Gareth could.

"Please stay," she said awkwardly, unsure of how to ask for help.

He did.

Gareth had never felt so useless.

For the past few days Joan had been tenaciously clinging on to life and he had been forced into the role of a mere spectator.

Still, he wouldn't have had it any other way. He had been so afraid that Zetta would shut him out that it had seemed like a very important victory when she had let him stay. But victory had quickly turned to frustration when he had realized that she wouldn't let him do anything to actually help.

She had closed out everything other than her mother.

Gareth had even been reduced to begging her to at least eat something. Sometimes she listened; most of the time she simply ignored him.

He was discovering a reservoir of patience he hadn't realized he possessed, but it was at a great cost. He stood staring out of the solar window, so caught up in his own bleak thoughts that he wasn't even aware of the cold night air. He had only been dimly aware for days that there was a world outside of the tragedy unfolding around him.

The evening meal would be finished by now, and no doubt the king was entertaining himself with one of the serving wenches, as he had done the previous few nights. Gareth knew he should feel at least a little guilty about leaving his royal guest to his own devices, but he didn't.

He might not be achieving anything much, but there was nowhere else he could be when Zetta needed him.

When he heard the door open, he turned away from his pointless contemplation of the night and smiled slightly when he saw the dejected look on Edrit's face as he limped toward him.

"You were right, Gareth," Edrit said without preamble. "The kittens are quite happy in the kitchens. The cook even lets them sleep in front of the fire. Can you believe that?"

"Good," Gareth murmured, glad that the cook had taken him at his word when he had threatened violence to anyone who upset Edrit.

They stood in silence for a moment; then Edrit leaned closer to Gareth and whispered, "Zetta needs to go to bed."

Gareth smiled faintly. "I was just thinking something along those lines myself."

"Well, then, go and make her."

Gareth shook his head. "I don't think the devil himself could make your sister do something she didn't want to."

"But you could," Edrit said earnestly. "She has never liked anyone as much as she likes you, and she let you stay when I know she would never have let anyone else. And if she doesn't sleep, then she might get sick too, and I don't want her to get sick."

For the first time, Gareth noticed the fear that clouded Edrit's eyes. "Don't worry; I won't let her get sick," he said with gruff reassurance. "I'll see what I can achieve, though after that vote of confidence, how can I not succeed?"

Very easily, but he kept that thought to himself.

He walked over to where Zetta sat. He crouched

down beside her chair and his jaw clenched as he saw the black bruises under her eyes and the gauntness of her cheeks; even her hair seemed to have lost its luster. Gently, he reached up and tucked a curl behind her ear.

She didn't move away.

"Zetta, you need to go and take some rest."

"No, I'm fine," she said testily. Before, that had been enough to make Gareth back down, but this time he couldn't afford to.

A muscle twitched in his cheek.

"You are not fine. If you carry on like this you'll be no good to anyone, especially your mother. She needs you to have as much strength as you can raise."

For the first time in days she looked at him properly and he almost flinched when he saw the raw pain in her eyes. "I can't leave her."

"You won't be leaving her if you go and get some sleep. You will just be making sure that you have the strength you need to keep on nursing her."

She swallowed hard and turned back to the bed. "I don't want her to be alone."

Gareth turned her face back to his. "She won't be alone. Edrit and I will stay here with her." He tried to smile. "I promise on the life of Edrit's kittens that we will not leave her alone for a second." He could see the hesitation in her eyes, and he couldn't let her brush him aside again.

"Go."

For a second he thought she was going to argue; then she closed her eyes and slowly nodded her head. "I'll go and rest for an hour. One hour," she said austerely, but she continued to sit as if her body didn't know how to function normally anymore. Gareth quickly stood up, and taking her hand, he pulled her to her feet.

"Go to my chamber. You can rest undisturbed there."

"And you will be here?"

"And I'll be here."

She looked deep into his eyes for a second, and before he realized what she intended to do, she reached up and placed a quick, hard kiss on his lips.

"Thank you, Gareth, for everything," she said huskily.

"I haven't done anything," he said throatily, but she just smiled.

Feeling slightly dazed by the sudden kiss, he watched her mutely till the door closed behind her.

"I told you that you could do it," Edrit said with satisfaction.

Gareth chuckled as he sat in the chair Zetta had just vacated. "Yes, but if I hadn't seen it with my own eyes I don't think I would have believed it."

Edrit grunted a laugh as he went and sat in front of the fire, both of them settling back into the by now familiar pattern of waiting.

The peace didn't last long.

Only moments after Zetta left, Joan opened her eyes and stared at the canopy over the bed for a moment in bewilderment, then slowly turned her head toward Gareth.

A smile spread over her tired face.

"Humphrey," she whispered and Gareth's brows shot up in surprise; then he remembered that she had made that mistake before.

"I'm not Humphrey," he said gently. "That was my father's name. Did you know him?"

Joan didn't seem to hear a word he said, her eyes continuing to move over him with wonder.

"Oh, Humphrey. I knew you'd come back to me eventually. I knew that if I waited long enough you'd find me again—" Her words were cut off by a heaving cough, and Gareth quickly shook off his surprise and went to her, lifted her up on the pillows and supported her head with his shoulder.

He looked down in surprise when he felt her weak hand run over the side of his jaw. "I love you," she said shakily, then swallowed hard and guiltily looked away. "But I couldn't wait forever. I had to look after our son somehow. I had to have money and I had nothing else to sell. I didn't like it, Humphrey, and I cursed you sometimes, but I do love the daughter it gave me. You will love Zetta."

Gareth felt as if his core had been turned to stone. "You and my father had a son?"

A faintly condemning look of disappointment filtered over her face. "Don't you remember the baby I was going to have? I suppose you did forget. That is why you never came back to me like you promised you would. You only went to Normandy for a month or two, you said, just so you could tell your family about us. But you never came back. I waited and waited, but you never came back. I had the baby. . . ." She hesitated for a moment. "I called him Edrit, after my brother, the one who died at the Battle of Hastings. He probably isn't all that you could hope for, but he is a dear soul and you will love him when you get used to him. Humphrey, why did you leave me? Why . . . ?"

Her voice faded away. She slowly closed her eyes and sleep claimed her again. Tenderly Gareth laid her back on the bed and stared at her with dumbfounded amazement.

He had another brother. He looked over to where

Edrit sat placidly by the fire, totally impervious to the truth that now rocked Gareth's world. Now he could suddenly see echoes of their father in him. And himself, Gareth realized with wonder.

His brother. Edrit, his eldest brother.

This poor, twisted man with his childlike mind had been heartlessly abandoned by their father. The resentment that filled Gareth was like nothing he had ever known. How could his father do such a thing? Gareth had never loved the man, but he had never thought him capable of something so callous. Edrit was a de Hugues. The blood of one of Normandy's noblest families ran through his veins and he had been raised in the gutter.

Well no more, Gareth promised Joan silently.

Then a horrible thought halted his righteous anger in its tracks. How was he going to tell Zetta? How could he possibly explain to her that it was his own family who had been responsible for the destruction of hers? It made him faintly sick to think about it.

But he would have to tell her. He couldn't love her and keep secrets from her at the same time. He would just have to make her see past all of her anger and resentment to the simple fact that he did love her.

Gareth smiled sadly down at Joan and gently covered her hand with his. This woman had suffered much at the hands of his family, but he was going to see that everything was put right. It was the least he owed her. But for a strange twist of fate, this woman could have been his mother, he realized numbly. Instead, she had been abandoned to raise his brother and had given birth to the woman he loved.

He owed her more than he could ever repay, but he was going to try.

Chapter 11

Joan died the next day.

Though it hadn't been a shock, two weeks had passed since then and Zetta still felt stunned, like someone had removed all of the air from her body. Still, that was an improvement on how she had felt the moment she realized that she was never going to see or talk to her mother ever again. In that second she had felt utterly paralyzed, incapable of even the smallest rational thought. All she had wanted to do was to curl herself up into a ball and will herself out of existence.

And if it hadn't been for Gareth, she might have done just that.

He wouldn't let her. Instead, without any fuss or bother, he simply took over. It was he who organized the small funeral mass and bribed everyone necessary to have Joan's body interred in the local Saxon convent. It was he who set Edrit and Zetta up in the smaller chamber beside his own, away from their sad memories. It was he who spent hours every day with Edrit, distracting him from his grief and giving Zetta the space she needed to grieve.

It seemed to her that his every waking thought and deed had but one aim, that of shielding her from the world for as long as she needed to be. He even seemed wholly content with this self-imposed task. His ability to give without expecting anything in return still awed her, and if she hadn't actually seen it all for herself she wasn't sure she would have been able to believe he existed at all.

But she was very grateful that he did.

With a soft sigh she closed her eyes and leaned her head back against the tree she was sitting under. This morning she had escaped for a few moments of solitude into the walled herb garden while Gareth and Edrit practiced archery. They'd been doing it every morning for the past week, and the fact that Edrit would now be better able to protect himself was just one more thing that she owed Gareth.

She wasn't sure if she would ever be able to repay him for every one of his small kindnesses and the old Zetta would have resented that. She would have hated the way he had taken her life so completely over and would have suspected him of all kinds of manipulation and done everything in her power to wrest back control.

To her own great surprise, she didn't feel like that at all. Just knowing him had made her grow and change beyond all recognition. She saw things now that she would never have noticed before. It was amazing to realize just how badly she had misjudged Gareth, even when she had been falling in love with him. She had actually believed he was at best an amiable man without depth. She would never have guessed his true worth, seen beyond the obvious to the reality that hid beneath the smile, if her world hadn't fallen apart at his feet and he hadn't done everything in his power to help her hold it together.

And that would have been a tragedy.

She would never have known that he could be endlessly kind and considerate, that his pigheaded stubbornness almost rivaled hers, that his intelligence was intimidating and that he was able to blush if he was praised. That, in short, he was everything she needed him to be. And more.

When she needed to smile, he was her clown. When she needed to cry, he was her tireless comforter. When she needed to be looked after, he was her tyrant. When she needed a friend, he became her best one. When she needed a lover, well, he was only all too willing to oblige then as well.

As impossible as it seemed, somehow, since that fateful day she had stolen from him, he had become her world. She hugged herself tightly, trying to hold it all inside. She drew a shaky breath, bathing her senses in the scent of the flowers that had started to bloom in her little wild garden.

That change, too, seemed miraculous. What before had seemed like a tangle of weeds had turned into an exquisite tapestry of wildflowers. The heady mix of their perfume filled her senses and she couldn't remember a time before when she had been able to enjoy such simple pleasures that could soothe her soul and ease her silent pain.

And for it all she had only one person to thank, she thought, with an awed smile.

"I seem to have found a fairy all alone in a walled garden waiting just for me," Henry drawled, jarring Zetta to alertness.

It just proved how she had changed that he had

entered the garden without her being remotely aware of him. Not that any warning would have done her much good, not when this meeting was long overdue.

Zetta hadn't seen Henry since her disastrous attempts to be a lady; Gareth had seen to that. She hadn't asked him to shelter her from her own folly, but she had been grateful all the same. She had almost managed to forget about the royal invasion altogether.

As she clumsily clambered to her feet and dropped into a hasty curtsy, she silently wished that by forgetting him she could have made the king cease to exist altogether. She wasn't at all surprised that her wish was not granted and a very much existing Henry strolled toward her, his tanned, lined face utterly relaxed. He gave her an easy smile as he lifted her from her curtsy.

"Now, now, no need for such formalities, my dear fairy, not when it is I who am a visitor in your kingdom," he said amiably and his smile broadened. "Indeed, now that I can see those lovely green eyes of yours again, I find I've a desire to dally in your kingdom for a little while, my enchantress."

"Sire, I'm no enchantress."

"I beg to differ, my dear fairy, because I certainly feel as if you have cast a spell over me," he said smoothly. "Indeed, since the night that we met, I have found it impossible to banish you from my mind. I feel very much like I have fallen under a witching spell."

Not that he hadn't been trying his hardest, Zetta thought dryly. Even she had been aware of the rumors that had been spreading round the castle about him. It was common knowledge that several of the serving wenches had warmed the royal bed, some of them at the same time, if the rumors were to be entirely believed.

Zetta very much doubted that he had spared her so much as a thought—till now, that is. Now, unfortunately, she had his full attention. She tried to hide the dismay she felt by lowering her eyes modestly, but she knew that she wasn't entirely successful. She also knew that Henry didn't really care that he disgusted her. She could almost feel his growing excitement at her reluctance like a physical presence in the garden. He was looking forward to the challenge.

She had to get away from him.

"Sire," she said, carefully keeping her voice neutral, "I have things I must do, so if you will excuse me . . ." Her voice dwindled away to nothing as Henry turned away from her and walked the couple of paces to the old stone seat. She dared to glance up, bewildered and entirely unsure of how to go on.

Slowly, as he turned back to her, Zetta realized that she was not going to be allowed such an easy escape— not this time. He smiled at her broadly. "No, my dear fairy, I don't think I will. The last time when I let Gareth spirit you away, you disappeared entirely for weeks. He kept you so well hidden . . . and entertained, so I hear, that I was unable to get better acquainted with you. I will not make that mistake again. Now that I have rediscovered you, my dear, I intend to take full advantage of your . . . company."

Zetta stared at him in amazement for a moment, almost unable to comprehend the extent of the man's gall, and then slowly she felt her jaw tighten as anger started its slow boil in her veins. "I would like to leave now." She carefully articulated each word, preparing herself to take advantage of her first opportunity to escape his advances.

Henry continued to smile at her benignly. "And I

would like you to stay." Leisurely he strode back over to her. Zetta's instinct told her to turn and run but she refused to give in to such cowardice. He stopped unnervingly close to her. "And I am sure that you wouldn't want to go against your king's wishes," he whispered huskily.

Her stomach knotted painfully and fear moved through her veins like ice. She had fallen into a very dangerous situation and she had no idea how she was going to extract herself from it. She stood frozen to the spot while the king slowly drew his gaze leisurely over her body, her hands clenched impotently at her sides. A hot flush rose over her face as Henry lifted his hand and ran a slow finger over her throat, stopping at the edge of her bodice before lightly moving it up again.

She swallowed hard. "Why are you doing this to me?" she said stiffly, her voice cracking with fear.

"Because this is what you want," he said simply as his finger moved down once more. "I saw it in your eyes that night at dinner. You wanted me and I would have had you but for Sir Gareth's interference. Your lover is protective—" His voice dropped to a throaty whisper. "But I think you will find that I can protect you far better."

As he lowered his head to hers she felt the heat of his words against her lip. She stood paralyzed as Henry's lips began to plunder hers, but when she felt his tongue start to force its way between her clenched teeth she seemed to suddenly come to life. With all of the strength she had she shoved Henry away. Taken by surprise that she was not submissively giving herself to him, he stumbled back a few steps and stared at her with amazement as she raised a shaky hand and began to scrub her lips free of the vile taste of him.

"I never wanted this," she spat out furiously. "All I wanted was to complete a task that my mother asked me to do. I thought that if I acted like a lady I could do it without any fuss. I never intended for you to feel that I was inviting any kind of . . . familiarity."

She glared at him defiantly, not caring for the moment whether he was king or pauper. She waited for the royal wrath to fall on her head but she couldn't regret causing it.

He appeared impervious to her anger and regarded her quizzically. "Task?" he asked slowly, his face showing nothing more than polite interest. "What task?"

Zetta eyed him suspiciously. "It doesn't matter anymore. I would just like to return to the castle now."

"But I think it does matter," he said firmly. "I would very much like to know what possible reason you could have for leading me on to such an extent."

Zetta crossed her arms defensively over her chest. "I didn't lead you on. You led yourself on with your seemingly impregnable belief that every woman wants you." She thought for a moment that she had gone too far and had to bite her bottom lip to stop anything else from falling out.

She needed to find some control. She took a deep breath and tried to find just some of that dignity her mother had always so prized.

"What task?" Henry said carefully, and Zetta knew that he was reaching the edge of his good humor. He wasn't going to let her go without a full explanation.

She sighed. "I didn't understand it properly myself," she said grudgingly. "But my mother said she wanted me to speak to you and tell you things like her name and my age. Really, it doesn't make any sense and it doesn't matter anymore," she continuted, with a wince.

Hearing it aloud made it all sound so strange and like a terribly feeble excuse. She wouldn't have been at all surprised if the king had laughed in her face right before locking her up as a madwoman.

Instead, his gaze sharpened and he stared at her face intently. "I have heard that your mother passed away," he said slowly and Zetta nodded her head stiffly. "And what was her name?" he asked softly.

"Joan." Zetta's throat tightened and she had to clear it before trying again. "Joan of Bovey."

Henry's eyes widened in surprise. "You're Joan's daughter?" He reached out and lifted her chin sharply so that her face was in the full light. "How old are you exactly?"

"Twe . . . twenty-one," she stammered, bewildered. It was as if the king had suddenly become unhinged, and Zetta didn't much like the idea of being the one closest to him as he went over the edge.

His eyes filled with horror and he dropped her chin as if he were scalded. She watched with mounting bewilderment as his face turned a strange shade of gray.

"Your father," he said through clenched teeth. "I must have his name."

"I don't know it. I have never known who my father was."

"You never asked your mother? She never mentioned him, never told you?"

"No."

"But she sent you to me when she knew that she was dying."

It took a second for Zetta to understand what he was saying. As enlightenment dawned, she found herself looking fully at the man in front of her for the first time, trying desperately to see if what he implied could possibly be true. All she could see was a stocky man of middle years indistinguishable from any other man of his class. He wasn't good-looking; he wasn't ugly. He was just a man.

But he was also the king and her mother had sent her to him.

"No," she said with a strangled voice as her breathing became shallow. She turned blindly away from this sudden threat to her sanity. "No," she said again through clenched teeth, wanting to believe in that denial with all her heart and soul.

"If only it were that simple, then there would be a lot more happy people in this world," Henry said dryly, his eyes searching her face for the truth, just as hers had searched his.

"It would seem that I should be grateful for Gareth's jealous tantrums," he said slowly. "It was only that, I fear, that stopped me from committing incest with my natural daughter. I believe incest is a sin that even the pope can't lift from your soul."

Zetta shook her head, staring in mute horror at the man in front of her. All at once she found it impossible to believe and also hauntingly true.

He held out his hand for her to kiss his coronation ring. "Well, daughter, aren't you going to give your father a proper greeting after all of these years?"

Zetta didn't stop running till she reached Gareth's room.

It was only when she had barred the door from the inside that she felt at last safe from the world that had inexplicably run mad. Her mind reeled as it tried to grapple with something that was too big for a mere mortal to comprehend.

It was too incredible, yet she was finding it all too believable. Her father could be anyone, she told herself sternly. Her mother had been a whore and her father could be any man who had been within the walls of London with the price of a woman in his purse on the day that she was conceived. That was how a street whore lived, by not turning anyone with ready cash down.

But her mother hadn't been a street whore back then.

When Joan had still been young and beautiful she had lived as a kept woman, choosing who she gifted her favors to. Her success had for a while seen her choosing her lovers from the cream of William the Bastard's court.

After a time her beauty had faded, and the wealthy protectors with it, but still Zetta had grown up with the mementoes from those better days. The mementoes may have been sold one by one to buy food, but she could still remember the feel of rich silk under her hands and the way real jewels caught and distorted the light. They had all been relics of a time long forgotten when Joan had known the security of a powerful man's protection.

And the son of a king was a very powerful man indeed, even if he was only a younger son destined for the church.

Zetta slumped to the floor and covered her face with her hands. She had never before given her father much thought. Somehow, he had seemed irrelevant. Her life had been hard enough just trying to survive without wasting valuable energy brooding on things she couldn't change. Besides, she had never really felt any lack, had never wanted more family than she had. Edrit and Joan had offered her all of the love that she had ever wanted and she had found no need for a father who'd had no need of her.

She still had no need of a father, but Henry seemed terrifyingly willing to become just that, she realized despairingly. The whole idea filled her with horror. Not that it was a certainty. She held on to the knowledge that any man could be her father like a talisman. The possibilities were endless and she refused to let go of that hope. She suspected, however, that hope wasn't going to be strong enough on its own.

That Henry had been so willing to accept it as fact only made the possibility that she was his daughter all that more unnerving. Not that she should be all that surprised, Zetta thought bitterly. After all, he had already claimed any number of children as his. He seemed to look on them as proof of his virility. What would one more matter?

No, now that he had claimed her as one of his bastard horde, there was absolutely nothing that she could do about it. He was the king of England, after all. A tremor started somewhere in Zetta's stomach and rippled through her. The more she tried to suppress it, the more she shook with it.

She needed Gareth.

She needed him to hold her, needed him to tell her that none of this mattered and for him to turn the world back to the way it had been only a few short hours ago. It was all too much for her to absorb. She had lost a mother she had loved with every particle of her being and gained a father she didn't want or like.

Perhaps God thought it was a fair exchange, that by taking with one hand and giving with the other he was keeping everything balanced. But He wasn't. She felt as if He was mocking her, trying to destroy her, and she needed Gareth to make it all go away.

He had become the one certainty left in a life set adrift.

She began to silently pray. She needed him, needed him not to let her down. She needed him so badly that it seemed to stretch her skin till she thought she would burst and be absorbed into the hollowness of her need.

She needed him.

Gareth frowned.

His chamber door was barred. From the inside.

Feeling a little foolish, he stared at it a second longer, then reluctantly reached out a hand and rapped his knuckles against the solid oak. He wasn't sure what response he expected, but all he got was silence. His first instinct was to kick the blasted thing down and have strong words with whoever was inside about the stupidity of locking the master out of his own rooms. He hesitated, somehow knowing who was hiding in his chamber.

After quickly making sure that no one was around to hear him, he called softly, "Zetta, are you in there?"

He heard no reply, if indeed she made one, but after a second he did hear the sound of the bar being lifted as it echoed through the empty corridor, but the door didn't move. With a sinking heart he pushed it wide open.

Zetta had moved away from it and stood near the end of the bed. As he entered she smiled at him, but it was such a travesty of her true smile that he felt as if he had been kicked by a mule. Gareth quickly closed the distance between them and gathered her into his arms. He didn't speak, just pressed her close to his heart and waited for her to tell him what she needed him to do.

Whatever that was, he knew that he would do it without question or reservation. He placed a gentle kiss on the crown of her head and waited.

After a little while she pulled away a little and drew in a deep, shaky breath.

"Thank you," she murmured huskily and gave him another small smile that was filled with the sadness of the ages.

"Anything to be of service," he said as he reluctantly let her go. He felt bereft without the warmth of her, but he could sense just how hard Zetta was struggling to keep control of herself. If he offered her too much sympathy, she would break down and would then hate herself for doing so.

He turned from her and walked the few steps over to the window. Casually, without looking back to her, he murmured softly, "But I'd like to know why exactly you have any need of my services."

Without answering, Zetta walked over to the door and quietly closed it. When Gareth heard the sound of the bar being returned to its hooks he turned to face her. She stared at him mutely and Gareth felt a block of ice start to grow in the pit of his stomach.

The stark, hopeless look on her face frightened him. Zetta had been consumed with grief for weeks, but he had never seen that look in her eyes. Not once.

"What the hell is it, Zetta?" he asked with gruff concern.

She struggled to find her voice to explain all that had happened. "It's the king. He found me in the walled garden this afternoon. He said he wanted to bed me."

Gareth's jaw tightened as he tried to stop his rising anger from exploding out of him. "He *what?*" he asked through clenched teeth.

Zetta flinched at the fury she could feel radiating off of him. "Oh, I fought him off, Gareth. As you will recall, I'm very good at that." She wrapped her arms around herself. "He was quite kind about it, really. He didn't get angry, he just wanted to know why I had . . . had led him on. So I told him. I told him that my mother had wanted me to speak to him, and I had thought that the best way of doing that was to pretend to be a lady. I honestly hadn't realized that he would assume I was available."

The relief that he felt that she hadn't been harmed was so all consuming that it took a second for the rest of what she had said to register.

"She wanted you to speak to him? Why?"

"She wanted me to tell him her name."

Gareth looked at her with blank confusion.

Zetta's laugh was high-pitched and brittle. "I didn't know why either. It didn't make any sense to me at all. I had really thought it was her disease speaking, that she had lost her mind." She turned away from him. "But it made sense to the king. As soon as I mentioned her name, he seemed to know exactly what was going on. You see, he knew my mother. Twenty-one or so years ago, she was his mistress."

"Twenty-one?" Gareth murmured, his mind making some rapid calculations. "You mean, she thought . . ."

Zetta nodded her head jerkily.

"Yes, it would seem that was exactly what she thought, what the king now thinks. He is quite prepared to claim me as his natural daughter." A single tear slid from the corner of her eye and traveled down her cheek. "Oh, Gareth, what am I going to do?"

He just stared at her dumbly, his mind trying to understand it all. The only thing he seemed to be able to comprehend fully at that very moment was that this one problem was entirely beyond his capacity to fix.

Chapter 12

"But I don't want to leave," Edrit said petulantly.

Zetta sat down on the side of the bed wearily preparing for yet another round in the battle that had been raging between them for days. They had been having this self-same discussion, or something very much like it, for several days now and she didn't know how much longer she could keep it up. She was finding it increasingly impossible to defend her decision to fall in with the king's wishes to herself, much less to Edrit.

She didn't understand it at all, though she suspected that it wasn't truly her decision at all. She had been swept along by a force far greater than herself and she didn't know how to even start to fight it, and if she had learned anything over the past weeks it was that you didn't say no to kings.

She ran a hand over her tired face and stared at her brother's determined face with a growing feeling of helplessness. "Edrit, we have no choice. The king insists we go back to London with him and we can't just say to him, 'Thank you very much but we don't want to go.'

It doesn't work like that." She smiled at him coaxingly. "Besides, we knew that we couldn't stay here forever."

"Well, I just don't care what the king wants. I'm not going." Edrit put his hands clumsily on his hips and glared militantly at her. She had seen that look before and knew exactly what it meant.

She felt a block of ice-cold panic begin to form in her stomach. Edrit very rarely put his foot down about anything. He grumbled and was as obstructive as he could be, but for the most part, he did what she wanted him to do.

Except when he didn't.

On those thankfully rare occasions when he set his mind to something, nothing short of the Almighty was able to move him. Certainly, Zetta had never managed it. She stared at him helplessly as she realized that this was one of those times when Edrit wasn't prepared to be cajoled.

It seemed that she was going to be trapped between two equally determined objects. The king said they must go; Edrit said they mustn't. She would be crushed between them if she didn't find some way of changing Edrit's mind, but for the life of her she didn't how she was going to achieve the impossible.

She couldn't seem to think properly at the moment. Her wits had entirely deserted her from the second her whole understanding of life and her place in it had fallen apart. Edrit deciding to rebel only confirmed what she already knew. Whatever luck she had ever had before was gone. Life now intended to take from her everything she loved and understood, to cast her adrift without so much as her soul. And there was nothing she could do to stop it.

She met Edrit's sulky stare and was almost overwhelmed by her own helplessness. What was she going to do?

Unnervingly his face split into a most beatific half grin and she became terrified.

"I know what you should do," he said with frightening maturity. "You should ask Gareth to let me stay here. I'm sure he would let me." Then he added confidently, "He likes me, you know."

"Edrit . . ."

"Go on, ask him."

Zetta looked into his hopeful, determined face and she wanted to cry. She could cope with the chaos, with the change, with almost anything provided she didn't let herself think of Gareth and of losing him. She had barely seen anything of him since she'd told him that she was the king's bastard. He had cut himself off from her entirely and the separation seemed not to hurt him at all. There were no more protestations of love, of wanting to marry her, of her being his whole life; instead, she had been all too easily put aside.

Now Edrit had decided that he no longer needed her either. He had replaced her and she felt like someone had slapped her. She was so used to being vital to Edrit that she couldn't seem to understand that she no longer was. She may have resented it from time to time, wanted just a little peace, but she would never have changed a thing.

And now he wanted things to change. He no longer needed her, not like he always had before. He had a new friend and supporter and that made her feel frighteningly disposable.

But this wasn't about how she felt, she told herself sternly. She shouldn't resent Edrit finding some independence from her, not when it was only perfectly natural. Edrit was a man grown in body if not entirely in mind, and for all her ever-growing doubts about Gareth's sincerity, she knew that he would always take good care of anyone as utterly vulnerable as Edrit.

"You will ask him in the morning, won't you?" Edrit asked again eagerly.

How could she say no?

Gareth noted with surly disinterest that the dawn light had finally reached his chamber window. It hardly seemed important that time was passing as it should when he had sat in the chair by his empty fireplace staring blankly at the stone wall while inside him all was chaos and gloom.

Would it be today? Would this morning bring with its old light a polite farewell and all the inanities that went with it? Would today he have to say good-bye to the woman he loved, with only impersonal disinterest between them as if they were nothing more than mere acquaintances?

If not today, then soon. He had been waiting for a week and he wasn't entirely sure how much more he could take without breaking down into a sobbing mess and begging her to stay with him. He almost wished that today was the day, and he could finally be done with it. This waiting was killing him. How much longer would he have to live with the pain and uncertainty of not knowing when the sword would finally sever him from Zetta forever?

It was surely like tooth drawing and much better to be done with a sharp if agonizing yank than this slow, lingering torment.

At least, that was what seemed reasonable sometimes, he realized with a dark frown.

Other times he found himself fervently wishing that time would stand still. At least, for all the pain it brought him, he could still see Zetta, be with her, breathe the same air as her. When she left, well, then even that small blighted pleasure would disappear forever.

He could have laughed at the impossibility of his confused desires if they weren't tearing him in two. He could do nothing but wait and spend his days watching over her from a distance. He couldn't even begin to understand the strange, perverse pleasure he found in the quiet, dignified way Zetta carefully accepted the heavy burden of responsibility that had been added to her already laden shoulders. She seemed barely to stumble as her world changed and became even more complicated.

Gareth ran a rough hand over his face, trying desperately to ignore the lump in his throat. He hadn't thought it was humanly possible for him to love her any more than he had already, but he now found his love growing as he watched with awe at her strength and determination. She had changed and adapted so quickly that the transition had almost been invisible, but sometimes he found himself missing the fey urchin he had first met. His urchin.

He slumped a little farther into his chair as he forced himself to face up to the dull pain of the fact that she would never be his, even as it was doubtful that she ever had been.

And soon she would be gone. She would disappear into a world where he couldn't follow her without betraying his brother and the responsibility that he had willingly accepted when he had agreed to look after this castle. Perhaps it was a blessing; perhaps it was just as well that he wouldn't have to watch her change in the septic air of the royal court.

Once Henry married her off to his own gain, all signs of the urchin would disappear altogether and she would become just one more brittle, aristocratic lady who lived for her lovers and small intrigues.

And then she would be lost to him with a finality that was stifling.

Watching her over the past week and knowing what lay in their future, he had wanted to roar out his anger or to cry with the pain, but he did neither. Instead, he stole every moment just being near her that he could. And he waited. It was all he could do. Henry had made it painfully clear to him that whatever relationship had existed between them was now over. It seemed he expected more from his newly discovered daughter's marriage than a mere younger son.

So he snatched every moment he could. Even if it was only across the merry chaos of the great hall at supper, he greedily stored up every aspect of her, every nuance and quirk, hoarding them faithfully in his memory, hoping they'd protect him from the bleak lonely future that lay ahead. Somehow, those little sunshine memories would have to fortify him against the desolation of the rest of his life.

And soon even the time to gather those memories would be over.

Although nothing had actually been said, Gareth had spent too long among men of arms not to notice the small signs of restlessness and preparation around the king's knights. Today, or maybe tomorrow, Henry would come and slap him on the back with that friendly camaraderie he dispensed so easily and thank him for his hospitality. He would then leave and take with him all of Gareth's happiness.

Gareth closed his eyes. Would it be today? Could it be today?

The terror of the future suddenly galvanized him into action. He got up from the chair, stretching out cramped muscles with a ruthless determination. His pain was too great just to sit and hold it all in.

The practice yard, he thought grimly. Perhaps if he worked himself to exhaustion going through the million activities that were second nature to him, then he would no longer feel this soul-freezing pain. He doubted it would work, but he had to try.

Somehow he had to find a way to survive this day. And the next.

He had no other choice.

Zetta found Gareth in the practice yard just before noon.

The sight of him standing in nothing but his breeches as he let arrow after arrow fly into the target forty paces away filled her with a soothing, gentle feeling and an agitated fear all at the same time.

After the odd events of the past week she was filled with strange, desperate hopes, needs and fears, and they were all centered on the man in front of her. She stood just behind him and found herself bemused by the realization that this was the closest she had been to the man she had made love with in days.

Suddenly there was so much more she needed to say, needed to ask.

It was a need that had been haunting her through the days spent without him, but it was at night when she was in her empty bed that it ruled her completely. It was in the darkness that all of the doubts and insecurities that had been steadily growing tried to crush her completely.

Did Gareth really love her?

He had said that he did, before everything had changed, and she desperately wanted to believe in him. But she didn't.

Why should he love her? Why should he bother to defy his king just to claim her? What could she possibly offer him that would in any way compare with all he stood to lose? What did she have to offer him at all? Questions tore at her, and no matter how hard she tried, she could find no answers to them.

But that was only at night when she hovered on the edge of that cliff of self-doubt.

During the day he became her strength. When she became afraid of the new world that now held her captive, all she had to do was to imagine Gareth's jaunty smile and the ever-present laughing glint in his eye and she would find the calm she needed to go on.

She felt like the two sides of herself were warring within and pulling her in two completely different directions. She needed Gareth like she had never needed anyone before, needed him to help her make sense of it all, but she had only seen him from a distance for days. And now that he was finally near enough, all of her questions remained trapped in her throat even as they plagued her.

She wanted to ask him which Gareth was he. Was he the man who could easily walk away from her or was he the only sane thing in a world gone mad? She wanted to tell him that despite all of her doubts, he meant more to her than anyone else in the world except Edrit, and now he finally stood before her.

"I've been looking for you everywhere," she said with cold formality, hating her own cowardice even as she gave in to it.

Gareth ignored her. Carefully he pulled back the bowstring and with a mighty thwack let it go again. The arrow shot through the air and stuck firmly near the center of the target.

Without a pause he reached behind to the arrow sheath on his back and took out another arrow, then fitted it onto the string with practiced precision.

Something inside her snapped. How dare he be so indifferent when she was all confusion!

Just as he had the string pulled out to its fullest extent, she kicked him in the shins. Hard.

He yelped in surprise and let go of the string. This time the arrow sailed gracefully through the air and landed well wide of the target.

He turned on Zetta with a growl, but she couldn't stop herself from admiring his fierce beauty even as she took a step back. She refused to let him know that he intimidated her and raised a brow imperiously. "Now that I have your attention," she said with apparent calm, "I wonder if I may beg a favor of you."

Gareth let out an exasperated sigh. "Don't be asinine. You know perfectly well that everything I have is at your disposal. You don't even have to ask." He paused a second before meaningfully adding, "or kick me, for that matter."

Zetta searched his face desperately trying to read its suddenly inscrutable features. Her own uncertainty made her feel gauche and insignificant and she found she couldn't quite meet his open, angry gaze.

"I wasn't sure, not when everything has changed so much;" she said awkwardly.

Gareth stared at her in bewilderment for a second, then with calm deliberation he reached out and grabbed hold of her shoulder. His grip was not gentle, but the warmth of his large palms flowed through her.

"Don't be foolish," he ground out. "What has happened doesn't change how I feel about you."

Zetta slowly lifted her eyes to his and summoned up all that was left of her tattered bravery. "Truly?"

"Truly," he said softly, giving her a small lopsided grin. "Though I have to say that had you asked me that self-same question at the exact second you were kicking me, then my answer might have been slightly different."

"Fickle," she said with an exaggerated sniff, but she found herself smiling as the tension started to ease away.

His grip on her shoulders softened and he began to slowly move his hands up and down her arms. "Now, what was the favor you wanted?" he prompted.

Zetta grimaced slightly. "It's Edrit. He doesn't want to go with me to London." She snorted derisively. "It's not as if I want to go either."

"Then why do you go?" he asked with careful indifference.

Her face stiffened almost imperceptively. "I have to. The king won't take no for an answer. And trust me, I've tried. Somehow I'll sort this mess out, but it is going to take time and Edrit doesn't have to endure life at court while I do. It isn't his mess to sort out and he has decided that he would rather stay here with you."

"Of course he can stay," Gareth said without hesitation, but Zetta quickly shook her head.

"I knew you would say that even after all that has happened, but you don't have to do this if you don't want to. Edrit is not your responsibility; you don't have to take him on."

Gareth scowled as he suddenly realized now was the time for him to tell her Edrit was his brother and he glanced down at his feet uncomfortably as he tried to find the words. "Well, actually, he is my responsibility as much as he is yours," he muttered gruffly.

"No, he's not. Just because you and I . . . well, just because of that doesn't mean you have to offer to look after him," she said gently. "It won't be easy you know. He is a lovely man, a kind man, but so many people don't understand that. Things just always seem to go wrong around him and you are not used to that." She smiled ruefully. "Hell, I am used to it, and I am still continually surprised by the trouble he can get into without even trying."

"Zetta . . ."

"I don't want you to feel that because of whatever may be between us you have to do this."

"Zetta, please."

"Of course, if you really don't mind and want to do this, we would both be very grateful. He would so love to stay with you. He says that you are the best friend he has ever had."

"Zetta, will you shut up for just one moment!" Gareth snapped, giving her shoulders a little shake in an attempt to get her attention. She looked down at his hands, then up at him in surprise. He quickly let her go. Her open gaze only made him feel guiltier about what he had to tell her.

"Don't look at me like that," he growled. "I'm feeling bad enough about all this without that."

"Bad enough about what?"

He had to repress the urge to shuffle his feet uncomfortably, like a naughty boy caught with his hand in the soup pot. Instead, he cleared his throat nervously. "Edrit *is* as much my responsibility as he is yours," he said, abruptly turning away from her. He couldn't bear to see the look in her eyes when he finally told her that he had been lying to her by omission.

He took a deep breath. "Just before your mother died she mistook me for my father."

"What?" Zetta frowned in confusion. "Did she know him? She never said."

Gareth closed his eyes, suddenly very tired and heartsore. "Zetta, she more than knew him. She said that Humphrey de Hugues, my father, is Edrit's father."

The silence that fell was like a roar. Gareth could stand it for only a few moments before he had to turn around. As soon as he saw Zetta, he wished he hadn't. Her face looked blank and brittle as she absorbed the news.

"Say something," he muttered hoarsely. "Yell at me, storm at me, hell, you can even kick me again, but do something. Anything."

She shook her head and he saw with desperate fear the black anger that had replaced the look of vulnerability. "What do you want me to say or do?" She smiled darkly. "Surely you don't want me to say 'Hello, brother' and welcome you into the bosom of our family?"

"Good God, no. I'm not *your* brother," Gareth said explosively, the image she conjured turning his stomach.

"I don't know why you sound so surprised," she said with mock innocence. "What else am I expected to call my brother's brother? If I can get used to calling the king 'father,' then I suppose I should be able to manage to call my lover 'brother.'"

"I'm not your brother," he ground out stiffly, trying to will her to understand.

"No, and you're not my lover anymore either." She turned her face away with disgust. "I'm sorry; I have to go. I can't do this. I know it is feeble of me, but it would seem that I can only deal with one long-lost relative at a time."

She turned to leave, then hesitated for a second. Without looking back at him, she asked coldly, "Why didn't you tell me this before?"

Why? There had been reasons—good, sound reasons—but for the life of him he couldn't seem to remember what they might have been. He stared at the ridged line of her back and suddenly it became the most important thing in the world that he make her understand.

"I don't know why," he said urgently. "It doesn't matter now. I just want you to know that I never meant to hurt you. Never."

"Well, you did."

"I know and I'm sorry."

There was so much more he wanted to say, but the words of explanation died in his throat. There was nothing he could do, and perhaps it was better this way. At least he now wouldn't waste years hoping against hope that maybe, just maybe, she would return to him.

"I will look after Edrit," he said with careful neutrality. "He can stay with me for as long as he likes."

She nodded her head and without another word walked away.

Gareth stood riveted to the spot. He watched her walk away from him, praying that she would at least turn to look at him, give him just one small moment of recognition.

She didn't. He continued to stare after her long after she had disappeared.

"We leave in the morning," Henry said, leaning back into the large comfortable chair and looking with a keen, calculating interest around the small room Gareth had set aside for his business affairs. "I have any number of things awaiting my attention in London and I see no reason to dally here any longer, as interesting as this visit has proven to be."

No reason now, Gareth thought bleakly, as if he'd ever revealed his reasons for being here in the first place. Gareth listened with something akin to despair to the sounds of the king's men preparing to leave rising up from the courtyard below.

It was hard to remember a time when he had actually been eagerly waiting for the king to grow bored of his petty intrigues and return from whence he came. Now Gareth would give him everything he had and more if he thought it would make any difference, but he knew that it wouldn't. When Henry left tomorrow he would take with him all of Gareth's hopes and dreams and somehow, as impossible as it seemed to be, he would have to start again with nothing.

Well, he had done it before, he told himself with stern practicality. After all, this wouldn't be the first time he had recovered from a broken heart. And he had managed before. Why should this time be any different? His jaw clenched compulsively, and he quickly moved to the window, looking sightlessly out at the activity below to hide from Henry his all too raw emotions.

Everything was different now.

Before, all he had really been feeling was sorry for

himself. Once that small grieving was over he had been able to move on unscarred. This time he felt as if someone had reached into his chest with their bare hands and yanked out his heart, and he knew that he would bear the deep scars of it for the rest of his life.

"I will be sorry that you are not leaving with us," Henry murmured, drawing Gareth's attention away from his own brooding thoughts.

When he was sure he was under control, Gareth turned and leaned against the casement. He shrugged his shoulders. "For the time being, my life is here." *If you call a life without Zetta living at all,* he added silently. After tomorrow he would be dead from the inside.

"If you should change your mind, you are free to join us at any time." Henry smiled slightly. "But I don't really mind if you stay here and continue to play house. As long as you don't decide to join with anyone else, I'll be content. If I hear that you have joined my brother, however, I will see that you are reduced to nothing more than a handful of memories."

"You are too kind, sire," Gareth murmured ironically.

"I know. If my father were here before you now, you wouldn't be given any choice at all." Henry pursed his lips slightly. "Of course, I must admit to being a little surprised that recent events haven't changed your mind."

Gareth continued to lean back against the casement with careful nonchalance, but inside everything tightened painfully, and his big hands gripped the stones tightly. "I don't see why I should have."

"I appear to have been wrong, but I thought that at one time you had feelings for my newly discovered daughter." He smiled broadly. "But all the same I am happy to see that you don't."

Gareth's eyes narrowed dangerously, and it took

every ounce of his willpower to keep his hands safely by his sides.

Henry seemed totally impervious to the sudden danger as he continued blithely, "I don't think you would suit me all that well as a son-in-law, not when you are so determined to follow your own path. No, I think that my Zetta will not be losing anything by not having you as her husband." He raised a brow satirically as he added, "Or as anything else, for that matter. Actually, while we are on this slightly delicate subject, there is something I would like to make clear."

"What?" Gareth growled with unhelpful belligerence.

"I will not inquire further as to exactly what . . . relationship you have had with my daughter, but I would like to make it perfectly clear that it is all absolutely over now. And I never want to hear of it again. I fear she may have been a little impetuous in this matter, which is hardly surprising considering her parentage, but that impetuosity stops now."

Gareth nodded his head stiffly, unable to speak through the anger strangling his throat. Henry's smile only broadened.

"Of course, if you decided to join me, well then, things might change. I would owe you very much then, and I am known for my graciousness in repaying all of my debts . . ."

He left the offer hanging and Gareth heard little of Henry's farewell through the roaring in his ears. It was only when he was finally alone that he dared to let his emotions rise to the surface.

With a strangled roar, he slammed his fist into the solid wood table. The pain that shot up his arm was nothing compared to the pain in his heart.

Everything was such a bloody mess!

Zetta was angry with him and preparing to run away. Henry was gleefully trying to manipulate him, using his feelings for Zetta as leverage. He was tied to a castle he was coming to hate and a family for whom he had long since stopped having any feelings. Everywhere he turned he found another wall hemming him in till he felt smothered.

If he had been completely sure that Zetta felt for him anything like his love for her, then he would have spirited her away from this endless mess and started their life anew somewhere far away from the machinations and mistakes of others.

It was what he should have done before Henry had arrived and ruined everything, he thought grimly. At least then they could have escaped the poison that now seemed to fill everything.

If only he were sure . . . .

But he wasn't. He had waited to find out, and by doing so, he had lost his chance. She probably would not believe him now if he tried to tell her again that he loved her with everything he had. He had lied to her once by not telling her all he knew, and he doubted she would ever trust him again.

He stared down at his bloody knuckles with a certain satisfaction. At least it was a pain he could see. It was the hidden pains that would kill him, he realized bleakly.

Chapter 13

The bustling castle was desolate and empty without Zetta's quiet presence. Gareth was being haunted by a silence that no one else seemed to hear. It was as if he was listening in the babble of all the other voices for the one voice that wouldn't be heard.

She was gone.

No matter how many times he told himself that since it had been her decision to leave he should learn to accept that she had rejected him and move on with the rest of his life, he continued to wake up each morning reaching out for her warm body.

And each morning his heart broke all over again, because she wasn't there. That fleeting moment of hope left his wounds raw, and the only way he knew to stop the pain was to cease to exist. If he could have, he would have willed himself to fade away. As it was, he did what was required of him without feeling. He had gone completely numb. It was a strange sensation to watch himself from a distance, but he was going to have to learn to live with it. He had to keep numb and moving, or else the pain would swamp him entirely.

He hated what he was becoming, what suffering was making of him. The only consolation he could find in the whole sorry mess was that no one else seemed to be aware that Zetta had broken his heart, which left him some semblance of dignity.

Except Edrit. He knew, but then he was fighting his own demons. At first Gareth didn't notice the change that had been slowly taking place in his brother, but eventually Edrit's unnatural quiet penetrated Gareth's shield of numbness, drawing him out enough to start him worrying.

After Zetta left, Edrit rarely spoke and spent the greater part of his day staring blankly out a window. Gareth tried everything he could think of to penetrate the walls that had sprung up suddenly around Edrit, but after a week of fruitless attempts he was about to admit to the full humiliation of his defeat.

Almost, but not quite. Today he had suddenly developed an overwhelming need to go fishing in the small forest stream that ran near the castle and had insisted Edrit join him. They had gone fishing several times before Zetta left, and Edrit had always seemed to enjoy it. But now he halfheartedly dunked his line in and out of the fast-moving water and looked the very picture of misery.

Gareth could only all too easily identify the long-suffering look on his face, and he suspected he had a very similar look on his own if he ever dared to take a closer look.

They sat in silence, each contemplating his own private, brooding thoughts.

"We are going to go, aren't we?" Edrit said simply, startling Gareth out of his thoughts.

He frowned at Edrit.

"What?" he murmured, grimacing as he realized how abstracted he sounded.

"We are going to follow Zetta, aren't we? I'm going to have to go back to London, aren't I?" He sighed tragically and tugged his line out of the water. With exaggerated care, he put it down beside him with his good hand, then stroked it lovingly. "I don't want to leave. I like it here, but you are going to leave soon." He frowned. "But it is okay, because, really, I do like Zetta better than I like any place, even this great place."

It was on the tip of Gareth's tongue to say that he too liked Zetta better than he liked any place but instead he shrugged his shoulders. "There is no reason why we should go, especially if we are perfectly happy where we are."

"But we are not happy. You are not happy. I am not happy, not really. I thought I would be. I thought that I liked you enough that I wouldn't miss Zetta, but I mustn't like you enough for that. Or maybe I just like Zetta better," he said. Then he hastily added, as if afraid that Gareth would misunderstand, "But I have known her a lot longer and she is my sister."

Gareth didn't misunderstand.

He mightn't have told Edrit the truth about their mutual father, not knowing how he could make him understand. But Gareth didn't believe for a second that even if Edrit knew they were brothers, he would allow Gareth to replace Zetta in any way.

"You have made a wise choice, my friend. You should like Zetta better," he said gently, and the two of them sat in silence for a few minutes, the only sound coming from the rushing of the little creek.

Edrit sighed again heavily. "I don't want to go."

"Then we won't. We will stay here and fish, and enjoy ourselves."

"We are not enjoying ourselves. We miss Zetta too much. We will go, Gareth." He glared up into the over-hanging trees. "We will."

Zetta decided that she would rather live among animals than courtiers. There was certainly more honor to be found in the occupants of the royal stables than there was among the fools who dared to ride the noble beasts, she thought with disgust.

She sat with apparent serenity beside Henry in the otherwise empty royal pavilion watching the jousting. Her gossamer veil fluttered gently in the light breeze, making her uncomfortably aware of the bejeweled gold circlet that secured it. She had to physically restrain herself from continually checking it was still in place. Instead, she sat straight backed, her hands held tightly in her lap against the stiff, heavy material of her skirts. It was Henry who had insisted that she dress in a manner befitting the daughter of a king and attend all of the tedious court activities. Zetta did what he wanted, but inside she seethed with rebellion.

She was very careful not to let what she really felt show in any way. Repression. It seemed to her that that was the one important skill every courtier had to learn. And she was learning fast. On the surface of the court everything appeared to be well, but underneath there was a poison that found its way into everything and everyone. It was a wonder to Zetta that they all didn't sicken of it and die.

She was beginning to believe that she had started to sicken already. She felt like she had some form of internal rotting disease. The symptoms weren't anything definable, but there was no denying the general sense that there was absolutely nothing right.

A genteel cheer went up from the gaily colored pavilions as one of the jousting knights was unceremoniously unhorsed. The pleasure on the faces of all the men and women watching this absurd ritual bewildered her. She just couldn't comprehend what they found to enjoy in this so-called sport. To her it was like watching small vicious boys playing at war, the only difference being that the weapons were not made of wood.

Yet all around her people were clearly enjoying themselves. Somehow, she just couldn't imagine Gareth would find anything to enjoy in this tomfoolery.

Damn! She had been trying so hard not to think of him. She hadn't been all that successful, but that didn't mean she was going to just give in to it. If she was to survive, she had to do everything in her power to forget about him. She couldn't spend her whole time with an aching hollow feeling inside her that only Gareth could remove or she really would rot away from the inside and die.

"My dear, please try not to look so ferocious. You are starting to scare people with that scowl of yours," Henry said softly.

Zetta felt a cold, nervous pain in her chest as she tried to smile. "Is that better?" she asked politely, horrified by the realization that she had been letting her real emotions show.

"Better, but not good. You are going to get yourself a reputation for being too serious if you don't start enjoying these little entertainments."

The whack of steel hitting steel rang out as another knight was unhorsed.

"I don't think of this as entertaining," she said stiffly, her stomach churning at the screaming sound coming from the horse that had gone down with its rider. A lance had shattered in its face and destroyed the animal's armor plating. Blood streamed over its face grotesquely.

A squire quickly and roughly forced the wounded animal back to his feet, making it scream again.

"It serves its purposes," Henry murmured as he thoughtfully watched the victor of the last joust ride over to present himself. "Not only does it help keep men ready for war, but I can think of no better way of introducing people away from the sometimes claustrophobic court protocol."

The knight acknowledged the king formally before lifting his visor, revealing a surprisingly mature face. Underneath the sweat that was streaking down the knight's face, Zetta could see clearly the lines and hollowing of a man entering his middle years.

"Ah, well done Baron de Hugues. You have fought very well today. You must now be glad that I managed to persuade you to come to England and . . . visit my court."

Zetta's heart stopped. She scanned the knight's face with dawning recognition. "De Hugues?" she whispered.

Henry looked at her with wide, innocent eyes. "Of course, you know Gareth de Hugues, don't you? What a fortunate coincidence. Let me introduce you to his older brother, Lanfranc." He turned and smiled even more broadly at Lanfranc. "Your brother gave my poor lost daughter his protection in your excellent castle at Bovey, where I was lucky enough to find her."

Lanfranc bowed his head slightly. "I'm glad my family could be of service," he murmured, but Zetta didn't hear the words. She couldn't help but stare at him, trying to see if she could find Gareth somewhere in this stranger's face.

It was there. Lurking beneath the lines and the wrong coloring there was a similarity. However, it was the differences that conjured Gareth's face most painfully. She knew Gareth's face better than she knew any other, and this variation was entirely alien, the lines and sculpting in all the wrong places.

Lanfranc's face was stern and unsmiling and made Zetta shiver. Gareth's face, by contrast, was made to laugh and smile. She longed for that now as Lanfranc regarded her austerely as if she was a puzzle he wanted to solve. She tried to ignore it, but she couldn't seem to stop herself from moving uncomfortably around in her seat, wishing him away even as a part of her wanted to eagerly grab at this one tangible link to Gareth.

Fate must have decided to take pity on her, because the herald announced that the next joust was about to begin. Hastily, Lanfranc rushed through his formal farewells and after a quick bow made his way back to his tent and the squire who waited to prepare him for the jousting lists.

Henry watched him leave with evident satisfaction. "I think I've got him," he murmured to himself.

Zetta frowned. "You mean you think that he will desert your brother, the Duke of Normandy, in favor of yourself?"

"Oh, yes." He turned to her and smiled brilliantly. "Especially if I can now offer him just the right kind of bait."

Very quickly, Zetta decided that she didn't like very much at all being the right kind of bait. Not liking it, however, didn't change the fact that she had now become just that—nothing more than bait. Henry took every conceivable opportunity to throw her into Lanfranc's path.

Every evening since her arrival she had taken her place at the second table a suitably discreet distance from Queen Matilda, who, although she had not made any public comment about the presence of another of her husband's bastard daughters, had also made it clear that she wanted nothing to do with her.

Zetta had been content enough with her polite exile until suddenly Lanfranc appeared at her side at every meal and insisted on making polite conversation. Before she knew it, he was everywhere she went. Every time Lanfranc competed in a tournament, Henry insisted that she sit with him in the royal pavilion. She danced with Lanfranc, talked with Lanfranc, did everything else with him that Henry could organize to be done in the social whirl that was court life.

When she had flatly refused to join a royal hunting party because she couldn't ride, but mostly because she had no desire to see some animal being torn asunder, Henry had just smiled at her and suggested that Lanfranc stay and keep her company instead. Perhaps he could take her for a walk through the gardens?

And he did.

For two hours Lanfranc had, with calm patience, guided her around the formal gardens as if he'd never had any desire to go hunting. He always agreed with everything anyone said. It was the thing she found the most unsettling about him. Not once did he demure from any of Henry's blatant maneuverings and intrigues. Zetta supposed she should have been flattered by his apparent contentment to spend all of his time with her, but she wasn't.

Not once did she ever sense anything real inside the

sterile shell of his body. He was polite and a perfect
gentleman, but he never let her see anything of the
man who might be lurking underneath his social mask.

He was the complete opposite of Gareth in more important ways than his lack of humor. Gareth had always
been open. He couldn't, or wouldn't, hide himself. She
had not once looked into his eyes and felt that he was
hiding himself. She had only to remember the worried
and reluctant look in his eyes when he had told her the
truth about Edrit's parentage to realize that although
he might not have told her the truth, he lacked Lanfranc's ability to be cunning and uncaring. Lanfranc's
face was always carefully blank. Even on those rare occasions when he smiled, she could never see the light
of it in his eyes. She never had any idea what he might
actually be thinking.

Even now, as he carefully guided her under a small
arbor as if she might get lost without his help, she
could only guess at what might be going through his
head. Her ignorance irritated her. She had no liking
for the vague feeling that she was somehow being manipulated by him, just as she was being manipulated by
Henry.

Well, enough was enough, she decided suddenly. She
had been passively letting everyone else make decisions
for long enough. She might still be intimidated by the
strange new world in which she found herself, but it
was time for her to start taking some control of it.

She was smiling as she deftly lifted her hand from
Lanfranc's arm and stood stock-still near a stone seat.
He turned and looked at her with surprise, and she
crossed her arms defiantly over her chest.

"I want to know why," she said stiffly.

"I'm sorry, milady, I don't understand. Perhaps if you would like to sit for a moment—"

Zetta cut him off angrily. "I don't want to sit down, and if I did, I certainly wouldn't need your help to get there. And I am *not* a lady; we both know that."

"You have never objected to courtesy before," he said mildly, but Zetta refused to let his calm, condescending manner embarrass her back into obedience.

"Well, I'm objecting now. And while I'm at it, I'm objecting to you going out of your way to be nice to me when I know that you don't care for me one way or the other. I know, you see," she said tauntingly, hoping to wipe that smug look off his face. "I know you are doing it only because the king, my father, insists upon it. That I know, but what I don't understand is why."

"The insisting of kings is normally seen as reason enough for obedience."

"Not for you. I don't think you do anything without good reason. You have some motive for all of this, and I'm going to find out what it is. Now."

For a second she thought she saw anger flit over his face, but he quickly masked it. His eyes narrowed as he looked at her warily. "You are not what I was led to expect," he said slowly. "I knew of your background, of course, but still I somehow expected you to be . . . different."

"I am as I am, but that is not what is at question here. I will know what game you play, and if you don't tell me, I'll do everything in my power to make it damn impossible for you to continue at it."

Lanfranc's lips turned upward, but Zetta would never have called it a smile. "Do you want to know why the king insists that we spend so much time together or why I let him?"

"Either. No. Both."

He shrugged his shoulders nonchalantly. "The first is simple. Henry needs me. When he marches into Normandy he will need as many of the Norman noblemen fighting under his banner as he can organize. The more important the family, the more he has need of their support. He has decided that the best way to get my support and, through me, that of my powerful family is for me to be tied as closely to him as possible. In short, he wants us to marry, the sooner the better."

"And you would agree to marry me—marry anyone— for such a reason?"

"Perhaps. I would have preferred any wife of mine to be unblemished by the stigma of illegitimacy. Certainly my first two wives came from the finest families of France and had been gently reared. But still, you do have something more to offer me, fortunately, other than your dubious origins."

Zetta felt her stomach clench in revulsion. She was hearing nothing she hadn't expected to hear, but she couldn't reconcile such coldness with marriage. It seemed impossible he could even be contemplating such a union if he saw her only as some bastard who had risen too far from the gutter.

Of course, her mother had often told her that such unions were common in the higher echelons of society, but knowing wasn't the same as experiencing it for herself. Having felt the coldness of such a life, for the first time she felt real pride in her mother. At least there had been more honesty and frankness in her prostitution than there was in this idea of marriage.

"What can Henry possibly offer you that you don't already have to make up for the horror of having to marry one such as me?" she asked coldly, her voice harsh and brittle, as she tried to match his ability to not care about such things.

"Stability," he said simply. "Robert of Normandy is a weakling, more concerned with crusading than ruling his possessions. The chance of Normandy being swallowed by one of her restless neighbors if he continues to rule is increasing with every passing year. And if Normandy as we know it ceases to be, then my lands are no longer secure. I can't let that happen."

Zetta stared at Lafranc disbelievingly, his ruthlessness astounding her, and then it suddenly dawned on her that Gareth would never be so callous. She hadn't truly realized just how amazing a man he was till now, when she could see what he came from, what he could have all too easily become.

"What happens if you marry me and you prove to be wrong? What if Robert has more strength than you realize and defeats Henry?"

He looked her over coolly and shrugged. "Marriage isn't for life. I have lost two wives already, one to childbirth and the other to fever, and if nature doesn't decide to solve the problem for me, then wives can easily be put aside in convents."

She could feel her face going white with rage.

However, she smiled at him sweetly, her jaw clenched painfully. "Well, you won't have to worry about killing me off or finding some far-off convent to hide me in, because there is absolutely no chance in hell that I am ever going to marry you. Aren't you lucky?"

He raised a brow. "Don't be foolish. It won't be your decision. *If* I decide to accept Henry's offer of your hand in marriage, then my wife you shall be. Accustom yourself to that fact, and it will save you all manner of outraged feelings later."

"Why you bandy-legged, fat-arsed, overweening son of a mongrel bitch," she spat out, deliberately trying to shock him. She felt marginally better as she watched his lips tighten into a white line. She wanted to wipe that smug look off his face. Perhaps then he would think twice about his mercenary plan.

Her disappointment was keen when his mask slipped quickly back into place.

"When we marry, I must see to it that you learn how to behave in the company of your superiors. I believe the pleasure in this stroll is over. I will now leave you to accustom yourself to the idea," he said mildly and with a perfect bow left her gazing after him in disbelief.

He was entirely serious! He really thought of her as nothing more than a mindless featherbrain who would quite willingly go whichever way she was blown.

And why wouldn't he, she realized morosely as she slowly began to make her own way back to the palace. It wasn't as if she had been making it all that evident that she was anything else. Since Henry had come into her life and accepted her as his natural child she had let herself be moved around without once giving any indication that she had wants and needs of her own. Everything, from the very fact that she was here at all, right down to what she wore and ate had all been decided by someone else.

Somewhere along the way she had lost herself. Well, not anymore. She straightened her spine and lengthened her stride purposely. From now on, she would be making her own decisions, whether they liked it or not.

They didn't like it.

When Zetta had informed Henry the next morning

that things were about to change, he had smiled at her indulgently and set about trying to organize her. It was only when she had refused to be ignored that he had realized that she was entirely serious.

It was her turn to decide how things were going to be played, and first things first: she was not going to be bait any longer. As sweetly and politely as she could, she avoided Lanfranc with a will. At first he seemed amused, but after a week of finding himself avoided, ignored and overlooked, his patience visibly started to fray.

And she couldn't have been more pleased when she noticed this weakness.

After that first taste of her own power, Zetta decided that she liked the heady feeling and set about exploiting every advantage she had. She no longer hung around in the background afraid of offending someone with her mere presence. If she was the daughter of the king, well, it was time for her to start acting like one.

It was then that Henry truly realized that she was his pawn no more, and silently he started to try to bring her back under his control. But Zetta was having none of it and decided that she was going to need supporters if she was to take on the war that was brewing between them. And she knew just how to get them. She hadn't spent most of her life surrounded by prostitutes without learning a thing or two about enticement.

It didn't matter that she would never be truly beautiful as long as she knew how to make the best use of what she did have. Using every weapon her mother had taught her, she could make every other woman at court look slightly frumpy. Men were drawn to her, not caring about Henry's growing fury when they were being entertained by the worldly, sophisticated woman she had become overnight. They wanted her and she knew exactly how to be delightfully coy about whether she wanted any of them or not. That was the greatest trick her mother had taught her—the ability to seem both available and untouchable.

Zetta did it all consummately well. She laughed gaily at the jester, cried prettily at the minstrel's sad stories and danced with more abandon than any true lady ever could.

And she flirted. She had never done it before and she had thought that such a thing would be entirely alien to her nature, but she found it wasn't. Some instinct that she must have imbibed with her mothers' milk came to her rescue and she quickly found herself the center of several romantic intrigues. Her vivacious new character began to create a new court around her, one that rivaled Henry's larger one in almost every imaginable way.

Although she hated the foolish games she was playing, she could think of no better way of making it absolutely clear that she was not going to be bundled off and married without so much as a gesture.

When Zetta received her summons to Henry's royal presence, she knew that her war cry was about to be answered in a very direct fashion. This time, she told herself grimly, she would not be dismissed as a pawn that only existed to be used.

Despite her outward confidence, however, she found herself almost afraid as she entered Henry's private chambers. When she saw the look on his face her heart pounded loudly in her ears. He sat behind a large desk staring at her enigmatically, his fingers drumming loudly on the solid oak. She swallowed uncomfortably past the lump of fear in her throat and quickly stepped forward to drop into an unusually clumsy curtsy.

Henry didn't invite her to rise, as he usually did. Instead, he just kept drumming his fingers on the table and regarding her balefully.

After a moment, Zetta dared to lift her head. "You sent for me?"

Henry narrowed his eyes carefully. "Yes, I did, and I am relieved to see that you at least obey me that far. I was afraid that you might decide to ignore my summons in the same dismissing way you ignore everything else I ask you to do lately."

He was angry, she realized, through the wave of panic that threatened to cloud her thoughts. Really, really angry.

She lifted her chin defiantly. "I have never ignored you. I have listened to everything you have ever said to me; I just have not always done what you have told me to do."

Henry suddenly stood up and strode around the table to stop directly in front of her. "How dare you!" he roared. "How dare you calmly tell me that you chose not to do what I tell you to? They are royal commands, God damn it, not suggestions! You owe me your obedience, both as your father and as your king. No one else has ever dared to treat me in such a fashion."

Owed him as a father? She stared at him incredulously, her own anger starting to rise. "I owe you nothing. You never gave me anything, and I'm far from obliged to give you anything."

"I gave you life, you ungrateful strumpet, or are you prepared to ignore that as well," he growled.

Zetta snorted. "Joan of Bovey gave me life. And love. And every other thing that I ever needed. Your contribution to my existence was over before it had ever really begun. You didn't even stay around long enough to find out I existed."

"Then if I am not to have respect because I am your father, then you can damn well respect me as your king." Zetta noticed a muscle jumping in his jaw as he bent his face down to her. "And as your king, I order you to stop undermining my authority. If you are not my daughter, then you are no more than a very lowly visitor to my court, and you can start acting grateful for the honor I bestow on you by letting you be here. If you don't, then I will take great pleasure in returning you to the gutter from whence you came."

Zetta decided that she'd had enough of groveling. She swiftly stood up and thrust her hands onto her hips. "Better the gutter than the wife of a block of ice like Baron de Hugues."

Henry's eyes widened with surprise. "Is that what your little temper tantrum has been all about?"

"It's more than a child's temper tantrum," she snarled out furiously. "Be warned, I demand the right to choose my own husband, 'Your Majesty,' and let me assure you I will never have that shallow ass of a man in my bed."

Henry turned away from her for a moment, and when he turned back, all evidence of his anger had vanished. "You will marry whom I tell you to," he said coldly.

Zetta shook her head.

"Don't be a fool. What you suggest is outrageous. No lady has the right to choose her own husband. They take whoever is chosen for them without comment or question."

"Then they are fools," she said simply. "Besides, I'm no lady. I will have the right. I did have the right till I met you."

"Yes, and look how you've used that right. You wasted your time on that 'shallow ass's' brother." He shook his head. "And that is the real problem here, isn't it? You

fancy yourself in love with the dashing Sir Gareth and
have been waiting longingly for him to come and claim
you as his, haven't you?"

Zetta blushed angrily, but she couldn't deny what he
said. A part of her *had* been waiting for Gareth to
come. If he finally appeared, he would put everything
back to rights no matter how hopelessly complicated it
had all become. If he came for her, she might finally
believe in the love he had dangled so tantalizingly in
front of her.

Henry eyed her pityingly. "You live in a dreamworld.
Gareth was never going to marry you and you are a
little fool if you think otherwise. At first you were too
lowly, only suitable as a diversion. Now you are too high
for a mere younger son to aspire to. Sir Gareth knows
all of this and will wisely leave well enough alone." He
reached out and cupped her chin. "Don't be an idiot
and throw away all that you can now aspire to just for
some foolish notion. Do as I say and take all that I offer
you . . . . or bear the consequences."

Had she been an idiot to believe in Sir Gareth for
even a moment?

Probably.

She shivered.

"I won't marry Baron de Hugues," she whispered defiantly.

Henry just smiled, his confidence fast returning. He
didn't believe her.

The strange thing was, Zetta didn't know whether
to believe herself, either.

Chapter 14

Gareth felt entirely out of place.

Henry's brother William had still been king the last time he'd spent any time at the royal court and that had been just the way he liked it. He'd always been grateful that the way he lived his life had mercifully never left any room for the royal court and all of its malignant frivolity. It seemed to him that he had spent the vast majority of his adult life trying to avoid this mass gathering of his peers, and he had been very successful at it.

Until now, that was.

He realized sardonically that his luck seemed to have well and truly run out. Here he was, surrounded by the noblest blood England had to offer, listening to a plump brunette ruthlessly proposition him. He wished himself almost anywhere but here, although he was the cause of his own suffering.

He deserved to have his head cleaved from his shoulders for being so foolish for deliberately ignoring the fact that he had been avoiding the royal court all these years for a very good reason. He knew these people too well, knew just exactly what they were capable of, and yet, despite all of that hard-won wisdom, this very afternoon he had ridden into the palace courtyard with Edrit in tow, and now he milled with the rest of the court in the great audience chamber.

In his defense, he was here for a very good reason. He needed to find Zetta, needed to know that she was all right. It hadn't been that easy, of course, but then nothing at court ever was.

The crowd was bigger than he had anticipated, and now he had been utterly cornered by this woman whose name he thought might have been Lady Mary of somewhere or other. Or it might not have been. He couldn't seem to remember even though she had introduced herself with coy aggression.

He didn't feel too bad about his ignorance, not when he knew that she didn't really care what his name was either. Instead, she seemed to be hell-bent on seducing him, or whatever it may be that her increasingly blunt invitations were inviting him to do.

And in another time and place, he might just have taken what she was so freely offering.

Instead, he took a fortifying sip from the tankard of cheap ale he had been given and looked her over critically. He had to admit that she was not all that bad for a plump little pudding. In the past, before Zetta had turned his world upside down, he would have at the very least been making further inquiries as to what exactly was on offer. Now it took all of his willpower just to be polite and not leave her in midproposition.

She didn't seem to notice his barely disguised impatience.

She continued to look at him coyly from beneath her long, tinted lashes and boldly reached out to place a possessive hand over his arm. He flinched instinctively, but he could tell by the satisfied look on her face that she had no idea what he was truly thinking. The silly woman probably actually thought she was driving him wild with lust, he realized incredulously.

"My, but you are very tense," she all but purred. "You should come to my room tonight and I could help you with that. I have a balm that my wisewoman makes for me that will soon make every last morsel of tension leave your body."

The ale Gareth had been swallowing went down the wrong way, but he was strangely grateful for the coughing fit that followed. At least it prevented him from having to reply to her outrageous comment for a moment. When he had himself back under control he tried to give her what he hoped was a consoling smile, the kind of smile that said "No, but thank you," but clearly she didn't understand. She beamed right back at him and moved a little closer.

"My lady," he began carefully, finding it slightly unnatural to be turning such an open invitation down but, at the same time, knowing absolutely no way in hell he was going to accept, "as grateful as I am, I cannot . . ."

His voice faded away to nothing and his brain went entirely blank.

She was here.

The crowds had parted just enough for him to catch a glimpse of Zetta across the great echoing chamber. Her head was thrown back and she laughed at something some unseen person was saying or doing.

He abruptly realized that he had never seen her laugh, not like this anyway. Her cheeks were flushed seductively, her lips parted and glistening alluringly in the candlelight. They seemed to him to be beckoning him, begging him to go over and claim them.

His heart started to pound in his ears as he tried to absorb every detail of her at once.

She had changed in the time they had been apart. She had gained an air of sophistication that she had lacked before. She wore her regal dress of sapphire with such confidence that he could almost forget that when he had first met her she had looked like a scruffy urchin. The only similarity that he could find was that she wore her hair swept up and hidden under a jewel-encrusted hat of a similar shade of sapphire to her dress.

She had a new confidence, however, and he instinctively sensed that she now knew exactly her worth. Yes, she had changed and he found this new Zetta as equally intoxicating as the old. He wanted to find out who she had become and to get to know her all over again. But it was those things that hadn't changed that made him ache and regret the time he had allowed to be wasted.

It was the lips he could remember possessing; the legs that had once wrapped possessively around him, which he knew now lay hidden underneath her new finery; the proud upthrust of her breasts, which he could clearly remember warming in the palms of his hands.

Want was like a hard fist to his stomach. All memory of the loneliness evaporated in the heat of the desire that was consuming him. He had never felt anything to match it in his life, and that knowledge of its uniqueness was an exultation through his veins.

Even when the crowd shifted and hid her once more from his gaze, he could still feel the need, feel her calling him.

His body knew that its other half was here and

wanted him to go and claim her again. His soul needed to look into her eyes and know she was safe, that she was his, if it was to ever be whole again.

"Sir Gareth?" the plump woman asked uncertainly.

In the chaos Zetta wrought on his senses he had forgotten that she was even there. He stared at her with some confusion as he tried to get his fuddled brain back into some semblance of working order.

The woman raised her brow. "A simple no would suffice," she said gently, then smiled slightly. "You don't have to look faintly panicked and dumbstruck. I won't eat you, I promise. Not unless you ask me to."

"My lady . . ."

"I know, you're not going to ask me to. Pity. I think I would have really enjoyed biting certain parts of your truly magnificent body. But I suspect that there is someone else with a prior claim." She sighed. "It's the king's wretched daughter, isn't it?"

Gareth grimaced self-deprecatingly. "It was that obvious, was it?"

"Well, I could say that I guessed from your body's rather interesting state where before there had been nothing, despite all of my best efforts"—she cast an appreciative glance at his erection, which was partly hidden underneath his long tunic and hose—"but the truth is I know who distracted you because every other man at court seems to have a similar problem where that woman is concerned. A lady has to be very careful not to be crushed by all the big feet that seem to lumber endlessly to that woman's side."

Somehow, Gareth didn't find that there was much comfort to be found in the fact that he was a lovesick fool in good company, but it also didn't surprise him. A man would have to be dead not to act a little foolishly over Zetta. Exactly what form that foolishness might have taken among the jackals of the court had him slightly worried, however.

"She is finding her way then?" he asked casually, as if only mildly curious, but his body tensed as it prepared itself for the worst even when he wasn't entirely sure what he wanted to hear least: that she had been ostracized, or that she had been all to readily accepted—by men.

"If you had asked me that when she first arrived, I would have had to say no. She was a sad little mouse who clung to the shadows as if she needed them. Now"—the woman shrugged her shoulders—"the mouse is gone completely."

She hadn't grieved for him long then, Gareth thought bleakly, then chided himself. It wasn't as if he had wanted Zetta to be miserable. He should be pleased that she had found some peace in her new life, but he couldn't help but wish that she had pined for him just a little. He was only human, after all.

"You had better go to her, I think, or you might miss your chance," the lady said briskly. "And I will stop wasting my time on what is obviously a definite no. There has to be someone left here who can see past that underdeveloped redhead."

Gareth heard the hurt dignity hidden behind her bravado and found he regretted having caused it. Oddly he felt grateful to her and he bowed over her hand with all the courtly flourishes he could remember.

"Don't judge all men by this fool. A woman as beautiful as you should have no trouble finding a man who will appreciate your . . . balms."

As she watched him stride away from her, she couldn't help but sigh wistfully. She didn't think that she would find anything that good anytime soon. She lifted her chin and began to straighten her hair.

That didn't mean that she was going to stop looking.

The jester did another tumble and Zetta laughed just as she was expected to, but inside she heaved a sigh. It was all she could do to stay awake. Tonight she had danced too much, eaten too little of the far too rich food, laughed too hard and said too much. She needed nothing more than to find her bed and some of the oblivion sleep gave her, but she couldn't retire for the evening before Henry.

Their fragile truce was far too tenuous for her to dare do anything that held even the merest suggestion of a slight. If she left the evening's revels before the king, then the whispering would start and all sorts of rebellion would be implied. Speculation would be insinuatingly deadly as courtiers tried to put the worst possible interpretation on why she had left. You moved with the pack or were savaged by it. She had learnt that much about court life early.

She would simply have to try to stay awake a little longer. She hid another yawn behind a brittle laugh and silently wished the obnoxious and very silly jester would go and torment some other poor victim. She didn't understand half of his sly jokes and those she did she didn't find amusing. After more than an hour of listening to his limited range she was reaching the very edge of her endurance.

But she had to keep laughing. In this surreal place, such frivolous things became imperatives. The next time she yawned she hid it behind a delicate cough. It was as she was looking surreptitiously around her to see if anyone had noticed that she saw Gareth purposefully making his way toward her.

In that moment everything fell into place.

All of her fatigue disappeared and the depression that had been her constant companion left her as if it had never really existed.

He was here.

He had come for her.

All of her uncertainty, doubts and suspicions no longer seemed relevant or real. He was here! He was coming to claim her, to make her whole, and on that thought her world righted itself.

Appearances no longer mattered. She turned and walked away from the startled jester. She didn't care what anyone thought—not when *he* was here. The joy of that revelation bubbled up inside her, and this time when she laughed, she did it because everything inside her was laughing.

He was here!

Gareth and Zetta both stopped near the center of the room, surrounded by candlelight and malicious curiosity. It was odd, but now that she stood in front of him at last, he had absolutely no idea as to what he should say. He felt like an awkward, untried boy, something he had never been, not even as a gauche young man.

He had always known what to say to a woman, and he could bring the world to its knees with nothing but the force of his charm. It was only with maturity that the doubts had arrived.

What if she didn't want him, didn't care that he had come for her, that he loved her? What if she rejected him again? What if she liked this life and wouldn't settle for the little he could offer her as a lowly knight? What if . . .

His doubts were paralyzing him. All he was capable of doing was staring at her mutely.

She smiled.

"I didn't think to see you here . . . Gareth." Her voice caressed his name and he leaned closer to hear it better. His eyes searched hers for some sign that she too felt the completeness possessing him. Slowly he began to grin like a fool.

"I didn't think to be here either, but I couldn't stay away from you."

It wasn't what he had meant to say. It made him sound like a fool, but for all that, he wouldn't have wished the words away even if he could. He *was* a fool for her and it was a relief at last to be able to admit it.

"I'm glad." She lowered her eyes shyly. "I have missed you."

Gareth's grin broadened even farther. From Zetta any admission of vulnerability meant so much more than any other woman's protestations of undying love.

"I love you and want you till I ache. I would give everything and anything I own to be with you in a bedchamber. Now," he growled, trying to keep his voice low. He was aware of the interested people surrounding them but he was unable to hold his silence any longer.

His words lacked any kind of polished finesse, but fortunately Zetta didn't seem to mind.

Instead, she grimaced in consternation. "We can't. I can't leave till Henry leaves."

"Why the hell not?"

"It is too complex to explain easily." She cast a furtive glance around her and leaned a little closer.

"And I certainly don't want anyone else to hear the whys. I just can't."

Gareth let out a long, explosive sigh, trying to untie some of the knots inside him. He needed to get in control of the burning rage of his desire or he was going to burst into flames before her eyes.

"We will wait then," he said through gritted teeth.

She stared at him and then began to giggle. While he knew it was at his expense, he couldn't help but smile back at her. He had never seen a sight lovelier than her honest amusement after so many grim days.

Still chuckling she patted his arm consolingly, not caring anymore about the raised eyebrows and muttered comments her actions caused. "Don't worry, Sir Knight, it is a noble thing you do by waiting and no doubt you will be rewarded, if not in this world, then perhaps in the next."

"I very much intend to be rewarded in this world, in this night, in your bed. And if you don't remove your hand now, we might very well end up being on this floor."

Slowly she ran her hand down his arm, then with devastating gentleness slowly ran it along the long sinuous line of his hand. Her face flushed gently and her eyes began to sparkle with repressed desire. Gareth supposed he should find some consolation from the fact that he didn't suffer alone.

"I missed you so much. I missed this"—she let out a small sigh and moved her hands firmly to her sides— "but we must wait."

"Well then, I had better go and wait somewhere else if you don't want me to make an exhibition of both of us. But I warn you; the second I see the king leave, I will come and get you. Be ready."

He gave her a quick formal bow before turning and striding away.

She followed his retreating back with her eyes till his powerful form disappeared into the crowd. It was then that she heard the excited speculation that was happening all around her, but she didn't care. Everything was different, she realized dazedly. The world had been made new just for them. Whereas before she had seen only a maze of darkness and intrigue, she now saw both light and hope.

Things were all going to be well; she would sort out the mess she had made for herself, would become the woman she knew she could be.

All because he was here and was hers.

She grimaced as she noticed the jester relentlessly approaching her, but she still smiled.

Gareth was hers.

By the time they were inside her chamber, Zetta was laughing so hard that she could scarcely breathe. She leaned weakly against the wall as Gareth put the bar firmly into place, trying to find some control over herself but failing miserably.

"Stop laughing at me, my little thief. It does a man no good to be laughed at," Gareth growled at her menacingly, but he too was smiling broadly.

"I'm sorry; truly I am," she said, trying to breathe, talk and laugh at the same time with little success. "B . . . but, I . . . I honestly don't think that the jes . . . ter will ever recover from the look on your face when you growled at him like that. Did you see the look on *his* face? Oh, my lord, I swear he was deflating before my eyes!"

"He was acting like a pompous peacock. He needed to

have a little of the pride let out of him," Gareth said defensively, and Zetta burst into a fresh wave of laughter.

"What about your pompousness?! You just all but frog-marched me from the hall. Here I was, expecting a discreet exit, and what did you do? You were as subtle as a battering ram. I suppose I should be glad you didn't just throw me over your shoulder and run from the room. I *suppose* I should be glad that instead you just acted like a snarling dog looking after its bone."

Gareth snarled at her in a poor imitation of a dog, but it set Zetta off laughing again.

It still amazed him, this new side of her. He had never seen her laugh with her whole soul. And she was teasing him, playing lighthearted games. Even though it was at his expense, he found that he liked it. Her green eyes twinkled like a forest after the rain and her cheeks were all rosy and warmly inviting.

But it was her lips that held him spellbound.

His need for her almost brought him to his knees. The numbness he had been feeling for the past weeks had disappeared in an instant and his senses were overwhelmed by her assault on them. It was like walking out into the sun after being trapped in a dark room.

His wants and needs must have been communicated to her because slowly she stopped laughing and her smile faded. With a shaking hand she reached out and ran her fingers over the tense line of his jaw up to the softness of his lips. Her eyes followed her fingers as if she was mesmerized.

"I have missed you so much," she said again, her voice as shaky as the hand he now held to his lips and worshiped with his kisses.

"And I you."

She laughed gently, her eyes filling with crystal tears.

"I didn't think I would. I thought that I had prepared myself so well for your eventual desertion that I wouldn't feel a thing when it happened, even if it turned out to be me leaving you. And I was so angry with you. After finding out about you and Edrit—" She stopped suddenly, a hot flush moving over her face. "I haven't even asked where he is, or how he is. I should have. It should have been the first thing I thought of when I saw you, not—"

"Shhh." He nipped the mound of flesh under her thumb gently to stop the inadvertently guilty roll of her thoughts. "Edrit is fine. I brought him with me, but the long days in the saddle wore him out more than he realized they would. When I left him, he was sleeping peacefully in the chambers they assigned to me. I think his bad hand and leg are paining him more than he will let on, but he will be fine after a few days of easier living."

She shook her head. "I still should have thought about him first, before myself. What kind of sister does that make me?"

"The best kind. You have looked after him all of his life. No one would ask anything else of you. I, on the other hand, didn't even know that he existed when I should have."

He had to look away from her beloved eyes. He cleared his throat. "I'm so sorry, Zetta, for what my family did to yours. If it hadn't have been for my father, your mother's life would have been very different. That is why I found it so hard to tell you. I was so afraid of what you might think. We were just starting to get somewhere; you were just starting to trust me. I couldn't bear to destroy it before it had even had a chance to begin. Forgive me."

"Of course I forgive you," she said tenderly, stepping

closer to him. "Because I can't stay angry and love you at the same time." She smiled tremulously. "Not for long anyway."

"Zetta," he breathed as he pulled her the rest of the distance till she was held tightly against his chest. He lowered his mouth to her upturned face, and she welcomed him with a moan as his tongue took possession of hers. He slanted his lips, trying to get closer to claim every part of her that he could.

His erection pressed tightly against her soft belly and he couldn't stop himself from thrusting lightly against her, groaning with frustration as it brought him both a relief and a greater need. With a nipping kiss, he quickly pulled away before he lost control altogether. Tonight was going to be special and he was going to make it perfect for her.

Or die in the attempt, he thought with harsh determination.

The sight of her ravished mouth almost undid his fragile hold on his resolve altogether.

"Turn around," he said hoarsely, but she only stared at him in confusion. He clenched his teeth as he slowly spun her around to face the door. "If I can see that look on your face I will lose control, and I need whatever power of self-restraint that I have left."

Not being able to see her face didn't help all that much. His lower body tightened unbearably as she lifted her hands and removed the silly, bejeweled cap. Slowly she began to take out the pins that held her hair.

He took a deep breath and when he was fairly certain that he wasn't about to fall on her and ravage her he removed her hands and took over the task himself. Frowning with concentration, he slowly undid the last few pins restraining her curls, luxuriating in the feel of the silky softness of her hair moving under his calluses. Abstractly he noticed that this act had at least partially helped him to gain back some control over his raging desire.

Carelessly he took the cap from her hands, then threw it casually among the rushes before he began to tunnel his fingers through her fiery curls. She sighed softly as his hands began to ease some of the tension from her scalp, and he smiled with satisfaction as he moved his fingers a little more firmly.

"I swear that if you were one of Edrit's kittens, which, by the way, I couldn't dissuade him from bringing with him, I think you would be purring right now."

"Well, I don't feel remotely like anything so innocent as a kitten," she said sharply over her shoulder, and Gareth chuckled.

"Good, because what I intend to do with you tonight" —he moved his hands away from her and began to undo the lacing on the back of her gown—"would make a poor little kitten blush."

She stepped out of the dress and he lifted the chemise over her head. She was naked and vulnerable to his gaze. The sight of her perfectly formed, alabaster white back tapering down to her waist and flaring out again into her womanly hips and buttocks made his mouth go dry. He swallowed compulsively.

"You are the most beautiful woman I have ever seen," he said hoarsely as he began to rain kisses down the length of her spine.

She leaned against the door, needing its support as he wrapped his hands around her hips and began to decorate her buttocks with more small, nipping kisses.

The cool of the wood against her breast, belly and thighs was an exciting counterpoint to the fire that raged through her skin. She closed her eyes and rubbed her cheek against it as his kisses started to move slowly down the soft insides of her thighs.

When he moved over the back of her knee with the flat of his tongue she arched into the wood of the door and moaned.

"You liked that, didn't you?" he said wickedly, then did it again.

She had no voice to answer him and could only nod her head in mute approval.

"Spread your legs, my little thief. I want to look at you."

Slowly she moved her thighs apart, the beating of her heart racing as silence filled the room. She knew he was looking at her, at the most intimate part of her, while she could not even see so much as his face. And even if she could see him, he was still fully clothed. The fact that she was naked while he was not made her feel a little vulnerable and very aroused. She could feel the dew of that arousal even now coating the insides of her thighs.

Gareth could see it, she realized with a shudder as her hand curled into the unyielding oak door. From him her body had no secrets.

"Enough," Gareth growled, and with one sudden, sweeping movement he stood up, lifted her into his arms and deposited her unceremoniously onto the bed.

Looking down at her, he began to remove his tunic, but she touched his thigh to stop him and slowly shook her head. The hard muscles under her hand leapt and his eyes blazed at her with aroused questioning.

"Leave them on," she said, scarcely able to recognize the oddly husky voice as her own. "I want you clothed as you come inside me."

He smiled wickedly and quickly joined her on the bed with a growl.

His kisses were now hot and fevered and his hands everywhere at once. He paused for only a moment to free his erection from the confines of his clothes and without a pause filled her achingly wet sheath to the hilt. As she arched up to receive him she exploded into a million pieces. The roaring in her ears drowned out everything but the man who was moving against her, inside her. Another shudder of fulfillment washed through her.

The feel of his tunic against her aching breasts and his clothed hips moving between her sensitive thighs turned all of her nerve endings to fire, building the passion inside her again. When Gareth reached down and lifted one of her knees so that it was under his arm, the scream of her next release punctured the silence to be joined by his roar of satisfaction. He buried his body as deeply inside her as he could and she wrapped her arms tightly around his shuddering body when she felt his seed spilling into her.

She could feel his heart beating against her, feel the sweat of his back under her hands, his breath over her face, and she realized that there was one more thing that she had to do to make this passion perfect.

She moved her mouth so that it was beside his ear, and after she deposited a small, licking kiss she whispered, "I love you."

The shuddering of his body started all over again and Zetta felt tears fall down her cheeks. Every muscle in her body held on to the man she loved with all of the strength she possessed as he began to spill his seed inside her again.

Chapter 15

"Now can I get undressed?"

Zetta smiled up at Gareth lazily as she arched her back, bringing her highly sensitized skin against the delicious abrasion of his clothed body one more time. A shiver went through her and she closed her eyes to better capture the lights that were bursting behind her lids.

"If you must," she said throatily, then quickly opened her eyes so that she could watch the glorious spectacle that was Gareth undressing.

Swiftly Gareth clambered out of the bed and threw off his clothes, and all the while Zetta watched him through her lashes. She could not help but admire the movement of his hard, well-developed muscles under his deeply tanned skin. It was like watching the shimmer of silk in the sun. If it was at all possible for a man as utterly masculine as Gareth to be beautiful, then he was beautiful.

She could never tire of watching his easy movements. For such a large man he had a grace that was riveting. To see him do even the most simple of things captivated her.

By the time he rejoined her in the bed, a low flutter of desire had started all over again in the core of her being. Her passion for this man was almost like a living presence in the pit of her stomach. He leaned up on his elbow and ran his hand too lightly over her already peaking nipple, turning flutters into a steady burn.

"You shouldn't have insisted on me keeping my clothes on. The fabric has rubbed your lovely white skin to a dusky pink. No doubt it will be hurting you soon, if it is not already."

"It was worth it."

He smiled at her lazily. "I agree. I liked the way I could see all of you and you could see none of me. It made me feel . . . good," he said huskily, his gaze avidly following the movement of his hand against her. "Although I don't think we will make a habit of it. I much prefer to enjoy the feel of your skin when you wrap yourself around me."

He flattened his hand and ran it over her stomach, leaving a trail of heat behind. He moved up onto his knees so that he could better watch as his hand moved down over the inside of her thigh. His smile broadened as he noted the subtle change in her breathing, but his touch remained light and teasing.

"You are red down here as well," he murmured as he lowered his head to place a light kiss on her exquisitely tender skin. Then he looked up into her half-closed eyes and added wickedly, "Now, I know a lady who would have just the right balm to help your poor breasts and thighs, only I can't seem to remember her name. Pity, because I think I would enjoy rubbing it all over you."

"What lady?"

"A lady who was kind enough to keep me company

till I found you," he said absentmindedly, his hand moving steadily up toward the damp juncture between her thighs.

"And I am sure she kept you well entertained," Zetta said acidly, not liking him thinking of some other woman while touching her. She knew it was slightly irrational, but she swatted his hand away from her as she quickly tried to sit up. "Perhaps you should go and find her and see if she and her balm will keep you entertained."

Gareth stared at her blankly for a moment and then gave her a gentle push onto her back. He quickly joined her and wrapped her in an embrace that she couldn't get out of no matter how she might try. "Don't be a complete idiot for one moment, and listen to me carefully. If I had wanted to be with that woman, then I would be with her. Hell, if I had actually wanted her, I might even have taken the time to find out properly what her name was. But, obviously, despite all that is rational, I don't want to be with anyone but you."

He placed a small kiss on the point of her shoulder and after a moment asked quietly, "Can you say the same?"

Zetta stilled and stared at him incredulously.

"What kind of question is that?" she screeched indignantly.

Gareth grimaced. "The question of a man who just may be having his own slight problems with jealousy where the woman he loves is concerned."

"No 'may' about it," she growled darkly.

"That sounds a bit harsh coming from someone who was struggling with something very similar just moments ago," he reminded her gently.

She ignored his coaxing smile for a moment and then relented with a long sigh. "Yes, I suppose it does, but for some reason I just cannot be happy with the idea of you enjoying some other woman's company."

"Well, how do you think I feel? You have been surrounded by every randy nobleman in England for weeks and you expect me to believe that not one of them has tried to seduce you?"

"Oh, many have tried," she said grimly. "They all know my history and assume that because my mother was a whore I too am available." She let out a cold chuckle. "One duke, well into his sixties, told me that he remembered my mother, remembered her *very* well. He had been a . . . client of hers when she had first arrived in London, and it had struck him as a truly delightful idea to have me as well. That way he would be able to compare mother to daughter."

"What was his name?" Gareth asked, a raw fury burning bright as he began planning just how he was going to remove such disgusting images from the dirty old man's mind.

Zetta smiled at him sadly and ran her fingers soothingly through the hairs on his chest. "It doesn't matter. It's not much worse than what everyone else has been thinking, and saying behind their hands."

His embrace tightened around her and his hands gently cupped the back of her head, as much for his comfort as for hers.

"You should never have come here." Gareth tried not to sound accusing and stroked her back to soften the words when he failed.

"Well, I certainly don't belong here." She breathed deeply of the scent of him and found the repressed anger and tension she had been carrying inside her since coming here easing. It was nice to finally have someone to share it all with, and she snuggled her cheek against his shoulder as she searched for the words to explain all that she felt. "I don't really understand these people. They live such futile lives, yet if they wanted to, they could change the world. I suppose they are no better or worse than the people I have lived with all my life, but I'm an outsider here. Hell, I don't know if I would change that even if I could. I already have a world I belong to, and need no other."

"Is that how you think of me?" Gareth asked gently. "Which of your worlds have you put me in?"

Zetta's eyes widened with surprise, and she pulled back so that she could look into his tense face properly. "If I have learnt anything by all this it is that I wouldn't want to live in any world that didn't contain you," she said, willing him to understand. "You are not at all like these people anyway. Having seen all this up close I can't understand how you managed to become such a good, kind man." She frowned up at him earnestly, trying to make him understand. "When I met your brother, I couldn't comprehend how different you are from him."

She held her breath until he asked with only mild curiosity, "Which brother?"

She let out a sigh of relief and snuggled against him again. "You don't know? Lanfranc has been at court for, well, since before I was here. Apparently he's trying to decide which side will be blessed with his support in the coming war."

"That is not good," Gareth said sharply, his mind making rapid calculations as to what this change would mean to him.

Nothing good, he realized grimly.

The balance of power must be shifting again, and if he didn't choose exactly the right path he could find himself involved in something he wanted nothing to do with. His fighting days were behind him, and he would do everything in his power to make sure that it stayed that way.

"You're not wrong. The man is completely horrible. Do you know that he actually thinks I am going to marry him?"

Gareth carefully made sure that the expression on his face did not change, but he felt his hold on reality slipping from his grasp. It was almost beyond the ability of his mind to comprehend. In his arms he held the one person in the world who meant anything to him and here she was, calmly telling him that he was going to have to give her up to his brother. It would be far easier if she would just pull his heart out and be done with it, he thought dully.

He didn't dare believe for a moment her slighting rejection of Lanfranc as a person. She was far too practical not to realize that in marriages such things as likes and dislikes really didn't matter. Wealth and position, they were the only things of importance in such decisions.

She had been at court long enough now to know the exact difference between a baron and the mere younger son of one. She would now know that it was an act of folly to waste everything on a man who had no more than a good name and a sword arm to offer her.

And Zetta had never been a fool.

Henry would be pleased, Gareth thought, and then bleakly realized that it had most certainly been his idea from the first. He had been so desperate to have a de Hugues on his side that he had actually been prepared to settle on a younger son. Now he had the baron in his sights and what better way to secure him than through marriage?

It was a situation that would benefit everyone. Gareth swallowed hard, trying desperately to remove the bitter taste from his mouth.

Zetta was entirely impervious to the dark emotions that were roiling through him. As she lazily ran her fingers over his chest she continued to muse aloud.

"It really has been quite funny. At first he only had anything to do with me because the king had insisted on it, but since I have told him what I really think of him, he has become almost ardent. It is getting harder to avoid him."

Gareth stilled her hand and carefully lifted it away from his cooling flesh. "That was a very good way to get his attention. And how long will it be before you stop trying?" She stared at him blankly and he gritted his teeth with frustration. "Tell me how long, Zetta, before you stop trying to avoid him and just give in to his undoubted charms?"

Her expression didn't change, but with a movement that he almost didn't see she rose up and slapped him across the face.

"You bloody idiot," she said coldly. "How can you honestly think I would let myself be used in such a way? Even if I didn't love you, which I do, I still wouldn't let my dear father and your big brother organize my life between them."

She lifted her hand again, but this time she ran it gently over the reddening mark on his face, trying to soothe away the hurt she had caused. "But I do love you. I have from the first moment I saw you laying sprawled out in the mud." She smiled gently. "I can understand why you possibly don't believe me. I haven't exactly acted like someone in love, but you must understand that it was because I didn't dare. I was afraid of losing you and had to pretend that it wouldn't mean anything to me if you did leave me. But I do love you and I always will."

Gareth softly covered her hand on his face with his own. "And I you," he said hoarsely.

"I know," she said simply. "I think I have always known despite all the lies I tried to tell myself." She smiled at him wryly. "That sounds a little more smug than I intended it to, but you know what I mean."

With his confidence returning in leaps and bounds he rolled onto his back and hauled her on top of him. "Yes, I know what you mean. You mean that you absolutely adore me and couldn't live a minute without me."

She rolled her eyes. "Only you can go from being eaten alive with self-doubt and jealousy one minute to being overweeningly confident the next. I can't even begin to comprehend what it must be like to live in your head." She finished with a yawn and tried to find the most comfortable place to lie on his body.

As her eyes started to drift shut she heard Gareth murmur, "It has been so much better living in my head now that I have you in my heart."

She was still smiling as sleep claimed her.

Zetta rolled her eyes and Edrit actually dared to laugh.

"I didn't think it was that bad of an idea," Gareth muttered defensively.

"I think it is the most spectacularly bad idea I have heard of since God decided to plant apple trees," Zetta said succinctly.

"I think it is very funny," Edrit said, with another appreciative giggle. "I hope I get to see Gareth ask the king if he is allowed to marry Zetta."

Gareth put his tankard down on the table with a bang and glared at the two of them. He was beginning to regret that he had thought it a good idea for the three of them to get together to discuss his plans for sorting things out.

He certainly wasn't getting the reaction he had been expecting.

What seemed the only sensible way to proceed now that Zetta had agreed to marry him was apparently endlessly hilarious to Edrit and Zetta. Reluctantly, he could admit that there might be some cause for their amusement. There was something incredible about the idea that he was actually going to ask the king for his permission to marry the woman he loved, and he could not honestly say that he was looking forward to the forthcoming interview. How Henry was going to react to the request was highly uncertain, but that didn't mean for a moment that he was going to back away now, Gareth thought grimly. Henry could rant and rave, forbid the banns, threaten all kinds of calamity and it wouldn't change the one glorious fact that still held Gareth spellbound.

Zetta was going to marry him.

He couldn't help but smile at the sense of satisfaction and completion that filled him. It still dazzled him that she had said yes when he had finally mustered all of his courage and asked her again just hours ago. The startled look of amazement on her face when he had knelt before her had given him pause, but gently he had held her hands and formally asked her to become his wife. It was only when she had said yes and started to cry that he had dared to start breathing again.

It was the final proof his cynical and rusty heart had apparently needed. Self-doubt and worry, however, had no place inside him if Zetta was prepared to throw away her newfound security, her newly discovered wings and her royal position just to be with him.

It now seemed foolish that he had actually waited three days before gathering the courage to ask her, but it really had taken three days of hearing Zetta tell him repeatedly of her love for him before he had been able to put his courage to the sticking place.

And she had said yes.

Even now it scarcely seemed real, and he would be lying to himself if he didn't acknowledge that some doubts still lingered in the furthest, most untouchable reaches of his mind. It was those doubts that made him decisive.

He was organizing their coming union with military precision. He needed to make Zetta irrevocably his, needed to bind her to him with all the laws that God and man had put at his disposal. He had to make certain that he could not be so easily abandoned again.

That was why he needed to speak to Henry. If the king gave them his blessing, even if only reluctantly, then nothing on this earth could take her from him. Not that the clever old bastard didn't already know exactly what was happening, Gareth thought wryly, and that he hadn't put a stop to it had to be a very good sign.

There was nothing that happened within the castle walls that Henry didn't know about almost immediately. He would have known the exact moment Gareth had arrived, would have known every detail of he and Zetta scandalously leaving the hall so obviously together. He would have known that they had been together every night since.

And if Henry knew all that and hadn't intervened, then perhaps there was hope that everything was going to be all right. The only way he was going to know for sure, however, was if he confronted the king and formally asked for his natural daughter's hand in marriage.

The possibility that Henry might say no was something Gareth prepared to contemplate, dwelling on it only long enough to make plans. If the blessing couldn't be procured, then they would have no choice but to run off to France, find the first priest who would be willing to marry them and live the rest of their lives as exiles.

Actually, he found something a little attractive about the whole idea and was tempted to do it anyway. But he couldn't, not when he wanted more than that for Zetta. She deserved more.

Well, she had until she had laughed in his face, he admitted to himself wryly.

"I'm still going to ask him," he muttered defiantly to no one in particular.

He knew he sounded like a petulant child, but he decided that he didn't really mind. If you couldn't be childish with the people you loved, then who could you be childish with?

Still laughing at him, Zetta got up and walked around behind his chair. She wrapped her arms around his shoulders and placed a quick kiss on top of his head. "I suppose you should do what you think is best," she said comfortingly, then ruined the effect by giggling and adding, "but I agree with Edrit—I would love to be able to watch the . . . confrontation."

With a mock growl, Gareth loosened her arms and pulled her around into his lap. She let out an indignant squeal but still settled herself more comfortably against him, her eyes laughing as they met his turbulent ones.

"Behave yourself, wench, or you will not like my punishment," he growled at her threateningly. She did not seem to be all that perturbed. Instead, she raised her brows at him mockingly as she moved her bottom against him intimately.

"Don't make promises you cannot keep right now," she murmured provocatively.

Heat thronged through his veins and all of his petulance was burnt away by the hard desire tightening his loins. He saw an answering passion in her eyes as he lowered his head to claim her lips in a searing kiss.

"Well, you could at least wait till you think I am asleep, like you did last night," Edrit said conversationally.

Zetta's laugh filled Gareth's lungs, and with a light nipping kiss she moved away. Her eyes twinkled merrily as she quickly arranged herself less provocatively on his knee, but while she might have looked prim, he knew only too well that she was anything but. He was all too painfully aware that underneath the table, out of Edrit's sight, her warm, soft hand was stroking the hard, tense length of his thigh even as she looked the picture of decorum.

Not that he wanted her to stop, he admitted to himself as the blood started to pound in his ears.

"Sorry about that, Edrit," she murmured politely. "I will try to make Gareth control himself better in the future."

"But who is going to make *you* control yourself?" Edrit asked with mild interest as he reached for more bread.

"No one has ever managed to control me so far," Zetta said with a shrug. "I don't see any reason why that should change now."

Gareth knew a challenge when he heard one, and he

smiled confidently as he lowered his hand to hers and stilled its torturous movement by holding it against his thigh.

"I intend to have control of you, Zetta," he murmured into her ear. "That is, after all, what marriage is all about."

She wasn't perturbed by his threat. Instead, she leaned back against him with a satisfied sigh, and the change of her weight pressed down squarely on his aching erection.

"You won't control me, any more than I'll control you," she said serenely, "but I will look forward to you trying."

With a chuckle, he lifted her off his lap altogether and slapped her lightly on her far too tempting behind.

"And my dear Zetta, I don't think I would have it any other way," he said with satisfaction.

With worrying speed Gareth was granted a private audience with Henry.

As he was escorted into the king's opulent private chambers by two silent guards, Gareth was actually glad that he had let Zetta talk him into buying a new set of clothes. At the time, he had just thought it was a damn silly waste of the money that had suddenly become so very important.

He couldn't say that he had ever worried about money before, but then his personal fortune had always been more than adequate. However, a couple of days spent with courtiers and all of their extravagances was enough to remind him that a nobleman's life was a very expensive one. Many a family fortune was lost paying court to a king, and Gareth could not seem to forget the fact that he didn't even have one of those. All the wealth he'd earned for himself and that somehow made it seem even more vulnerable. For the first time in his life he found himself trying to husband his resources and make them as impregnable against the vagaries of fortune as he could.

He would never let Zetta regret having settled for a mere younger son. She had suffered enough already. He could only all too easily remember the fragile existence she had been living when first they had met, and he was bound and determined that she would never live like that again. Those days were behind her now and, as he saw it, it was his job to make sure that it stayed that way.

If that meant that he had to go without, then so be it. Unfortunately, Zetta had not seen it as that simple. Her amusement at his plan to confront her father had faded as she had realized the enormity of what he was doing. It was then she had started to fret about the incidental details and insisted that he needed to have some better clothes for the task that lay ahead of him.

With great reluctance and much grumbling, he had let Zetta have her way and grudgingly he was now glad that he had. The black cloth of his tunic was bedecked with gold and it felt comfortingly like a kind of armor. Just the thing a knight needed when he was off to slay a dragon for his lady.

Not that Henry was looking all that much like a dragon—more like a scholar, Gareth realized, with an uncomfortable frown. It didn't bode well. Gareth knew all about slaying dragons but nothing about the strange world he had stepped into. The king's chamber held more manuscripts than Gareth had ever seen in his life before outside of a monastery. He couldn't even begin to calculate just how large of a fortune lay scattered absentmindedly over the top of the large, solid table that occupied the center of the room.

In the middle of all this mess Henry sat with evident ease, ignoring Gareth's presence as he made copious notes on a sheet of parchment, referring occasionally to the manuscript open in front of him.

Gareth, however, was anything but at ease.

He would much rather have been facing an executioner at this moment. He could feel every last ounce of his ignorance pressing down on him as he nervously cleared his throat, needing to get this over and as quickly as possible if he wasn't to be entirely swamped by his unexpected nervousness.

Henry didn't look up but continued to scratch away with his quill.

"So, Sir Knight, can you read?" he asked suddenly.

"Enough," Gareth said reluctantly.

Henry finally looked up and pinned him with a hard stare. "Enough? What do you mean, enough? Do you mean enough so that you know your name when you see it written or enough so that you can actually read anything put before you?"

"I mean enough to know that I would not understand more than every second word of most of the manuscripts in this room."

Henry let out a short laugh and put down his quill. "I knew I liked you. No, no. We will have no more bowing after such an honest answer. Come and sit over here near the window."

With great congeniality, he directed Gareth to the only other chair in the room. Henry, however, remained standing and Gareth found himself in the unaccustomed position of being forced to look up to someone.

The king regarded him curiously as he leaned back

against the windowsill but said nothing. He seemed to be waiting for something, but it took Gareth a moment to realize that he was waiting for him to speak.

"I . . . ah . . . I would . . . I . . . ," Gareth stuttered clumsily and hating it.

"A first, I think: Sir Gareth actually lost for words," Henry observed dryly. "Let me help you a little bit. You have come here to explain to me why I should not cut your balls off and shove them up your nose for the fact that you have disobeyed my express orders that you leave my daughter alone. Does that about cover it?"

Henry smiled at him, but Gareth couldn't help but notice that it didn't reach his eyes.

Strangely, this sudden aggression made Gareth feel a little more comfortable. Scholars, it would seem, made him nervous. Crowned thugs, on the other hand, he knew how to deal with. He leaned back into the chair and raised a brow admiringly.

"You are direct, Your Majesty," he murmured laconically.

"It seemed the best way to deal with it. So explain."

"I'm going to marry Zetta," Gareth said simply, finding he liked hearing those words, even in this uncomfortable setting.

"Mmmm," Henry murmured noncommittally, crossing his arms over his chest as he continued to regard Gareth closely. "And what exactly makes you think I will let you?"

"I have so thoroughly compromised her that I'm your only chance of having her decently married now."

"Don't be a simpleton," Henry said with a tired sigh. "I can make any perceived stain on her reputation disappear just by saying that it doesn't exist. You will have to come up with something much better than that if you hope to convince me to allow this . . . misalliance."

Gareth's mind went suddenly blank.

He had assumed that Henry had allowed them to so blatantly flaunt their relationship because he intended to ultimately endorse it. Now, he realized, he had misjudged the situation entirely and had blundered into very uncertain terrain. Somewhere, he had made a wrong turn and he was trying rapidly to think up some way to make it all all right again.

His mind was frighteningly blank.

"Can I make a suggestion?" Henry asked softly, and Gareth thought that somewhere he could hear the sound of a trap snapping shut as he nodded his head awkwardly.

"Now, what you need to do, Gareth, is to offer me something *I* want if you want to have even a chance of getting what *you* want. My daughter's reputation is not that terribly important. If she were legitimate, things would be different, of course, but then I would also not be considering you as a son-in-law if she were. And I am considering, Gareth. So what you have to do now is come up with something to persuade me to your way of thinking. Something a man with your background and, shall we call them, your professional connections, can offer very easily."

Gareth's face didn't change, but his gut tightened unbearably.

He didn't know whether Henry had set it up all along or whether he was just taking advantage of an opportunity as it presented itself, but that hardly mattered when the final result was exactly the same.

"You need me as a mercenary," he said slowly.

"Not a mercenary, no, because I have absolutely no

intention of paying you. Think of it more as a favor to your soon-to-be father-in-law."

In short, Gareth realized numbly, if he was to marry Zetta he was going to have to become once more the thing he had come to hate. He had left behind the knight's life with relief. He'd been good at it and, in his youth, had even enjoyed the camaraderie and action of it, but that soon had waned. It had taken him years to get his soul back, to fill the dark spaces with just a hint of sanity. And yet, here he was, actually contemplating returning to it all. No, more than contemplating.

For him there was no other decision he could make.

Zetta would always be worth whatever price he had to pay. If to have her as his own he had to become the despised mercenary again, then so be it.

"You do realize that my companies have long since been disbanded," Gareth said with cold practicality, deliberately pushing aside the welter of emotions that would only cloud his judgment. "Besides, the only man they ever called leader was Robert Beaumont, not I. It is only for him that they could be reformed into fighting companies."

"I don't see any problem. Robert has always been your close friend. Doubtlessly he will agree to help you now that you have need of him," Henry said with apparent reasonableness, and Gareth was not in the least surprised that all of the possible problems had already been solved.

Well, Henry wasn't going to have it all his own way, Gareth decided suddenly.

"It is not enough," Gareth said conversationally, grimly amused to throw Henry's sentiment back at him. "I'll need more than a wife to entice me back to the life of the sword."

Instead of being irritated as Gareth had hoped, Henry rubbed his hands together eagerly. "Good. There is absolutely nothing I love more than a good haggle. So, what else is it that you think you need?"

"Land. I need a castle, preferably in the north. I need it made over to me and to my descendents so that no one can take it from me or mine. And I need your word that once these wars are done, you will never again interfere in either mine or Zetta's life again."

"You do put a very high price on your services, Sir Gareth."

"I have to. I'm very good," Gareth said with a confidence he didn't entirely feel. It wasn't wise to show any weakness in front of monarchs.

Slowly, Henry nodded his head. "We will call the castle Zetta's dowry. I had intended to give her something of its like anyway."

Whether that was true or not, Gareth decided it didn't really matter. The only important thing was that he now had something to offer Zetta besides himself. They would have a home.

Now all he had to do was try to stay alive long enough to actually enjoy it.

Chapter 16

Gareth continued on as if he had made no bargain with the king.

He wanted to share the turmoil of having struck a deal with the devil with Zetta but he needed to keep her as far out of Henry's dark web as possible. There would be time enough for her to worry about it all later. For now, Gareth tried simply to enjoy the precious time they had without having her fret about something that neither of them could change, no matter how much they might want to.

To that end, when Robert finally arrived at the royal court several weeks after he received Gareth's desperate request for his help, he treated it as a pleasant surprise. In fact, he had been impatiently waiting for him so that he could get Henry's planned hell started. He sighed as he realized that even with that he was going to have to wait. Zetta's curiosity had been pricked and wouldn't just go away because he willed it to do so.

If it weren't for the desperate, frustrated feeling he had, he would have actually smiled at the way Robert and Zetta both carefully sized the other up when he introduced them. Robert actually looked stunned when Gareth informed him that Zetta had agreed to marry him. And for her part, Zetta made sure that she was standing pointedly close to Gareth after she finished her curtsey.

She kept her face carefully blank as she murmured, "I'm pleased to finally meet you, Sir Robert, after having heard Gareth speak so highly about you." She paused and shot Gareth a pointed look. "When he just happened to mention you out of the blue yesterday evening."

Robert raised his brow skeptically. "I, on the other hand, have heard absolutely nothing about you," he said, his voice steady and reserved, "and I know for certain that I would have remembered even the slightest mention of so lovely a lady in Gareth's message . . ."

"Well, it was only a short note of greeting," Gareth said hastily, sending Robert a quelling glance, which was acknowledged with a small, almost imperceptible nod of his head. Gareth sighed with relief.

The last thing Gareth needed was Zetta asking why he'd sent a message to Robert and not mentioned it to her. If she found out that he had sent anything more elaborate than a short greeting, she would be suspicious. He already knew to his cost that she was far too clever by half and would no doubt very quickly start asking the uncomfortable questions that Gareth just didn't want to answer.

No, the best way was to make everything seem cordial and unimportant.

Robert frowned speculatively. "Yes, well, I still think you could have mentioned that you were about to take a wife. Imogen will give you hell when she finds out that you have kept such a secret from her."

Gareth pulled a face. "I will just have to make sure that I am nowhere near her when she does find out about my small omission. If I give her time to cool off before I head north into your territory again, she might just be able to resist the urge to pull my head off my shoulders as punishment."

Robert laughed, but Zetta frowned in confusion.

"Who is Imogen?" she asked quietly.

Gareth didn't quite know why, but he found he couldn't quite meet her eyes, even though he knew it made him look guilty as hell. There was something about the questioning, vulnerable look he knew he would find in Zetta's deep, green eyes that made him wish rather strongly that he was somewhere else, which he knew was a strange reaction. His feelings for Imogen had long since mellowed into respect and friendship, but he almost felt like he had been unfaithful to Zetta because there had been a time when he had wanted so much more.

Fortunately, Robert came to his rescue.

"Imogen is my wife, and the mother of my two children." Then he added, with a deep smile of satisfaction, "Actually, that is soon to be three children."

Gareth looked over at him with surprise, and then slowly a large lopsided grin spread over his face as he pulled the other man out of the chair and gave him a big, all-encompassing hug. "Congratulations, my friend. So when is the next little Beaumont nightmare due to descend on Shadowsend?"

"In six, maybe seven months' time," Robert said, pulling away from Gareth with an embarrassed shrug. "Imogen has been a bit coy about the exact details. She has been too busy haranguing me for daring to get her pregnant again."

Gareth chuckled, all too easily imagining Imogene's ire at being slowed down by yet another pregnancy. "As I recall, it does actually take two to create a new life. So why is she blaming you?"

"Your memory, as always on such matters, is in the right. And I certainly don't remember her complaining while we were making this one." With a frown he sat back down and took a long drink from the tankard beside his chair. "No, I think the real reason she is being so cantankerous about the whole thing is that she is trying to make me feel so horribly guilty that I will let her redecorate the keep again. She has been begging me to let her do it since, well, since almost as soon as she had finished the last round of rather startling changes."

Gareth laughed out loud. "What, again? I thought she would never tire of that deep green cloth with gold thread shot rather expensively through it. God knows she hung it from every surface that would support its considerable weight."

"I'd almost gotten used to it and all," Robert said wistfully, "but this time she has her heart set on red and blue everywhere and some extremely elaborate and, needless to say, expensive tapestries from Flanders that some fool merchant brought to us last month." Robert shrugged fatalistically. "Honestly, I was glad to get away just to escape her impressively persistent nagging for a week or two. Every time I speak to her of late all I can hear is my poor tortured purse squealing in pain."

"You don't mean that," Gareth chided gently.

Robert sighed with resignation. "No. I probably don't mean it any more than I mean it when I tell her I'd rather be painted blue myself and paraded through the streets of London like a northern barbarian than let her yet again create her rainbow nightmares with our keep."

Gareth laughed, but Zetta frowned with concentration. "You are going to let her do it?" she asked with ill-disguised curiosity, daring to interrupt their easy flow of conversation for the first time.

Robert smiled fondly. "Eventually. But it wouldn't do to say yes straight away or I'd be ruining all of her fun. I believe she spends many hours fantasizing just how exactly she will make me give in this time."

Gareth could see that Zetta didn't really understand, for all the fact that she nodded her head at Robert knowingly. That something so normal and mundane puzzled her made his chest tighten. He couldn't stop himself from slipping his arms around her waist and pulling her back against him. He smiled lopsidedly at Robert. "She doesn't understand now, but no doubt she will soon come to learn all of the wiles a wife needs to have proper control over her husband."

"I think you have enough trouble with the wiles I already have without wishing me any more," Zetta said tartly but leaned back into his embrace all the same.

Robert stared at her blankly for a moment, then started to chuckle. "Imogen is going to like you. You will have to come and visit us when all this is over."

"All of what?" Zetta said, leaping on to Robert's inadvertent lapse with frightening speed.

"Oh, the wedding and all of the nonsense that seems to be unavoidably involved with them," Gareth said airily, hoping to distract her by raising the one thing that had been causing any irritation between them of late. He succeeded all too well, he thought ruefully, as she turned around and glared at him indignantly.

"All of the . . ." She shook her head with disgust. "It's

you who are the one turning our marriage into some kind of mummery show for all and sundry. When I suggested a parish church, it was you who demanded an abbey. And the . . ."

"Shhh," he said softly, placing a finger over her lips. "We don't want Robert to get the wrong idea about you. He'll start worrying that I'm marrying a harpy."

"That is fine, just as long as he also has the idea firmly established in his mind that you are totally mad."

"Oh, Gareth's not mad, not really," Robert said, then chuckled when he saw Zetta's skeptical look. "Honestly. He is only a little eccentric at best."

"You find him that way too?" Zetta said. "Maybe we should sit down and compare stories."

"Not while I am listening, you will not," Gareth said with a smile. "You can do it later on when I will make sure that I am nowhere near to hear my reputation being torn to shreds. But for now, there are some things that Robert and I need to talk about, my little thief, if you wouldn't mind finding something to entertain yourself with for a while."

Zetta's eyes widened in surprise. "Are you trying to get rid of me, by any chance?"

"Maybe." Contrarily his embrace tightened slightly. "Is it working at all?"

She lifted his arms from around her middle and turned to face him fully.

She considered him suspiciously. "Not particularly. Perhaps I had better stay and find out what is really going on here behind this deliberate display of frivolity," she said slowly.

"Nothing is going on other than two old friends wanting to bore each other with reminiscences." He lightly ran his finger over her cheek. "Just for a few hours. Then you can come and grill Robert to your heart's content."

Gareth could tell that she didn't believe him for a second, and it was with evident reluctance that she finally let him gently push her out the door.

Robert looked at the closed door thoughtfully.

"Do you think it is a wise idea to leave her in the dark like that? In my experience, women only make more of a fuss when they do finally manage to wheedle the truth out of you." He paused for a moment while he emptied his tankard. "And believe me, she will wheedle it out of you before too long."

"What else can I do?" Gareth said with a long sigh as he walked over to the jug and poured them both another drink of ale. "If I tell her what is happening, I run a very real chance of her deciding that it is not acceptable, and then she will do some foolish thing to fix it." He smiled fondly. "She has a bit of a reputation for that sort of thing. Trust me."

"Of course I will bow to your doubtlessly superior knowledge of your lady, my friend," Robert said as he accepted the drink Gareth offered him, "but I still think that in this you are entirely wrong."

"Well, it wouldn't be the first time." Gareth wandered over to the window and stared out of it unseeingly as he finally asked the question he needed to know the answer to so urgently. "So, how well did we do?"

Robert grunted with what sounded like satisfaction. "Most have agreed. The one or two who haven't are no great loss and they can be replaced easily enough. Most of them should be replaced, to be honest." Robert sighed tiredly. "Even those who have agreed to join you are not in the best condition, from what I have seen of them. I warn you now—don't go expecting miracles. It has been nearly seven years since our company last fought. Some have continued to fight for others, but most have retired to a less taxing life. We have all gotten a little older since then. And fatter in most cases. These are men who haven't picked up a sword in a very long time, and it shows."

"It would serve Henry right to have a company of overweight ancients fighting under his banner. Maybe they could destroy the enemy by making them laugh themselves to death."

Robert smiled only as a reflex as he thoughtfully stared intently into the distance. Gareth knew what was coming, but he waited patiently for Robert to come to it in his own time.

"I can't fight with you," he said suddenly, shaking his head ruefully. "I have promised Imogen that I won't. I had to or else she was going to have me chained to the wall till I got over the folly of even contemplating it. She sent me off with a rather extensive list of instructions that also included making you give up what she calls 'a damn fool idea.'"

Gareth smiled slightly. It didn't surprise him for a moment that Imogen wouldn't let the man she loved to distraction put himself in any kind of danger. That he too was included in her ring of care was nice to know. It didn't change anything, but it was nice all the same.

"Well, it looks as if you are going to have to fail in that particular mission, I am afraid, my friend. I will fight. I suppose I should be grateful that I haven't gotten as fat as everyone else," Gareth said lightly.

Robert frowned intensely. "While I would hack my tongue off rather than admit it to her, Imogen is right. This is not your war. You are a fool if you let yourself be dragged into something that could tear this island apart." He shook his head. "I knew something like this was going to happen as soon as you got that message from your brother. I knew then that things were going to go spectacularly wrong. You should have listened to me. If you had never left Shadowsend, you wouldn't be in this mess now."

"But if I hadn't left I would never have met Zetta," Gareth said quietly, "and that would have been a real tragedy, far greater than the one you imagine me to be heading toward now."

Robert grunted sympathetically, understanding all too well what his friend meant. "If that is the way of it, then I can only give you all the help I can and wish you all the happiness you deserve."

"I have the happiness, so perhaps you should be wishing me the time I will need if I am to enjoy it to the full."

"But they are just cats," Edrit said morosely, his chin resting on his good arm as he lay sprawled on the ground, impervious to the damage he was doing to the fine fabric of his breeches and long tunic.

Zetta tried to suppress a smile as she continued to tease one of the now nearly fully grown cats with a piece of grass. "Yes, well, what else did you think kittens were going to grow into?"

Edrit sighed and rolled onto his back. Zetta noticed with resignation the green stains marking the front of his expensive tunic. Edrit just had no concept of how fine fabric was to be treated and Zetta had given up trying to explain it to him. She, however, was sitting carefully on a fur rug, making sure that no part of her own pale blue gown touched the grass at all.

"I didn't want them to grow up at all," Edrit grumbled, ignoring the cat that had plonked itself on the flat, wide expanse of his belly and had started to purr contentedly.

This time Zetta couldn't stop a laugh from bubbling forth at Edrit's petulant scowl of annoyance.

"I'm sorry, Edrit, but there is no way to stop that from happening." She picked up the cat she had been teasing and nestled its warm body briefly against her chest. "And besides, who would complain when instead of kittens you have some very nice cats that absolutely adore you?"

"I suppose," he said grudgingly, reaching down his good hand to chuck the cat resting on his stomach under the chin. Its purr went up a notch and its eyes closed with contentment.

Zetta carefully sat back against a tree, a small smile still playing over her face. She could feel the warm dappled sun on her skin, could see Edrit playing gently with his cats and felt so content that she could feel even some of her earlier anxiety dissipating a little.

But not entirely. She felt as if she was deliberately not being told something very important. She could feel it growing just out of her sight, and not knowing what it was and how she was going to fight it made her alternately frightened and very, very angry. She couldn't quite put her finger on what exactly was wrong with Gareth, but she knew with a bone-deep certainty that right now Robert and Gareth were talking about far more serious things than old memories.

But she had to learn to trust Gareth, she thought with grim determination. She had to find it somewhere within herself to believe that if it was anything she needed to know, he would tell. And she was trying, but it was driving her mad all the same.

For now, however, all she could do was wait for him to come to her in his own time. Waiting had never been one of her strengths. But as the pale autumn sunlight fell through the leaves of the tree, and she watched Edrit play with his cats, something inside of her fell into place.

She had a future, and she found that she liked that feeling of certainty.

When she heard footsteps approaching through the long grass, she felt only a mild curiosity. This little wilderness was avoided by the courtiers, which was why Zetta had used it more than once as a retreat, for the first time in her life seeing the value of trees. Anyone who found them here would have to have been looking.

Perhaps it was Gareth.

Perhaps now that he had spoken to Robert the darkness that had become so much a part of him over the past few weeks was gone and he had come out to enjoy the sunshine with her, she thought with lazy anticipation.

Her senses sharpened, however, when it was Lanfranc who stepped into the small clearing instead of his brother.

His stride was casual and relaxed and he smiled pleasantly as he came to a stop just in front of her, but Zetta found herself tensing, some instinct warning her that this was no accidental meeting. Nothing was ever accidental with Lanfranc.

He bowed graciously. "Ah, my lady, I had been hoping to find you. We have much to discuss, you and I."

"I cannot think of anything I need say to you," she said stiffly, suddenly tense.

"But I might have much that you need to hear." He held out his large hand for her. "Come, leave this half-wit to his games and walk with me a while."

She stared at his hand as if it were a viper. "He is not

a half-wit," she growled, but Lanfranc just shrugged his
shoulders. A part of her wanted to tell him to go to
hell, but a more rational part warned her to be cau-
tious. Her soon-to-be brother-in-law was a very powerful man, and if she angered him, there was every
chance he would use that power against Gareth. She refused to let a war start between the two brothers because of her.

Reluctantly Zetta put her hand in his.

He helped her to his feet and waited with impatience
as she told Edrit to return to Gareth's chamber when
he was finished playing with his cats. She could tell by
the worried look on Edrit's face that he didn't want her
to go, but he nodded his head obediently.

She tried to give him a comforting smile as Lanfranc impatiently wrapped her hand over his arm and
began to walk farther into the little forest. Zetta could
do nothing but follow him. After five minutes of
pointless wandering through the forest's undergrowth
she felt like a bowstring pulled tight. She waited for
him to say what had brought him so far from his natural environment, but instead all he did was make idle
conversation.

She waited. This was a game that had to be played his
way. She smiled sweetly and joined in with his pointless
prattle by faking an interest in his nonsense, but all the
while she waited with growing irritation for the blow
that was coming.

"So Gareth's old commander has joined him at last,"
he said suddenly.

Zetta stiffened, her mind searching frantically for the
hidden meaning as she said stiffly, "If you mean his old
friend Robert, then yes, he arrived earlier today."

Lanfranc smirked. "Robert Beaumont is no friend,

not in the way you mean. He is the leader of the battalion of bachelor knights Gareth used to fight with, back in the days when he made his living as little more than a mercenary for hire. Any friendship they have—and I do have my doubts that they have any—is based exclusively on their shared memories of their days as mercenaries."

Gareth a mercenary? She knew that he had fought in several wars but she had never thought of him as someone who would fight for mere gold. The whole idea seemed entirely foreign to her, and yet exactly right. There was darkness to her laughing man, a depth of understanding that was rare.

Carefully she made sure that her face showed none of her confused surprise. Instead, she said calmly, "I believe that shared experiences are often the basis of very good friendships. From what I have seen, Robert and Gareth are most certainly friends."

Lanfranc's brow rose skeptically. "Well, there might be some truth in what you suggest, but I can assure you that 'friendship' has nothing to do with this little poignant reunion. After all, this isn't a social call, now is it?" With studious care he helped her up a small incline that she needed no help with, then silently directed her down a small, dark path that she had never noticed before in her wonderings.

An uneasy shiver went down her spine and she felt as if a suffocating silence had wrapped itself around her. "I think we should go back now," she said sharply, trying to pull her hand from his. He did not let go. All pretense to civility disappeared as he began to ruthlessly drag her along, Zetta struggling to keep up with his long stride.

Suddenly he stopped short and hauled her so that

she stood in front of him, then grabbed her other hand in his iron-tight grip.

"I'm sorry for my brusqueness, but I can't let you leave until I have made one or two things perfectly clear to you," he said pleasantly, his cold blue eyes boring into hers. She had never before realized how soulless his eyes were and she wanted to look away but didn't dare.

She returned his stare defiantly, refusing to be cowed. She could not let him know just how afraid she was. Instead of crying, screaming or fainting, as a true lady would have, she said coldly, "Say what you have to say and get on with it."

Lanfranc's lips turned up into one of his rare smiles.

"That is one of the things that I like about you. You never play these little games by the same rules as the rest of us. You always seem to manage to act with amazing unconventionality. I like that." Zetta continued to stare at him unemotionally, making him sigh. "And I find it very irritating that you never react to a compliment the way you should."

"I do when I actually receive one."

"Well then, let me give you the greatest compliment that you will ever receive." He brought the back of her hand up to his lips, ignoring her ineffectual struggles to prevent him from kissing it. She shivered with revulsion as she felt his cold, moist lips on her skin, but he smiled down at her with satisfaction as he murmured, "I am still prepared to marry you, Zetta, regardless of the life you have led up till now."

Whatever she had been expecting to hear, that wasn't it. She stared at him blankly and was unable to stop a hysterical laugh from escaping her.

"I am sure I should be flattered," she said as she struggled for breath, "but as you know, I am going to marry Gareth in three weeks' time, so I don't understand what you think to gain from this little drama."

"Oh, I know that my little brother has made some sort of preparation, and that you may even actually manage to spend some time as his wife, but I am prepared to wait."

"Wait? Wait for what?" Zetta asked, a sudden watchfulness stilling the rapid beating of her heart.

"Wait until Gareth dies, of course."

For a second Zetta could not believe what she had heard. It seemed impossible to her that someone could mention death so casually, indeed to admit to be looking forward to it. It was perverse, and she felt bile rising in her throat at the thought that she breathed the same air as such corruption.

She tried to repress her shudder of disgust. "Well then, you can wait forever. There is absolutely no reason to believe that Gareth will not outlive you."

"But, Zetta, the life of a mercenary is never a long one," Lafranc explained patiently, as if to a child. "They are the expendable forces in any army. A wise general puts them where the fighting is at its worst, where the fatalities are the highest. That way, he will make sure that as many of his loyal men survive as possible while cutting his expenses. Dead men rarely demand payment for gold owing."

"As Gareth is no longer a mercenary, I hardly see that your little lecture on military tactics has anything to do with me."

But even as Zetta said those brave words, a sick feeling started in her stomach as she suddenly understood exactly what it had to do with her. She knew why Henry had suddenly removed his objections to their marriage and why Robert had appeared seemingly from nowhere.

She knew now what Gareth had been trying to hide from her. Even as Lanfranc gloatingly told her that Gareth had agreed to fight for Henry in exchange for her hand in marriage, she found she knew it all already.

She knew that her love for him was going to lead Gareth to his death. The pain of the realization was so enormous that she couldn't even begin to try to hide it, and Lanfranc pounced on her vulnerability eagerly.

"Poor Zetta, the last to know." He leaned forward till she could feel the heat of his body against hers and the whisper of his breath as he murmured into her ear, "But I still want you. I have wanted you since I realized there was wildness inside you that only I could tame. Together, we would be a truly interesting match."

She pulled back so that she could see his gloatingly cold eyes, and with all of the venom she could muster, she spat at his face.

She watched with distant satisfaction as he started with shock, dropping her hands to wipe the spittle off his face.

Her instincts kicked in. She took full advantage of his moment of confusion to turn and run back the way they had come, hauling her skirts up ruthlessly. As she crashed through the undergrowth, her only thought was of her need to get away from this cold, twisted threat. She dared to slow only when she reached the formal gardens and the relative safety of being in the full view of the castle, but she still didn't dare stop or return to the rooms she had been sharing with Gareth. Instead, she searched desperately for a small corner of the garden where she could shatter into a million pieces unseen.

But by the time she found the deserted kitchen gardens the pain became so unbearable that she didn't care who could see her. She fell to her knees, tears streaking down her face as the enormity of what was happening slammed through her. Lanfranc's words kept playing over and over in her mind, and she was entirely unable to make them or their dark meaning go away.

Gareth was going to willingly die, all because he loved her. If she let him make that sacrifice it would be she and she alone who would take the life from his heart and leave his body to rot on some Normandy battlefield. The whole idea barely seemed real, yet it was all too frighteningly real.

It was happening now.

Zetta knelt up and wiped her eyes with her fists as she tried to find some sense in the chaos that surrounded her. She couldn't afford to let go of herself—not like this. It was self-indulgent and self-defeating. First, she had to find a way to stop Gareth from going through with this nightmare. Once he was safe, she could indulge herself all she wanted.

The cold reality, however, was that there was only one way to save Gareth. He was doing this for her. It was for her; her safety; for love of her; and for her father. It was she and she alone who had brought him to this point. And it could be only she who could make it all go away again.

She had to leave him.

The tears dried on her face quickly in the gentle breeze and she swallowed hard. It was the only thing that she could do. She had to make Gareth safe, and the only way to do that was to remove all the reasons he had for putting himself in danger in the first place.

It wouldn't be hard. She could just disappear as if she

never existed. In no time at all this would all seem as no more real to either her or Gareth than a dream.

That's what it had been, she realized bitterly. It had all been someone else's dream; a beautiful unattainable dream where she had loved a man and had been loved in return. A dream of a life where she had dignity and acceptance from another human being simply because she was worthy of it. It was a dream where a man loved her so much that he was actually prepared to kill and be killed.

Zetta stiffly got back to her feet and began to mechanically dust off her gown.

She would have to quickly forget such dreams, she told herself sternly, and welcome the numb, hollow feeling that was even now spreading inside her. If she was foolish enough to live inside such dreams she would only go mad.

No, it was better to forget than to slowly bleed to death from the thought of what might have been. If there was something life had taught her, it was that she couldn't let in any weakness if she was to survive.

And she would survive. She had to. That was what living was all about. Dreams of love were nothing. No, in the long run, it was the dumb, animalistic survival that counted in this meaningless world.

And she would survive.

Chapter 17

Zetta found it physically very easy to leave.

It seemed oddly right that for all of its pomp and circumstance, the royal court was vulnerable. Any castle that it was easy to escape from could just as easily be got into. The high stone walls of Henry's London castle offered only a false sense of security.

Of course, her ability to disappear was aided by the fact that she didn't look like herself. Or more accurately, she thought with grim amusement, she did look like herself, her real self, the person she had always been until Gareth had turned her life on its head.

In the dark of the early dawn, when she was certain that Edrit had finally fallen into a restful sleep, she had snuck into his room and quietly rummaged through the chest at the end of his bed. It had taken her only a moment to find what she was looking for. At the bottom of the chest, under all of the fine clothes Gareth had fitted him out with, sat folded Edrit's old clothes. Silently, so as not to disturb him, she had stripped off every last vestige of the elegantly dressed woman she had become and slipped into them.

After she had closed the sturdy but worn cloak around her shoulders, she looked down at herself and grimaced. It was like slipping back into her own skin, but there was something wrong about how she looked. For all its familiarity, it all seemed to be utterly alien. Suddenly, it had occurred to her what was wrong.

She no longer had the straight lines and sharp angles of the boy she had always in the past so effortlessly pretended to be. There were curves and valleys where before there had been none, but more than that, there was something else. Something about her had changed beyond all recognition, but she could find no name for what it was.

She took a shallow, shuddering breath and tried to remain focused on all that lay before her. She could not afford to let herself be distracted by mere details and introspection when there was so much else at stake.

No doubt the curves would disappear soon enough, she told herself with harsh practicality. Besides, it was not as if anyone else was going to look close enough to even notice them. Edrit's large, shabby clothes hung off her loosely, hiding her new body from the world. It was only because she knew they were there that she could see them, she told herself sternly.

Only Zetta knew how much she had enjoyed being Gareth's woman. She threw back her head, trying to get some air into her suddenly starving lungs. A pain settled deep inside her chest and it felt like it was trying to tear her apart.

As she struggled to swallow the tears that welled in her eyes she could almost find it within herself to hate Gareth.

Because of him everything was so different now and not knowing herself and where she belonged was pulling her into a million disjointed little pieces. She was lost. No matter how she might pretend otherwise, the life she had always inhabited so easily for so many years now seemed entirely alien to her, the clothes of that life a strange costume that disguised nothing.

She forced her tears away and stared blindly into the darkness. She drew in a shaky, shuddering breath. Strange or not, she would simply have to relearn everything. She couldn't afford to waste precious time mourning over things lost.

They were gone and there was nothing left here for her. She had said all of her good-byes, albeit silently to herself.

Gareth had seemed surprised by her decision to spend the night in Edrit's room but hadn't tried to change her mind. His kind understanding had made her want to cry. It seemed unbearably tragic that he was entirely impervious to the fact that while he had been kissing her good night, she had been kissing him good-bye.

He had held her gently in his arms and lowered his lips to claim hers. It had been a sweet possession. The slow movement of his warm lips against hers had been like a brand in a way that no violent plundering ever could be. It had been a fragment of time that had seemed to last forever.

Yet it had ended all too soon.

When Gareth had started to deepen the kiss and moved his hands to cup her backside, pulling her more intimately against the heat of him, abruptly she had pulled away. She had seen the startled, puzzled frown start to form on his brow. She had swallowed clumsily as she had stepped away from the warmth of his embrace.

"I'll see you in the morning," she had said in a stiff monotone, trying not to stumble over the lie, but still it had left a rusty metallic taste in her mouth. Gareth's concerned frown had deepened.

"Zetta . . ." he had murmured.

"I'm fine," she had interrupted hastily. "I just promised Edrit I'd spend the night with him. He says he's been missing me. It will only be for just one night."

"I suppose I can manage just one night." He had smiled as he had run the back of his hand gently over the line of her cheek. "Well then, good night, dear one."

"Good night," she had said quickly, then turned and fled, leaving his chambers without a backward glance. It had been the only way she could keep herself moving.

When she got to Edrit's chamber she had to get herself back under control quickly. An even harder task had awaited her because she couldn't leave her brother without some kind of explanation.

She had sat him down and told him everything as clearly and simply as her jumbled mind would allow. She had told him all about his real father and that Gareth was his brother. He had smiled happily at the thought of his idol being his brother, but his smile had faded when she had tried to explain what Henry was doing and what she was going to do to stop him.

By the time she had finished, tears had been rolling down his face and he had reached out for her hand and held on to it tightly while mutely pleading with her not to leave him.

Firmly she had pried his fingers open and gotten up and left him. She could no more stay and watch him grieve for her than she could let Gareth hold her through the long lonely night and then leave with the scent of him fresh on her skin. Still, the memory of his grief-stricken face had haunted her as she had filled the long hours waiting for him to go to sleep by flitting around the castle.

Moving unseen, she had watched from dark corners as the noblemen and noblewomen had played their endless games of seductive intrigue and betrayal. It was just as poisonously captivating as she had always found it. No, she wouldn't miss it. It had never been her world. It was the people she would long for, the people she loved with everything good inside her.

Now, she hesitated beside Edrit's bed but didn't kiss him for fear that he would wake up and plead with her again when she didn't have the strength left to fight his fears as well as hers.

And Zetta *was* afraid. It terrified her to think she might never see his dear face again, and no matter how often she told herself that he was better off here, that if he returned to the streets he probably wouldn't survive another winter, it broke her heart to leave him.

She said her silent good-bye to him, then, like a ghost, crept from the room.

Dry-eyed, she stole down the drab, ill-lit servant stairs that led to the vast kitchens. Even though the sun had yet to rise, they were already bustling with the multitude of servants preparing the massive amount of food required for the royal court. It was childishly easy for her just to blend in. None of the servants questioned her, too busy with their own tasks to worry about the pale stranger who held his shabby cloak so tightly that his knuckles where white.

Still, she felt conspicuous. As unobtrusively as possible she joined the group of cook maids and kitchen boys who were preparing to leave for their daily visit to the London markets. Hoisting a basket snatched from a table onto her shoulders, she followed them out through the plain wooden doors into the torch-lit bailey and out of the gate.

She was free.

For the first time since the fateful day she had robbed Gareth, she was in full control of her life again. Just the memory of it made her want to turn around and run straight back into his welcoming arms.

When they reached the market Zetta faded into the early morning crowds as unobtrusively as possible. She looked around helplessly. The sights and sounds were so achingly familiar—hawkers trying to entice passers-by, servants and peasants mingling freely. For the first time in more than six months she heard the accent of her childhood in the mouths of others. Excrement and sweat mixed with the tantalizing aroma of herbs and spices on a nearby stall. It was everything she had ever known it to be, but she felt like she wanted to throw up. She forced herself to remember that she was doing all of this to keep Gareth alive.

And for him, she found she would do anything.

Gareth woke suddenly but didn't open his eyes.

He could feel someone watching him.

Instinctively he knew Zetta was not in the bed beside him, and for a moment he couldn't remember why not, but then it came back to him exactly why.

Every sense pricked as he tried to discern who the intruder was, but the only thing he could tell for certain was that it wasn't Zetta. Her absence from him was like a hole inside his core. There was a special something about her that called to that part of him that he hadn't even realized existed till he had met her.

But if it wasn't Zetta, then who?

Once he was sure he was fully alert, he slowly opened his eyes, regretting that he had left his sword in the chest at the end of the large brocaded bed. He couldn't actually remember when he had stopped putting it near him at night, but he had gotten very lax about that of late. His body tensed, automatically readying itself to fend off any kind of attack.

Edrit sat in the chair near the window, his brow was furrowed with confusion and his eyes were red, as if he had been crying. He glared at Gareth with a strange coldness that had never been in his open gaze before. Even so, Gareth's body immediately eased out of its taut lines and he smiled.

"You are my brother," Edrit said accusingly, his good hand clenching and unclenching rhythmically on his knee.

Gareth's smile faded and he eyed the other man warily. He wasn't sure if he was prepared for this discussion yet, but ready or not, it seemed he was going to have it.

Slowly he pushed himself up till he was sitting, the furs dropping to his lap. The frigid air of the chamber was chilly on his naked chest, as the fire had long since gone out, but he scarcely noticed the discomfort as he searched his mind rapidly for something to say.

"Yes," he said finally, wincing at the feebleness of his answer, but unable to think of anything better to say.

Edrit's frown only deepened.

"Why didn't you tell me? Why didn't you want me to know?"

"I didn't know how to tell you, what words to use to make you understand," Gareth said weakly. "I tried several times, but for the life of me I couldn't think of how to explain it all to you."

"You were ashamed of me, weren't you? You didn't want me to be your brother at all." Edrit's calm matter-of-fact voice was entirely at odds with the pain that shone from deep in his sad eyes. Gareth felt as if a lifetime of rejection was staring out at him, and it was his turn to frown intensely. Suddenly his own ineptness irked him intolerably.

He pulled back the bed furs, threw on a discarded tunic, and strode restlessly over to the hearth. He bent down and halfheartedly poked at the smoldering embers, trying to revive the fire as his mind flayed forward, trying to find some way to explain the seemingly inexplicable.

The fire remained determinedly dead, however, and Gareth finally stood up, no longer able to delay the inevitable. With a deep sigh of weariness, he turned to Edrit. The pain in his brother's eyes was like a slap across his face, and suddenly he became very angry at himself.

"Don't be an idiot," he growled. It wasn't quite what he had wanted to say, but it was all he seemed able to come up with through the mire of his tangled thoughts.

Edrit shrugged his shoulders. "But I am an idiot, and my face is no good and I walk funny. Everyone treats me bad. And that is why you don't want to be my brother."

"None of that matters to me, you fool," Gareth said through gritted teeth. "I'm not perfect, so how could I dare to judge you? What counts is what is on the inside. Nothing else."

Edrit looked at him disbelievingly, and Gareth realized that he needed more reassurance. Deserved more. He took another deep breath and said with steady sincerity, "The reason I didn't tell you was that I was ashamed, but not of you. Our father was a complete bastard and I resented him all of my life, but I at least had the chance to find that out for myself. You, on the other hand, were given nothing, not even my rage. That shamed me. I am ashamed of him; I am ashamed of the life that I have been privileged to live. And I am damn guilty of not once questioning my right to any of it." He ran an agitated hand over his face. "Hell, I told you I wasn't perfect."

Edrit's expression didn't change as he continued to regard Gareth solemnly. "I think I would rather be your sort of not perfect than mine," he finally said slowly.

Gareth's lips tightened. He just didn't have the words to take away the lifetime of hurt that Edrit had suffered. This was his brother and he didn't know what to do to make it better. He desperately searched his mind to find some way to tell the gentle man-child that he was so proud to be able to call him brother. And he really was proud, he realized with a start. His mind warily circled around the entirely unfamiliar sensation. For the first time in his life he was actually proud of a man he called brother. This man had suffered so much yet he sat and asked his questions with a quiet dignity.

And he knew that no matter what else he achieved in this world, if he could ever say that he had become as good a man as Edrit he would be content. Even now, when he should be railing against all of his injustices, Edrit actually had hope slowly dawning in his eyes as he digested all that he had just heard.

"So you don't mind being my brother, then?" he asked. Gareth could see the fear lurking behind the hope. Fear that he would be rejected. But still he asked.

It was one of the bravest things that Gareth had ever witnessed in his life.

The least he could do was respond in kind.

"Edrit, I would be honored if you would call me brother."

Edrit's twisted face turned into an eccentric grin. "I think I might like having a younger brother." His face suddenly dropped. He swallowed hard as tears gathered in his eyes. "But not in the same way I liked having a younger sister. Zetta looked after me and I looked after her. Nothing will be the same now that she is gone."

Gareth felt himself go very still. "Gone? Gone where?"

"Gone back," Edrit said simply, the tears starting to fall freely. "She said that she couldn't stay because if she did the king would make you fight and then you would die and it wouldn't be right. So she had to leave and it was better if I stayed because I'd be better off because I'm not very strong and you would always look after me because you are my brother. I'm sure you will look after me though Mother left and our father left before I was ever born and now Zetta's left." Edrit seemed to shrink into himself. "And how am I to know for sure that you won't leave me? Because if you do, I'll be all alone and I have never been all alone."

Through the haze of raw panic that was stripping his emotions to agony, Gareth could hear Edrit's own pain. There would be time enough for his own confused hurt later, Gareth decided grimly. Right now Edrit needed him.

He went over to where Edrit sat huddled in the chair. His cheeks were wet with tears as Gareth crouched down beside him, his knees cracking a loud protest. He grabbed hold of Endrit's hand gently, carefully folding his long fingers along Edrit's twisted ones.

"I'll never leave you," Gareth said hoarsely, his large hands squeezing Edrit's hand slightly, trying to make him believe what probably seemed impossible. "No matter what happens, from now on, you and I are a team. Together we will bring Zetta back. She has gotten things a little confused, and when we find her, I will make her understand that she didn't have to leave you and me. Somehow we will work everything out. I promise."

Edrit considered Gareth's words for a moment and Gareth felt himself holding his breath. Slowly he nodded his head. "I will trust you."

Gareth closed his eyes for a moment, relief flooding through him. He knew the true value of those simple words. It was a blind leap of faith that humbled him. He could feel his throat thickening, and when he pulled away he had to clear his throat before he could speak.

"Thank you. I won't let you down."

Edrit shrugged his shoulders. "If I thought you would, I wouldn't have said that I trusted you," he said with simple, ruthless logic.

Gareth managed to chuckle dryly as he stood up, but inside his blood was racing through, spreading in its wake an icy panic. Zetta was out there somewhere all alone. The knowledge that she had survived many years on the streets of London without him offered no comfort. She could be in danger and that thought possessed him completely.

And she had done it all because she thought it would save him.

He had to find her.

He grabbed some leggings from his wooden chest and began to throw them on with careless haste.

"I only wish," he said as his tousled head poked out of the top of the tunic, "I knew what exactly Henry told Zetta that sent her off like that. And why, for that matter."

"It wasn't the king who told her. It was your brother." Edrit stopped and frowned with worry. "Does this mean that he is my brother too? I don't like him very much. He called me a half-wit."

Gareth's face hardened, a disturbingly clear picture forming in his mind of exactly what had happened. Lanfranc was playing his games, manipulating things to suit his own ends.

He should have seen something like this coming, Gareth thought grimly. The signs had all been there. A part of him had been aware of the icy anger that had radiated from Lanfranc since Henry had announced the impending nuptials to the court, but he had chosen to ignore it. He had never thought it was important because he hadn't thought there was any way he could harm Zetta.

But he'd been wrong. He had entirely underestimated the extent of Lanfranc's twisted, icy anger. It had led him to drive a wedge between them by telling Zetta of the schemes that were being hatched behind her back. It had probably never occurred to his cold, selfish brother that Zetta's reaction would be one of horror and guilt rather than anger. Lanfranc had miscalculated, and now Zetta was going to pay the price unless Gareth could find her.

But before he pulled London apart stone by stone he was going to have a little word with his brother. It seemed that they had one or two things that needed to be made clear.

Once that was done, Gareth would never see Lanfranc ever again.

* * *

Gareth found Lanfranc with Henry. The king had decided to take advantage of the relative peace of the early morning to have a friendly completion on the archery range. Lanfranc had doubtlessly volunteered with practiced flattery.

His brother, Gareth noticed as he strode toward them, was ever so politely losing. It didn't surprise him in the least. Lanfranc was nothing if not the perfect courtier. He played the meaningless games with a consummate ease.

Well, this time he was going to be playing someone else's game. Gareth stepped in front of the straw target directly in the path of the arrows.

Henry was just about to let loose a shot, and he swore loudly as he hastily lifted his bow, sending his arrow harmlessly over Gareth's head. He lowered the bow and glared furiously at Gareth.

"What the hell do you think you are doing, you madman? I might have shot you." He let out a shaky breath and muttered, "Not that you wouldn't have deserved it after doing such a damn fool thing."

"I needed to get your attention. It seemed the quickest way," Gareth said mildly, but a thread of steel ran through his voice. "And now that I have it, I would like you to answer exactly the same question for me. What the hell do *you* think you are doing?" His eyes bore into Lanfranc's, who merely raised a brow.

Though Gareth was clearly asking Lanfranc, it was a still-shaken Henry who answered.

"I have no idea what you mean," he said with ill-disguised impatience, looking between the two brothers as if trying to work out what was going on.

"He does," Gareth growled, taking slow, measured steps toward his brother. "He knows why he told Zetta all about our arrangement, and because he told her, she has disappeared into the stews of London. I simply want to know why the hell he interfered in something he should have just left alone."

Henry stilled. "Zetta has gone?"

"Yes, she left sometime this morning, snuck out disguised as a boy," Gareth said bitterly, all the while glaring icily at Lanfranc, trying to discern the least sign of human reaction on his face.

"Well, what the hell are you doing here then? You must find her and bring her back," Henry said fiercely.

"I have every intention of doing just that, but first I have to hear what possible excuse my elder brother can come up with for his actions."

Gareth stopped just in front of Lanfranc, his hands clenched at his sides as he tried to control the unholy rage that was swelling inside him. Looking at Lanfranc in the harsh, early morning light, he felt like he was truely seeing him for the first time.

When they had been boys Gareth had actually worshipped his dashing older brother, who seemed to embody all the grace of the courtier while also being a knight of some standing. Lanfranc had seemed so unattainably noble as he had gone off to fight the incessant warring between the barons of Normandy.

Gareth had seen in him everything he had wanted to become, the personification of all that was great and good in the world.

Now all he saw was a cold, ruthless man who manipulated the people to suit his own twisted ends. What kind of man was it who saw no harm in terrorizing a woman just so he could have a little petty revenge for her rejection?

If his rage hadn't been so all consuming he might actually have pitied his brother.

"You actually loved the silly wench, didn't you?" Lanfranc said with sneering amusement. "Have you not learnt anything of the real world, little brother, or must I teach you about this just as I taught you everything else?" He shook his head with mock compassion. "Women are so terribly disposable, Gareth. They come; they go. It does not pay to give one of them too much importance. There are always plenty of others to choose from. It's not as if you can really find any difference between them anyway. Lady or serving wench, they are all the same."

"If you truly believe that, then why the hell didn't you just leave Zetta alone?"

"She chose to shame me by publicly choosing you," he said as if it explained away every sin he had ever committed. "So yes, I stirred the waters a bit. And if what I told her had actually come to pass, well then, I would have taken full advantage of it. I never, however, expected the silly wench to take flight." He shrugged his shoulders. "You should be grateful. Now you can say that you have laid the royal bastard with her father breathing over your shoulder, but you won't actually have to marry the whore. I've given you back your freedom and added to your reputation all in one fell swoop. You should be thanking me."

Rage clouded the last rational part of Gareth's brain, consuming him completely. He pulled back his arm and with one long, powerful swing slammed his fist straight into Lanfranc's face. The sound of bones breaking rang out, making Gareth smile with grim satisfaction.

Lanfranc stumbled back as blood spouted from his damaged nose, but he remained standing, a look of pure hate filling his eyes. Carefully he dabbed at the blood with the edge of his sleeve.

"Careful, little brother, or I will be forced to make your life very uncomfortable indeed," he said with a lethal stillness.

"Very likely you will, but you will be doing it from some other kingdom," Henry said with emotionless authority. "You are no longer welcome at my court, or in my kingdom. Do I make myself clear? I want you gone from this place by sunset, and by the end of the week I hope to hear news that you are back in Normandy spreading your vile poison through my brother the duke's court."

"You dare expel the Baron de Hugues?" Lanfranc asked incredulously.

"A baron is a baron and a king is a king. I dare very little in the scheme of things, I think you will find."

An angry flush moved up Lanfranc's neck as he glared impotently at Henry. "You will regret this, Your Majesty. When you finally get around to this long-awaited battle with your brother, you will regret that you don't have me fighting by your side. I just hope you live long enough after that to truly regret your decision."

With that, he spun on his heel and strode away.

"You may have made a mistake there, Sir Gareth," Henry said with deceptive mildness. "You should have thrust a knife between his ribs when you had the chance. As it is, not only is a mere broken nose too good for the bastard, but it won't slow him down for long."

"Don't tempt me."

Gareth watched his brother walk away, and he realized with a cold, detached amazement that it would probably be the last time he would ever see Lanfranc unless they chanced to meet on a battlefield. There should have been some sadness or regret at such a moment. Instead, he felt absolutely nothing at all.

And that was exactly what Lanfranc was to him now. Nothing.

"Where has she gone?" Henry asked, not taking his gaze from Lanfranc's retreating back, but Gareth could sense the studied tension radiating from the king. Gareth could even feel some sympathy for the turbulent and strange emotions that were no doubt going through the king, but he didn't have time to worry about them now.

"I don't know," he said starkly, his feelings of futility controlling him for the moment. "She has chosen to vanish rather than see me fight as your mercenary. She thought that if she wasn't here, you wouldn't be able to use her to manipulate me, and then I would be safe."

Henry scowled. "That wasn't what I was doing. I wasn't just using her for that. I was thinking of her future, of where she would be safest, happiest," he growled defensively.

"No, you weren't. You knew that I would do anything for her and you used that knowledge against me. You were making my decisions for me."

Henry looked over to him. "And you say that because of this she has thrown herself back into the stews of London? All just to save your sorry hide?"

Gareth nodded his head.

Henry exploded. "Damn, what else was I supposed to do?! It is done all the time and not for such good causes as mine. I need the men and the arms if I am to have a hope of getting my incompetent brother out of the way before he grinds Normandy into dust. You wanted Zetta. It was only logical."

"She is your daughter. Did you even for a moment think of finding out what *she* needed, what *she* wanted?"

"She wouldn't have suffered," Henry said stubbornly.

Gareth hesitated a moment, then said softly, "But because of what you did, she *is* suffering. Right now, wherever she is, she is completely alone. I don't even want to begin to imagine what kind of danger she is in, the danger if anyone should work out who she is and try to use her to get at you. Trust me, she *is* suffering now."

Henry stood still for a second as Gareth's words slowly sunk in; then suddenly he began to stride away from Gareth and back to the castle.

Just as suddenly he stopped and turned back.

"Find her," he ground out. "Marry her, and take her up to your cold north lands and give her what you are so certain that she wants, and I will see that you will not want for anything while I am alive."

Gareth considered the other man carefully. "Thank you. You will not regret this," he said simply.

Henry didn't acknowledge his gratitude. Instead, he pointed his finger at him and said severely, "But before you go, you had better organize some kind of regiment from your mercenaries or I will make both you and Zetta stay at court forever just so I can truly appreciate the happiness that you are so certain you will find in each other's company."

With that he turned and followed the path that Lanfranc had taken just moments before. Gareth supposed he should have felt some sense of victory. After all, Henry had just given him everything that he hadn't even dared to hope for.

Instead, his mind raced through all of the fears that

had taken hold of his heart the moment Edrit had told him that Zetta had left. He had to find her. He had to make her safe. Logically, he knew that the task before him was almost impossible, but logic had nothing to do with what he was feeling right now. He couldn't even contemplate the idea that he might not find her.

He had to find her or his life just simply wouldn't be worth living.

Robert absentmindedly ran his hand down the flank of Gareth's large gray warhorse. The stallion threw his head restlessly.

"Where will you begin?"

Gareth shrugged his shoulders, mechanically tightening the strap that held his bag to the saddle. "We will start with all of the places Edrit remembers."

"And if she doesn't turn up at any of them?"

"Then we will pull apart every hovel and slum in London. Every lane, alley and muse will be searched until there is not a stone in the damn place that I'm not intimately familiar with."

Robert frowned and lowered his voice so that Edrit, who was sitting uncomfortably on the horse that Gareth had just helped him up onto, couldn't hear.

"It is no easy thing that you plan to do. Why not leave Edrit with me? I will be staying at court for a few more weeks while I sort out a regiment for Henry. Then I will be heading back to Shadowsend. If Edrit came with me, I would look after him, and I know Imogen would be more than happy to take him under her wing for a while." Robert smiled slightly. "She does so love having people around her to mother."

"Thank you, but no," Gareth said firmly. "I promised

him that we would stay together, and I intend to stand by that promise. Where I go, he goes."

Robert nodded silently, but Gareth knew only too well what he was thinking. It didn't matter. It might sound insane to anyone else, but as far as Gareth was concerned, it was the only way. Edrit was family, and a real family, as Gareth was fast discovering, was too precious a thing to be thrown over just because it was easier without it. Besides, Edrit would be able to show him places where Zetta may have taken refuge.

Robert's frown returned. "I hope you find her soon, my friend," he said awkwardly.

Gareth nodded and gripped Robert's forearm in his own. "I will. And thank you once again for all of the help that you have given me." He smiled lopsidedly.

"I wish that I could do more."

Gareth's smile slowly faded. "There is nothing anyone else can do. From now on it is up to me." He cleared his throat and suddenly changed the topic. "Send Imogen my love and look after yourself. Henry is still plotting, I suspect, and you could be an even bigger prize than me."

"You are not usually so modest," Robert said with a gruff laugh. "You look after yourself and Edrit," he added as he pulled Gareth into a rough embrace.

After a moment, Gareth pulled away and quickly mounted his horse. Without another word, he grabbed hold of Edrit's reins as well as his own and nudged his horse into motion.

Robert watched them till they were over the drawbridge and it was closed behind them.

Slowly, he turned around and began to walk back toward his chambers, frowning grimly. He knew that the task his friend had set himself was far more difficult than he would admit. If he failed, then Robert didn't know how Gareth would go on. He needed his lady like he had never needed anything before, and that Robert could understand only too well. He felt the same way about Imogen.

Robert rubbed his eyes, suddenly tired to the core as he realized there was only one thing that he could do to help Gareth, and that was to wait.

Chapter 18

"I'm hungry," Edrit said hopefully.

Gareth looked over to him with a frown of concern but continued to walk briskly down the darkening street. The rain of the past three days had turned everything to mud. Gareth could feel it clinging to the edge of his cloak in a wide band, dragging him down. And it was getting colder. Maybe tomorrow there would be an end to the rain, or perhaps the cold meant that it would snow instead.

In the month that Zetta had been missing, Gareth had found that he had developed a whole new passion for discerning and anticipating the many faces of the weather. Each night, when sleep eluded him yet again, he wouldn't find himself drawn to the window of whatever dank inn chamber they were inhabiting, trying to gauge what the weather would give them the next day. He would stand looking out into the dark London streets for hours trying to convince himself that despite the steady, relentless onset of winter continually dropping the temperature, Zetta must have found somewhere warm for the night, that she knew the world she found herself in well enough to survive.

Despite these carefully drawn images, the possibility that she could be out there somewhere shivering and afraid haunted him. She had taken only one frayed and elderly cloak with her, and if she had managed to hold on to it, which was doubtful in a world where preying on the weak was a way of life, it would still be inadequate to protect her from the intense cold of a London winter. Each night as it grew steadily colder, Gareth felt the urgency to find her growing inside him like a destructive cancer.

He had to find her, he thought grimly, his stride lengthening.

"Gareth," Edrit said softly, his breath wheezing as he struggled to keep up, "it is getting dark now and I am really hungry."

"I know, Edrit, I know," Gareth replied patiently, deliberately shortening his stride again. "But we will just check out the last merchant in this area before going to find our supper. It was you who said that she sometimes sold the things that she . . . acquired in this area. We will just go and ask the man if he has seen her at all and then we will return to our lodgings. Promise."

"All right," Edrit said with a sigh of defeat, chafing his bad hand through the woolen glove, trying to warm it up.

His limp was also becoming more pronounced, as it often did at the end of a long day, Gareth noticed with growing frustration. No doubt the pain in that twisted limb would keep him awake, as it had done every night over the past week and a half. The only thing that seemed to soothe away at least some of the pain was to have the leg rubbed continually, and Gareth had quickly learned how to do it. It wasn't that dissimilar to the way a squire rubbed down a knight after a day spent in armor, and he was becoming quite proficient at it. Still, it killed him to see his brother in such pain. And he *was* in pain, no matter how much he stoically tried to deny it.

Every time he suggested that Edrit should spend the day resting instead of searching, however, it was rejected out of hand.

Each morning Edrit dragged himself along behind Gareth, seemingly only the sheer force of his will keeping him upright. That, and an indestructible optimism. He told Gareth every morning that he was certain that today was the day they would find Zetta, because that was what Gareth had promised him.

Such simple faith almost brought Gareth to his knees. What made it all seem so much worse was the fact that day after day that faith was proving to be entirely misplaced. With each successive failure, Gareth could feel his own faith corroding inside him, poisoning him with its bitterness. His self-doubt was almost all consuming, and he was now relying on his grim determination to find Zetta to keep him moving forward.

They had searched for her in all the places Edrit actually remembered, and they were now searching in places whose links to Zetta were tenuous at best. When those places too were exhausted, well, then they had the whole city of London to hunt through.

But what if she was not actually in London?

What if she had run farther?

What if she was somehow entirely out of his reach?

What if he was too late?

Gareth began to walk a little faster again, trying frantically to outstrip his doubt. He had to find her and she had to be all right. Anything else just was not an option, not if he wanted to stay sane.

Zetta shivered as an early morning breeze swept through the market. The walls on all sides hemmed it in, cutting off all natural light. She wrapped her arm around her middle and scowled ferociously at the man who regarded the silver jewelry she had just brought him skeptically. She had thought he would be less discerning. Normally a merchant in a second-rate market stall in the middle of the city's poorest areas couldn't afford to be as exacting, but that wasn't proving to be the case this time. The longer she waited for his answer, the more nervous she was becoming.

When he finally gave her an amount her scowl deepened.

"It's worth three times that," she growled, carefully making sure that she sounded like every other occupant of the slums. That was probably the only thing that had returned to her quickly.

The stall owner shrugged his shoulders. "Not to me it ain't. If you think you can get more money somewhere else, then good luck to you, but that is all I'm prepared to part with for a bit of stolen silver from some street brat."

Zetta didn't even bother denying that the jewelry was stolen, there was no point when the origins of the jewelry were so obvious. Instead, she grudgingly accepted the small number of coins the man gave her for it. She couldn't afford to be picky.

She slipped the coins into a small cloth pouch around her neck after hastily checking around to make sure that no one was watching her too closely. When she was sure that the other denizens of the market were too caught up in their own personal dramas to worry about hers, she slipped back into the crowd and began to make her way back to the single room she was now sharing with four other people.

Her hands were still shaking when she finally closed the door of the small chamber. She leaned against the rickety door and tried to force them to stop. Fortunately, she was alone. If anyone else saw her at such a moment that person would have easily been able to move in for the kill.

The shaking didn't stop.

She slipped her hands up her sleeves, pretending to herself that she was shaking only because of the cold. It didn't work. Her hands were cold, but that was not why they shook. She was afraid.

Something as basic as selling stolen goods had never made her hands shake before. She had never liked thieving and the industries that surrounded it, but she had understood the practicality of it and had always been very, very good at it. There had never before been any nervousness or moments of self-doubt of any kind. She had done what needed to be done.

That acceptance seemed to have entirely deserted her now, along with everything else. Every tolerance she had ever possessed seemed to have evaporated. Only that afternoon, as she had walked through the all too familiar streets and back alleys, it had taken her a surprisingly long time to realize that she was being followed.

She should have been on the lookout for it. The jewelry that she had just sold for a pittance had not only been stolen, but it also had not been hers to sell, not by the harsh laws of the street. She hunched her shoulders and cursed her own folly.

She might have been the one who had physically lifted the third-rate piece of silver, but she had not done it under instruction from the man who ran this area of the slums that hugged the city's eastern wall. Todd controlled the area and every thief, whore, assassin and petty criminal had to give him all of the fruits of their labors. They then had to wait for what Todd considered their fair share. It was always just enough to keep body and soul together so that everyone could keep earning Todd his fortune. It was never enough so that anyone could escape the web of deceit that bound them.

The man was a greedy, evil bastard as far as Zetta was concerned, but the only way to survive was to work for him. Anyone who tried to escape paid a very bloody price and was found the next day floating near the docks. It was the way things were done. Zetta had worked for others like Todd before and had never found it that hard to conform when conformity meant survival.

But this time, she was desperate.

She needed as much coin as she could manage to scrape together to get out of London as soon as possible. The meager amount that Todd and his minions let trickle down to her just wasn't enough. And she had to move on—soon. The longer she was forced to stay in one place, the greater the chance of Gareth finding her.

She never doubted for a second that somewhere out there he was looking for her. If he found her, then she didn't know how she could save him because she couldn't turn him away. No, it was better if she left and started a new life somewhere else.

She had thought that she might head to France or go up north to York, but it didn't really matter which. Anywhere. Just as long as it took her away from the temptation of falling into his arms again.

Whatever her destination, Zetta knew that the one constant was that she would need more coin than the small amount she could earn stealing for Todd. In order to get what she needed she had to steal from the thief master, then so be it. A shudder went through her as she realized how close she had come today. If she hadn't been able to shake off whoever had been following her, Todd would have found out about her double-dealing. It was a very fine line she was balancing and if she wasn't careful she would end up facedown in the Thames, like so many others who had dared to defy the great man.

Perhaps the most truly terrifying realization, however, was that the idea didn't frighten her at all. She continued to move forward because there was no other choice, but inside she was empty. A hollow numbness had taken over full possession of her and she felt nothing. Not even mortal fear.

"Do you have anything to report?" the messenger asked stiffly.

Gareth continued to stare out the window, wondering idly if it would be possible to deflate the man's blatant pomposity without actually spilling any blood. It might even have improved his evening in a way, listening to yet another of Henry's messengers. Not that he was listening.

There really wasn't any need to.

He had heard it all before. Every evening Henry sent

a messenger to inquire how the hunt was going, and every evening Gareth sent back the same answer that they had found no sign of Zetta anywhere. He hated having to admit his defeat yet again. It all only served to remind him just how little he had achieved, something he certainly had no need of. The knowledge was like a brand on his skin.

"Sir Gareth, you must have something that I can report back to His Majesty."

Slowly Gareth turned around to face the frustrated, impatient messenger. "As usual, I have nothing to report except that we now have fewer places to look."

"He won't be pleased," the little man said fussily.

"I'm not exactly jumping for joy myself," Gareth murmured dryly, but the messenger just continued to frown at him furiously.

"I don't know now if I should give you the information the king told me to give you, seeing as you are continuing to be so unhelpful."

Gareth tried to keep hold of his fraying temper. He raised a brow inquiringly and crossed his arms over his chest. It seemed the only way to stop them from reaching for his sword.

The messenger paled and gulped nervously.

"The king just wanted you to know," he said hastily, "that your brother the Baron might not have left the country, because, according to the king's . . . ah . . . informant, he has yet to reappear back in his Normandy stronghold."

With that, he bowed hastily and all but fled from the room as if chased. It might actually have amused Gareth if he hadn't already been trying to untangle the mess of his brooding thoughts.

This new information might mean nothing but, at the

same time, it could mean everything. Lanfranc could very easily be anywhere else on the continent making his deals and playing one of his endless intrigues, and if that was the case, then Gareth would have nothing to worry about.

Somehow, he didn't think he would be that lucky.

Bad omens had been dogging him of late. Everything he touched seemed to turn to basest lead, and if that held true, then the odds were on Lanfranc still being in London, preparing to revenge himself on Zetta any way he could. God alone knew what hellish plans Lanfranc was already concocting.

Gareth could almost feel his time physically running out.

He had to find Zetta before Lanfranc did.

In theory, at least, Gareth had the strongest chance of finding her first. Edrit knew her better than anyone, and they methodically searched every area he suggested, hoping against hope that she had returned to her old haunts or places very much like them.

But theory was proving to have very little to do with reality. And Lanfranc was not a man to be underestimated. He never started something that he didn't already know he could succeed at. He had no doubt spent the time Gareth had been fruitlessly searching exploiting his own nefarious contacts. There was nothing his brother wouldn't do, no depth he wouldn't lower himself to, in the name of victory.

Restlessly Gareth began to prowl around the small chamber. It was going to be another long night. He had seven hours to wait before he could wake Edrit and they could begin their searching once more. Just as they had every other day for the past, long weeks.

But now there was an increased urgency about what they did.

Any time they wasted could be time Zetta would pay for if Lanfranc found her first.

Zetta moved quickly through the muddy streets, carefully avoiding the foul drain that ran through its center. Someone was following her. For the past three days there had always been someone there. She caught glimpses of the person, the same face wherever she went, following her every step.

Today's shadow was better than the others had been. She hadn't spotted him once, and whoever he was he did not make a sound, but she could still feel him, a menace at the back of her mind. The sensation brought the hairs on the back of her neck up.

A strange, excited fear started penetrating the numb fog inside her as she turned a corner and felt the person behind her drawing closer.

She quickly headed toward an alley, trying not to break into an outright run, but the menacing presence was too close to be lost so easily, following her with disconcerting accuracy.

But once she hit the alley she did begin to run, no longer caring how it looked.

She came out onto another busy street and ducked along it, then went down another alley, but nothing she did seemed to shake the feel of her follower.

Suddenly, she stopped.

Trying to control her panting breath, Zetta realized that running was not getting her any farther away from the threat, and she certainly did not want to lead whoever it was straight back to her lodgings and the things she had stashed under her straw pallet. She had been selling them slowly so as not to draw attention, and she had to keep it that way if she wanted to survive this.

Her only chance was to brazen this out. Slowly she turned around.

There was no one there.

A shiver ran down her spine and the sound of her labored breathing echoed eerily around her, filling her ears with the sound of her own fear. Perhaps it had only been her mind and paranoia playing tricks on her. She ran back up to the mouth of the alley trying to see where the threat was hiding. On the busy street people moved quickly about their business, no one paying the least attention to one more waif and stray.

Gradually her panic began to fade and she turned to walk toward her lodgings.

She had taken only a few steps when a solid object slammed in her back and pushed her up against one of the wooden walls that hemmed her in on two sides. Her head slammed against the solid structure with a sickening thud.

For a second she could feel herself slipping into a black void, but she struggled to fight off its dangerous allure. Roughly someone turned her around.

She could not see the face of the man who held her pinned up against the wall, the weight of his large body smothering her, but she could smell the liquor on his breath and the sour sweat that threatened to suffocate her more quickly than the forearm he was pressing against her throat.

"So you thought you could double-cross me," she heard him say as if from a long distance as she struggled to fight off the fog that was filling her brain. "And now I realize that you did more than cheat me out of a bit of nicked silver."

Careful to leave one arm on her throat, he shoved up her long tunic and grabbed her cruelly at the juncture of her thighs. He smiled.

"They were right; you ain't no boy."

As his fingers began to insinuate themselves crudely against her, some latent instinct rose to the surface. With a strangled shriek Zetta reached up both of her hands and tried to lift him off of her, digging her nails helplessly into the thick leather of his forearm bands.

He just laughed and leaned more of his weight on her throat.

"Don't be thinking me a fool. I've been dealing with bitches like you for too long to let one of them get the better of me now."

"Get off me, you bastard," she managed to squeeze out through her constricted airways, her voice hoarse. It took up almost all of the meager amount of air he was letting through and she could feel herself getting light-headed, but she refused to give in to it.

He leaned forward into the dim light so that she could almost make out his sneering face.

"I have me a friend, a nobleman who talks to kings. Now this friend, see, has asked me to find a woman hiding herself as a boy. And if the story he spun me was true, then it would seem that it's you who are the bastard, a right royal one at that. He promised me a great deal of gold if I would give you to him."

He finally moved his hand away from her crotch and grabbed hold of her hair, making her scream. With professional, economic movements he cracked her head back against the wall with just the right amount of force to send her tumbling down into a dark void that she couldn't fight her way out of.

"And Ben Todd never disappoints."

Gareth found Lanfranc with surprising ease.

Unlike Zetta, Lanfranc had not lived in London all his life. He was a stranger to the impenetrable slums that were hiding Zetta so well. Instead, he had made no more effort to hide himself than to take private lodgings and to live discreetly away from the court.

It certainly had not been enough to hide him from Gareth for long. Henry should have nailed the bastard to the underside of a ship headed for Normandy, Gareth thought grimly.

As it was, it would seem that his own desire never to see his brother again was not to be realized. He stared up at the comfortable house Lanfranc had hired and struggled to understand the welter of emotion that filled him at that moment when his brother had turned predator and was threatening Zetta. Everything had changed so drastically since he had made that silent vow never to look his brother in the eye again that it was almost incomprehensible.

Indeed, he was actually relieved to have found Lanfranc. At least he knew for certain that he had not located Zetta either. If he had, no power on earth would have kept him in London. It meant, of course, that she was still in mortal danger, but at least Gareth knew he still had time to find her and make her safe.

But that time was rapidly slipping through his fingers. He would have given everything he possessed for the chance to go in and confront his brother anyway. After asking him a few pertinent questions, he could then enjoy himself by pounding him until he got it into his head to leave well enough alone.

He wanted to do it so badly he could almost taste it, but common sense told him that to do so would obliterate what was fast becoming his best chance now of actually finding Zetta before she did something foolish.

So instead, he gave some coin to a street urchin to watch the house with the promise of even more when he actually had something to report about the man inside.

That night, when the royal messenger came for his daily update, he made no mention of having found Lanfranc. Henry's emotions on the subject were running high and Gareth didn't want him interfering, not right now anyway.

Instead, Gareth spent the next couple of days searching with Edrit as if he knew nothing about Lanfranc and was still searching blindly for Zetta. The truth was, however, that Gareth was going mad. But for the fact that Lanfranc was obviously also still looking he would have sunk under the weight of the futility of their search. They could still find no trace of her, and the more Gareth saw of her world, the more vivid his nightmares were on those increasingly rare occasions when he did actually manage to find sleep.

Tonight's nightmare had been the worst. With a shaking hand, he poured himself a large dose of spirits, but he left it untouched as he began to pace around the room. He was haunted by the image his mind had conjured of Zetta's battered body lying in the mud while rats consumed her. He drew a shaky breath and buried his face in his hands. He needed her, needed to know that she was safe. The not knowing tied his stomach into one endless knot, and his heart was beating in his ears so loudly that he almost didn't hear the timid knocking on the door.

When the noise did finally penetrate the clamor of his senses, his hand dropped to his side and all emotion wiped from his face. Only when he was sure that he had himself back under perfect control did he open the door.

The street urchin he had set to spy on Lanfranc stood nervously outside.

"Sorry, sir, but you told me to get you if that man you had me watch did anything unusual. Well, he left his house an hour ago and I followed him to old Ma Rose's tart house down near the dock. He met a man there and I managed to hear the man whom you made me watch say that he was pleased the parcel had arrived just before I hightailed it over here to tell you." He paused from the garbled rush, drawing in a deep breath before plunging on. "Can I have me money now?"

A battle calm settled over Gareth. This was it. This was what he'd been waiting and hoping for since he had heard that Lanfranc had stayed in London. The searching was over. Now he had to be ready.

"Wait here," he said to the boy with perfect calm and went into the next room to wake Edrit from his own troubled sleep. He then went to his own chamber and quickly gathered up his cloak, scabbard and sword and slipped a dagger into the leather band around his bicep.

He smiled at the urchin, who stood shuffling his feet uncertainly by the door, obviously impatient for his reward.

"I'm going to give your coin to Edrit here," Gareth said simply, "and he is to give it to you only if you go with him to see the king. You will wait for him while he tells the king about this development. You are both then to come back here. Only then will Edrit part with the coin."

Edrit limped into the room, a frustrated frown appearing on his face. "But I want to come with you and find Zetta."

Gareth shook his head. "Trust me; you can be of more help to Zetta this way. I'm going to need some backup and Henry will know just what to do."

He could see that Edrit wanted to protest, but instead he grabbed his cloak and clumsily threw it around his shoulders. He did not like it, but if Gareth said it was for the best, then it was for the best.

"Now, boy," Gareth started to say, but the urchin interrupted.

"Me name's Marcus, sir."

"Well then, Marcus, I want you to tell me where exactly you saw the man go."

"Right you are, sir," he said with an impish smile, well pleased with himself and no doubt already counting the coin this night's work had brought him.

Gareth listened to the boy's directions carefully, but in a cold, empty place of his mind he was already playing through this last confrontation with his elder brother. It would be bloody and final.

For the first time in his life he found himself looking forward to inflicting a great deal of pain and suffering.

Zetta didn't like the hollow stone chamber that she found herself in after regaining consciousness.

It was dark and smelled of dank corruption. Water seeped continually through the stones, and Zetta had lived in London too long not to recognize the smell. She was somewhere close to the Thames, if not directly under it, as water trickled from the ceiling as well as the walls. She huddled on the meager pile of straw that had been dumped in one corner, all fight drained from her. Or perhaps it had just been frozen inside her.

She tried to keep her blood circulating by chafing her hands and feet, but while she had been unconscious someone had stripped her of her clothes and replaced them with an aged, thin chemise. The chill of the room penetrated it easily, the threads seemingly held together only by filth, as far as Zetta could tell. She scrunched herself up and tucked it around her feet but it did absolutely nothing to repel the cold, just as the single candle that had been left for her did nothing to dispel the gloom with its flickering light.

She sat huddled with the moving shadows it cast all around and strange, seductive terrors began picking away at the edges of her mind. At the same time, her whole life seemed entwined with the candlelight and she dreaded the moment when it would go out.

Maybe when it did she would start to scream and never stop.

When she had first slowly regained consciousness she had banged on the door, begging someone to open it and let her out. But the door had remained resolutely closed. The screaming had stopped when her throat could take it no more, and her hands, bloodied from where she had banged on the rough wooden door yet still strangely ice cold, had dropped uselessly to her sides. It was better to save her strength for whatever was coming, though she could scarcely imagine what exactly that could be.

Whatever her fate, she hoped it would claim her before the candle went out. Better to be dead than mad. She supposed she should be relieved that they had given her food, even if it was only black bread and stale water. At least that meant they were not intent on starving her, though she could find no relief in that fact.

Zetta wrapped her arms around her knees and began to rock gently. She might not like heights, but she was finding the knowledge that she was under the ground, under the river Thames, frighteningly suffocating. She stared at the candle trying to guess how many minutes and seconds she had before it went out.

When she suddenly heard sounds of movement beyond the door she quickly stood up, her legs shaking precariously. She cast her gaze around, trying desperately to find something in the room that she could use as a weapon, but she already knew there was nothing.

The door opened, and even though the only light came from a blazing torch, Zetta found herself shading her eyes and blinking them rapidly. By the time she had adjusted to the light, Lanfranc was already in the room closing the door behind him.

He looked around in distaste.

"To think if you had come to me when I had asked, I would have given you a palace to live in." He shrugged his shoulders, his gaze raking over her assessingly. Carefully he put the lit torch into a wall sconce and then began to languidly walk toward her. "Why you chose to run instead I will never understand, but I am sure I will make you reconsider the folly of your ways before this night is over."

As he reached her she felt herself tensing as she waited for a blow to fall, but she still was taken by surprise when he casually backhanded her, knocking her to the ground. The metallic taste of blood filled her mouth as she struggled back up to her knees. She wiped the trickle away with the back of her hands, her anger suddenly burning into life.

"You spawn of hell," she snarled up at him. "What do you want from me?"

He was smiling as he reached down and jerked her back up to her feet by her hair, ignoring her outraged scream of pain.

"First, I'm going to teach you a lesson," he said mildly, "and then we are going to get on my ship and head to my estates in Normandy. Once there, you are going to be my insurance. With you as my . . . guest, I need not worry overly about what happens between the royal brothers. I can declare myself for the duke, but if he should lose, I will have no concerns about Henry extracting any revenge. He will not jeopardize your precarious existence. However the dice fall I will win."

"You evil bastard."

He slapped her across the face with his other hand, the force causing a resounding crack. "You are starting to repeat yourself and that is not like you."

With her hands she reached out to claw his face, but even as she tried to fight back she knew that she could never hope to overpower him. She refused, however, to make his victory too easy for him.

He grabbed both of her hands in one of his and, letting go of her hair, jerked them high above her head, causing a tearing sensation in her shoulder socket. The pain took away her breath and her stomach clenched as if she was going to throw up.

She continued to struggle, her desperation rising as he slammed her against the hard, unforgiving stone wall and loomed over her.

Suddenly, the door flew open.

The noise of the wood hitting stones reverberated

through the small cell deafeningly. Before the sound had even stopped echoing Lanfranc let her drop to the floor and turned quickly to face this new threat. Zetta's world tilted. All breath left her body as it slammed onto the stones.

Lanfranc bared his teeth in a feral smile when he saw Gareth standing in the doorway.

"So, you have come to find your bitch."

"Get out of here," Gareth said through gritted teeth. "I gave your men some coin so that they could enjoy the pleasures of the docks. The royal guard will be here soon. If you don't want to die, leave."

"You don't frighten me, little brother."

"Well, I should, because not only am I longing to put my sword deep into your guts, but I have also let the king know that you have lingered in England and deliberately flouted his exile edict. If he finds you, you will find yourself longing for the relatively quick death you would find at my hands."

Lanfranc regarded him through narrow eyes, then smiled faintly. "Well, if you put it like that," he murmured with a shrug of his shoulders, then walked toward Gareth as if he was going to leave. Abruptly he turned and with one powerful swing knocked Gareth's sword out of his hands.

With a roar, Gareth threw himself at Lanfranc and the two men fell to the floor. Zetta, struggling to stand using the wall as support, watched in horror as they writhed on the floor in a deadly struggle. She couldn't tell who was winning.

When the world stopped swimming she grabbed hold of her battered ribs and went as quickly as she could to where Gareth's sword had landed. She bent down and grabbed it with both hands and struggled to lift its weight.

Lanfranc had Gareth on his back, one hand wrapped around his throat, the other tangled brutally in his sandy hair. Gareth was trying desperately to pull him off, but Zetta was not sure whether he would manage it before Lanfranc successfully throttled him.

With the last of her own strength she pressed the point of the blade between Lanfranc's shoulders. A distant memory of a similar scene played tauntingly through her mind. The last time she had pointed a blade against a man had been the fateful day she had first met Gareth. She swallowed hard against the tears that she refused to let fall.

"Let him go," she said, her body shaking with the sobs that rose through her, but she held the sword as steady as she could.

Lanfranc paused for a moment, then with a crack brought Gareth's head down against the stone floor. He moved off of Gareth, who lay ominously still, and stood up. As he turned, Zetta backed away, carefully keeping the blade pointed directly at his heart.

"And just what the hell do you think you are going to achieve by this?" Lanfranc asked with sneering condescension. "You don't think you can actually find the bravery to kill me, do you? My God, you can barely hold the blade of the sword straight."

"Try me," she said through gritted teeth, desperately struggling to keep her sweaty hands on the smooth hilt.

She couldn't stop herself from taking a step back when he moved toward her.

"You are a weak, stupid woman. You don't have what it takes to run a man through in cold blood, so you might as well give that to me and end this silly game."

"I don't play games."

Lanfranc ignored her desperate warning and took another step toward her. And another. Zetta felt a tingle of panic rush up her neck and swallowed compulsively. Lanfranc stopped when the point of the sword pressed against his belly.

"Give it to me now and you can watch me kill Gareth." He smiled at her and Zetta realized in a flash that he actually planned to do what he said.

For a second the world went black, then brilliant white. With a strange sense of detachment she heard her roar as she used all of her strength to thrust the sword through the fine weave of Lanfranc's tunic. She watched in bewildered detachment as the blade disappeared inside him. The sound of a man dying surprised her. It was an oddly silent noise, one that couldn't be heard and yet it echoed off the stone walls.

Her eyes were locked with Lanfranc's. She couldn't look away. She saw his surprise, the horror and the pain. Then nothing. She would remember the exact moment his eyes lost all soul for the rest of her life. It was a blankness that looked into eternity.

His lifeless body slid to the floor, jerking free of the sword, but the weight of the sword still brought her to her knees. She knelt beside him, still staring into his eyes. She felt as if the death in them had branded her, had sucked out her soul, and now she was floating somewhere above everything.

She watched from her detached distance as Gareth struggled to his feet. He held the back of his head gingerly, as if trying to make sure that all of his brains were still held within, as he quickly went and knelt down beside her. She watched as if from another room as his hand touched her shoulder.

Abruptly she could feel her heart beating again. Her breath came in tearing sobs and she couldn't stop shaking.

"Gareth . . ." she pleaded without even knowing what she was asking for.

"I know, dear one, I know," he said soothingly as if he understood every one of her jumbled thoughts. "Give me the sword. Just let go and everything will be all right."

It was only when she looked down to where her hands remained clamped over the hilt that she realized his other hand had covered hers and that they were both covered in blood.

A hysterical giggle rose up inside her. "It's strange. I can see my hands—I know they are mine—but I can't seem to make them do anything. I . . ."

"Shhh," he murmured. Then he gently pried her fingers from the hilt all the while whispering, "It will be all right, Zetta. Trust me."

Freed of the weight of the sword her hands started to ache as if the bones had all been bent. She lifted her hands and suddenly the scent of blood hit her senses. Her stomach spasmed. Hastily she stumbled to her feet and lurched from the room. She leaned against a wall and tried to control the roiling of her stomach, dimly aware through the retching that Gareth had wrapped an arm around her middle. He held on to her forehead and whispered nonsense into her ear.

When the dry retching finally stopped the sobs started.

She turned and tried to burrow herself into his chest. His arms enclosed her and held her safe as he gently rocked back and forth.

"What have I done?" she asked, even though she

knew the answer. She needed to hear it out loud before she could understand it properly.

"Something I should have done the second I realized what a bastard he was. He got much more than he deserved."

Slowly Zetta lifted her eyes to Gareth's and slowly the anger faded from his face. She couldn't quite believe that she was in his arms again when she had thought she would never see him again in this world. Hungrily she absorbed every detail of his beloved face.

He had changed. His face was more finely chiseled and slightly harder than she ever remembered her laughing man to be. Pale lines of tension radiated around his mouth and eyes, whereas before there had only been signs of laughter. But the depths of his eyes were the same. In them she saw the only thing she had ever wanted for her own—his love.

Shakily she lifted a bloody finger to his lips.

"I shouldn't be," Zetta said, her voice sounding raw, "but I am very pleased to see you."

A smile suddenly burst to life on Gareth's face.

"What, you are not excited, elated, overjoyed? Just *pleased*? I am crushed."

She pulled back and, wiping the tears from her cheeks with the back of her hand, regarded his face with a loving sadness. "How can I be any of those things when I know I can't stay with you?" She quickly stilled his protest by pressing her finger against his lips. "Shhh. Don't say anything that will break my heart. I can't take much more, not when I already know that I can't stay with you. How could I when I know it might mean your death?"

Tears began to fall unchecked down her cheeks as she struggled to catch her breath. "I don't know how I will ever manage to leave you again"—she stiffened her spine—"but I must."

Gently Gareth lifted her finger away from his lips and engulfed it in the security of his hand while he ran the back of the other over her already discoloring cheek. "You won't leave me again. I won't let you. Instead, we will marry and you will be mine." He smiled wickedly at her incredulous expression. "I intend to keep you so distracted and worn out by our lovemaking that you won't have the energy to ever leave me."

"You can't do that if you are off fighting in some damn fool war and get yourself killed," she snapped, her anger sparking into life as he taunted her with possibilities.

He bent his head and kissed her nose. "Henry and I have come to an agreement, dear heart, and I can now promise I won't be fighting his wars, not unless I want to because I believe his cause to be just."

"And you trust him to keep to this bargain?" she said with a derisive snort.

He regarded her solemnly. "Of course not. The man is as slippery as a snake. What I intend to do is stay as far away from London as possible so that he forgets either you or I exist. He has promised to give you an estate somewhere in the north as a kind of dowry. Once ensconced we need not travel any farther south than York if that is what you wish."

She looked into his beloved eyes and for the first time, felt herself daring to hope. "Are you sure?" she asked hesitantly. "He really meant it?"

He wrapped his arms around her more firmly and pressed her cheek into his chest, bathing his scent in the essence of her. "As sure as I am of my love for you," he said hoarsely.

Zetta closed her eyes, relief flooding to fill every

hollow space inside her. She felt entirely safe and secure, for the first time in her life. It was like a waking dream. She could feel the wonder of it radiating from every part of her. She lifted her head and reached up to kiss the man who had somehow managed to achieve the impossible.

Gareth met her halfway.

He plundered while she consumed. She angled her head to get even closer, raw desire burning her. When at last he raised his head, the sound of their ragged breathing echoed through her.

"I love you, Gareth," she said with wonder. "I love you with all of my heart and soul."

"Well then, my darling little thief, there is nothing in this world we cannot conquer as long as we are together."

He lowered his lips to claim hers again. This time the kiss was as much about love and hope as it was about passion. She returned it with a fervor that burnt through him like a fire.

Zetta pulled away and looked into the eyes of her laughing man and smiled back at him.

He was right. As long as they were together, they could conquer the world.

Epilogue

Zetta's eyes flew open. For one heart-stopping moment she thought she was back in the dank cellar. The cold of it oppressed her as she once more stared into Lanfranc's eyes as the blade of her sword slid into him. But he wouldn't die. That was the horror holding her heart in a vice as reality slowly replaced dream fears. He wouldn't die and she would be forever caught in his web.

She forced herself to breathe and tried to will away the panic lodged inside her core. *It was a dream,* she repeated to herself like a prayer as her eyes adjusted to the dark. From the gloom arose not the remembered prison but the simple shape of the cottage she had called home for nearly six months now.

And this small cottage was her home in a way nowhere else had ever been.

The walls might not be entirely straight and the roof might be inclined to leak during the frequently rainy weather, but every inch of it, each imperfection, was dear to her. How could it be otherwise when Gareth, with Edrit's enthusiastic help, had built it with his own hands? It had been the first self-imposed task he had completed when they had finally reached the northern holdings that were her dowry lands. Of course, there had been many offers of help for the new lord and master, but he had been adamant that it was something he had to do.

Zetta smiled as the nightmare faded finally into the shadows as gloriously different memories claimed her, memories of those first days spent together as man and wife. That time of awakening had been a revelation to Zetta, but at the same time bewildering. Changing from a life with nothing to live for to one where every second was precious had been frightening in its own way. It was a bit like having the whole world tipped on its head. What she'd need was time to make some kind of sense of it all, but Gareth had been surprisingly ruthless in his determination to sever all ties with their past. With breathtaking speed he'd organized everything.

It had all happened so quickly that there had been no chance to talk to her father, much less say goodbye. Not that she knew what she would to say to the man who, by some random accident of happenstance, called her daughter. Everything and yet nothing. How could it now be possible to fit two lives into one mere conversation? It wasn't, of course, and she knew that, but the small girl who stubbornly remained part of her wanted to try and mourned yet another missed opportunity.

There would be other chances, of course, Zetta thought with a small sigh. Gareth had grudgingly agreed that they might be able to present themselves to the king in high summer if the harvest was going as planned, but he did little to hide his reluctance. He wanted to put it all behind him and never look back, as did she. Sometimes. At others, she wanted to know more of the man who had sired her, even though rationally she knew it would now be impossible. The man had become lost in the crown too many years back for the deed to be undone now.

She sighed again and snuggled down in the warm furs to escape the sudden chill that swept over her. The movement, or perhaps the melancholy direction of her thoughts, disturbed Gareth. Exhausted though he was, he grumbled something, rolled over and hauled her against him. In seconds his breathing evened out and he started to snore once more. Zetta smiled as she smoothed a wayward lock of hair off his forehead.

Her husband. Those words still had an unreality about them that could catch her unaware with their awesome splendor. Just as the man himself did. She pressed her face into the comforting swell of his throat and couldn't stop herself from placing several featherlight kisses over the warm skin of his neck. She didn't worry about the action waking him from his much needed sleep. Nothing short of the apocalypse could disturb him before dawn these days.

She had never seen anyone work as hard as Gareth did to build for them a home out of this rugged, untamed landscape. From dawn till well past vespers, when he crawled into their bed, he worked to make them a prosperous, safe haven. Zetta helped where she could, and while the role she found herself in was entirely alien, she was starting to learn. And day by day

Gareth's fortress was making its mark on the wild landscape of their new home.

Only to herself could she admit that a part of her never wanted it to be finished. She would miss this simple cottage when it came time to leave. After all, it was these very walls that had sheltered her while she'd leaned the infinite range of glory and happiness that were now hers.

Even this simple embrace, being held close and safe by the man who had pledged his life to hers, was a beautiful moment to be treasured. It certainly shouldn't be squandered on dark memories and haunted dreams, she thought as she curled her arm around Gareth's waist and closed her eyes. There were still several hours till dawn, when Gareth would wake her with warm kisses and subtly decadent caresses. And that time would go faster if she was asleep.

This time her dreams were filled with memories of love and passion, and just before dawn she awoke to the feel of Gareth's lips pressed to her own and his large, calloused hands stroking the sensitive skin of her inner thigh.

"Good morning, Sir Knight," she said with a half-awake, sultry smile when his lips finally released hers. "Is it possible you have finally had enough rest to see to your husbandly duties at last?"

"Don't tease me, wife," Gareth growled as he lowered his head and began to place fevered kisses over her breasts. "I need you, now."

"As I need you." Zetta moaned, and arched her back when Gareth's hot mouth began to suckle on her nipple. Through the haze that was raising to possess her she realized that dreams, good or bad, in no way measured against the reality of living and loving the man who was now torturing her with desire. He alone was able to bring light into the dark cavern that had been her heart. He had given her life.

And she knew that was a miracle never to be squandered.

More Historical Romance From
Jo Ann Ferguson

Discover the Magic of
Romance with
Jo Goodman

Discover the Romances of
Hannah Howell

Put a Little Romance in Your Life With
Georgina Gentry

Cheyenne Song
0-8217-5844-6
$5.99US/$7.99CAN

Apache Tears
0-8217-6435-7
$5.99US/$7.99CAN

Warrior's Heart
0-8217-7076-4
$5.99US/$7.99CAN

To Tame a Savage
0-8217-7077-2
$5.99US/$7.99CAN

To Tame a Texan
0-8217-7402-6
$5.99US/$7.99CAN

To Tame a Rebel
0-8217-7403-4
$5.99US/$7.99CAN

To Tempt a Texan
0-8217-7705-X
$5.99US/$7.99CAN

Available Wherever Books Are Sold!

Visit our website at **www.kensingtonbooks.com.**